MOON

DARK

SMILE

ALSO BY TESSA GRATTON

Night Shine
Strange Grace

The Blood Journals Duology
Blood Magic
The Blood Keeper

The Gods of New Asgard Series
The Lost Sun
The Strange Maid
The Apple Throne
The Weight of Stars

MOON DARK SMILE

TESSA GRATTON

Margaret K. McElderry Books

NEW YORK   LONDON   TORONTO   SYDNEY   NEW DELHI

V50

MARGARET K. McELDERRY BOOKS
An imprint of Simon & Schuster Children's Publishing Division
1230 Avenue of the Americas, New York, New York 10020

MARGARET K. McELDERRY BOOKS is a trademark of Simon & Schuster, Inc.
For information about special discounts for bulk purchases, please contact Simon & Schuster Special Sales at 1-866-506-1949 or business@simonandschuster.com.
The Simon & Schuster Speakers Bureau can bring authors to your live event. For more information or to book an event, contact the Simon & Schuster Speakers Bureau at 1-866-248-3049 or visit our website at www.simonspeakers.com.
The text for this book was set in Bembo.
Manufactured in China
First Edition
2 4 6 8 10 9 7 5 3 1
Library of Congress Cataloging-in-Publication Data
Names: Gratton, Tessa, author.
Title: Moon dark smile / Tessa Gratton.
Description: First edition. | New York : Margaret K. McElderry Books, [2022] | Audience: Ages 14 up. | Audience: Grades 10-12. | Summary: After discovering a dangerous way to bring the demon of the palace with her, Raliel, the heir to the Emperor, sets out on her coming-of-age journey, accompanied by her demon-kissed bodyguard Osian, who secretly plans to act as his mother's weapon against the Empire.
Identifiers: LCCN 2021052679 (print) | LCCN 2021052680 (ebook) | ISBN 9781534498150 (hardcover) | ISBN 9781534498167 (paperback) | ISBN 9781534498174 (ebook)
Subjects: CYAC: Demonology—Fiction. | Princesses—Fiction. | Voyages and travel—Fiction. | Names, Personal—Fiction. | Magic—Fiction. | Fantasy. | LCGFT: Novels. | Fantasy fiction.
Classification: LCC PZ7.G77215 Mo 2022 (print) | LCC PZ7.G77215 (ebook) | DDC [Fic]—dc23
LC record available at https://lccn.loc.gov/2021052679
LC ebook record available at https://lccn.loc.gov/2021052680

TO ROBIN MCKINLEY
AND KAREN LORD

The river is a flat, shining chain.

The moon, rising, is a white eye to the hills;

After it has risen, it is the bright heart of the sea.

—LI PO,
TRANS. FLORENCE AYSCOUGH AND AMY LOWELL

MOON
DARK
SMILE

NAMES

SUNRISE

S UNRISE WAS A COMMON name throughout the empire. Likely because it represented hope and joy, just like the dawn. Many children with the name were firstborn or born after a long struggle. Most grew into cheerful, happy adults, though a few took the name and ran in the opposite direction. Contrariness was always a risk with such an obvious name.

But this Sunrise, the first—and only—child of Syra Bear Mistress, was given the name because he was born several months after his father died in a violent magical battle with the sorceress of the Fifth Mountain. Syra had clung to the growing spark inside her through her desperate grief, keeping herself alive for the child of her defeated lover, Skybreaker, the sorcerer of the Fourth Mountain. She swore the child would grow in remembrance of the sorcerer's glory, a monument to it, and a gift of revenge.

Thus Sunrise was named Sunrise, a promise of that soaring splendor.

By the time her child was six years old, Syra sent him down the mountain to be raised by her sisters, a coven of some seventeen witches and priests vowed into service and scholarship.

Syra had been one of them, but she had abandoned their work when she fell in love with the Fourth Sorcerer.

As the only child in the enclave, Sunrise was entirely spoiled. Fortunately, the abundance of love only polished his laughter into something easy to share and filled with compassion. He never knew suffering, always was encouraged, and when the aunties laughed at his escapades and mistakes, it was done with an air of familiarity. They taught him to read and cook and clean, to punch and dance and wield a sword. They taught him history and music, how to draw, and how to win graciously. Among the seventeen of them there was very little they could not teach. Sunrise learned it all, and though he had his preferences for warfare and music, his strangely perfect memory meant he could recite or re-create even what he considered boring.

He was so pretty, dimpled, and friendly, his aunties always took him to the market with them, to visit nearby manors for tutoring rich children, or to replenish blessings at crossroads shrines or scholarship temples. He chattered away as they traveled, held their hands or darted ahead, smiled innocently, and never realized it was his adorable charm that helped this aunt haggle or that aunt squeeze into the last room at an inn.

The only scar on this surprisingly idyllic childhood was his reluctance to ask his aunties to stop treating him like a daughter. It was not their fault; they did not know, because he never corrected them when they assumed he was a girl like them. Sunrise did not truly believe they would flinch, much less judge him for being his true self. It was only that this was an enclave of women, and he feared he would be asked to leave if he told them he wasn't one, and never would be.

4

So Sunrise left the secret a secret, only curling up at night and wishing for a day when he was old enough and brave enough to confess to the family he loved.

His mother made it easier to hold tight to his secret, for Syra was sharp and violent in her expectations. The widow was determined to carve her child into a weapon against those who'd caused Skybreaker's death. When she was not up the mountain wrestling with wild sorcery, she told Sunrise tales of his father's vast strength and clever machinations, of shape-shifting and intricate spells that took months to carefully draw to completion. She said Skybreaker had been the most handsome person, the tallest and most ambitious—too bad Sunrise was delicate and compact like his mother. But she said that Skybreaker had loved three things: his great spirit, Syra herself, and Sunrise even unborn. "They took him from us. You are alone because he is dead," she whispered late at night when she came down the mountain for a visit. Then she sang a soft, strange lullaby in a language he should have learned from his father.

Sunrise did not think he was alone at all: he had his aunts, his dogs and canaries, the little mice in the fields, and the juniper spirits with their tiny blueberry eyes. Why, if he felt alone he need only look up at the stars in the sky—or the sun!—and see that he was not. But he stopped saying such things to his mother early on, after she locked him in a dirt cellar for three days to prove to him what loneliness was, to show him how he must rely on her.

(After, his nightmares involved the dark and being lost forever, but he refused to explain what had happened to his favorite aunts Tali and Windsong, even when they hugged him tightly and promised to protect him from anything. Even his mother. He assured them with large, shining-brown eyes his mother had not hurt him. Sunrise refused to imagine what his mother would do to retaliate if he snitched on her.)

Syra's determination to pull apart the remnants of Skybreaker's spells to try to find a way to bring him back, or to destroy the imperial family, obsessed her: she ate little, only enough to live, and filled her body with shards of power in every way she could think of: wearing charmed bracelets or eating farsight apples—though they showed her nothing because the thing she desperately wished for had died. The great spirit of the Fourth Mountain was named Crown, and because Crown also missed Skybreaker, sometimes it laid its scraggly head upon her lap and listened to her rant and wail. She lost herself in memories, grasped at the bear spirit with hungry fingers, trying to swallow parts of its magic.

She could not. She was not a sorcerer and could not make herself into one.

Often she grew violent when she failed, lashing out at the spirit. She accused it of failing Skybreaker and screamed that it should have died when Skybreaker died—then it would be a great demon and could devour the empire! Beginning with Kirin Dark-Smile and his family.

The fights between Syra and Crown froze the peaks of the Fourth Mountain and set the alpine grasses on fire.

Syra stumbled down the mountain every few months to recover, and Sunrise nervously cared for her, mopping her brow of aether-fevers and helping her sip medicinal teas. She often grabbed him too hard, bruising a wrist, and he never pulled away. He remained huddled at her side because when he was beside her she breathed easier. His mother murmured in her sleep, and tears fell down her temples. She begged him not to die, begged him to stay with her, and late at night she hissed plans for what they would do to his father's enemies. "They did this to us. To me! They don't even care, down in their glorious palace. If we all wasted away, what would it matter to the Moon! We must destroy them—we must. I'll never live otherwise!"

Sunrise promised to help her. The empress and her heir certainly didn't seem to care what had happened on the Fourth Mountain, or this fallout. If nothing else, they were indifferent. And maybe when Syra's vengeance was satisfied she could rest. Maybe someday she could look at him and see him for who he was, not only as a weapon.

Maybe. He hoped so. Prayed so, making dangerous offerings of his hair and blood at every spirit shrine he found. *Let my mother love me. Let her see me.*

When he was eleven, his mother said, "Prove to me you can do what is necessary," and offered him a small canary in a cage.

"Mother?" he said, confused. It was one of his, which he'd raised for over a year.

"I want to roast it for dinner."

Sunrise froze, lips parted. He understood this was a test, and one he would fail if he did not harden for her. He blinked, tried to stall. "It is mostly bones."

Syra Bear Mistress stared at her son, cold and ferocious, until he took the cage with shaking hands and removed the canary. He stared at its little black eyes, its body twitching in his gentle palms. Then he snapped its neck.

7

Fast.

Before he had even consciously ordered himself to do it.

He dropped it to the floor; it barely made a sound, it was so small.

"Good," his mother said. "Now get better at such things. No hesitation."

Sunrise nodded, flushed with panicked relief she'd not demanded he kill one of his dogs. He would have hated proving himself to her over one of those sleek, loyal babies. After waking in a cold sweat imagining it, Sunrise gave the dogs to a neighboring farm with children the right age to adore them.

His aunt Windsong—who did not know about the bird— began to teach him everything she knew about blades and fighting. That took many months. When Windsong declared she had no more to teach, they hired a retired soldier who worked at one of the nearby inns to teach Sunrise more. That took another two years. The work was grueling, and Sunrise never hesitated to push too hard. He broke his wrist. He did not sleep. Until Aunts Tali and Windsong threatened to refuse to let his soldier mentor enter the enclave again if Sunrise did not rest and take care. Sunrise fought them until Tali said, "What good will you be to your mother if you are weak and exhausted?" She said it with an uncertain frown, but it worked.

Then, for no reason Sunrise or the aunties could see, Syra came down the mountain entirely calm. For two years she smiled at her old sisters; she laughed sometimes and petted her Sunrise with a tender familiarity. Hope burned in her gaze, and in turn, lit a spark in Sunrise. He said, "What happened, Mother?"

She giggled like a maiden and said, "We are not alone, baby."

She refused to say more but put her finger to her lips as if to keep a secret between them.

On his thirteenth birthday, Syra brought him flowers and strange food, as well as armor and weaponry, showering Sunrise with gifts and laughter.

Sunrise flushed with joy, held her hand, and showed her his hard work. He'd recently learned a new set of sword-forms, and excelled.

Syra kissed him on both cheeks, then held him close all night.

In the morning Syra took Sunrise by the hand and led him toward the paths up the Fourth Mountain.

"Where are we going?" he asked.

"To meet some friends and finish forging you."

Sunrise swallowed anxiety at the obscured answer. It could mean anything, but he went with her. What other choice did he have? He needed her to love him.

As they trekked up, he wandered off the path sometimes to caress a lovely fern or pluck a tiny flower for Syra's hair. Together they sang rounds, their voices weaving around each other into weak spells for blessing. Syra could see scraps of aether sometimes, when they glinted in the shadows, and Sunrise could anytime he tried—but he hid it from his mother, preferring to use his slight gift to mess around with funny spirits like raccoons and sparrows and foxes.

It took them a day and a half to reach the Fourth Mountain gate, where Crown, the great bear spirit, awaited them. The bear stood on its hind legs, its rough fur black as night but glimmering with stars the blue-silver color of aether, and its eyes swirling pools of the same. Sunrise had met the great spirit before, of course, but rarely and not since he was much younger. For some reason, being nearly thirteen years old did not make him feel stronger or taller or wiser in the presence of such a neat, powerful creature. So Sunrise gaped gently and tried not to put his hand on his knife.

daughter of Skybreaker, the spirit said.

Sunrise carefully knelt. "Great spirit," he said.

you are here for our gift

"What gift?"

transformation

Sunrise gasped. "Mother?"

"Not a dramatic one, daughter. You will recognize yourself, and all your aunties will, too."

The bear turned those swirling blue eyes to him. *you do not wish to change?*

Its voice reverberated softly in Sunrise's skull.

"I . . . wish to be the best I can be, for Mother. And Father," he added earnestly.

Syra nodded firmly, and Sunrise knew he'd answered as she liked.

The bear tilted its head and then dropped onto all four paws. Turning, it walked through the gate. Syra took Sunrise's hand and pulled him after.

Inside it was cool and shaded. Dark.

Syra spoke a word he did not know, and a row of tiny lights sparked to life, curling up the walls of the cavern until the whole place was lit silver-blue. It was a workroom, lined with shelves carved right into the walls, piled with books and jars, items he knew like knives and wands and mirrors, and items he could not name, with strange shapes and colors.

And two men stood shoulder to shoulder, staring at Sunrise.

He froze, pinned by their twin gazes.

Like mirrors of each other, the men smiled: they were pale and handsome, young, with bloodred hair and dark eyes, wearing elaborate suits of black and white. Barefoot, Sunrise noticed. With rings on several fingers, exactly the same.

"You are Sunrise," one said.

The other said, "We are When the Wind Stills the Stars Dance."

Sunrise swallowed.

"Lord sorcerers," his mother said sweetly. "Here is my daughter, and she is ready."

"We will begin," said the sorcerers of the Third and Second Mountains.

The bear spirit settled in a bright furry curl and pulled Sunrise onto its lap. Two flashes of aether forced him to blink and shield his eyes. When he lowered his hands, a great spirit sat to either side of them: one a large, sleek tiger, the other a bird of prey combing its curved beak along the feathers of its blue-silver wing.

Heart pounding in his ears, Sunrise stared. He could feel their power radiating against his skin, lifting the hairs along his arms and neck.

He fisted his hands in the cloth over his knees and nodded to each great spirit.

They ignored him.

So Sunrise watched as his mother moved across the flat stone floor with a wand, drawing a diagram. She giggled to herself, and a shudder coursed down his spine. The bear spirit grunted. It was staring at him with one vivid aether-blue eye.

"Hello," Sunrise whispered.

hello, it said.

"Thank you for caring for my mother."

our interests align

"Oh. You . . . want revenge for Skybreaker's death."

your father looked like you before he bound himself to me

"Really!" Sunrise grinned in sudden relief. That was the nearest anyone had come to treating him like his father's *son.*

"Sunrise," Syra chided sharply. "I am concentrating."

"I apologize, Mother," he called before softening his voice again, attention on Crown. "He was small?"

the shape of his mouth was like yours. The color of his eyes. Your hair and stature are not from him, though. He was always tall.

"That's nice, though. Thank you, great spirit."

It nodded and went back to ignoring him.

But shortly, Syra beckoned him over to stand before her and the two mirror sorcerers. "Strip," she commanded, and he did not hesitate.

Naked, Sunrise stood where he was told, in the center of the diagram. He studied it: the dark silver lines spread from his feet out in loops and jagged letters of some kind, barely visible against the granite floor.

His mother took the wand and pressed one end to her palm, then switched to press it into her other. She passed the wand to one of the sorcerers, who tucked it into a sleeve. Then each sorcerer took one of her hands, palms up, and whispered until her hands glowed.

Before Sunrise could move, a flash of brilliant aether-light flared from the diagram: it burned with blue-silver aether. He gasped, and his skin pebbled as the air crisped; his hair rose down his neck and along his arms. "Wow," he whispered.

His mother walked to him, placing her toes carefully, and with those glowing hands she began to touch him: first his temples, brushing down to his cheeks and along his jaw. She brushed fingers along his neck, then back into his hair, combing through tenderly. Following the lines of muscles, she traced swooping lines across his shoulders, down his spine, along his hips and thighs and ankles. Sunrise closed his eyes and melted into the gentle warmth: he felt loved, finally, as his mother painted him over with magic.

To finish, she caressed the tips of his eyelashes and said, "Open your eyes, my Sunrise, and hold them wide for me. Trust me, and be strong."

He did so and bit back a slight whimper as she oh so carefully touched the pad of her forefinger first to one eye and then the other.

At her nod, he squeezed them closed again as they filled with thin tears. He took a deep breath, and his mother held his shoulders, breathing with him.

"Good girl," she murmured. "You're all done."

When Sunrise looked again, the aether had faded and his mother knelt, leaning back on her feet. Behind her, the mirrored sorcerers clapped their hands together once, hard and in sync.

Pain flared in his bones. Sunrise dropped to the ground. He felt drained and bizarre, his skin tingling. He leaned forward, and Syra held him as he pressed his cheek to her lap, shaking. She petted his hair, drawing the long strands apart, letting them slide through her hand and skim his back.

For a long time Sunrise shuddered and sweated, so very cold. A burning kind of cold that raced through his body like the worst fever.

Then it stopped. Someone spoke. Sunrise shook his head to clear it. His mother lifted him, helped him move his noodled limbs. He moved without thought, dull and exhausted. As he tied his pants, Sunrise realized it was not the spiraling aether-lights on the cave walls tingeing his knuckles blue-violet. His skin was changed.

Shocked, he turned his hands over and studied the subtle lines of dusky color against the suntan of his skin. Then he bent to look at his belly and chest, twisted his neck to try to see his shoulders and spine. It was so bluish all over.

"Mother!" he said, and one of the mirrored sorcerers offered a small silver mirror. He handed it to Syra, who angled it to Sunrise.

His eyes were dark purple and flecked still with the warm brown they used to be. The blue-violet lined his cheeks and jaw and streaked back into his hair. He looked demon-kissed. "It is perfect," his mother said. "You must stay away from amulets of transformation, if possible, which might undo the spell."

"Why?"

One of the sorcerers flicked a dismissive hand. "Sorcery can be fickle."

"I mean . . ." Sunrise tried to bow but tilted with vertigo. His mother caught his elbow. He said, "I mean why make me like this?"

"You will be accepted faster into the palace," Syra said.

"Being demon-kissed will make up for being a woman warrior. And your background will be less investigated."

Sunrise licked his lips, ignoring the prickling discomfort of *woman warrior*. "But I'm not fast or strong. I have no demon-kissed talent."

"Your memory is extraordinary," said one of the mirrored sorcerers. Maybe the same one who had spoken before.

"Oh." Sunrise stared at the sorcerer, at the strange smooth features, like an unfinished painting. The sorcerer smiled, and glanced at Syra.

Her eyes shone with a strong emotion Sunrise didn't understand—but he found himself suddenly ill at ease all over again.

"Sunrise," she said, "it is like proof of your father's power. He was not demon-kissed, but he was a sorcerer. Marking you with magic is a way to show people you are born of it."

Sunrise touched her cheek with his knuckles, as he did when she was ill. Her skin was flushed, her gaze wild. Then he nodded. "I understand, Mother," he whispered.

demon-kissed would have a different name, the great bear spirit said.

Sunrise jerked, surprised.

Even Syra looked up sharply.

The bird of prey spirit spread its wings lazily, and the tiger spirit stalked toward Sunrise. He did his best to remain still as he carefully said, "What was my father's name, before he was your Skybreaker?"

"Good," said one of the sorcerers, and the other said, "Very good."

The bear spirit, lifting to its full height, nearly brushed the ceiling of the workroom—it had to be twelve feet tall suddenly.

Sunrise leaned his head back and gripped his mother's hand.

Osian, the bear said. *Skybreaker's first, human name was Osian.*

"Osian," he repeated.

"Osian," his mother murmured, long and mournful. "Osian will destroy the family of Kirin Dark-Smile."

And Osian imagined he felt the slick sensation of the name— as if it were alive to choose—claim him, sticking to his palms and the bare soles of his feet, diving into his chest to find his heart.

ONE

RALIEL DARK-SMILE MET THE great demon of the palace for the first time face-to-face when she was seven years old, just after she'd given herself her name. Of course, she'd seen scraps of the demon's aether and slippery dark shadows in long hallways and pockets of the palace gardens. She'd felt it humming as she learned to play the harp at her mother's side. But it wasn't until that night, seven since she'd declared her name, two since her father had been enthroned as the Emperor with the Moon in His Mouth, that the demon appeared.

She woke from a dream, and there it crouched upon the foot of her bed. It was the size and shape of a child her age, made of shadows and darkness, with seven round silver-white eyes like seven moons clustered on the flat plane of its face.

Raliel had been startled but not afraid.

She knew it was the great demon, as she'd lived in the Palace of Seven Circles, which was the demon's house, for all her life. It slept, her nursemaid had told her, far below in the foundations of the palace. It slept like a serpent guarding its nest, rolling over sometimes so the palace floors trembled, and hissed its breath in the occasional cold wind gusting through the smoke-ways in the sticky summer. The demon only woke, her nurse said, when a new emperor took the Moon into themself and at the heir's investiture ritual—or if it was needed to defend the palace, which had not happened since the great demon of the Fifth Mountain had tried to kidnap the emperor, years before Raliel had been born.

Of course, that wasn't the way her father the emperor told Raliel the story. He said he'd not been kidnapped at all, not exactly, and that Night Shine, the great demon of the Fifth Mountain, had saved him, been his good friend. The emperor also said their great demon, whose name was Moon, rarely slept these days, rather slipped through the walls from shrine to shrine, listening intently to gossip. Moon brought some of it to the emperor, if the demon thought he should know a thing. "That's our secret, little moon, yes?" the emperor told her, and she asked, "Except from Mother and Father?" The emperor smiled his tilted smile and whispered against her ear, "No exceptions."

So Raliel learned sometimes the emperor kept secrets from his consorts. She had tried to speak to the great demon herself, but it never said anything to her, or seemed to notice her back.

Until that night it stared at her from the foot of her bed. "Hello," Raliel whispered, pushing sleek black hair behind her ear. It always escaped her night braid.

hello, the demon whispered. No part of its face moved: no gash of a shadow-mouth appeared, no flash of fangs or forked tongue. The whisper simply formed itself like delicate glass filaments, and Raliel could not be sure if she heard it or felt it.

Resisting the urge to draw her legs up to hug her knees to her chest (which would be a sign of emotion), Raliel peered at it. Throughout her room, moonlight reflected: in her mirror, gleaming against the polished cheeks of toy dancers and carved rain forest animals in the corner, shining off the crystal globe etched with a map of Heaven, and highlighting the gold ink tracing the lines of imperial ancestry along scrolls spread over her tea table. Everything in her bedroom shone or sparkled as it caught hints of silvery moonlight. Except the demon. Its small form swallowed light, a child-shaped void, darker than anything.

Raliel shivered, rather excited. "What are you doing here?" she asked softly—her mother instructed that a cool, soft tone was less revealing than a whisper.

I like your name. It is a dragon's name, the demon said.

"Thank you. I picked it myself," she answered, unable to stop the pleased blush of her cheeks. It had taken her years to find a name she liked, that sounded the way she felt, and meant something she wanted.

the emperor did not give you a name.

"He told me my name should be the responsibility of nobody but me." Raliel did not truly understand such reasoning but could repeat the words her father the emperor had spoken again and again.

Until recently she'd been called nicknames and endearments—"little moon" by the emperor, "my sweet" or "little empress" from her father Sky, and simply "daughter" from her mother. Her grandmother, the previous Empress with the Moon in Her Mouth, called her "darkling smile" with resignation, and her grandmother Love-Eyes called her "child." Her grandfather Sun-Bright called her "Kirin's reward," which she didn't realize was sarcastic until she was a lot older. To her cousins and aunts, to the Lord of Narrow and witches and dawn priests, she was "the princess." Everyone was frustrated and everyone complained, but her father (now the emperor) insisted she find a name for herself only when she was ready.

She found her name in a song, one she had plucked from the library for its simple melody with which she could practice her fingering on the lap harp her mother had given her. When she realized she knew her name, she declared it to her parents in the Moon's Recline Garden because this had been the garden where her father, who had been Kirin then, had taught her that she could be anyone she liked. She would be known as a girl, he said, because that was expected, but it did not mean she *was* a girl, or had to be. Not in chosen name or identity. "You listen to yourself," he had told her, snuggling her in his lap, her cheek pressed to embroidered bluebirds along the lapel of his elaborate morning robe. "That's what I've always done, little moon, and I'm perfect for it."

With the name finally ready on her tongue, she tugged his sleeve. Kirin had set down his bowl of tea and flicked his fingers for the attention of First Consort Sky and Second Consort Elegant Waters. Lifting his unpainted face into the cool cast of listening, Kirin said, "Our daughter has decided who she is. Tell us, little moon."

She straightened her back, pressed her palms to her folded knees, and said in a voice she tried to make as easy as his, "Raliel. I am Raliel Dark-Smile, after my father and the great dragon of the Tylish Lake, who was murdered and became a great demon to wreak vengeance upon its enemies. After they banished it"—her smile widened with childish bloodthirsty wonder—"the dragon demon became a *song*! And if you sing the song, you'll die within seven days!"

Kirin's expression cracked instantly, and even a little girl could recognize the sheer glee lighting him up. He laughed, raising perfect eyebrows at Sky.

Sky had given both Kirin and their daughter a shared look of resignation. Elegant Waters had hummed, considering the situation. She lifted her tea to her pink lips—she already was painted for the day, in sweeping lines of black and pink like wings spreading from the corners of her large dark eyes—and tilted her head without disrupting a strand of intricately looped hair. "Tell me, my daughter," she said, "if you are a dragon, what sort of dragon are you?"

Raliel bit her lip before she remembered that would muss her own makeup, and even though she wasn't wearing it yet, she must always bear in mind how she touched her face. In the same cool voice, she said, "A beautiful one."

Her mother had smiled just slightly. "Come here, little dragon, and I will help you with that."

Now in Raliel's midnight bedroom, the small shadow-form of the great demon wrapped its arms around its knees and seemed to stare at her. She was glad it approved of her name.

"Did you choose your name?" Raliel asked.

Instead of answering, the demon said, *you were thinking about the sky.*

"I was asleep," she reminded it. "Thinking of nothing at all."

at the ritual. You were thinking about the sky.

Oh, Raliel recalled that: it had been so boring, the elaborate ritual making her father the emperor. Boring but crowded, and Raliel disliked the press of courtiers and witches, the spark of aether knotting itself up with all the various intentions and antagonizing. She'd had only one small part to play—giving her name and making her vow to be the pure Heir to the Moon— and otherwise she'd stared up at the tiny windows at a very faded half-moon in a very blue sky. And wished to fly like the dangerous dragon of her same name. Or be anywhere else, really.

do you dream? the great demon asked.

Her fingers itched to reach up and tug on the end of her braid for comfort. She stared at the seven moon-eyes, wondering if there were one or two she should focus on. They clustered together in what might've been a spiral. The more she stared, the more she could see shapes in them, white on white. Her father the emperor had a voluminous black robe embroidered with a garden of black flowers. Even when he was still, the robe seemed to shimmer with a dark life of its own, but when he moved and it caught sunlight or aether-lantern glow, the black flowers danced, the illusion of deepening jungle drawing the eye further and further into the emperor's power.

The demon's eyes were like that: seven moons each with a pale world inside them.

Raliel shivered again and said, "Do you want a piece of candy?"

It said, *I cannot eat candy, but you can, and I will like that too.*

She narrowed her eyes, wondering where the trick was, but when she couldn't find it, she slipped out of bed, pulled on a thin robe, and tiptoed out to the small sitting nook between her room and her mother's. A dish of hard honey petals sat on the writing desk near the window, and she plucked out a dark one she hoped was red, but the moonlight washed the colors into shades of gray. Then she turned and gasped, for the demon had followed her. It hovered right there, exactly her height and its shoulders the same width as hers, and Raliel got angry that it was imitating her. But she did as her mother expected and made her anger cold instead of hot, then put the candy in her mouth and rolled it with her tongue as she glared at those seven moon-eyes. Shadows moved across the lower portion of its face as if it had a petal rolling in its mouth too.

They stood there, mirroring each other, while the candy melted sugar down Raliel's throat.

Then she opened her mouth to show it the candy was gone and her tongue was much darker than before.

The demon sank away into the parquet floor.

Confused, Raliel remained standing there until her toes were too cold, and she tucked herself back into bed.

TWO

I F THERE WAS ONE thing everyone in the Palace of Seven
Circles agreed upon, it was that the Heir to the Moon was
perfect and good but too cold.

The Lords of Narrow and Every Star, the Ladies Peach
Blossom and Falling Red had nothing but compliments for the
heir, for her poise and politeness; the lesser courtiers appreciated the clear notes of her music, the way she poured her father
tea; the guards and generals found her sword-forms impeccable;
the palace poets said her early efforts at composition revealed
the potential for greatness; the tailors and cooks and ink maids
enjoyed their turns painting her face or embroidering her
gowns or adding just the right amount of pepper to her food
as she was unerringly kind and remembered everyone's names
and relations and even some distant relatives or stories they'd
spoken of once and assumed she'd forgotten. The scholars and
priests who tutored her praised her memory, too, and her precision and clever mind. There was a retired battle witch called
Immli who was suspicious of the speed with which she picked
up complicated aether-work and drew sigils that ought to have

been beyond her, but it was his job to be cautious with magic, and he was correct, in any case: the great demon of the palace helped the heir with her sigils and taught her the languages of spirits, which was a language that could not be spoken by human mouths and voices but written well enough, in ink or sand or pollen or blood.

Raliel grew accustomed to the great demon's voice in her head, tingling in her palms or down her spine as if the demon held her hand or nudged her between her shoulder blades. When she knelt at one of the altars carved in alcoves in every level of the Palace of Seven Circles, she felt it kneel beside her, and as she prayed, it drank up the aether that gathered in candle flames or swirled in the thin lines of incense. That was how it ate: the prayers and offerings of every human in the palace increased its power, tying their lives to it with thin tendrils of magic. It drew from the imperial family, too, but that was a circuit, and when Raliel prayed, when her fathers and mother prayed, it returned strength to them sevenfold.

Palace gardeners worked constantly, for flowers and trees with their roots in the palace soil were slowly drained of their aether to feed the demon. Mice that died in the walls fed it, and baby birds that fell too soon from nests in ornamental pear trees in the fifth circle, and any spirits that managed to live in the Lily Garden or dawn sprites fluttering in the chapels had to work triply hard to maintain their connections to the aether, lest the demon make little demons out of them, too. There were no ghosts in the palace, for ghosts cannot exist where there is a great demon to chew up their final spark at the moment of death, regardless of how or why they die. The priests in the palace mostly had forgotten how to make ghost amulets, focused instead on charms that could shield a dying old tailor or a gravely injured palace soldier from the demon so that their spirits could dissipate into the world and their names be recorded in Heaven.

Despite earning the admiration of nearly everyone Raliel Dark-Smile met, she did not quite manage friendship. When she played her harp, she sounded as good as her very gifted mother but lacked something nobody could quite name. (Perhaps her true audience appreciated the music differently than human ears.) When she discussed historical tactics or legal reform, her words were smart and sharp but lacked fire. (Arguing at night with a demon taught one to be very careful and precise with weaknesses.) Her poetry, while technically superior, was strangely abstract. Beautiful yes, graceful yes, but the subject matter was more suited to obscure ancient texts than youthful wonder or exuberance. How much of an old soul she seemed—yes, that was it, the courtiers murmured among themselves. An old soul.

Returning favors to her or giving her gifts was difficult, for no one knew what the heir liked. Oh, she might say she liked pale silks and white orchids in her hair, she might say she preferred the essays of Andel Aged or the styles of the water painters from the eastern canyons, and when she played she certainly gravitated toward haunting, yearning songs over joyful ones. She was diligent in her calligraphy and put constant effort into sword-forms, surpassed her peers in aether-work, but could any of that be proven a passion or merely duty? She was the only choice for Heir to the Moon, after all, and required to excel.

Her father the emperor, who tutored her personally in politics (mostly by asking her questions about what was actually happening and helping her map out patterns of internecine favoritism and grudges) was unconcerned. His daughter did not know who she was yet, and her bold choice of name promised when she was ready, she would blossom spectacularly.

But the emperor was not Raliel's only parent, and both the First and Second Consorts were worried.

First Consort Sky spent part of every day working with his daughter on warcraft and meditation; he was satisfied by Raliel's efforts in sword-forms and privately considered her better than him at any meditative techniques that allowed for stillness. Combining the two in Sky's preferred style of mindful movement proved more difficult for her, but she tried. The first time Raliel smiled at him with *distance* on her face, Sky nearly fell over. It was an expression he'd never seen her wear, though Second Consort Elegant Waters looked similar sometimes when she herself was hiding a sudden surge of emotion. Sky knew both he and Elegant Waters were reserved people—one had to be, paired with the emperor—and he knew Raliel styled herself after her mother in poise and expression, but he'd thought it was a sweet imitation. He had thought he understood his daughter. And then appeared that cool smile.

The First Consort summoned his courage and told Elegant Waters, who lowered her lashes and said she'd spoken at length with Raliel about relaxing sometimes or allowing herself to grow angry—it was perfectly normal to be angry, or hurt, or desperate for something. And Raliel had frowned prettily and asked what could possibly anger or hurt her in the palace? When she wanted something, she could have it.

Mother and daughter knelt on cushions in the Second

Consort's favorite garden, in the fifth circle, where she'd stayed upon her first visit to the city. It had been for the emperor's birthday, and she'd been invited along with many other eligible young women from around the country. Elegant Waters, a second daughter who had been raised in a silent monastery high on the Mountain of One Thousand Falls, had been overwhelmed by the ornamentation of the Palace of Seven Circles as well as by the eager, boisterous young women, and found refuge in the moss garden. The peaceful beds of cultivated moss were artfully arranged around a central ancient nurse log covered in tiny purple flowers and rainbows of lichen. Elegant Waters found it endlessly soothing.

There she gently dug at her daughter, insisting in several subtle ways there must be something Raliel wished for, wanted only for herself.

Raliel said, "I . . . What should I want, Mother?"

Pursing her lips to display a hint of displeasure (it would not do to scare Raliel away), Elegant Waters said, "When I was thirteen, I wanted a friend. A dearest friend."

"Oh. I see." Raliel glanced down at her hands, folded casually in her lap. "I am sure I will make friends. Father had not met his First Consort when he was thirteen."

"No, but he had his Night Shine already."

Raliel's eyes lifted to her mother's then, as if finally understanding something. She nodded and said tentatively, her pale cheeks flushing a delicate peach, "I would like to see your family's home. The Mountain of One Thousand Falls, with all its cold springs and winter flowers. I wish I could go—I wish you could take me. In the winter when there would be snow."

28

Of course such a request was impossible: the bargain with the great demon of the palace kept the Imperial Triad bound within its walls, just as the demon was bound, and the heir could not travel until the traditional Heir's Journey the summer she was nineteen. Elegant Waters did believe it was a true desire on her daughter's part, and also that it was a safe confession because it couldn't be granted.

The Second Consort tried again. "You do not want friends, Raliel?"

Raliel's mouth moved as she stopped herself from biting her bottom lip. She shook her head. "I have the great demon, Mother. It is my friend."

Elegant Waters could hardly argue, when she got along well with the great demon herself and had just mentioned the great demon Night Shine as the emperor's first friend. So the Second Consort did not challenge her daughter again. She did, however, send for her cousin's children and one of Sky's nieces to be companions for the heir.

So by the time she was fourteen Raliel had a coterie of three: Salri was a stout, merry boy with the same cool brown eyes as Elegant Waters but even whiter skin and the same gift for music. Averilis was the least bold of the three but pretty as a songbird. The demon-kissed Rose Blue would have been plain if not for the streaks of purple in her hair and bluish shading to her copper skin. It was said the demon-kissed families had been cursed long ago by a Queen of Heaven, marked for an ancient crime, but now they were often admired for their unique looks and whatever magical gift came with it. Raliel's father Sky was demon-kissed, and stronger than any twenty men together. Rose's gift was perfect aim and would've been better suited to the army—Sky had been a soldier before he was the First Consort—but Rose disliked exercise and warcraft and had learned to harness her gift in the delicate work of makeup and accessories. If she could hit a target with an arrow from too far away for Raliel to see, she could also use a needle to thread minuscule seed pearls onto a single strand of hair or paint perfect, unwavering lines of goldfleck in repeating patterns down Raliel's cheek.

Raliel appreciated her new friends, though she did not forge intimate connections with any of them because the great demon was uninterested in Raliel's coterie, and they were afraid of it, which allowed Raliel to keep those parts of her life severed. She arranged time every day to be alone in the Garden of the Seas in the third circle, supposedly in meditation and prayer but truthfully playing games with the demon.

Sometimes the emperor joined her, and he was the only person in the world she could not order to leave. The third time he surprised her there, Raliel realize the demon had invited him. "Did you play with the demon when you were my age?" she asked, tucked on a pillow beside a bed of waving rows of blue-leaf and vivid midnight flox.

Her father smiled the smile they shared: tilted to a wicked degree, with the slightest hint of teeth. "I played with *a* demon," he said. "Not the Moon. But that other demon lives in the Fifth Mountain now."

"Why doesn't *our* demon leave the palace?" she asked the emperor. "The priests and Immli say that great demons can leave their houses, and it's what differentiates them from lesser demons who must remain physically connected to the house they possess."

"Our demon doesn't have a sorcerer to anchor it in the house while it leaves," her father answered, playing with one of the three ruby rings on his left hand. That hand was only ever decorated with ruby rings. Sometimes each finger was adorned, sometimes only a few, rarely a single half-moon ruby glinted alone on his forefinger. That coincided with the days the emperor wore robes cut in feminine style or a lady's gown tailored perfectly to his masculine-shaped body. Averilis, who collected gossip for Raliel, said a few years ago a courtier had whisperingly called him the Empress with the Moon in His Mouth, and when the emperor found out he'd gifted the person to blame with a box full of pearls.

Raliel said, "It has us. We aren't sorcerers, but we're tied to it by the palace-amulet. Shouldn't we anchor it well enough?"

The emperor shrugged elegantly. "We are none of us anchors for the others, but all bound together. We make the house; we do not simply live in it."

"Do you regret it? Being stuck here?" she asked, lowering her eyes because she knew better than to ask.

Her father tugged the drop of rainbow glass hanging from her earlobe. "Never, little dragon. Here is where my family lives, and my power."

Though Raliel wished to draw her knees under her chin and hug herself small, she kept her spine straight and her hands gentle on her thighs. She let her lashes flutter and pursed her coral-painted lips as her only sign of displeasure. Her mother had been helping her learn to control her face with exercises and mirrors—because political power was not the only sort she had available. "Beauty is power, and you should wield it,"

Elegant Waters had said. "Do you know how I earned my title?" Raliel had not, and her mother smiled a beautiful cool smile, like a perfectly shaped ice sculpture. "I told your father, when he still had his old name, that I was the only other person as beautiful as he, and our children would be even more so. I appealed to the side of him that most saw but refused to acknowledge."

"Am I?" Raliel had asked.

"More beautiful than myself or your father?"

"Yes," she'd whispered, not believing it but hoping nonetheless.

Elegant Waters had inspected her, bright brown eyes a bit too warm with humor. "We shall see," she had finally answered, and would give no more.

In the Garden of the Seas, Raliel asked the emperor, "What is your power, Father? Is it the demon?"

"The Moon represents my power and the power of the empire. But our power itself comes from our prosperity and our strategies, from the farmers and soldiers and merchants and priests, little dragon. My power comes from everyone who speaks my name with respect and trusts in me to hold my promises. When I became emperor, I became power. I embrace it, as you will in turn."

Naturally, Raliel found a moment to ask her father Sky about power too. He frowned so deeply his chin puckered and she feared she'd misspoken. Though at fourteen she was getting better at invulnerable, icy expressions, Sky must have seen her distress; he hunkered down and cupped his wide hands on her face.

"Dada!" she shrieked because he would certainly smear the soft silver Rose had painted on her cheeks.

Sky released her, grumbling only a little, and said, "Liel, you already know about power—you were born to it, and since you were anointed as the Heir to the Moon, you've worn it. You need to understand that it already is part of you, a part you must temper, or you will hurt people."

"Have you hurt people?" she asked in her smallest voice.

He did not answer directly, and that usually meant he was covering for the emperor.

The great demon told her power was food and showed her a sigil to draw excess aether from the wind to give it a snack.

As Raliel grew older, she became more involved in the public face of the imperial family, joining her mother for gossipy lunches and her father Sky with the inner troops and the emperor at banquets and more and more afternoons of correspondence and meetings. She moved through it all gracefully, imagined herself to be a cool moon, like Moon, a silent observer, and to never give herself away with a gesture or expression. To never laugh when the demon tapped something through the floor that sounded like the language of spirits or even blink when it distracted her on purpose by purring against her skin. That made her shiver, made her learn more flirtatious mannerisms to cover it in public.

It was a challenge she relished. The world would be vibrant and loud, and Raliel would be snow on a cold night, a winter moon drifting among rowdy suns and summer flowers.

With practice, she made herself more beautiful, following her parents' examples to create her own aesthetic for the younger courtiers and palace folk. Where the emperor favored a bold, traditional contrast of color, black and white, red and mint, sunrise-violet and vivid marigold, shaped in sweeping layers and elaborate styles, and her mother made herself untouchable with striking headdresses and encrusted jewels, Raliel began to put herself exclusively in white, silver, or gray. Her coterie held on to color, but gray-washed as if seen by moonlight: seafoam greens, silver-evening blues, pale-pretty pinks. They made of themselves a moonlit garden with her. It was oh so rewarding to draw the eyes of everyone like she was the moon and they were winking stars.

Only, the more she created an image of herself, the more Raliel *became* that cold moon soaring high over the palace, the less she felt attached to anybody, including Salri, Averilis, and Rose Blue. She knew the emperor and her mother kept themselves aloof on purpose, because of their titles and what they meant to the empire; she also knew that when alone they shed such trappings for each other. Though her father the emperor never would be caught dead in anything less than the creamiest linen shirts or slippers of embroidered silk, even just with his family, it was the masks he put down, to allow his consorts—and his daughter—to know him. In private he removed his rain veil and makeup. He laughed and teased and *fussed* constantly. He climbed into Sky's lap and melted after a long day. Elegant Waters sometimes dug her toes into the moss in the garden despite staining them, or held her hands over a candle flame because she truly enjoyed the warmth she did not display in public. She fondly pinched the emperor's thigh or sighed dramatically when Sky was too jealous. Even Raliel's father Sky wore a mask of himself before the world—a mask he'd created when he was a soldier, a young bodyguard for a prince he was forbidden to touch. But he had always shed it for the emperor, given his true self to at least one person.

Raliel did not know how to do that with Salri, Averilis, and Rose Blue. Or if she even should. Her coterie *were* friends, but also they were accessories. She listened to their stories and family histories, she knew of them, she knew *them*, but she rarely gave herself to them in the same way—any personal family stories were either well known already or too private. Potential weapons, potential gossip. Raliel told them the things her parents wanted for the empire, her opinions on art and poetry and historical edicts, scheduling changes or gossip requests, the things she wanted to eat or drink, and they saw to it. But none of that was who she was or could be.

Slowly, Raliel realized her parents were able to remove their masks because they knew themselves underneath. And Raliel did not. Beneath the mask she was building, she was a cavern. And the weight of her emptiness dragged her down, deep into her thoughts, where she couldn't escape.

Only the great demon saw her when she shed everything and lay listless in her bed, staring at the distant stars and listening to the hush-hush of the ocean.

"I think you are my only true friend, Moon," she whispered to it.

good, it whispered, purring through the walls just for her.

Perhaps its possessiveness should have concerned her, but instead, she liked it. This she did not have to share. It did not have to share *her*.

Well into her sixteenth year, after a long morning of sword work and math, of an interminable lunch with her mother and seven bickering courtiers, after an afternoon too rainy to study in her favorite gardens, after spilling ink on her hem, and a whiplash of aether when she tried too sharp a sigil over an unstable net, after a performance by the emperor's favorite poet before the entire court, in which the poet described a wilderness so evocative Raliel's teeth hurt with longing she could not express—the heir returned to her bedchambers only to send her maids and Rose Blue away and tear free of her headdress and outer robes by herself. Violently. Crushing the fine boning and silk flowers as she threw them to the floor.

"I have to get out of here," she hissed, shoving the latticed shutters open to lean into the warm sea air.

She closed her eyes and pressed her temple to the black-lacquered windowframe. Her half-undone braids listed to the side, dragging at her sore neck, and she wrapped her arms around her waist, curling her fingers angrily in the too-fine layer of sheer linen. She could tear it. She could.

But she didn't.

Tears pressed behind her eyes, thickening her throat, and Raliel wondered what was wrong with her. She had everything. Family. Power. Beauty. Lavish rooms, plentiful foods, friends and servants, and the promise of an even better future. She wanted to be good, but what did that *mean*? What did she yearn for? *Snow?* It was selfish and ridiculous, and she hated it. She hated being unable to breathe it away, to accept this was all she would ever be. But she would be the empress of all the land between the Five Mountains someday! How dare she be unhappy. How dare she long for more.

More *what*?

Just more. No wonder she'd not been able to express to her mother what she wanted those years ago!

Laughing angrily at herself, she peeled open her tear-sticky eyes and looked out at the blue nighttime, the glint of stars and the mirroring sea on the horizon. Below, the palace spread downward in all its circles, peaked walls and gardens and towers in red, white, black, all washed gray like midnight wounds. And beyond that, the city with its wide avenues and market squares, the broad parks lush with rain forest trees and sheets of vines, flowers and fountains, and aether-light lanterns. The Selegan River wound a wide ribbon along the west side of the city, a night-silver road flowing to the sea. She wanted to sail against its current: north, up through the farmland and into the rain forest, cutting through that thick jungle and against the foothills of the Fifth Mountain. Her fathers had done so once, both of them. With the demon Night Shine and a dragon.

Was that dragon nearby now? Could she summon it along a string of aether? She'd like to meet it, but Moon did not allow other spirits of such power into its domain.

Raliel closed her eyes again and listened with her skin and other senses for the unsound of ready aether. She reached out and plucked a strand that tangled in the breeze. At her touch it hummed, and she wondered what it would be like to grasp it in her fist and pull. It would not tear but stretch, and jagged bursts of her power would flow along it in either direction until it hit a knot or a high note or until something else—some spirit or witch—tugged back. She wanted to try, to tear at the aether no matter the consequences from here. Her tutor, Immli, would be furious, and her father the emperor, too, for not taking care.

Every action of hers would ripple out into the world, even to the smallest and least of their people, and she was not allowed to hurt anyone. But Raliel needed to tear into something. Even if that something was the whole empire. Even if that something was herself.

From here, with the vast network of aether, with the roads and messenger witches, army scouts, traders who carried letters, and even farsight spells, Raliel could seem to be anywhere. Could speak with anyone across the empire. This was the heart of the land, this city, and this palace. She wasn't *trapped* here; she would be *enthroned* here. Why did that infuriate her so?

The demon's touch settled cold on her neck.

Raliel whispered, "Everything here is theory, Moon. Words and books. Stories I'm told but can't possibly know. Everything is handed to me: knowledge, power, friends. What have I earned? What have I even experienced? What is my own? *Mine?* I have everything, but it tastes like ashes."

yes, it agreed.

Just that acceptance made her lean into its cold, amorphous but solid touch. "It is not that I want more—but I want less. Something, any small thing, just for myself."

The great demon slid cold fingers up her neck against her scalp. Raliel's eyes fluttered closed.

"Moon, do the walls of the palace feel like your home or your prison?"

When it answered this time, the word came from many mouths around her head. Seven pairs of lips and seven whispered voices.

they are both.

Raliel nodded slowly. The cold slipped down her neck, down and down her back to pool at the base of her spine. Settling her. Her breathing smoothed and her hands relaxed. "I hope I find something, on my Heir's Journey, to satisfy us both. To make us want to be here and work here for the rest of our lives. And I wish I could take you with me," she murmured. "When I go on my journey."

maybe you can, the great demon said.

THREE

O N A COOL SPRING day, when the clouds hunkered low over the city cliffs and the ocean ruffled like an irritated old chicken, an assassin attempted to murder Second Consort Elegant Waters.

Raliel was seventeen, and for several months had been conducting experiments with the great demon of the palace in order to find a way to take it with her on her Heir's Journey. She'd been surprised when it first made the suggestion, but she threw herself into the idea. Their theory that it was possible rested on her being the heir and therefore already tied to the demon's house—the palace—through the enthroning ritual. Her father had become the Emperor with the Moon in His Mouth, and his husband and wife the First Consort and Second Consort, the three of them bound to the demon and palace with ancient magic known as the palace-amulet. During the same ritual, Raliel had traded her name to the demon and become the Heir to the Throne. It was, essentially, her real name. Until one day her name would become the Empress with the Moon in Her Mouth.

The great demon, standing before her in a black void exactly her height with seven moon-white eyes, had said, *because of this, when you go for your journey, a piece of my house will go with you. What if I can put some of me into a thing you can carry?*

"Make yourself my familiar?" Raliel bit her lip, a habit she simply could not rid herself of, even by wearing the bitterest of lip paint. "Witches have demon familiars. Immli's first familiar is a demon mouse."

yes.

"I am as good with aether as any young witch."

yes.

"But you are a great demon, not a demon. Will you be able to survive in the form of a mouse or even something stronger, like the spirit stags?"

only one way to know, the demon whispered.

And so the experiments had begun. In the Garden of the Seas, when they were alone, the demon practiced putting itself into flowers at first—but they withered and died. It tried with beautiful river rocks and a ring with a massive black pearl, but neither had enough aether of their own to support it. The star-flower tree lived for nearly an hour with the demon inside, though Raliel could never take a tree with her, so she brought the demon a snake. For nearly a day Raliel wore the snake demon around her neck and shoulders, a blue-scaled living stole that disturbed almost everyone, and she was hopeful. But as she slept that night, the snake on her pillow turned to ash.

Averilis refused to clean it, and Rose Blue only jumped in to help when Raliel began to do it herself, but Rose Blue disapproved, unsure Raliel ought to be encouraging the great demon so. Salri asked why they were doing this, and Raliel told him everything in the palace was a part of the great demon's house. "Shouldn't it be allowed to know the sensation of scales and warm skin rather than only damp basalt and rain on roof tiles?"

"Knowing such things and devouring such things is different," Salri said.

Raliel knew that. She nodded, lowered her eyes. She said, "We are learning."

The next month, before venturing just beyond the palace walls to attend a fancy duel for Lady Falling Red's nephew's wedding, Raliel went into the cellars of the palace to find a chunk of the foundation. She dug free a sharp piece of limestone, enough to fit in her hand, heavy and porous, and took it with her. The great demon tried to hold on to it, given it was a chunk of its bones, but none of its consciousness remained once Raliel passed through the gate of the seventh circle.

Though the experiments failed, the demon was delighted, and continued to catch what it could: a dozen pink butterflies swarmed around Raliel's head like a living crown; a trail of mice that raced in her footsteps. A sleek black hound that belonged to the Lady Crane and sat at Raliel's heel with its eyes gone moon-white. It sat so still while the heir poured tea that Rose Blue and Lord of Narrow thought it was a toy, or a trick. But when it died, it cried out, and Raliel's expression was so coldly disappointed, rumors spread fast she'd poisoned it somehow.

As the imperial family ate their supper in private that night, the emperor ordered her to stop playing such games with the great demon. Their people knew the demon protected them, they knew the empire's prosperity was tied to the Moon, but reminding them it was a dead old thing at the heart of their power chipped away at the people's love and trust. Raliel's mother agreed, appalled by the ugliness of the entire situation. "Harming those weaker than you is not what you were made for," Elegant Waters chided.

The emperor scoffed. "And worst of all—you were caught!"

First Consort Sky glared at the emperor for that. "This is not a game or political maneuver, Kirin. It is horrifying." Then he turned to Raliel. "I am disappointed in you, daughter," he said. His demon-kissed gaze bored into hers. "You might as well have killed that hound with your own hands."

Cut by his words, Raliel silently left the dining room without finishing her meal, hurrying up to the Moon's Recline Garden. Thick moss softened the ground, and Raliel fell to her knees upon a pillow to avoid staining the pristine gray-white of her layered gown. The garden was open to the night on three sides, facing south and the sea, so the breeze was tinged with salt as it blew past, spreading fine clouds across the sky. Only the imperial family and one gardener were allowed here. No one would disturb her.

Raliel drew a long breath, and as she exhaled, she made herself go still. She imagined she was one of the paintings in her mother's rooms, white parchment and fluid black ink against the vivid nighttime colors of the moss garden. Her hollow insides became a valley of snow and stark winter trees.

It calmed her. Stillness; careful, slow breathing. Her pulse slid clear and cold like tiny mountain streams. She breathed in gentle sea breeze and the sweet scent of the rainbow balsam at her knee and the cloying star jasmine that twined up the rail.

Her father Sky was correct: she was willingly—actively—using her power to hurt others. There was no excuse. They could not cause harm to achieve this goal.

The demon slowly rose through the garden floor, coating the moss with frost. The wind fell silent. *I am here* was all it said.

"I know," Raliel whispered. "And I know what we must do."

With the patience of the moon, the demon waited, as Raliel stared out at the night sky. Eventually, she said, "It has to be me."

Because the great demon had so quickly devoured the aether of every living creature it attempted to possess, they needed to be careful. Theoretically, they both understood how a demon made a house of a living creature—it involved death, always. Often demons made their houses in hollow trees or stagnant ponds, natural meeting places between life and death, with deep roots and access to aether—and to bright living things. Great demons required mountains or entire palaces, as well as a sorcerer for channeling great quantities of aether. Raliel was no mountain nor sorcerer. She had no aspect of death to herself. How could they keep it from killing her?

On the day of the assassination attempt, Raliel knelt amid a stack of old scrolls and delicately preserved books in the library, conducting research.

The great demon rarely joined her in the library, unable to read without eyes, unwilling to expend the energy to manifest itself only to be caught out by nosy priests or tutors. So Raliel did her reading between meetings and lessons, tucking books into her pockets to take to her room at night and read when she could whisper to the demon as it pooled like an oily shadow at the foot of her bed. She read about demons, of course, but spirits, too, and the history of witches both in the Empire Between Five Mountains and beyond. For studying possession, she had sent away to a couple of monasteries for the journals of old dawn priests who dealt with possessing ghosts as well as demon banishment if there were no witches to be found.

That day she'd just fallen into an essay from a survivor of demonic possession—a rarity indeed. The woman had lived a century previous, and met a curious newborn demon in the aftermath of a drought that had killed the demon's living house. It had been a juniper spirit, hearty and usually quite good at surviving droughts, but when the rain had finally come the ground had been so abused and dry a flash flood had destroyed the entire tree. The demon, unable to find a house, had driven painfully into the young woman, rooting into her lungs when she gasped to scream. Fortunately for her, the town had three visiting priests who'd been reblessing the crossroads shrines after the rain, and they pinned her—and her juniper demon—down, tearing it out with a blood ritual. Raliel was disappointed the ritual was not described in detail, worried the woman was exaggerating. But if a demon could be drawn out of a delicious, aether-filled house like a young woman with blood ritual, could her demon be drawn into her somehow, safely, with the same?

The library floor trembled beneath her.

Raliel glanced up in shock. She felt the tremor again and saw the ink pooled in the shallow stone at the corner of her desk ripple.

"Moon," she said, flattening a palm to the floor.

"Moon."

Nothing responded.

Raliel frowned. She dipped her finger into her cold tea and drew a sigil for echoing against the wooden panels of the floor. Imbuing it with a wisp of aether, she said the great demon's name again.

The sigil snapped to life, biting at her!

Snatching her hand back, she curled it to her chest to protect it. Her skin ached as if she'd been burned.

Just then she heard muffled cries from a distance.

Raliel stood and strode out of her private study room. Two librarians caught her gaze, each wide-eyed before they bowed and stammered, "Heir."

She moved past them into the hallway. Only one palace guard stood at attention: her jaw was clenched, and when Raliel said, "What do you know?" she looked immediately down the long corridor to the sound of rushing footsteps.

When Raliel started toward the noise, the guard darted around and bowed. "Heir, please, remain in the library. Whatever happened, you mustn't go toward it."

Raliel ignored her, sweeping around her with the knowledge the guard would not touch her nor block her way. The guard trotted after Raliel, who wanted to run but held herself to a steady quick walk.

At the broad juncture of staircases leading between circles of the palace, one of the small shrines cut into the plaster walls was *on fire*.

Dawn priests knelt, praying as if prayer could put out the fire, and servants held water jugs and blankets to keep the fire from spreading. They allowed the shrine, with its triad statue and delicate paper flowers, to burn.

More guards rushed up the stairs, ignoring the fire. Raliel followed them, past the fourth and third circles (where more shrines burned!) and into the second circle. The imperial family's private residence.

Raliel's heart thudded painfully, and she could not believe Moon did not hiss at her or cry out to tell her where to go.

"Let me past," she commanded the crowd filling the landing in the second circle—the only part of this level open to courtiers and palace attendants or ministers who were not specifically assigned to the family.

Several fluttering lords and ladies stepped out of her way, distress plain in their drawn expressions and clenched hands. Seven Warriors of the Last Means blocked the red lacquered panel doors that opened to a beautiful greeting hall for close guests of the imperial family. One of the doors bore a scorch mark the size of Raliel's hand.

"Heir," said one of the warriors, an older commander named Whorl.

"Commander," she replied. "Is my family within?"

"The emperor just arrived."

She lifted her eyebrows to indicate she wished to be allowed through. The commander hesitated, then gestured for his subordinates to move. They slid back the heavy door, and without another glance, Raliel entered.

More guards and warriors stood inside, and several of her parents' attendants knelt making tea. They glanced up at her, appearing shaken but not afraid, nor sad. Raliel decided no one had been harmed, or this would be a very different greeting.

But the great demon still had said nothing to her.

She strode for the entrance to the Consorts' Bower, then stopped in the doorway as two people in physician's robes and a Warrior of the Last Means escorted a young demon-kissed man out past her. They nodded respectfully, but the younger man, in the uniform of the palace guard, didn't catch her eye. He slumped between the healers, seeming exhausted. Raliel chose to ignore it and entered the Consorts' Bower.

The chamber seemed entirely normal: The silk curtains that could be used to separate the bower into sections were tied back in luxurious falls, the floor pillows arranged around the low tables exactly as her mother liked them. Simple paintings of the northern mountains graced the walls beside mounted lap harps, flutes, and even a small guitar, as well as the First Consort's collection of antique weapons. Arched doorways on either side of the bower led into their private bedrooms, and directly across from the entrance was a small garden.

Right now, all three of her parents knelt together near the center of the bower. Elegant Waters between Sky and the emperor—the latter of whom wore all his layers of formal robes, fit for high court but for his rain veil tossed upon a low sofa without concern for how the fine chains would tangle. The emperor held Elegant Waters around the shoulder, though she sat with good posture, barely leaning into him, her expression cool. But a strand of hair clung to her neck, and one small smear of paint marred the corner of her slightly glassy left eye. First Consort Sky poured clear wine into a shallow cup for her, and she took it. Before she sipped, she looked at Raliel.

"What happened?" Raliel demanded. "Are you hurt? Where is the great demon?"

Just then a doctor emerged from where she had knelt at one of the side tables, where Raliel had not noticed. It was one of the older palace physicians, slightly bent and very silver-haired, but with hard-knuckled hands that brooked no insolence from feverish children. Raliel managed not to recoil from sheer sense-memory.

"Here, Second Consort," the doctor said gently, kneeling before Elegant Waters. "Drink this before wine."

Sky took back the wine, and Elegant Waters drank her medicine instead, knocking it back rather dramatically. She only pursed her lips slightly in reaction.

Raliel folded her hands behind her back, eyeing her parents urgently, though doing her best to appear patient. The emperor's mouth turned up on one side, a very slight wry smile, and Sky said, "Someone attempted to murder your mother."

Cold horror grasped Raliel, her mouth going dry, her muscles rigid.

"They are dead," the emperor said calmly, bright honey gaze sliding from Raliel to his Second Consort. He shifted in order to slide his arm lower, holding on to her waist rather than her shoulder. Possessive.

"I am fine, Emperor," Elegant Waters murmured.

"Thanks to that guard," the emperor said.

"What guard?" Raliel asked. She still did not move toward her parents.

It was Sky who said, "A palace guard, demon-kissed. He recognized the trap and set it off before it could ensnare Elegant Waters."

"The scorch marks?"

"Yes."

Raliel licked her bottom lip and immediately froze again at the gesture of distraction. She took a deep breath. "And the shrines?"

"This guard—Osian," Sky said. "Osian Redpop. His demon-kissed gift is his perfect memory. The scorch mark on the door was the result of his setting a sigil ablaze—a sigil he recognized because he'd seen them appearing on the palace shrines and not thought anything of them. But he knew it did not belong on the consorts' door. He claims he acted upon instinct, ordering the Second Consort away in a huddle of guards and activating the sigil with his own aether. He is no witch, and it drained him badly, but he is well. When the assassin was discovered in this very room, he had no place to go and was executed immediately." Sky glanced toward the brazier, and Raliel followed the look to see several flecks of still bright blood against the polished floor.

She said suddenly, "The sigils were to contain Moon!"

The emperor grimaced in agreement.

Raliel fell to her knees and pressed her hands to the floor. She reached with aether again, a sharp stab of it. "Moon," she snapped. She listened. Heard nothing but birdsong from the garden beyond.

Just then a dawn priest entered. He bowed, pastel pink and gold jacket and skirts pooling around him. When the emperor gave him permission to speak, he said, "Emperor, Consorts, we have identified the sigils."

Raliel moved to the sofa where her father had tossed his rain veil. She lifted it as the priest spoke, moving behind the emperor to carefully arrange it back over his elaborate hairpiece. A few of the very delicate strands of silk and silver had indeed caught together, but it would do. The emperor huffed quietly but did not shoo her away.

The priest said, "It is a locking pattern, we believe to muffle the power of the great demon. When the fires go out—and they will, when the energy of the pattern is entirely consumed—the demon should be released, and perfectly well."

"If greatly annoyed," the emperor said.

Raliel touched her father the emperor's shoulder in agreement. She swallowed her anxiety and remained standing there, behind her parents. The priest said they predicted the fires to last only another quarter of an hour, and each was entirely contained.

The emperor said in the future the dawn priests of the palace ought to pay much better attention to how their shrines were being manipulated.

The dawn priest bowed deeply, and when he was dismissed, Raliel thought he looked very green around the lips.

Once the doctor had departed as well, instructing Elegant Waters to rest for the evening, the emperor requested his family's meal be brought here and they then be left alone.

Raliel sank to one of the floor pillows beside the emperor, wishing she could lean against her mother instead. She helped the emperor remove his rain veil only after food had been brought and laid out for them upon three low tables. Wine and tea as well, and Raliel asked for Averilis and Rose Blue to be allowed to come with a change of clothing for herself.

Once they had arranged themselves, just the four of them, with wine poured, and begun to share around a first-course salad of onions and cucumbers in vinegar and coriander, the great demon slipped up out of the floor.

"Moon," Raliel murmured, relieved enough to slump.

I dislike this, it said, a small fox-shape shadow with seven full-moon eyes and a tail longer and more sinuous like a snake. It moved to the emperor, nosing at him, and the emperor scratched where its triangular ears met its head.

"You are well?" the emperor asked.

no.

Elegant Waters reached out a hand. "I can play for you, something soothing."

"After you eat," Sky warned.

would like that, said the demon, flicking its tail around her wrist. Then it trotted around to Sky and butted its head to his hip. *wish you'd left the witch for me to eat,* it hissed.

"Me too," Raliel said, low and angry.

The great demon looked at her; then it circled the family twice more, shadows rippling like ruffled fur. It came to rest at Raliel and climbed into her lap, curling there, cold and heavy. She wished she could gather it up and press it into her stomach, into her body where she could keep it safe.

FOUR

THE FIRST TIME THE great demon possessed Raliel Dark-Smile, it killed her.

FIVE

T HE SECOND TIME, RALIEL was more prepared.

For a few weeks she and the great demon met at night, curled up at her tea table with only a single aether-lantern glowing. The heir drew sigils and ideas on the lacquered wood with warm water, while the demon used smoke and streaks of white-blue aether as they worked out what had gone so very wrong with its first possession of her. They suspected it was related to the same reason they'd believed it would be possible in the first place:

Raliel was the Heir to the Moon and so there already existed an aether connection between her and the demon. It was bound to the palace by the palace-amulet, which also bound her father, the Emperor with the Moon in His Mouth, and his First and Second Consorts. Raliel's connection was less firm, less binding, because she was not yet invested as part of the amulet—only her blood and her childhood vow linked her to it, not the demon's full true name. It was just enough for the possession to work, but it also made her vulnerable. When Moon had pushed into her with the force it expected to be necessary to possess a living witch, her blood and vow had welcomed it so enthusiastically that the demon miscalculated the strength it could exert and it lost control. Her heart had stopped. Fortunately, the demon realized what had happened and shoved aether back into her. She gasped to life after hardly a moment had passed, aching and cold.

To prevent a reoccurrence, Raliel constructed an amulet of her own with a small circle of pounded silver. She etched *Raliel Dark-Smile Heir to the Moon* into the metal with a needle, using the language of spirits the demon had taught her—a language no human could speak, but only write—then she said, "Great Demon, for this to work, tell me your true name."

Silence answered her.

She worked in the Moon's Recline Garden, under a low waning moon that shone boldly down at her and upon the amulet cupped in her hands.

"Moon," she said softly.

The demon was listening. She felt its presence around her in the garden. A cold tingle, a press of a needle at the nape of her neck. Sensations that brought her comfort.

She waited.

It would choose to trust her with this if it wanted their plan to work.

why? it asked so softly it was barely a sound. *why are you willing to take this risk again?*

That was an easy answer. "You deserve to leave sometimes—I get to go, my father did, and his mother. We all have a chance to see the world, to expand beyond the walls of the palace at least once. It's unjust, it's wrong, to never let you do the same."

unjust.

"Yes. And—out there . . ." Raliel hummed in thought. Eventually she said, "We can learn ourselves better out there. Here we are one thing, but in the world . . .What else, who else can we be?"

Slowly the darkness just before Raliel solidified into a shadow with seven jagged legs and seven round eyes mottled silver and gray like the moon above. It parted seven slashed mouths to whisper through tiny black teeth: *"Moon Caught in the Tide."*

Raliel shivered and bowed her head, let her eyes fall closed. She breathed gently and deeply, overwhelmed by the name, by the trust even though she'd expected it. To calm, she imagined her skin hardening in thin flakes of ice, frost forming in beautiful, intricate patterns.

"Thank you, Moon," she said.

When her eyes opened, its face was too close. Her lips fell apart, and she gasped air tasting of honeyed candy rose petals. Those seven eyes stared at her, and its seven legs bent as it hunkered down to kneel.

Taking up the amulet again, Raliel carved *Moon Caught in the Tide Great Demon of the Palace* over and in between the forms of her name, then wrapped delicate threads of moon-gray silk across the silver amulet's face to hide them. She tied it to a braided cord of black silk and looped it around her neck. Raliel pricked her thumb, then with blood wrote a sigil for drawing aether onto the amulet. Her blood flared silver-blue, imbuing the amulet with power.

They were ready.

The sweet salt breeze blew the carefully tended sprays of early-summer moon lilies and flares of rainbow balsam, tugging at the vines of star jasmine wound to the thin pillars raising the ceiling. Raliel could hear distant laughter and muted conversations floating up from the third circle of the palace, as late night-courtiers finished their dinners, and from a window just below the garden slipped a pretty melody played upon a harp. She recognized the delicate style of her mother and wondered if both her fathers reclined to the eddies of music, or if the First Consort dined late with the Lord of Means as he often did, or the Emperor with the Moon in His Mouth sat with his old mother Love-Eyes who had been ill recently and liked the lovely sound of the emperor's voice to soothe her into sleep.

If Raliel had told any of her parents she intended to spend the night here, they'd have joined her. For most of her life this garden had been where they'd gathered at dawn. At first it would be just Raliel and her father the emperor, preparing tea while he chose his rings for the day. Then the two consorts would wander in for tea and breakfast. The four of them snatched what little family time was available before the demands of the day pulled them in various directions. Her mother would comb her long black hair while her father Sky asked about her lessons, and her father the emperor fussed with the amount of honey in his evergreen tea until it was perfect and ready to share in shallow ceramic bowls.

But she was doing this part alone. Or rather, partnered only with the great demon. Even her father the emperor would not approve.

It would be all right.

"Are you ready, Moon?" Raliel asked as she knelt on the moss with the amulet over her heart.

I am, the great demon replied in its softest voice, the one like tiny claws on the lacquered floor of her bedchamber.

Raliel drew a careful breath, filling her lungs with the smell of flowers and the distant ocean, and as she let it out through carefully pursed, unpainted lips, she looked up at that oblong moon.

The amulet tingled in her palms. Her spine grew cold, like a narrow birch tree slowly freezing from the roots up, frost forming pristine crystals along her bones, spreading from her center out in branches. The fingers of ice slid up the nape of her neck and sank needlelike into her skull. Raliel focused on her breath and the amulet in her hands. She imagined the little pains dissipating and in their wake leaving space inside her for the demon.

I am here, it said, and this time the whisper came from within.

"Oh," she said, folding over her lap so her forehead brushed the cool moss. She cradled the amulet in her hands, clenched between her small breasts and as near her heart as it could get. She curled there, a ball swaddled in rich gray silk and fine linen, and felt the demon curl along with her, a sensation as if her spine elongated, each individual vertebra lengthening into long draconic spines. It did not happen, but she imagined it and felt strangely better.

The garden seemed to spin sunwise in a dreamy whirlpool as Raliel breathed shallowly.

Maybe she was going to throw up.

Maybe not.

it works, said the demon, the pleasure in its voice a fissure along her skin, down to the tips of her bare toes.

The demon withdrew from Raliel like ice melting in the sun.

She stretched her arms, unfolding until she lay on her stomach in the middle of the garden, cheek to the moss and amulet in one hand, fisted against her heart. She tasted cool floral air on her tongue as she smiled. "I'm so tired," she said too softly for anything but a demon to hear.

when we are outside I will take life from the world, and it will not drain you so badly.

Trusting, Raliel nodded and let herself drift into a dreamless sleep.

SIX

O N MIDSUMMER EVENING, RALIEL knelt in the
Court of Seven Circles half listening to a poet
recite odes to the sun in ever-more-complicated
rhyme schemes, half meditating in perfect posture as the poet's
voice lent cadence to her breath and heartbeat. The banquet
was laid out in the court in seven semicircles of tables arcing
from the emperor's throne, facing a length of stage constructed
just for the occasion and striped with billowing curtains of gold
and red and white. Raliel was a pale slip of moonlight among
bold summer colors, kneeling just to the side of the Imperial
Triad. Her coterie and their pastel compliments were several
rows away from the center.

All her life, banquets had made Raliel restless. When indi-
viduals became a crowd and food was served at an exacting pace,
and conversation relegated to that tense form where everyone
could be overheard by everyone else but one was required
to pretend at detailed knowledge of one's neighbors. During
the meal, the emperor wore an even more elaborate headdress
than usual. It lifted the rain veil away from his face with wide

spines that allowed him to eat delicately beneath. The First and Second Consorts fed him finger foods from tiny plates, a well-coordinated display of intimacy made more impressive by their own massive gowns and layers of robes, embroidered with sunlight and stars against vermilion and spring-green silks. After the meal, and a brief costume alteration, the emperor lounged easily at the low table for the conversations and performances, his expression safe behind the simpler veil. He said what he liked, of course, warm voice reaching to tease a courtier or lord even at the farthest semicircle of tables. To make up for it, the First Consort said nothing at all, while the Second soothed and coolly flirted, and promised to take her turn on the stage with her harp.

Raliel had no prescribed role here, except to be present and well behaved.

Someday, she would be the one safe behind the veil. Someday, if she was lucky, her consorts would balance her just so well.

Someday.

Someday. It rang in her mind, a gong that grew and grew in low reverberations like a meditation bell.

She did her best to keep her face still as she breathed more deeply, as she listened to the poet and kept her spine both relaxed and also straight. She studied the occasional burst of aether from one of the familiars holding wards at the entrances and high tiny windows. She thought of snow falling onto the loops and combs of her hair, slipping down her body to fill her up: only her, it was a private snowstorm.

It helped.

Then, *Raliel,* whispered the demon from the floor. *go with me.*

She tapped a finger to the tiled floor twice in agreement.

As it had practiced these past few weeks, the great demon of the palace slipped in through her finger and coiled into a tiny egg at the base of her spine.

Raliel bit the tip of her tongue to halt the gasp—she wasn't surprised, and yet she always fought a physical reaction.

The demon curled inside her, expanding in her awareness as it felt with soft fingers against her bones and organs, stretching her muscles like a newborn kitten, learning her. It touched her stomach and said she could eat more, slithered down toward her hips and bladder and reminded her she'd need to relieve herself soon.

A soft flush crept up her neck—it felt that, too, and dismissed it with a little laugh.

Raliel was learning. Primarily how to accept this intimacy. That was the price of possession, or at least of this sort of aware, awake possession.

She breathed. She imagined snow. Moon sighed into the snow, and inside her helped spin a nest of ice for them to share.

When the poet finished her recitation, after the applause, Raliel stood and excused herself with a small bow as a new performer took the stage.

Averilis lifted her brow at Raliel as the heir passed her coterie, asking if she needed them for anything. Raliel shook her head in very slight negative and continued out. Her gown dragged behind her, whispering nearly as tenderly as the demon, and once she was past attendants and guards, she murmured, "Where are we going?"

down, the demon said.

Raliel removed her outer robe, a sleeveless silk train crusted with glass beads and embroidered orchids. She hung it on an incense hook, where it would soak up the jasmine and musk of the shrine cut into the wall beside it. Then, in only three simple layers of gown and robe, she followed the great demon's directions. Down.

They walked into the sixth circle and to a narrow panel in the wall hiding a staircase for attendants and messengers. The demon directed her down and down, without hesitation, into the lowest foundations. It was a warren of cellars and storage down here, for ice and cheese and delicate liquors, as well as a few magic rooms carved into the bedrock for specialized aetherwork. Raliel assumed it was to one of these Moon took her, but instead, the demon nudged her through a dank closet filled with barrels of preserved vegetables and to a corner behind a shelf of pickled eels. A crack in the basalt proved to be a crevasse that led into a cave.

Raliel's lips parted, and she could taste salt in the air. She did not have her sword, which would have been best for lighting her way, already attuned to aether with sigils carved into the steel and pommel. Nor could she summon her own inner aether to make her hand glow—not with the demon possessing her. It ate up every extra scrap of aether she had.

So she bent and tore the hem of her organza robe—it was easy but unfortunate. The fine material was expensive, the embroidery thick. Raliel chose a scrap with no extra stitching, and then with a hum said, "I don't want to bleed on it, Moon. I don't have a blade of any kind."

The demon sighed. *spit.*

Surprised such a thing would work, Raliel licked her finger and drew a sigil for light on the organza. With the demon's direction, she breathed on it, and the demon reached a tendril of itself up her throat, tickled across her tongue, and gave her breath a spark.

The sigil caught with a faint glimmer, and then Raliel crumpled it into her fist, commanded it, and a small bauble of blue-silver aether-light appeared.

Raliel smiled.

it was not necessary, the demon grumbled as she walked on, down a long throat of rock. *I know the way.*

"I like to see with my eyes," Raliel murmured. "Where are we going?"

Moon did not answer.

She walked carefully over uneven, slick stone, long enough to know the palace no longer sat above them. It was city and docks, and soon Raliel could hear the tide and feel the demon inside her murmur back to it.

Orienting her breathing, Raliel let anticipation build—hers or Moon's or both—and when they reached the mouth of the cave she extinguished the aether-light.

While to the west of the city the Selegan River spread wide into many fingers before smoothing into the sea, here there were low, old bluffs. Soft in many places, crumbling, pocketed with tidal pools and shallow caves. A wide beach of gray-white sand spread in front of Raliel, flat and smooth for a hundred paces before the ocean broke against it. "Will this work?"

we will find out.

She stepped out under the sky. The sand was dry and her

slippers sank with a hiss. Raliel removed them. The beach was deserted in both directions. Dark and perfectly quiet, she was alone except for Moon inside her.

An hour ago the sun had set, leaving only a soft gilding of the horizon, and there was a crescent of the real moon hanging sharp and bold, surrounded by stars and stars and not a single wisp of cloud.

The air was thick with summer, though, and a salty breeze pushed the humidity into Raliel's face. She tasted it on her lips, and it made her eyelashes feel heavy.

Taking a deep breath, she walked out. The ocean purred at her, grasping at the sand, and the soft moonlight caught the rough waves that reached, curled, crashed, dragged again and again. Beyond them, the light reflected off the wide glassy ocean until she could no longer distinguish water from stars.

It pulled her, that blurred horizon—she couldn't see it, could only trust that it happened. Sea to stars, or else the sea became stars, glittering against the soft black night, reaching up in a massive, world-eating wave—reach, curl, curl up and up over her, bending in an arc over the entire world.

Raliel thought of the sky as a geode then, a huge rock sphere with an inner core of smoky crystals, each tip a sparkling star.

As she walked she felt *something* in her stretch. Sticky aether-cords, pulling like taffy. "Moon?"

yes it is strange.

Soon she reached the damp sand: pressure from her feet pushed water out in pretty arcs. Lily pads of sand as if she walked across a pond.

When the water first rushed up to touch her toes, she danced back instinctively. She spun, lifting her skirts, but the torn hem of her gown was already wet.

Turning, she saw behind her: the city and palace rose off the bluffs, a bright silhouette of peaked rooftops and temples and the great teeth of the palace, lit up with winking orange torches and the stable silvery glow of aether-lamps.

my body, said the Moon.

Raliel touched her fingers over the amulet she wore under her clothes. "My body," she said. Then, with a cheeky smile, "I live in yours."

I live in yours, Moon answered, its laugh a series of soft puffs against the inside of her spine.

Cool water clutched at her heels, grasping her ankles in foam hands. Raliel gasped and hopped away. Then she turned back to the sea. She stepped in, letting her gown and robes drift around her calves as the tide pushed and pulled.

Ahhhhh yes ahhh, said Moon.

"The tide?" Raliel nodded. She did not wade in farther, though the water felt good. She tilted her chin up and glanced at the stars. "Why did you bring me here?"

wanted to feel it.

wanted to touch it.

"The sea?"

the tide, my tide.

Raliel remembered the great demon's name: *Moon Caught in the Tide*. She looked over to the crescent moon, then down. There was no clear reflection, but a wide blur of moonlight on the sea. Maybe when the moon first rose, or as it fell closer to the western horizon, the reflection would solidify, would consolidate itself. But now it was too much, just jagged rippling light.

She said as much, and Moon sighed down her legs. Her tiny body hairs lifted at the sensation. Suddenly she felt liquid herself, mutable, changeable. Between.

It frightened her, how sharp and good the feeling was, and Raliel wanted to bend down into the water, to crouch and become more of the sea; or dash onto the beach again and become more of the shore. But she did not move. She remained there, both and neither, sinking slowly into the sand as the tug of the water pulled around her feet, and matched her breathing to the tide. "Is it coming in or out?"

in.

Raliel thought, *coming in for us.* But Moon could not hear her thoughts.

"Is this what you want from . . . this? Me?" she asked instead.

I want to go with you. And this.

"Does it feel different, when you feel wind on my skin or wind on the palace walls? Does it look different through my two eyes than through your seven? Do you really have seven eyes or make it so because the palace is seven circles?"

different. But good. More like wings and scales and teeth and tongues. No—scales are more like the wall. The tiles of the roof.

Raliel understood.

All she could hear was the ocean, and she liked it. A gentle but loud voice it had. Salty, insistent, but patient, too.

It wasn't like her imagined snow, or a mountain, she thought. It moved and changed too quickly. It was warm and variable. Filled with life. "Is this where you come from?"

67

tide. beach. wind. clouds, Moon said. *Don't remember, except I remember everything, too. I slept for a long time.*

"What woke you up?"

nothing.

"You just . . . woke up?"

Under her heart, the great demon grumbled. *Night Shine,* it said. That was the great demon of the Fifth Mountain.

you, it said after a moment.

Pleasure stuttered Raliel's breath. "Me?"

you were thinking of the sky. I wanted to think of the sky, so I paid closer attention and that was enough.

Raliel smiled. She spread her arms, and her fingers, as if to catch the wind.

help me, Raliel, the great demon whispered. *I want to be able to come here again. After we go. I want to feel the tide. I want to move and be free. Like Night Shine. She is no prisoner. She can do anything.*

"I will. We'll find out how to change the rules for both of us. So that we can be strong *and* free."

promise.

Taking a deep breath, she said what she'd been thinking for months: "Moon, you know I believe it is unfair to keep you here always. Without a choice. We—my family and I—we choose to be bound here. It doesn't always feel like a choice to me, because I was born for it, but . . . it is. I could leave, walk away and never return. But you, however you were bound the first time, you never get to choose again."

I do not remember clearly.

"Exactly. Every generation you are rebound to the palace-amulet, but nobody lets you choose. I can't rule that way. I . . ."

Raliel closed her eyes, concentrated on the feeling of salt breeze touching her cheeks and the curling surf at her ankles. The breathing sound of the tide. "I want you here. I want you to be with me, for my turn on the throne. But I won't make you. It has to be real, for both of us. And so, I swear I will find an option for us, for you. We'll find a sorcerer to help. Or another great demon. Someone must know more about this palace-amulet. I'll find you your choice. If I have to discover a new kind of sorcery, that's what I'll do. Instead of our bound demon, you'll be our familiar. Like Night Shine and her sorceress. Like The Scale and their great spirit."

yes, Raliel. Yes.

"Only we have to protect the empire too. My family, the people between the Five Mountains. Keep them all safe. Do you promise?"

I do.

SEVEN

THEY RETURNED HOME BEFORE Raliel could be missed. If the demon had been in the walls of the palace, it could have whispered to the emperor that his daughter was safe. But the demon was in the walls of Raliel's body and could not.

In the cellars, Raliel chose a dusty round bottle of sweet barley wine and cradled it in the crook of her arm as she climbed up the stairs. This time she startled attendants moving to put the palace to bed after the end of the banquet. She stepped aside and remained silent, nodding only if they seemed to require permission to pass. The demon slipped out of her, skating against a smooth wall of red-washed plaster before sinking in. Raliel continued up, heading for the shrine where she'd left her outer robe—in case it remained.

It did not, but she knelt before the alcove shrine and lit an hour candle for the great demon, even though it did not need such devotions from her.

As she approached the imperial chambers at the heart of the sixth circle, she paused at the sight of three strangers in cerulean jackets cut in a style she did not recognize from among the various families welcome in this circle. They were youths, her age or just older, with golden circles painted on their cheeks and combs shaped like cats pulling dark hair away from their faces. Before Raliel decided whether to speak with them or sweep past and go to her room to change out of these salt-water-ruined clothes, the doors to the foyer slid open and a taller young man appeared.

He sparked with aether. Aether visible to anyone, Raliel thought, shocked, not just to witches or priests. As he moved, the aether burst around him like fireworks. As if the sheer volume of his power could not be contained in his body.

"Raliel Dark-Smile," he said softly, his eyes yellow and ensnaring as a cat's.

She lifted her chin and made herself go cold, considering her response, but suddenly the great demon of the palace surrounded her, visible ribbons of darkness in the air. It scratched quietly at the walls and parquet floor, creaking the beams of the ceiling. Candles wavered in a breeze none could feel as shadowy tendrils fluttered in the corners of her vision. *the Second Sorcerer*, it whispered to her.

A Dance of Stars. That was his name, Raliel knew. She held her back straight and her expression cold. Despite her damp hem, her lack of over robe or jacket, her wind-tossed loops and braids, she was the Heir to the Moon.

The sorcerer strode toward her slowly, studying her as she studied him. He was tall and blandly handsome. His hair was a vivid dark red, and when he smiled she saw his teeth were sharp. But his jaw was uninspired, his nose elegant but plain. A set of gold-shot outer robes billowed around him, sleek and shifting with sunlight that seemed to fight against the great demon's shadow-ribbons. He had several amulets hanging from his neck and rings on some fingers. No face paint. She wondered why he did not make his face sharper or sweeter or uglier or anything at all. A sorcerer could look like anything they wished.

Maybe he was so powerful he did not have to.

Raliel said nothing, holding his gaze even as he moved nearer. Her pulse hammered, but she kept her chin raised and pretended she was finely dressed, not bedraggled: pristine as snow.

A Dance of Stars tilted his head as if to speak again, but all around them the air suddenly crackled with cold. Shadows appeared in jagged lines down the walls.

The sorcerer paused, a tiny smile puckered his lips, and several things shuffled in his eyes. "I had hoped to meet you, Heir," he said. "But it seems my time in the palace has come to an end."

Moon darkened the corridor further, with creeping snakes of blackness.

Raliel said nothing.

A Dance of Stars bowed to her, and with a snap of his fingers, he led his attendants away.

She did not move. Nor for fear, exactly, but a sharp expectation— like something irrevocable had happened.

The air lightened again, warming, and the shadows faded. Raliel murmured, "Moon."

your parents are in the garden. Kirin is drinking. Because I wasn't here, they thought I did not mind the sorcerer's visit. Moon snarled wordlessly then.

Raliel decided to go to her rooms and change before joining them.

Averilis and Rose Blue both waited for her in her room. Salri probably had sought the tipsy company of the son of the Lord of Narrow, whom he was wooing lately. The two girls perched on one of the short couches under Raliel's sitting-room window, Averilis holding a pillow against her stomach and laughing at something Rose had said.

When Raliel entered she set the bottle of liquor down soundlessly and waited for them to notice her, with a soft—false—smile on her face.

"Raliel!" Rose said, standing in surprise. She laughed at herself, and Averilis put her hand on Rose's elbow as she stood too and set the pillow on the couch.

"I want to change into something casual, not for sleeping," she said, "and I don't need a bath. You two should go back and enjoy yourselves if there's still enjoyment to be had."

"Can I redo your hair?" Rose Blue offered dubiously.

"You can take it down, but I'll ask my mother to comb it."

They nodded and set to work. Rose, always the talker of the two, exclaimed at the state of Raliel's hems, and Raliel only said she'd been in the cellars, some of which contained puddles. Averilis hummed and held up the inner robe. "It can be cleaned," she said, but the organza was doomed. "This could be cut into panels for something else."

Raliel nodded. She didn't care. As long as what she wore reflected the moon and the Moon.

Listening to the two talk soothed her. Averilis mentioned that Lady Glass Peach was gathering funds to purchase a row of properties for a new city temple. Rose Blue said Maris Fire of Sunrise challenged the Air Lord to a pageant duel, and it would be in three days in one of the market courts—did Raliel wish to attend? No, but she would if they thought it best.

It did not take long for her to be undressed and redressed, her hair down but in three loose braids held together at the ends in a small club that brushed past her tailbone. She kissed both of them on the cheeks and shooed them away.

Barefoot, in three thin layers of diaphanous gray robes, Raliel took up the barley liquor and walked down the private corridor to the Consorts' Bower.

She moved silently through the bower and to the open silk door leading into the inner garden. Spare moonlight and seven tall candles lit the edges of the garden, and her three parents reclined upon pillows and blankets spread over woven mats in the center. They were surrounded by rays of vibrant purple flowers, moon lilies, and blush-pink orchids, glittering granite, and calcite pebbles that reflected the moonlight rather like ocean waves. Beside the single juniper, a short table held bowls of nuts and cheese, sweet petals, and candy, as well as both tea and a wine carafe. The emperor lounged with his legs outstretched and his head in the First Consort's lap, staring up at either Sky's chin or the sky itself beyond. Elegant Waters sat upright, her lap harp against her thighs, and plucked a soft, slow melody to accompany her gentle singing.

Raliel waited until the sun psalm faded, and her mother set her fingers to the strings of her harp to settle them.

Her first step into the garden shifted the pebbles, and all three of her parents glanced at her, and all three of them smiled welcome. She knelt before the low table and put the bottle of liquor down.

"Yes, please," the emperor said, and Sky and Elegant Waters hummed their similar assent. Raliel had not brought fresh cups or bowls so gestured they should finish their previous drinks and she'd serve them. Together the four of them saluted the moon in the sky and sipped the liquor. It was sweet and sharp on her tongue, and Raliel dipped her finger into the clear liquid before dripping some on the garden rocks for the great demon.

"Are you well?" her father Sky asked quietly.

Raliel nodded. She looked up at Sky's eyes and the flecks of ghostly blue glinting in his pupils from his demon-kissed blood. "What did the sorcerer want?"

The emperor sat up swiftly. "Did he say something to you?"

The soft demand surprised Raliel enough to frown. "Moon pressed him to leave."

"Jealous demon," the emperor said fondly.

"It's too jealous," Sky said.

Elegant Waters added, "Not in this case."

The three of them fell silent, into their own thoughts. The emperor slumped slowly back onto the ground, letting Sky guide his head again to his knee.

Raliel waited a long moment, in case one of them might answer her initial question. When they did not, she repeated it.

Both her mother and father Sky looked to the emperor. His eyes were closed, but his lips tilted up into an almost-smile. "He wants the Fourth Mountain."

"He already has the Second."

"Yes."

"He must know if he took another, he would be too powerful for . . ."

"For us to ignore him," the emperor agreed. "The Fourth Mountain has been empty since Skybreaker died."

"But why did A Dance of Stars come here? What can you do to help him plant a new spirit in the mountain?"

"He doesn't want a great spirit," her father the emperor said darkly.

"He wants a great demon?" Raliel was so surprised her voice cut across the garden like an axe.

Elegant Waters strummed a bittersweet chord on her harp. "He wants us to want a great demon there—he wants it to seem to be our idea. To realize that a great demon would balance the mountains better than a great spirit. It would be three and three, then."

The emperor studied Raliel intently. Waiting for her to work her way through it. She sipped her sweet-sharp liquor and considered. Then she said, "How would that give him any advantage?"

"Perhaps he is only looking out for the empire, as he claims," Elegant Waters said, shifting to pluck an old lullaby.

"What do the others think? The other sorcerers?"

Sky, his blue-knuckled hand on the emperor's shoulder, said, "Shadows of the Fifth Mountain will say the sorcerers cannot be trusted."

"Including herself," the emperor murmured.

"A Dance of Stars will be colluding with A Still Wind, somehow." Sky continued as if his husband had not spoken. "They have always worked together toward their own accumulation of power. It is only the Moon keeping them in their place."

"The Moon and Night Shine," Elegant Waters said.

"And The Scale?" Raliel suggested.

Sky nodded. "And The Scale, perhaps. Their motivations have never been clear."

"They are as intentionally mysterious as Esrithalan," said the emperor. His eyes fluttered closed.

"The Scale is ancient and sees far into the past and the future and rarely offers advice," Sky said.

The emperor said, "They are the one Night Shine trusts."

Raliel, rather surprised the great demon of the palace had not come to vibrate the garden floor, nor to possess her and have its say, folded her hands in her lap around her nearly empty cup. "Should we be worried A Dance of Stars will attempt to make a new great demon? Or try to steal ours?"

All three looked at her. Then her father the emperor laughed. "You should not be, little dragon. The Moon is entrenched in the foundations of this palace. It is a mountain itself and cannot be forcibly removed—not without destroying everything and everyone. The sorcerer would not risk that—not when Shine would destroy him in return, and even The Scale might act in the face of such aggression."

"Someone . . ." Raliel hesitated, but her parents gave her space to gather her words. "Someone invented a sigil to bind the great demon here in the palace, as a distraction. When they tried to kill Mother. Could it have been A Dance of Stars?"

The emperor pressed his mouth into a line.

The First Consort nodded.

Elegant Waters said, "Perhaps that was the real test, and I was the distraction."

Before Raliel could say more, the great demon appeared. The Second Consort gasped softly at the sudden clot of shadows, at the seven round moon-eyes as it crouched on seven spindly arms beside the heir. "There you are," Raliel said, reproachfully enough her mother and her father Sky frowned.

The emperor laughed again, under his breath, and sat up again too.

I would eat that sorcerer alive, it hissed from all around them, blowing out the candles.

In the new darkness, with only the faintest moonlight and glow of the city, Moon's shadows vanished and the great demon was nothing but seven coin-silver eyes hanging in the air.

"We'll keep that in mind," the emperor promised, grinning.

EIGHT

I N THE WHOLE EMPIRE, it only snowed in the far northeast, near the Third and Fourth Mountains. Elegant Waters
had grown up at the foot of the Third, under the eyes of the
sorcerer A Still Wind and his great spirit. The hills and valleys of
her family's estate produced winter wheat and redpop, rare silver
wood from the shimmering forests, and they administered over a
mine with the most yielding vein of amethyst in the empire. But
Elegant Waters had loved winter best, and when she married
Kirin Dark-Smile, preparing to become the Second Consort and
never again return to her homeland, she commissioned a series
of paintings of the view from her bedroom window: her favorite
garden, and the best landmarks of her estate—all blanketed with
snow and depicted with nothing but thin black and gray lines
against white silk. They hung in her private bedroom, and she
used to bring Raliel there to bathe in a cold bath and wash her
hair with juniper berry soap. As they snuggled dry, her mother
combed Raliel's hair and told her about real winter, about sharp
biting winds and the tender peace of snowfall: silence and whis-
pers, delicate, tinkling ice, the clarity of the stars at night, how

vibrant the world grew under the moon alone when it reflected against layers of snow on the garden and eaves and forest canopy.

Her mother's soft words, strangely warm for all the icy details, had settled into Raliel until snow meant love and safety, meant perfect beauty and quiet longing. Nothing disruptive, but the kind of cold longing necessary to living a full life.

Raliel was too young for her Heir's Journey, by nearly a full year, but she argued to her parents that she wanted to go this winter, because if she waited for the summer before she turned nineteen, she could not see snow.

It was not the real reason, though she did long to experience true winter. But she feared if she and Moon waited more than an entire year to leave, they'd be discovered. The emperor would notice the demon possessing her, or she'd slip with her mother or father Sky. If they knew, they'd forbid it. When they found out—inevitably, once the great demon of the palace was no longer in the palace—they'd be furious. Raliel needed to leap off this cliff before it crumbled beneath her.

When she said it, she met Elegant Water's pale-brown eyes and did not let go. She remembered the paintings and lines of poetry, the rhythm of having her hair combed for hours, the tug and tickle of tiny braids, and the tangle of her fingers in her mother's hair instead, as she learned to braid and loop and pin razor-thin amethyst lace into place.

"This is a good idea," Elegant Waters said, nodding to Raliel, and with that shift of alliances, the emperor and First Consort Sky were doomed to agree.

Of course, winning that so easily set Raliel up to lose the fight when she argued she ought to journey alone. All three of her parents were adamant she required a companion—a friend or a bodyguard, they had different opinions about which was more vital, but it must be someone. Raliel couldn't very well explain she was taking the great demon with her. When she said she liked to be alone, Elegant Waters said that was bad for her heart, her father Sky said it was too dangerous, and her father the emperor said she was already isolated enough and lacked loved ones besides themselves.

At her protest that she had friends, the emperor slyly asked if she would take some or all of her coterie?

Raliel instantly—silently—rejected the idea, but tilted her head as if in consideration and sifted through the personalities of Salri, Averilis, and Rose Blue. She thought of Salri's earnest music, his eager smile and how easy it was to smile back at him. She thought of Averilis's sharp mind and long-winding understandings of court politics and how much Raliel enjoyed arguing with her. She thought of Rose Blue's passion for paint and fashion, how proud she grew when the four of them drew the attention of the court away from even the Imperial Triad. Raliel relaxed under her skilled ministrations one muscle at a time, able to let go of her worries as her hair was let down, as her makeup washed away, as they massaged each other's hands with creams to soften the calluses of art and sword work.

Yet none of them knew the demon. None of them knew *her*. She hadn't allowed it—hadn't known how to allow it. Besides, none of their skills would suit the long road, camping and walking hours. None of them had ever been alone in the wild before. Not that Raliel had, but that was the point of the Heir's Journey: hardship and winnowing herself down to who she was, in order to cut herself against the people and landscape of her empire. She couldn't imagine doing that with one of her coterie at her side. And so she softly told her parents no.

"You prefer a stranger?" Sky asked.

With a breath deep enough to lift her shoulders, Raliel had nodded.

At least with a stranger, she could start fresh, and they would learn who she was as she did, with the demon a dark slick of ice under her skin.

The afternoon before she was to depart, she was presented with the warrior who would be her companion. Osian Redpop was his name; he had been the demon-kissed guard who noticed the pattern of sigils the assassin had inscribed into the palace shrines and activated them early to thwart the assassin, thereby saving her mother's life. If Raliel must take someone with her on her Heir's Journey, he would do, she supposed.

But her first thought upon officially meeting Osian was not relief, it was merely,

Oh, adorable.

It was not a word she often considered, nor one she'd ever associated with the demon-kissed before, or soldiers in general, and yet Osian was exactly that.

He was half a head shorter than her, slight but carried himself with strength, with lovely dark-brown hair half braided up and wound with purple ribbons, the rest tumbling in gentle curls down his back. His shirt, vest, and uniform jacket were tightly layered over trousers and bound against his arms for easy movement, in shades of pale and dark blue, edged in black, his boots polished, and he had seven small knives sheathed in a delicate leather harness down his left thigh. He wore a sword, too, short and heavy, and a small aether-bow hung off his right shoulder. Just enough black paint lined his copper-brown eyes to make them into brilliant half-moons against the pale-blue undertones at his high white cheeks and narrow, sharp jaw. The blue faded into violet shades as it vanished into his hair. He smiled, and it was perfectly even, perfectly sweet, revealing deep, impossibly pretty dimples.

Not just adorable: beautiful.

This was what a demon-kissed doll would look like if they were made, molded, and painted for children to love. Except for the weapons, Raliel supposed.

He bowed to her, lowering his eyes demurely. The dimples didn't fade.

"Osian Redpop," she said coolly. It was a name with both nothing and everything to hide. Many people shared the surname, those without lineage to trace, or generational farmers.

Standing, he caught her eyes with his once again. "I don't know who my father was," he said by way of explanation and guilelessly, as if he simply understood people wanted to know.

From within the nest of ice it had created under her heart, the great demon snorted. She felt it shiver up to the nape of her neck. She did not react except to say, "We leave tomorrow with the sunrise. I will meet you at the Seventh Gate."

Osian's nod was short and sharp. His smile brightened. "Would you have me pack anything in particular?"

"Only what you need for walking. We'll be gone until the spring. I will have money."

"Do you like music?"

Raliel blinked, then inclined her head, *Yes.*

"Then I'll bring my whistle, to serenade the Heir to the Moon on sleepless nights." The young demon-kissed soldier grinned at her again and, with another bow, departed.

"Cheeky," she murmured to the demon.

The demon purred. It curled around her spine, sinking low through her back, almost like the weight of menstrual cramps about to bite. The discomfort was becoming a relief, though, as she grew accustomed to it.

Nearly every day the demon possessed her for a little while, learning to share physical space with her, to see through her eyes and listen with her ears, without blocking her own sight and hearing. She controlled her steps and breath and actions, though the demon could stutter her or stall her, could force her silence. It only had done so once—for the sake of experimentation, it said, and Raliel believed it. Mostly.

And tomorrow they would finally walk out of the Palace of Seven Circles and onto the open road.

Raliel smiled into the empty greeting room, at the door Osian had closed. If nothing else, he was extremely pretty to look at, and a demon-kissed warrior probably knew how to live off the land.

She wondered which of her fathers had chosen him.

you like him, the demon said, somewhere under her heart.

Raliel hummed agreement as she returned to the bedroom to finish packing. The demon startled her by falling through her feet to spill back into the floor. The slats of polished wood trembled as the demon settled back into the palace, and Raliel felt briefly hollow before her own breath filled her back up again.

She was alone.

Already she had said her formal farewell to the court and personal farewells to her coterie and tutors and favorite priest. Now all that remained was to tie up her bag, lay out tomorrow's clothing, and have her evening meal with her parents before trying to sleep.

A dart of anxiety hooked itself in her left lung, making it difficult to breathe.

She was leaving. She was—

Instead of sitting down to breathe, to imagine her snowy internal landscape and find her balance, Raliel picked up her mostly packed bag and took it to the second circle. It was early for dinner, but she found the First and Second Consorts both in the Consorts' Bower.

They sat at opposite ends of the long, curving room, as usual, the ceiling lattices thrown open along with the garden doors to let in light and a breeze. Elegant Waters plucked at her harp, marking a page of music as she composed; The Day the Sky Opened frowned over an array of letters and maps spread across a low table. On the tea table in the center of the room, a pot still steamed, none of the cups used.

Part of her wondered if she'd ever see it again.

But of course she was coming back. She was the only Heir to the Moon. She had to return. So did the Moon. Even if they found a way to change the palace-amulet and make it freer to move, to fly, it had to return with her.

"Raliel," Sky said, noticing his daughter caught at the threshold by her own feelings—hidden though they were by a still, cool expression.

Elegant Waters glanced up, setting aside her charcoal pencil.

Raliel swallowed. She stepped inside and carefully set down her mostly packed bag. "Will you—Dada, will you look this over for me?"

Sky smiled and flowed to his feet.

"The tea is fresh," her mother said, standing as well, and moving gracefully to kneel and check the pot. She poured for the three of them as Raliel began to entirely unpack.

The emperor found his family in a well-organized sea of water-resistant underclothes and money, letters of introduction and spice packs, boxes of tea with a tiny pot and two cups, a warmth-charmed blanket, and tools and a cooking pot. He swept in and stopped. Raliel glanced up from where she knelt rolling several sheets of fire sigils together as tightly as possible so they would slip into one of the external pockets of her bag.

"Fire charms?" the emperor said, masking his feelings with skepticism. He raised graceful arms to carefully unpin the silver rain veil from his crown. "Can't you spark salamanders? What have I been sending you to study with that witch for if not?"

"Spirits aren't always to be found," Raliel said, and thought, *Especially when one is possessed by a great demon.*

"We were doing fine without useless input," Sky told his husband.

"Tea?" Elegant Waters offered.

The Emperor with the Moon in His Mouth set the veil over the stand beside the door, then plopped onto the floor in a flare of his elaborate skirts. He tossed back his long sleeves and reached for the neat, small stack of clothes.

Raliel pressed her lips together but did not protest.

"This is a man's cut," the emperor declared, flicking the gray top robe open.

"Warrior-cut," Sky corrected, pointing at the eyelet for tying the flared skirt back.

"Hmm." The emperor rifled through the stack. "No gowns? You look pristine in a lily skirt, and you will be meeting justiciars and local gentry."

"Skirts sound terrible on the open road," Raliel said. She waited for her father the emperor to look at her. "Besides, I'll be wearing my hair up." With a flick of her brow, she told him everything he needed to hear.

The emperor smiled. "I'm sending off a son, am I?"

"More of a dragon," she answered lightly. But her own smile cut at the side of her mouth, and up it curved into a mirror of his.

Sky hummed warily, and Elegant Waters offered a delicate sigh.

Raliel's heart beat hard, loud in her ears. This was too much. She felt too much sitting here planning to leave them. Lying to them. It hurt. She breathed in imagined frigid air, filled her stomach with the cold. With that icy food, it was less overwhelming and her smile faded into gentler being.

The emperor's smile softened too, but there remained a sharpness in his gaze: he saw what she was doing—the rigid control—and didn't approve. But neither did he complain. Instead, he reached out and stroked his finger down her cheek.

Sky grunted softly to regain her attention and, ignoring the emperor, helped her finish repacking. She'd done well, and he rearranged only a few little things, but removed the tarp, suggesting she double the sigils on the blanket so that it served for warmth *and* rainproof shelter. It would save both space and weight, and for warmth she'd have Osian if she was caught out away from a crossroads sanctuary or inn. Raliel widened her eyes at that, fixing her gaze on her father Sky's hands, especially the blue tinge at his knuckles.

At the last moment, Sky added a small worry stone of a pure sky-blue agate. "I would give you my sword if I could."

"I know," Raliel said. Her father's sword was much too heavy for her. And it had a little bird spirit imbued into the steel that would not like to travel with the great demon, she was sure.

"Are we doing this now?" the emperor asked. "Before dinner?"

Sky shrugged.

With a greatly put-upon sigh, the emperor stood and swept toward his bedroom. Elegant Waters came to Raliel, pulled her to her feet, and tucked her under her arm. In her bedroom, she gave Raliel a tiny pot of perfumed white paint, the kind that went on rather sheer and could be spread on her lips, under her ears, or pinched into the ends of her hair. It smelled like juniper. Then her mother handed her a small folding fan made of strong lacquered oak and silk, painted with a pale ocean. "Your father sent this with me, before we were married, when I returned briefly home to the Mountain of One Thousand Falls. Your father Sky," she added, knowing Raliel would assume she meant the emperor.

Raliel cradled the smooth, worn wood.

"He meant it to welcome me, and I hated it at first, but I kept it and used it, and I cannot imagine who any of us would be without it," Elegant Waters said.

"I will keep it safe and use it," Raliel promised, almost understanding the message behind it. The need to work at family. At making an empire.

Together they returned to the bower where the emperor waited, chin raised. He held out his hand, and in his palm was a long white ribbon tied to a ring. Raliel approached and carefully plucked it up.

The ring was three strands of twisted silver, sweetly cupping a very tiny diamond. Except for the stone, it was identical to the ruby rings the emperor wore to denote how he was feeling about being a man or a woman or both or neither at any given moment.

It fit her first finger perfectly. And the diamond glittered like a shard of ice.

NINE

T HE NIGHT BEFORE LEAVING on the Heir's Journey, Osian Redpop prayed all night in the oldest mountain shrine in the capital city.

Tucked near the palace, toward the river where the city itself was the oldest, its gate nestled between two close-pressed shops, each with apartments stacked atop like a series of hats. The lintel of the gate glowed softly with aether-sigils, the only thing setting it apart from any other neglected shrine. Osian strode under just as the sun was about to set and made his way along the cobblestones past several sigil flags, and tiny shrine alcoves cut into the sides of the shops. At the end of the alley, another gate spread. This one was closed, the thin slats of wood painted red and white.

Osian opened it gently and put a small chip of copper into the offering bowl beside a fountain that trickled softly. Reaching into the cool water, he withdrew an aether-stone from among the three dozen or so huddled in the basin.

Beyond, a hidden courtyard opened into a garden.

Six tall, wide-based obelisks spread before him, arrayed

exactly around the space. At the base of each was a miniature shrine, and at the tip of each, a spirit statue. The stone pyramids were streaked with greenish-white lichen and old moss, the mortar between their building blocks cracked with weeds and a few tiny pink flowers. The gravel spread between them all was rough and uncombed, and trails of weeds marred what should have been gleaming pale seashells only. But at the center, the well was clean, its roof peaked in a pattern of six that matched the six pyramids, and tiny bells dangled from each peak. The low sun cast the place with an even, gray sort of light, despite the brilliant orange sky above, despite the shining white clouds edged in gold.

Osian was alone.

First Osian went to the well and crunched around to the other side, where he could touch the bell carved with the number four. Its chime was tinny and plain but faded very slowly. Osian ducked under and drew up the cup of water. He wet his fingers and touched his lips with them.

Then he turned to the obelisks again. Each represented one of the Five Mountains, plus the deep red obelisk at the entry gate for the palace itself. They were crowned by statues for the spirits that inhabited them—or in the case of the palace, a round bright mirror, and a small flame for the Fifth Mountain's demon.

Each tiny shrine carved into the base of the obelisks was filled with ashes from burned sigils and fruit and saltcake crumbs. Someone was tending to them, but not well, Osian thought as he approached the Fourth Mountain. It was because there were prettier mountain shrines in the capital city. Prettier, larger, more popular. With gold-tipped obelisks and spirit statues that moved, with strings of aether-lanterns and sparklers and priests who helped with lighting candles and singing prayers, who told fortunes and shared slivers of candy.

But this one felt older to Osian. More real. He knelt before the Fourth Mountain and set down the aether-stone he'd pulled from the gate fountain. "Thank you, Spirit of the Fourth Mountain, for watching over me." He put his hand against the inner curve of the shrine carved into its base. The stone was cold and rough, and this shrine was empty. While the bear spirit stood strong at the pinnacle, there had not been a sorcerer in the Fourth Mountain for more than twenty years. Since Shadows of the Fifth Mountain murdered Skybreaker.

From the pocket of his outer robe, Osian withdrew a strip of paper, then unwrapped a charcoal stick from the writing set he kept in the pouch sewn onto his sword belt. Carefully, he wrote: *Mother, I was chosen to go with the heir on her journey. We leave immediately, though it is nearly a year earlier than expected. You wanted me in the palace, but this will serve us better. It will be only Raliel Dark-Smile and myself. I will have every opportunity to be the weapon you forged. I will contact you when I can.*

Folding the paper into a tiny square, he placed it into the empty shrine of the Fourth Mountain, set the aether-stone atop it, then settled back on his heels. This was the difficult part for him. He breathed deeply, slowly, and removed one of his throwing knives. With the tip, he cut his tongue. No matter how often he did it, tears sprang to his eyes. He rolled his tongue in his mouth until he tasted enough blood, leaned forward, and spat it on the paper and stone.

Osian slammed the butt of the knife into the aether-stone.

It shattered, and the magic released flared along the splatter of his blood and spit: everything flashed, and when he blinked, the paper was gone.

Mother would have it, far in the north, in her shrine at the foot of the real Fourth Mountain.

He tilted his chin up and looked at the sky. The west remained edged in pink-orange, but the clouds had lost their luster, and beyond them the luminous blue of the sky turned purple. From this hidden temple courtyard, the sounds of the city were muffled, as if by aether-threads, and he could only vaguely hear the cries of evening, the rumble of city life.

Taking a deep breath of the thick ocean air, he did taste smoke and some spicy tinges from cook fires or the apartments around. His tongue hurt when he pressed it to the back of his teeth, feeling he deserved the ache a little longer. He'd been raised to do this, sent here as a child to earn a place in the palace, in order to be ready to serve his mother's revenge. "The Fourth Mountain has been weak for too long," she had told him every time he forgot himself and smiled, or failed to perform any task to perfection. "You will not be weak. You will not hesitate. This is what you are meant for, what you were born for. To make Kirin Dark-Smile suffer. To take from him what was taken from us."

Osian looked down from the sky to the shades of similar violet and blue at his fingernails, at his knuckles. And he wondered if he would be able to kill the Heir to the Moon, or if once again he would fail his mother.

All night long, he wondered.

TEN

THERE WAS A MOMENT as she left the city that Raliel felt the palace-amulet scramble to keep the great demon. Like claws of salt, the power dug into her guts, tugging, stinging, but they crumbled, not as strong as ice or bone or the silver amulet she had made and bound between herself and Moon.

She stopped, taking a sharp breath.

"Heir?" Osian Redpop asked, hand hovering beneath her elbow. He did not touch.

The sun glittered down upon them, bright and gilding the clouds of just-past-dawn.

"I am well," she said, turning away from him—no, turning to face back the way she'd come, toward the city.

Inside her, Moon said, *I am in no danger.*

Raliel nodded, her attention entirely caught up in the sprawling layers of the capital city: perched on the cliffs overlooking the sea, it fanned inland in long, graceful spokes made of broad avenues capped occasionally by temple arches. The tiled roofs gleamed in the low sun, bold colors against the pale sandstone and polished wood of the buildings. The Palace of Seven Circles itself rose over everything near the cliffs, red-washed and tiled in black and green, each level taller than the last, all enclosed by a thick red wall. Banners in colors so bold she could easily make them out from this distance fell from each level, painted with massive sigils for prosperity and blessings. As the city spread, dipping toward the wide Selegan River in the west, buildings grew closer together until they became warehouses and docks cluttered with ships. In the districts nearest the palace, Raliel could see gardens overflowing their yards with vibrant greens, and beyond those, wide community parks and city forests bound by corner shrines with their copper bells and white spirit flags lining many of the streets.

She had never looked at it from outside—always from her bedroom window, high in the palace. This view overwhelmed her: markets and temple complexes and dueling arenas, huge moon gates and a constant shifting motion from all the people she couldn't pick out individually but contributed to the living, breathing city.

Raliel pressed her hand to her stomach, against the buttons of her red leather jacket, over her diaphragm, over the nest of ice where the demon curled.

This was her home. The heart of the empire. That layered palace had been like her spirit house. And it *was* Moon's. Its bones, its ligaments and muscles and pulse. How could her body fit the immensity of the great demon, when the *entire palace* had for so very long housed it.

Her body was not large enough. It never could be.

When she returned, everything would be different. She'd

make it different. No more prison for Moon. She would excise that injustice, or let it all burn without them.

"Heir," Osian said gently. He stood just behind her, small and lithe, exactly the size to put his cheek to her shoulder if he wished. If she would allow.

"Let's go," she said, spinning. She strode away from him, from her family, from her home, and up the King's Road into the rest of the world.

BLUE

THE SELEGAN RIVER

THE SELEGAN RIVER ADORED gossip.

Maybe because gossip was messy and tickled, flowed hard when obstructed or spread fingers in every direction when let loose. It babbled and roared and could worm its way into the stoniest heart or carve pits and canyons into the most stolid and hard reputations.

It was like a river.

Today the Selegan held the most delicious—dangerous—gossip it had heard in years. So, naturally, it swam against its own currents north to the base of the Fifth Mountain to tell its friend the great demon *immediately*.

Well, not immediately. If it wished, the Selegan River dragon could literally be anywhere along its river the instant it considered doing so. It was the river, after all, and so if it had been all the way south at the sea, bobbing among the docks in the capital, it could summon a flare of aether and be in a different part of its winding, strong water body, even miles and miles and miles north at the pinnacle of the empire where the Fifth Mountain bubbled and smoked.

But the pleasure of swimming upstream was such a treat—and the gossip so good—the dragon indulged itself. Its water slammed against its scales and tugged at the feathers of its eye-flares and beard. It drove itself faster with all three tails, though that was for show and exercise: aether alone could speed it up. The dragon tucked its silver feather wings against its sleek snaking body and opened its mouth to let water slide between its fangs, then arced up and leaped into the sky, spraying the water into the air over the twin villages of Silverbank and Pearlbank that squatted on stilts to either side of the wide Selegan. The spray caught sunlight and became rainbows just as the dragon dove back into itself, carefully avoiding the flat-bottomed fishing boat filled with cheering humans.

Oh, the Selegan was giddy with its news. Maybe slightly because the gossip was dangerous, and maybe because the dragon knew his friend would be so shocked. It was not often Selegan was able to surprise Night Shine.

Or maybe the Selegan River was so excited by this gossip because it involved the Heir to the Moon. Selegan had what Night Shine laughingly called *a crush* on the heir. But how could it not? She'd named herself after a dragon!

The river remembered when the heir had been born eighteen years ago, and the dragon had wiggled around the docks, trying to get as near to the castle as it could to hear more. The great demon of the palace disliked spirits tugging at the aether in its city but didn't mind the dragon as much—though it refused Selegan entry into the palace proper. While the Selegan had wanted to dart to the Fifth Mountain right away with the news, it had waited and waited to hear what the baby's name would be. And the name never came.

Nearly everyone and certainly every spirit was shocked—how could a living thing be safe without a name? they wailed or whispered, tingling with nerves. And Kirin Dark-Smile had sent out messages to the whole empire declaring that his child was healthy and strong and would grow to choose her own name. The Selegan was scandalized, and when it finally told Night Shine, the great demon's mouth had popped open to reveal teeth like tiny white mushrooms, and she'd fluttered eyelashes as long and curling green as ferns—she'd been making her shape out of only plant life for a few months, as sort of a game and experiment, and the Selegan had already been subjected twice to an argument concerning whether fungi even counted as plant life.

In her surprise, Night Shine's form had melted into that of the girl she'd been when they'd first met, and so the Selegan had put itself into their human form, too. Night Shine threw thin arms around them and hugged tight enough that tears leaked from her human-looking eyes. She'd whispered, "Oh, dragon, did Kirin really say that? That his child would name herself?"

"Yes," they'd answered, patting her back in little off-rhythm taps.

"It's because he really messed up with names once."

"Yours?"

"Mine." And Night Shine had smiled and smiled until her mouth curved too big for her face and she burst into a new shape: all smile, with a hundred mouths—human and dragon and wolf and duck and eagle and tiny butterfly and fish, oh, several fish, and all of them full of teeth and laughing.

Then the mouths started talking at once, with several threads of thought, and the Selegan had to pay attention to track them all and answered only one at a time, because they were a dragon, not a great demon, and had only one mouth for each shape.

Then, eight years later the little heir had finally picked a name, and the Selegan River had heard the story from folks swimming in a sandy little bend of its waters north of the city. It raced north again to tell Night Shine, this time finding her up at the lake in the heart of the Fifth Mountain, surrounded by dawn sprites in every color of the sun, and the sorceress Shadows reclined on pillows beside a grove of shivering silver birches. The Selegan had splashed into the lake and swam to the edge, crawling out onto the sun-warmed rocks of the shore, and said, "The Heir to the Moon named herself!"

Shadows, always scary and elegant and solicitous of the river, leaned forward and tossed it a pear. Snapping it up, the Selegan enjoyed the crisp flavor and burst of aether imbued in the seeds.

As it crunched, considering a request for another, Night Shine plopped down beside its long scaly head and petted the crest of feathers arcing over one big blue eye. The great demon had been shaped like her girl-self, but her skin was dark-blue gemstone, glinting and faceted like cut and polished spinel, and her hair was long filaments of the finest crystal structure, pale as aquamarine. Her eyes were a gentle, sparkling brown, as usual. "What is her name?"

The dragon made itself smaller but remained sinuous and dragon-shaped and curled its body around Night Shine to properly settle its long muzzle against her thigh. She smelled like singed earth and sweet fire balsam. The Selegan twitched its tails excitedly and said, "Raliel Dark-Smile," with relish.

"Very pretty," Night Shine said, clearly not impressed enough.

The Selegan leaned up to explain, just as the sorceress Shadows snorted.

"Raliel is a dragon's name," the sorceress said.

"Raliel," said the Selegan, carefully pronouncing it through its long fangs, "was a dragon who lived in a lake called Tylish and was murdered by a terrible witch—it became a demon and swallowed miles and miles of aether from fields and forests and the whole entire lake before it was stopped!"

Night Shine's eyes widened.

"But!" Selegan shivered in delight. "When it was stopped, its name—its aether—did not dissipate but became a song! And not only that but a song so pure and perfect and deadly, if you sing it, you'll die within seven days."

"Very impressive choice," the sorceress drawled. "Especially for a child."

"Wow!" Night Shine said breathlessly. "A dragon, a demon, and a murderous revenge song!"

The Selegan River rolled away, half into the water. This lake was not *its* water, or even connected to the spring down the peak that originated its river, but water was its preference no matter what, and this lake had no spirit of its own. Unless Night Shine counted, which maybe.

Night Shine asked, "Why did Raliel the dragon have a different name than its lake?"

Selegan said, "Oh, I am not certain. Perhaps it was not born of that lake, or perhaps humans renamed the lake. That might have weakened it enough for the witch to kill it."

"Really! If the empire collectively decided to rename your river, that would weaken you?"

Turning mournful eyes upon her, the Selegan transformed into its human shape. They preferred a plainly lovely form, neither particularly boyish nor girlish, pale like sunlight on water. Over the years they had aged themself up to a youthful sixteen or so and lengthened their silver-blond hair to fall past their waist. "Why would humans do that?"

"Oh, I don't think they would, Selegan! I'm sorry. I only want to understand," Night Shine said, petting their cheek with warm gemstone fingers. "Names, names, names, you know!"

The Selegan River nodded slowly, wisely, but did not know. Night Shine had had several names before Night Shine, and each one accompanied an iteration of herself so wildly different it seemed obvious to the dragon that there was such a connection between the self and the name. With a name, one could remake oneself. Literally if one was a spirit or demon or sorcerer— or aether creatures like dragons or unicorns or lions. And even humans could change with new names—new definitions of themselves. A person with a new name created a new perception for others, a new performance, a new perspective. Names came with histories, like Raliel and Dark-Smile; they came with homes, like the Selegan's own name. They came with families, like the great demon of the palace, whose true name the Selegan River did *not* know but assumed tied it to the emperor and his consorts and his heir. (And *Moon* was probably part of it.)

Night Shine watched the Selegan with large eyes that seemed to gradually get even bigger, taking over her face. Fire flickered in her pupils, and little bright lights popped in and out of the browns of her irises, like fields of wildflowers budding and blossoming and fading in whole seasons as they stared back.

The Selegan River said, "I think if humans renamed my house and nobody said Selegan River anymore, it would not weaken me. It would kill me."

"No!"

"Not turn me into a demon but into something else. Either I'd have to break free and keep my name as a dragon of the sky and winds, or let the new name remake me."

The sorceress Shadows approached them, bare toes peeking out from beneath vivid purple skirts. She lifted the skirts and knelt beside Night Shine. Her cheeks were inhumanly sharp, with tiny black streaks like baby feathers slicked back toward her hairline, and one eye was as green as hemlock needles with a red-slitted pupil; the other white as seafoam, with the same red pupil. She said, "If Raliel Dark-Smile named herself, then nobody can take it from her."

The Selegan River laughed in delight. "Good! That will keep her safe."

Shadows grimaced. "Hardly."

But Night Shine nodded eagerly. "Oh yes, it will keep her safe."

"Foolish children," the sorceress told them, placing fond hands on both their shoulders.

"I know!" Night Shine said, leaping to her feet. "Selegan, you should name yourself too, and then you will also be safe."

"But—" they said.

"Curls of Light!" Night Shine suggested. She backed away, tilting her head this way and that. "Rainbow Lure! Um, A Single Silver Feather!"

"It doesn't work if you make the name," Shadows reminded the silly great demon.

But the river dragon basked in the names and flapped their hands at Night Shine so she would continue. Even if they liked their own name and never wished to be anything but the mighty Selegan River, it was nice to feel the love that flavored every offering. Better than juniper incense, better than aether-coins or honey cakes. Better than pearls.

Today, a decade after the Heir to the Moon named herself, the Selegan arrived at the lava meadow that blanketed the base of the Fifth Mountain. The meadow rolled away from the riverbank in emerald and pink and violet, fanning outward and up to the dark, sharp fangs of the vicious volcano. The Selegan burst out of the water and spun. Droplets of water became another cloud, and it roared through the rainbow for the great demon. Its roar was a high trumpet that echoed toward the mountain as they landed lightly on their feet in their preferred shape of the lovely youth.

Folding their legs, they sat on the crown of a knoll and played with matching the color of their trousers to the grass and their tunic to the exact shade of tiny purple alpine daisies. The Selegan closed their eyes and made their eyes purple, too. That wouldn't last, they knew from experience. Their eyes always dripped back into watery silver-blue, rain-blue, the flashing white of sunlight ripples.

They heard a very soft trill of laughter. Opening their eyes, the dragon found themself surrounded by a swarm of butterflies!

The butterflies were small, indeed, the wings only the size of their thumbnails, and beating slowly in all sorts of colors, but especially amber, gold, and dark red. They swirled around the Selegan River, and the dragon grinned. The little wings beat in time with each other, in a heartbeat rhythm.

"Hello, Night Shine," the dragon said in their gentle voice. They kept their tone even, though they vibrated inside with the gossip they'd carried here. So delicious! So thrilling!

"Hello, Selegan!" screamed the butterflies, but it was not very loud. Just squeaky and shrill.

The dragon laughed again. "Are you relearning this, or rediscovering it?"

Suddenly the butterflies were gone, replaced by Night Shine's girl form. She collapsed in a heap, then swooned back with her wrist pressed to her forehead, landing with her head in their lap. She rolled her dark red eyes up to them, and it was the only thing standing out in an otherwise perfectly respectable human form. "Practicing. It's terribly difficult, I don't know how you manage it."

"I don't do that," the Selegan River said, surprised. "I am only ever a river, a dragon, and a youth."

Night Shine spread her arms expansively, despite her swoon. "But when you're a *river*, and I know you're *always* a river—it's your *name*—you're so much."

"So much?"

"Water. So much water!"

"Am I?"

The great demon narrowed her eyes at them. "Selegan."

"I'm not water. I'm a river. You said so yourself, just now."

Heaving a great sigh, Night Shine sat up. "All right." She stared at them, studying the details, and the Selegan River bit their lip and just knew their eyes were already bright with rain and dappled waves.

"You have news." Night Shine pounced forward.

The dragon nodded regally but kept quiet, drawing out the suspense. Oh, it was delicious. They shivered dramatically at the wiggling gossip that skittered down their spine, squeezing their guts and heart.

Night Shine bounced in place.

"It's about the Heir to the Moon."

"Yes?"

"Who left on her Heir's Journey several days ago."

"Oh, oh, Queens of Heaven, is she going as a boy? Is she taking a false name?" Night Shine clasped her hands over her mouth. "Is she coming here? Does she want to meet me? I want to meet her."

The Selegan River grinned with all their teeth and slowly shook their head no.

"What!" shrieked Night Shine, hands wound tight together under her chin.

"When she left the city, Raliel Dark-Smile *stole the great demon of the palace*."

ONE

ONCE THERE WAS A happy, clever spirit inhabiting a twisting stream that coursed along the southern edge of ShrineTree Forest. The stream laughed and sped over bright pebbles and long mudflats, curving sharply before it spilled into a larger river, and there at the riverbank was a town called Crescent Meadow, built up around a series of mills. This spirit's name was Merry Cold, and it liked to splash children—or anyone really—who dunked their ankles in or flipped over rocks to find crawfish or tadpoles. The local people made it grand offerings every spring and autumn, wine and sparkling quartz chunks, and shoring up a few of its muddier banks.

But a late-summer storm shoved over one of the ancient sugar trees shading its most prominent bend, and the tree cut the stream off from itself. Rain and mud and fallen detritus from the storm firmed up the dam before any of the locals could spare time to notice—they had their stronger river after all—and when they did finally, it was too late. Merry Cold had died, and in its place a starving demon was born.

A demon born of a happy, narrow stream might not ordinarily have been a problem, but this demon was fast and just as clever as it had been as a spirit. So it thrust itself with watery fingers into the mud and swallowed up not only the aether churning in its own water but eggs and hibernating creatures and hollowed out more of the banks to stop the stream even more. It made for itself a large pond, and drew long grasses to itself, pulling on threads of aether as it devoured: soon its blight caught up an oak spirit, and with that the demon grew. Next it ate a family of raccoon spirits and withered a garden of flowers. Those flowers, which had been lovingly tended and therefore brighter in aether, gave the demon an idea: it leapt through its water from root to root, over the dam and to the mightier river. Rot followed, and animals fled if they were not eaten.

The demon soured the first mill, giggling and spreading beautiful blue-green mold. Then it found the first field of luscious, heavy redpop, ready for harvest.

Those seeds, those grasses—plus a little deer caught in the drag—were a feast, and the demon gorged. It was too fast, too strong, and while the people sent for help from the nearest justiciar, the demon slid through the river, strong enough now to fight the current, and was ready when a young man filled a bucket and took it to the trough to feed his pigs.

Oh, the demon enjoyed the pigs. They shrieked as it snapped their aether up, as their body-waters dried and their flesh desiccated. Maybe, the demon wondered, it could eat the entire village. It remembered them, after all, the people who had shored up its banks and played in its ripples.

That night the demon spread itself through water and roots,

waiting for the people to emerge in the morning. It could not maintain this for very long, it knew, because this water was a thinner and thinner connection to the water that was its house—back in the slowly stagnating pond. But if it ate enough strong aether, it might take the river! What a strong demon it would be then.

Unfortunately for the demon, the sun rose upon visitors to Crescent Meadow.

One was a tall, beautiful youth with deep-black hair tied atop their head like a soldier, a dark-red jacket, and a large backpack on their shoulders. The other was the most adorable demon-kissed warrior anyone had ever seen. Swiftly, the youth dropped their pack, drew aether-sigils into the road, and held out their sword. With a yell, they made it glow bright blue, and it was so pure, so delicious-looking, the demon showed itself with a hungry gasp.

The demon-kissed warrior moved to flank the demon, and the youth told him to get a bucket of water from the river. Then they planted their feet and faced the demon. "Little water demon, you have taken too much. Come here, and I will put you to rest."

The demon sneered, bending water-vapors to make a hiss. It wanted that sword, but turned and fled. As it snapped back to its pond, it hooked claws and teeth into everything it could, devouring threads of aether from grasses, trees, and all the tiny life residing within. Then the demon sank to the bottom of its pond to sulk.

The demon-kissed warrior brought a bucket along with a handful of witnesses from the village.

The beautiful youth walked around the pond, one hand on their sword, the other out before them, and the villagers watched as they gathered aether around the blade like spooling thread. Seven times they paused to tie an aether-knot and drive it into the ground with the sword. They climbed onto the dam for the final knot, and as they did, the demon sprang up, sensing the knots: the youth swung their sword and caught the demon in a net; then, as they fell back, dragged the demon with them.

The youth landed on their shoulder, rolled through the mud, and got to their feet again, teeth bared.

The warrior threw them the bucket, and as they caught it, they climbed back onto the dam. The demon thrashed in the pond, tossing scum and rotting grasses, but it was trapped by the net of aether-knots. The youth hopped down and scooped up water in the bucket, then asked the warrior to distract the demon. He did, pulling out a small whistle. With a shrill note, he played for the demon, and the villagers joined in, for they knew the bright jig. It was a song about laughing water and pretty rain, about taking water to drink and leaving a pearl, about borrowing water to make into wine and spilling the sweet alcohol back in. The demon was distracted because it remembered those things.

That gave the youth the moment they needed to bless their sword with sigils and the pond water from the bucket, then they sliced the sword across the surface of the pond.

Blue-white light flared, and, as if a boulder had been thrown into the center, the pond splashed: droplets caught the sun and tiny rainbows fell like confetti.

Then the villagers heard a pop, and everything was still.

The youth was nowhere in sight. The demon-kissed warrior's jaw dropped, and just as he struggled into the scummy water, the youth leapt up out of the pond.

Drenched, muddy, and pale, the slightly-less-beautiful youth wiped water from their face and tossed their soaked hair, loosed from its knot, over their shoulder. They held out a hand to stall the warrior and glanced at the villagers huddled eagerly on the bank of the pond. With a very slight smile, they said, "The demon is gone."

A cheer rose, and the villagers insisted their savior join them for the day and remain for a meal that night. The youth demurred, insisted they did not need to rest, that the demon truly had not been as strong as it seemed. The villagers might have let them get away with it had they never learned their name. The moment the demon-kissed warrior said it, *Raliel*, their eyes popped and they smiled and fluttered, and one young woman took the heir's hand and Raliel no longer had a choice about spending the night.

They threw her a harvest feast, gave her a room in their finest house—not an inn, but the top floor of their richest miller's home. The heir bathed and allowed the people to take her clothes to be washed, and they insisted on her doing nothing to help with the food but sitting with the cooks for company to hear tales of her journey thus far. Luckily for her—and them—the demon-kissed warrior Osian Redpop was a very good story-teller. He charmed all the grannies and uncles and young men and women, while the heir sipped a cup of beer and managed to smile at the babies.

The heir remained quiet but smiling as they ate stuffed

chickens and candied apples, little nut cakes and purple potatoes, as everyone toasted their fortune—and especially the Heir
to the Moon and her friend. The moon rose, and the villagers
played music, accompanied by Osian Redpop on his whistle,
while the heir listened. To them she seemed cool and shy, but
the coolness did not matter, for hadn't she thrown herself into
the filthy pond just to rid them of a hungry little demon?

Late into the night they played, and the heir's eyes drifted
closed, but her posture never flagged. Finally she was shown to
her bed, where she slept until dawn, then left with her demon-
kissed friend at her side and a kind bow of thanks to the miller
and his husband.

Within days the story spread across the south, and in weeks
it was everywhere: the Heir to the Moon was on her journey, and you'd know her by her elegant looks, handsome in
face and stature, by the dark-red coat she wore, the skirts of her
robes tied back like a soldier, the sleek man's topknot, and the
aether-sword. You'd know her by the single silver ring with its
gleaming ice diamond on her first left finger. You'd know her
by her pretty demon-kissed young man, whose vibrant grin was
like a sun and revealed dimples sweeter than your grandma ever
saw. You'd know her because she'd jump into mud to save your
village, tie aether-knots around any mischievous demons, and
all she asked in return was a bed for the night and a chance to
wash her hair.

TWO

THE GREAT DEMON OF the Fifth Mountain vibrated with excitement. And when one was a great demon, that meant if you weren't careful the air around you heated rather fast and maybe you were going to cause a huge storm if you didn't rein it in. Night Shine was almost never careful.

She hovered a hundred feet over the Palace of Seven Circles, darting back and forth in addition to vibrating, and transformed into a gigantic dragonfly just so she could spend the energy batting her wings instead of ruining the balance of weather.

The palace was gorgeous from this height. She'd lived inside it for seventeen years, growing up in the gardens and bathrooms and especially in the smoke-ways between walls, crawling through secret doors and climbing across the ceiling beams. It was mapped perfectly in her memory, but from the ground. From inside its hollows and atop its bones. She'd never seen it in such entirety, from high above, until now: red-washed layers in massive concentric circles reaching up to her with towers like fingers; flares of green gardens; dark peaked roofs. The sun caught the blue tint in those ceramic tiles in a way that almost rippled.

And beyond the palace the city sprawled, from the bluffs in the east to the Selegan, a bright silver river in the west, and in the south, oh, the ocean! The ocean a mirror of green-gray-silver expanding outward and forever until it was just a barely curving line and sky.

The world was beautiful. Night Shine adored it. Especially she adored this city and palace and the people inside it.

Too bad she kept hovering up here, staring down, pretending to be awash in love and expectation. Actually, she was terrified.

The Selegan River had told her that the Heir to the Moon had stolen the great demon of the palace! The great demon had been her friend, inasmuch as it had been capable, when she'd been a child here, and so Night Shine was a little worried about it, but also—also!—it had forbidden her from returning ever, cutting her off from her family for the last quarter century! So she was here to see if it was gone and then, if it was, to absolutely take complete advantage of that absence to visit Kirin. Or rather, the emperor. And Sky.

What heart she had fluttered, and Night Shine turned into a girl in order to clutch romantically at her chest. Immediately she began plummeting through the air.

Laughing in shock, she remade herself again out of feathers and bird bones and spread her wings to soar. She tilted, turning in the wind, and shrank until she was about the size of a chickadee.

Thus, she flew toward the little garden in the back of the second circle, the one that made up the verdant heart of the imperial quarters. She landed in the only tree—a small, gently cultivated juniper—and hopped on her little bird feet, and tried to decide what to do.

Either wait for Kirin or Sky to just appear, or fetch them, or tug on the aether to drag Kirin here—though he'd think something was wrong.

Night Shine realized there had been no pulse of magic from the great demon when she landed on the tree.

In an instant she stood on the soft grass, in her old body—or rather, her young body. A plain seventeen-year-old girl, but quick and strong. She wore a simple dress, layered under bright-blue robes, and left her dark hair down. To anyone younger than thirty, she'd seem like a weird servant. Others older might recognize her.

When she dug her bare toes into the grass, she felt only the coldest, most distant echo of the great demon.

Biting her bottom lip as she knelt, Night Shine flattened her palms to the ground, too, and sucked on the palace aether.

It was delicious. It lit her up with energy and satisfaction.

But there came no response.

Night Shine pushed back, grasping threads of aether. She wound them about her fingers and tugged in the rhythm of a lullaby the great demon would know.

Nothing.

As she thought it, she smiled a little. Then laughed. Then fell over on her side, holding her stomach and laughing as she spread out, legs and arms splayed, just laughing laughing laughing at being here.

Night Shine was not a normal great demon.

A million years ago—no, just a few hundred, ha ha ha—she'd

been a tiny flower spirit, fire balsam, bright and content with sun and wind and dark, fertile earth. So happy she'd been that she collected more and more of herself, more aether-flowers, growing stronger, until she charmed and befriended more spirits and subsumed them into herself. She'd been a meadow then, a bright-red meadow of fire balsam on the slope of a mountain. Even before all that, she had been fire, maybe. A spirit of deep creation, violent life, forceful transformation. But Shine didn't remember it.

So she'd been fire, and her heat seeped up into the earth and found a flower, making her fire balsam spirit. Then she slowly grew and joined with other spirits until she was the focus of so much aether she popped one day into a great spirit. Her tether to the brightness of aether was strong enough she could leap up into the sky or rush down the little river barely sparkling from a spring near the volcano. She was a great spirit, mischievous and joyful, and not very old when the volcano erupted. The explosion was so violent, so hot, it snapped her tether.

She died, but dug flower claws into the world and held scraps of aether in her teeth until the violence was past. Dead, but also powerful, she'd become a great demon. And she took the Fifth Mountain for her own and got a new name, which she told to only one person, decades later: a young person who climbed her mountain and convinced her that a great demon needed a sorceress. The great demon had said her name was Does the Spider or the Universe Have More Patience, and the young person said her own name was Sudden Spring Frost. They used their names to marry, and it had been wonderful. Until Patience realized she knew what love was and wanted more. She wanted a heart of her own, and the sorceress Sudden Spring Frost promised to make it so. After an incredible, devastating spell, Patience died again and was reborn again, this time a weird little human girl with a sorceress's half-heart, in the Palace of Seven Circles, where that great demon Moon could guard and guide her. She'd been called Nothing and bound accidentally to the Heir to the Moon.

Well, that heir was the emperor now, Nothing had rediscovered her sorceress and died and been reborn a third time: today and for more than twenty years she'd been Night Shine Over the Fifth Mountain.

Everything was wonderful, and Shine didn't need more.

Except it would be good to see Kirin again, and Sky, even if it had taken the great demon of the palace being kidnapped. That was funny, too. She wondered why the Heir to the Moon had done this thing. It sounded like the sort of wild idea Kirin himself might have had when he was young but never acted on because of all the potential risks—and here Kirin's daughter had ignored the risks to the palace, to the empire, to her own family's health, and done it anyway! How fantastic, how dramatic. Oh, Night Shine needed to know why.

(Night Shine could not be certain there would be terrible consequences. Maybe the heir had done her due diligence and knew this was safe. But it seemed to Night Shine there were too many unknowns, because even the origins of the palace-amulet and the great demon itself were unknown! At the very least there ought to have been some backlash in the amulet, rippling out to catch Kirin and Sky and their Second Consort up in it?)

Getting to her feet, Night Shine headed for the archway that led into the Consorts' Bower.

The great room was empty and decorated so differently from when she'd been a resident of the palace. Simple low tables in dark wood and floor pillows in every shade of blue from ice to the vibrant demon-kissed blue that would perfectly match the First Consort. She recognized Sky's side of the room immediately; the walls were covered with armor and beautiful swords, and very vibrant rain forest paintings with bright-red and orange birds. The other side held several instruments and two large wall hangings painted with lovely watercolor snowscapes. Night Shine had a terrible urge to mark one up with a scarlet handprint.

Instead, she puttered around until she found a teapot and pulled the top off a table to find a brazier for heating. She'd just poured water over some leaves that smelled earthy and sharp when a startled gasp came from the front doors.

Shine grinned at the tall, beautiful woman stopped in the frame, with several attendants clustered behind her. She looked at Shine with large dark eyes, but her expression quickly fell into cold disapproval. Her hair was gloriously arranged around bright jasper and gold combs and dangled with black pearls. Pink painted her bowed lips and flared around her lustrous eyes in swoops edged vermilion. Her gown was stark evergreen and white in intricate layers, lace and on lace, with tiny shimmering jewels sewn in. This had to be the Second Consort, and Night Shine thought she was absolutely perfect. Kirin would almost look normal next to her!

"You're even more beautiful than Kirin!" Shine said, clasping her hands under her chin.

The Second Consort—Elegant Waters! that was her name!—blinked slowly, full of condescension. She stepped into her room. "The emperor," she said in a lovely voice, and firmly taking

Shine to task for using his old given name, "is the glory of the empire. Perhaps you have not seen him in some time to forget he is unmatched."

Shine laughed.

"Ask Lord Every Star to have tea with me," Elegant Waters said without looking away from Shine. "And The Day the Sky Opened. Hurry, please."

Two of the attendants vanished.

"Oh," Shine said. "Oh, don't worry. I mean, you should send for Sky, and the emperor! I'm Night Shine. From the Fifth Mountain."

One of the remaining attendants covered her mouth with a delicate hand, shocked, but Elegant Waters said, "You were not invited into this bower."

Shine grimaced. "I know! I'm sorry, but I had to land in the garden and didn't want to upset anyone—which, of course, I've done now, and I couldn't be sure it was true what the Selegan River told me. That . . ." She licked her lips. "About the great demon of the palace."

Finally the Second Consort pursed her lips and dismissed her attendants, first telling them it was unnecessary Lord Every Star come, and the emperor should be told his oldest friend was in the palace. Night Shine approved with a nod, and Elegant Waters coldly pretended not to see.

"Tea?" the demon asked, smiling her least feral smile. She hoped. (She should practice in a mirror.)

Elegant Waters inclined her head and gracefully drifted in. She knelt on a pillow so perfectly, skirts pooling in exact ripples— Shine thought of her sorceress, who was actually the most

123

beautiful, with her monster eyes and feathers in her hair and black claws. But Shine only poured tea carefully, hoping it was the right strength.

They lifted their cups together and drank. The Second Consort did not complain, and no slightest hint of displeasure showed on her face, which told Shine absolutely nothing at all.

"It is true," Elegant Waters said softly.

Shine sucked air in through her teeth very inelegantly. Her eyes widened. "I can feel it's mostly gone—but not all gone?"

"I am uncertain. I feel fine." Elegant Waters sipped again, obviously giving herself time. "The connection I have felt since the enthroning ritual is unchanged."

"So the bargain—the amulet, whatever—is intact." Night Shine nodded, very glad about that at least.

Elegant Waters studied Night Shine for a long moment. Almost a rude amount of time, Shine thought, but this was the Second Consort, so she could do whatever she wanted, and her gaze was arch, just slightly condescending, cold, and distant. It was impressive. A little scary. Night Shine could admit she thought it was sexy. That made her happy because, to be honest, she'd been burning with curiosity and jealousy for twenty whole years about the woman Kirin and Sky married.

"I will not say more," Elegant Waters finally said, almost gently. She lowered her lashes and finished her cup of tea.

Night Shine approved of that, too, and knocked back her own tea. It wasn't great—too sharp. Kirin had always liked tea that tasted like chewing on pine cones.

An aborted grunt near the door startled both of them. Shine was up in a flash, throwing herself at Sky.

He caught her, of course. He was so big and strong, and Shine wrapped her arms around his neck like he was a tree and she a strangling vine. He smelled like incense and leather and something really pretty, and Shine rubbed her cheek on his scratchy jaw—oh, he was so old now! Twice the age he'd been when she'd hugged him last. Tears pinched in her eyes, and Shine squeezed them shut, hugging.

"You're too—strong, Shine," he whispered. "Demon."

With a gasp, she threw herself back. "I didn't hurt you!"

The fondness in his dark-brown eyes, those familiar flecks of demon-blue, warmed her so much she thought she was flushing involuntarily, and Shine let it happen. She stared up at him, at the soft changes to his stony square face. Just as large, just as muscled, his skin light copper with those luscious violet-blue highlights sweeping back into his hair. Tears plopped down onto her cheeks, and Sky reached out a hand to brush them away with his thumb.

"None of that," he chided.

"I love you so much and never get to say it," she whispered around the pocked lava rock in her throat.

His eyes softened even more, and his mouth.

Night Shine snapped herself out of it by transforming into a girl-shape made of obsidian. A cutting shape, harsh and beautiful.

Sky's brow lifted as if he was as unimpressed as always. When she turned back into her old self, he laughed happily. Low in his belly. "Night Shine," he said, and took her hand. Then he looked at the Second Consort, and Shine followed the gaze.

Elegant Waters was perfectly still, watching like a cool, beautiful statue.

It was worse a moment later when the Emperor with the Moon in His Mouth barged in, threw his rain veil headdress to the floor, and kissed Night Shine full on the mouth.

His hands cupped her face, his long fingers slid back into her hair, and he bit her, sighed into her. He tasted like—like—like himself, and Shine hadn't thought about this in so long, or even realized she *knew* what Kirin Dark-Smile tasted like! And just as she thought it, he pushed her back, hands on her shoulders. He stared into her face with those piercing amber eyes, and his mouth twisted, and with almost a sneer, he said, "I knew it was you. I cannot believe I have to thank my terrible daughter for making this happen."

Sky snorted and then hugged them both, and Shine felt so good, as if years melted away. She wished Shadows were here, to be part of this, a big four-way hug. But the sorceress had not at all been interested in coming.

Then Kirin slid away and went to the Second Consort. He stood beside her kneeling form, with her perfect posture and folded hands, her unconcerned expression, and he touched her cheek. "Come here," he said.

She stood immediately, fluid, and Kirin took her hand, then faced Shine again. "Night Shine, this is Elegant Waters, my Second Consort." He said it like, *You didn't want the job, so I had to find someone better.*

"She made me tea," Elegant Waters said, and Shine smiled just for her.

"It wasn't very good," Shine said.

The Second Consort bent her lips in agreement.

"Raliel likes it," Kirin said, as if his demon-kidnapping

daughter's opinion mattered more than all the rest of them put together.

Elegant Water's tight lips tightened even further.

"What did she do, exactly?" Shine asked.

Kirin leveled a stare at her. "Can't you tell even better than us?"

With a huff, Night Shine rather melodramatically exploded herself into a dozen tiny ruby-red birds. She scattered out the doors and windows (and behind a curtain into a smoke-way) and re-formed herself into a hazy kind of light in the third circle of the palace.

Such a display exhausted her, being so far from her house and sorceress. But it was worth it to show off.

Night Shine sank through the floor, spreading herself thin along grains of wood and falling down chimney shafts, smoke-ways, curling through steam pipes and down root systems, into cellars, and finally the basalt foundations of the palace.

She felt the aether-bindings, the pins and strong wards holding power in place. A cage of aether, an elaborate diagram of overlaid sigils making something old and complex that was . . . empty? Not quite. Hollow.

Was this what the Fifth Mountain felt like when she was elsewhere? No, she doubted it, because she wasn't bound to the mountain like this. It was her house, not her . . . prison.

"Oh my," she whispered to herself. They were all firmly bound here, by this ancient amulet. The demon, the emperor, the consorts.

Trailing a few threads of aether that wiggled oddly, Night Shine found the little knot that the heir had exploited. A back-door in the spell. The great demon was here, because it was part of the cornerstones and part of the Imperial Triad. But the great demon was gone, because it had found a way to make a little house—a subhouse—inside the Heir to the Moon.

Night Shine really didn't want to be the one to tell Kirin.

At least she could add that she knew exactly how to force the great demon to snap back here. It would take preparation and probably they should wait for the right phase of the moon, but together the triad should be able to drag the great demon home.

Hopefully, the heir would follow.

If not, it was only a matter of time before the threads snapped. The backlash would likely kill them all.

THREE

RALIEL WAS DISCOVERING THAT she loved to wake slowly with the whole world.

As the light changed, as the frogs and crickets ended their singing, she woke and listened to the shifting rhythm of dawn. She thought of her father the emperor who had told her the times and places between things were the realm of sorcerers. "Sorcerers step between life and death, between spirit and demon. They are shape-shifters because they loose themselves from dualities," he'd said when they were alone one dawn, his voice wistful.

Raliel understood why he was sad when discussing sorcerers— he missed his friend Night Shine, and part of him would have liked to be a sorcerer, a shape-shifter, able to form his body daily to match his changing inner self. It was in those early mornings that the emperor would bring his silver box of rings, and while his tea steeped, while Raliel sighed with her head on his thigh, he tried on his rings, as if they were all new. Three on his first three fingers, one on his thumb, another on his second finger, a single ring gleaming on his forefinger. Then reverse them, or slip them on and off in a pattern that seemed to mean something to him, but to Raliel, dazedly watching the play of dawn against the rubies, it was a language she didn't understand.

The scent of his tea would reach them, and he'd stop playing, sliding the day's rings on with conviction and putting the rest away. *Here is who I am today*, those rings declared. *Or who I think I will be today. Who I choose to be today.* He served them tea with the exact amount of honey and watched her with a tenderness she saw in his gaze only when they were alone.

Waking up in the distant forest, to birdsong and gradual rising pink light, Raliel remembered those mornings as she breathed in the transitory space. Before anyone looked at her and decided who she was, when she was only herself: a being of thoughts and feelings, desires and fears, nothing that could be pinned into a body, into a word for physical impressions and instincts. Not boy or girl, not a princess or hero. Just herself. If only she knew what that meant. Who and what she was under all those trappings and titles.

She thought about her father the emperor, who had taught himself to wrap this liminal feeling around his body like a mantle. Made it real, and because he was the emperor, that rippled out into the world. Raliel wanted to do that, find herself and make it ripple out into the world. Find herself, change the world. That seemed like the only point in becoming an emperor.

But first she had to save the great demon. If she couldn't, there would hardly be a throne to go home to. Not one she could comfortably claim. Raliel hoped the sorcerer of the First Mountain would be able to help. For finding information about great demons and ancient amulets, a sorcerer was the best bet:

the twin sorcerers, A Dance of Stars and A Still Wind, were out of the question, being obviously suspicious, and Moon itself refused to seek aid from Night Shine and her sorcerer of the Fifth Mountain. So The Scale it would be. The Scale, who her father the emperor said was nearly trustworthy, who had lived for centuries in their mountain, in peace.

If they knew of any other great demons, besides Moon itself and Night Shine, they'd have more options.

"Moon," she said quietly in the rising dawn.

Raliel.

She stood and stretched, glancing at Osian, who sat up already. He nodded and began poking the fire. Raliel offered him a fire-starting sigil, which he took. She put on her boots and grabbed her water skin before wandering toward the creek.

"Moon," she said again, picking around brambles and fallen branches. The demon answered by filling her with its tingling cold. Raliel's skin burst into tiny bumps, and she shivered down her spine. She smiled. As she found a place to relieve herself— necessarily accustomed to Moon doing it with her now—she thought about moving through the forest with only Moon, changing her shape, taking aether from the world to feed the demon, to feed them both, moving on, moving through, moving everywhere.

you love it out in the world, the demon said.

Raliel smiled—and it was easy to smile feeling like this. "Don't you?"

it feels like the ocean.

"Massive," she murmured. "Limitless."

yes. We need to get rid of the warrior. Go forward on our own.

"Soon," she promised, still smiling. Moon certainly knew Osian's name, and even liked him. Because Osian could make the demon laugh.

They'd discovered it three days into their journey, mid-afternoon when they reached the first primary fork in the Way of King Trees. Raliel intended to take the eastern-bending way toward the First Mountain, but she paused to sit and have a snack first. A large market popped up at the crossroads every day, with vendors selling anything from chicken on a stick to new boots and painted fans. There were stalls specializing in spirit-offerings too: blessing amulets and good-luck charms and strings of salted meat to save for any encounters with roadside demons. Several benches had been set up for eating and rest, and there was a pavilion serving wine, tea, and hearty broth. Beside it, a cluster of mossy boulders was currently occupied by children playing a loud wrestling game. Colorful flags fluttered in the wind, and the King Tree here had been carved through at its base into a shrine itself. Apparently, it was good luck to walk through and ring one of the bells hanging from a net across the ceiling of the hollow. Raliel did so, appreciating the clarity of the bell she chose, and behind her Osian hopped up to ring five in a row. The demon huddled inside the nest of aether that she'd constructed for it just under her heart, pretty as an amethyst geode, and grumbled it wanted to eat the entire resonant King Tree.

Raliel petted the silver amulet through her tunic, then moved toward spirit shrines stacked atop each other at the northeast corner of the crossroads. Each little arched shrine was inhabited by a shrill but happy raccoon spirit. Osian tossed pine nuts up into the shrines, one at a time, and Raliel watched the slippery spirits snatch them, invisible to any humans who could not see into the aether. Raliel remained back, uncertain how the spirits would react to the presence of the great demon—or if they could sense it.

try, the demon whispered mischievously.

But it wasn't the moment for experimentation. She instructed Osian to light incense on her behalf, unsure whether or not he saw the raccoon spirits. Some demon-kissed—like Sky—did, but not all. Instead, Osian tried to coax her over with the promise of a pine nut for her, too.

"I prefer sugared petals," she said.

"In that case," Osian said, and dropped to his knees facing her, tilting up his head to offer his lips.

Raliel did not quite manage to silence the indignant half laugh she made. As she shook her head at Osian, she felt a long, low purr just beneath her heart.

Moon, laughing.

And Osian laughed, too. It brightened his brown-purple eyes, and Raliel discovered she was not annoyed to be laughed at. He was too pretty—too good-natured—to be mean.

"My kiss would dissolve such sugar," she said coldly.

Osian laughed once more and nodded in agreement.

As they walked on, Raliel said, "Which of my fathers chose you?"

The demon-kissed warrior slid her a look, and before he could answer, Raliel guessed: "Sky."

Osian nodded.

It made sense: her mother had given her three friends already, each interesting and good, and suited to court. Father Sky would choose such a blunt instrument as Osian Redpop.

When they'd first started out on the Way of King Trees, they'd constantly been surrounded by other travelers, and Osian made friends with them all. While Raliel was not often recognized as the heir, Osian wore his identity on his skin. Demon-kissed warriors always worked for the emperor, and despite his doll-like size, his warrior status was clear by the weapons he carried and his always moving eyes. Most assumed he escorted a refined son of a noble or rich merchant. Some looked long enough at Raliel to question the man's topknot pulling all her hair off her face and neck, to wonder if the delicately curving sword at her hip meant she was a warrior too. Some suspected she was a very tall, very beautiful rich girl, but most were put off by her face, which she held in a mask of ice.

Raliel did not realize her expression was so cold, because she was *working*.

It was work to walk and walk for miles on end, to listen to every word spoken, to take in the passing villages and tiny roadside shrines, marking details of crops being harvested and already razed fields, the kinds of trees pressing under the towering red King Trees that lined the road. Raliel remembered the names of every village and every road that turned off (aided by memorization of maps, of course), putting colorful details into her memories of those maps: a flashed smile, a fox shrine nearly overtaken by a rose bramble, a village sign with recently carved graffiti, the laughter of their fellow travelers when someone recounted a tale about this particular tree and the jocular jay spirit that inhabited it during his grandmother's time.

By early evening, she was exhausted. Her feet hurt, her entire body felt sore, and her mind narrowed to food and sleep before the sun had even touched the distant horizon.

The great demon paid attention with her, occasionally commenting on things that surprised it, or that had changed from what it thought it had known of the world. Once they left the Way of King Trees for the eastern Path of Fire Trees, the road remained paved with large stones for a few days, though it had naturally widened at either side into hard dirt, where people walked, out of the way of carts and caravans. Moon said, *that is like a river, pushing at its boundaries when it is strong.*

Most nights they camped in crossroads shelters with other travelers. The small huts and wells were kept up by imperial money, and wayfaring priests and witches usually invigorated the aether-wards protecting the thatch from rain or the corners from mice. Raliel always claimed a corner and meditated to soothe the ruffled edges of her aether caused by the very large presence of the great demon in her stomach, or if she was too exhausted from feeding it in fits and starts all day, fell directly to sleep. Osian woke her when there was food, and she ate, and sometimes she made little sigil papers for the people they shared shelter with. Fire sigils and blessings were the most common, and easiest. Raliel enjoyed silently drawing and imbuing the sigils, not required to say much. It was basic witch work. And helpful. Then she would go to sleep, and Osian stretched beside her, sometimes continuing whatever conversations with their fellows he'd been engaged in until fading into sleep himself, or the entire party decided it was bedtime. Raliel did not exactly make friends, but who needed to when Osian was right there.

"Why don't you speak to anyone?" he asked her after enthusiastically waving farewell to a trio of brothers they'd sheltered with who were heading home after a summer of itinerant farming.

Raliel said, "You ask everything."

Osian laughed of course. "I thought your Heir's Journey was to allow you to get to know the people."

"I am," she said, surprised.

"But they aren't getting to know you."

Raliel frowned.

He let it drop, and Raliel was grateful to mull on her own. Was that important? For people to know her? Yes, but . . . she couldn't do that by pretending to be something she was not. She was learning what she was good at, though, out here in the world.

She liked helping people: hands-on, with the sigils or banishing cranky pond demons. Once she and Osian propped up part of a wagon while the owner fixed the cracked wheel. The satisfaction of watching it drive smoothly away had buzzed Raliel for hours. Raliel thought she'd have made a very good itinerant witch or graveyard priest in a different life. But she did not like having to talk to strangers, tell stories to them or explain the work, or flirt back, or endure the teasing of grandmas pinching her cheeks and telling her the names of their cleverest grandsons.

The great demon liked it, too, because work like that generated aether, which it ate gleefully.

Once or twice they stayed at an inn for proper baths and to have their clothing washed, and there had been the night they'd slept in Crescent Meadow, when Raliel had drunk slightly too much beer. Otherwise, as they moved eastward, more and more often they camped under the forest canopy, either passing up crossroads shelters or stopping before they reached one. Camping was harder work, but Raliel enjoyed hauling water and building fires and seeking out soft needles for a bed. The chores gave her opportunities to mark sigils where Osian couldn't see, in order to help feed the demon and relieve herself of the constant drag on her energy. Most of all, though, Raliel enjoyed the lack of roof, so she might sleepily watch the stars blink into existence one at a time through the high leaves of the canopy. Osian played his whistle, a surprisingly lonely, yearning instrument, even when he chose jigs and celebratory songs.

"You're very good," she said after a particularly intricate song that seemed to play over itself.

He nodded his thanks, ducking as if to hide a blush she doubted would show on his demon-kissed face. "My aunts taught me."

"My mother taught me," Raliel said, and Osian's chin jerked up. "What?"

"You . . . offered something," he said with a wry smile. "*Shocking.*"

She scowled by narrowing her eyes. "Everyone knows Second Consort Elegant Waters is skilled at many instruments and a composer."

"Oh yes," he said, laughing again before he put the whistle to his lips. This time his song was melancholy, and Raliel closed her eyes, drifting as she listened.

if I could eat music, his would be the kind I wanted, Moon said.

Raliel hummed agreement under her breath.

but I cannot and so we need to leave him. If we are alone, I can feast, and you will be stronger. We can talk.

She frowned, but swept it away, centering herself again with hands folded in her lap. She focused her breathing, practiced drawing extra aether in with only her breath to feed to the great demon. It was frustrating not to be able to speak back to Moon, but she could not do it without Osian hearing.

During the day, Osian told her stories about his childhood and the demon-kissed warrior barracks, about the two years he'd spent with the army and tales from the village in which he'd been born. Whitelar Town, north near the Fourth Mountain. He told her stories about great spirits and tragic love, as if he himself were fed by the simple act of talking. Raliel listened, and Moon whispered counter-stories, sometimes outright disagreeing with the details of a story—it was a great bear spirit, not a great stag spirit that formed in the Rainbow Forest, and in the Tale of Twin Dragons the lady was called Potential of Melting, not Melting Tears, which made no sense whatsoever according to Moon. Raliel wished they could speak directly to each other, imagining the wild course of arguments Osian and Moon would share. She wondered what would happen if she told Osian about Moon.

Moon complained as they moved farther from the King Tree forest into a softer kind of forest, made of spreading trees with broad leaves turning gold and orange, that if it could slip out of her and possess one of those oaks or capture a flock of crows or one of the cranky badgers shuffling around at night, then it could learn in one swallow everything about the forest, its needs and names and relationships—and the local spirits and demons. Her burden would be somewhat relieved if Moon could eat a tree or two, or a hive of wasps they passed or slip into the creek and snap up fish or a restless water spirit. But Moon did not believe it could leave the harbor of Raliel's body without being snapped back to the palace immediately. They had no way to know if the palace-amulet was weakened by Moon's distance, though neither of them had felt any urgency or thinning of their connection, or tugs from the direction of home to suggest the amulet was overly affected.

Twice Raliel tried to slip away from their camp while Osian slept, to find a strong source of aether to steal for Moon. The first time he followed her, calling out her name, and she had to tell him she was relieving herself. The second time Raliel found something all right: a wolf demon that had been minding its own business until Raliel and Moon tripped over it, and she spent fifteen minutes in a fight for her life. She'd come away with three deep gouges down her shoulder and a tear in her red jacket, and only that because Moon had helped her trick it into trying to use that bloody wound to suck on her aether: they'd turned on it, and once the wolf touched her blood and got its fangs in her aether, Moon devoured it instead.

Osian had found her in the immediate aftermath, shocked and angry she'd left him, and they went to a nearby village to ask for medicine. Of course, the wolf demon had been the bane of that village's shepherds, so instead of apologizing to Osian for not letting him do his job, Raliel was rewarded with another story of her heroics spreading like wildfire.

The next day, Osian asked if Raliel had a plan for her journey, or if she was just wandering around looking to kill demons. She said there was no plan, which was a lie. They were on a quest to change the palace-amulet so that Moon could manifest outside of the palace, could run and fly and be free. To give Moon a choice about its house.

But Osian nodded like he believed her lie. "The Heir's Journey is supposed to be the summer of their nineteenth year. Why are you going early?"

When she didn't immediately tell him, Osian invented reasons: A quest from a unicorn. A lover she wished to marry urgently. A threat from outside the empire. Raliel kept her mouth in a cold line throughout his elaborate guesses. At the end of the day, once he'd fallen silent for the time it took them to set up their camp in a grove of maple trees with leaves turning the vibrant color of cinnabar, Raliel said, "I want to see snow."

"Oh!" he said. "Snow. Yes. Very compelling."

She didn't bother with a response to his sweet sarcasm. Instead, she filled her mind with cold winds and tiny ice flakes, swirling in a gentle ballet through the darkness. Little falling stars, cold and bright. They fell through her mind and slowly filled her body, starting in her toes, layering over themselves up her ankles and calves, knees and thighs, up through her hips and waist until it snowed around the amethyst geode she'd imagined under her heart for Moon's nest. Raliel breathed slowly and easily through the cold, even as it filled her shoulders and slid down her arms to her fingers and wrists. It crept up her neck, frosting her ears and crawling in pretty ice spiders along the black strands of her hair to her topknot, kissing her jaw, up her cheeks to her eyes, spilling over her nose and lips until she was solid, bright snow. Raliel smiled slowly, peacefully, and under her heart, Moon snapped its teeth like a spark.

Because the sun was not yet down, Osian unsheathed his sword across the fire and started a run-through of exercises. Raliel watched his forms, so like her demon-kissed father's, except looser and, well, smaller. Osian remained like a doll, especially compared to The Day the Sky Opened's broadly muscled self.

But with sword in hand, concentrating, Osian was anything except cute. He was deadly. Precise and fast.

Of course he was: Sky never would have sent his only child out with anyone other than the best. Oh, and very clever, too— he'd been the one to save her mother from that assassination attempt.

Osian swung around, stabbing invisible opponents, and his lips moved a little, as if he counted a rhythm to himself. That, on the other hand, *was* cute.

"What is your demon-kissed gift?" she asked when Osian had slowed to a stop, and, with his sword resheathed, was stretching out. Her father had said something about memory.

His mouth pursed in hesitant amusement. It had been a rude question, but she wanted to know. And he'd invited her more than once into conversation. "Memory," he admitted, his smile widening in apology.

"Memory?"

"I can remember anything I see, anything I hear. Word for word, or line for line."

Raliel allowed her eyes to widen. "That sounds extremely useful."

"It is. Maps, commands, messages—I can replicate them, or pass them perfectly. I should be a courier, not a royal body-guard," he said with soft self-deprecation.

"Hmm," she disagreed. "You saved my mother from that assassin. You're well suited to the palace. My father Sky knows what he is doing. He knows what I am interested in."

Osian stopped stretching and flopped onto the ground. "Oh?"

"Useful friends, future advisers. Soldiers can be found in the palace by throwing a grain of barley in any direction."

"And . . . you can use someone with perfect memory."

She smiled. A winter smile, compared to her other father's fox one.

And Raliel began to test Osian's memory as they traveled, making a game of it: inventing poems and reciting long strings of musical notes for him to recite back, asking him to retell her conversations they'd had, that others had had with him, and sometimes when they took a break, she drew elaborate sigils on the dirt for him to redraw later. She taught him a few phrases in the language of spirits, though what use that would be to either of them she didn't know yet.

Three weeks into their journey, Osian bullied her into sparring with him.

Having her sword in hand again reminded Raliel she'd been absolutely stupid: her sword was attuned to aether, and she could use it to focus her efforts to draw in extra aether for Moon. While she practiced forms and defense with Osian, she also pulled new threads of aether from the air and forest into the sword, using it as a focus to channel power into her hands and arms. She slid the blade into the earth sometimes, drinking up excess energy from the cycles of decomposition always surrounding them; she unsheathed it at streams to let the wilder liquid aether cling and kiss the steel. That was how she took the first spirit: it was a slow, happy spirit of a turtle, guardian to this bend of the creek. Raliel saw it, reached for it. It was drawn to the shimmering brightness of her sword, and when she touched just the sharp blade to its blue shell, the turtle spirit shattered into strips of power.

Moon jumped and laughed in her belly, ate it right up, and both of them were stronger for hours. She did not need to end the day as early as usual, being flushed and full of aether-power.

That night in her dream she knelt in the Moon's Recline Garden. Moss swallowed light as it rippled over rocks, in between clusters of moon lilies and bright balsam. Across from her was Osian—no, not Osian. This one's face was pale as the moon. His hair was pure black, eyes black, robes and coat darker than Osian's, and the knives on his thigh were shards of broken mirrors. When Osian himself smiled, it was always full and sunny. This one smiled too sly, the dimples a promise of shadows, not laughter.

"Moon," Raliel said.

Osian—Moon—blinked slowly, with long black lashes, and its smile twisted. "Raliel," it said. "I'm strong enough to do this, because of the spirit you killed for me."

Because of the dream, her feelings were even more distant than usual, but she knew that would bother her when she woke. *Killed for me.*

"I want to do that again," Moon said. It was, at least, not Osian's voice. It was lighter, more of a whisper.

"I said Osian looked like a doll," she said, "but you make him look like a demon."

Moon tilted its chin, showing her a strong line of pale neck. It carefully licked those pretty lips it wore. Smiling, the dimples pressed deeper, and Moon lifted a black eyebrow. "Do you like it?"

Raliel didn't answer.

Snow began to fall.

Tiny white flakes drifted down, catching her lashes and dusting Moon's hair. It did not melt on either of them, for they were made of ice and winter in this dream, and Raliel stared at Moon, into the demon's eyes, which glinted eerie blue in the pupils.

She stared, and it stared back, and then she reached out with her palm up.

Moon put Osian's hand over hers, palm to palm. "Do you like it?"

Raliel pursed her lips, slightly embarrassed, and struggled to remember this was a dream. They knelt so that their knees nearly touched, and her hands were still in Moon's. "It is fine. Strange."

Moon's smile spread with mischief, and it bent closer to her. "Strange? Or . . . good?" it coaxed, letting its expression soften and its lashes lower. They fluttered, then Moon glanced up, and Osian's dark eyes were wide and flirting. Raliel felt her neck warm.

"Moon," she chided.

A sharp laugh bit out of its lips, and Moon settled back on its heels. But it did not shift its shape. "I liked that stream spirit," it said. "I want to eat more. I want to taste the forest, Raliel. A great owl spirit, a collective of roots or a meadow spirit. We'll pass shrines, and there will be spirits."

"We can't eat spirits out of their shrines." The idea unsettled her, and the edges of the dream wavered.

"Why?"

"Those are their houses. It's . . ." Raliel paused. "It's rude."

Moon tilted Osian's head to the side. It looked inhuman despite the facade, because its expression was so flat and innocent. "I don't care."

"I do."

"When will we get rid of him?" Moon's frown pulled Osian's face into a pout. It rubbed its thumbs along the back of her hands. "When we are alone we can do so much better. Move faster. We could already be at the First Mountain!"

Raliel pressed her lips together.

"I could eat him, you know. Overnight. Just lean in close, and I'll drink up his aether."

"Moon," she snapped. "No killing people—absolutely not. If you do, I will destroy our amulet and you'll be snapped back to the palace forever."

"You promised," the demon hissed. "You promised to change the bargain, to help me fly again."

"And I will, Moon. But not if you kill anyone." Raliel felt the air growing even colder and ice crawling down her cheeks like frozen webs of tears.

Moon lowered Osian's lovely lashes again, then bowed to her. "Keep your promise, Raliel," it murmured dangerously.

"You keep yours," she threatened in turn.

Then she woke up with a gasp, staring up at the black night sky.

FOUR

THE GREAT DEMON OF the palace did not have a plan.

It just wanted so much.

Wanting was akin to hunger, and demons were always a little hungry. Being dead spirits without their own core of aether, they constantly required a source. Most demons could only survive with a permanent spring of constant aether—a house. But great demons managed to make their own connection to aether, so all they had to do was eat.

The great demon of the palace did have its own connection, but that connection was the palace-amulet binding it to the palace and the imperial family (and more loosely to Raliel). Moving so far away drew its connection taut and tenuous, and dangerous, and it was difficult for it to feed without drawing aether straight through Raliel, which in turn exhausted her. Though it wanted so much, it did not want to hurt her. *Only* because she was its best link to the world. Its only chance at freedom. If it broke the amulet accidentally, there was no telling what would happen to it. Though it did not remember its death and birth, it vaguely recalled a world-ending hurricane, wild hunger, and desperation that dwindled smaller and smaller toward total annihilation. It did not want to find itself unhoused and similarly desperate again.

It *wanted* to get to The Scale and demand the old sorcerer tell it how to break from the amulet. (That had been Raliel's idea, that they ask the old sorcerer. She'd suggested Night Shine and the sorceress Shadows at the Fifth Mountain first, but Moon refused to speak to that terrible little demon. Night Shine had *tricked* it for years, eaten its aether-food, seduced away its prince, disobeyed it in its own house! It might ask a different great demon, if such a creature existed, but not Night Shine!) It *wanted* to make its own house with its own sorcerer, sink into a mountain or ancient king tree or vast lake or, even better, the cliffs at the beach or an entire island—it certainly fantasized about being an entire island. It *wanted* to reach out with teeth of aether and chew into the whole world, sucking power into itself, infusing its being with light. It *wanted* to stretch its wings and fly. Take Raliel with it, up into the clouds, out over the ocean, listen to her scream like it was a roar.

But in order to do all of that—any of that—they needed to ditch Osian Redpop, who held them back.

If Raliel would only leave the little blue warrior behind, the great demon could show her how to eat enough aether that they could make her light on her feet, make the forest bend around them, turn her arms to wings maybe, tug on aether-winds and fly there in two days!

The demon told her that for the sixth time today.

"Moon," she breathed, barely putting any sound to it at all.

The demon liked the way the name shivered in her throat, a self-contained breeze, her lips touching briefly, her tongue tip at the roof. Its name.

Moon.

It didn't think about its name often. Or rather, it hadn't thought about it often. Moon Caught in the Tide was just its name, and it had a different one once, before it was . . . this. Before it was a great demon, before it was part of the palace. For years (decades, centuries) it had vaguely considered its name to be the Great Demon of the Palace. But it wasn't. Sometimes people called it Moon, like the emperor, and *Night Shine* had before she was Night Shine. But sometimes she'd called it Great Demon, too. A title, if not a name.

But Raliel said *Moon* like it was all the name the demon would ever need.

Usually she said it softly like just now: so Osian Redpop didn't hear. Sometimes, though, she paused in her walking and looked up at the sky. She said, "Moon," looking up at the curved fang rising against the blue. Or at night, as they traveled on and the rising time changed. She sighed, said its name, and Osian didn't think it strange; nobody did. Raliel was only pointing out the moon.

The demon knew otherwise: she was giving herself an excuse to say it. Moon. Like an invocation. A summoning. Or just a sweet hello. Cold and sweet like fresh mountain water, not warm and sweet. Raliel was never warm. Just like Moon was never warm.

Moon did not like her. Not exactly. It appreciated her. That was all. She was clever, sharp, beautiful, and spoke to it without fear or inflection. She gave it what it needed: attention and aether. She was wonderful.

It did like possessing her. The sensations of sore muscles and deep breaths, the slow descent into sleep and the flush of heat in her cheeks that was so rare it still surprised the demon. But the demon wanted so much more. Its own body, beyond its house. Like Night Shine. It was a great demon—why could it not do what Night Shine did? Simply because it did not have a sorcerer? It had a palace! It had the emperor and his family. Why wasn't that enough to let Moon taste with its own tongue, not the off-center possession of taste? Laugh aloud because it was startled into amusement—not Raliel's muffled giggles. Not the way she swallowed laughter back—and cries of pain, too. Also not the purr the demon made when it tried to laugh, to make Raliel feel how it found something funny.

Usually what it found funny was Osian Redpop. The demon could admit that. They still needed to ditch him.

Moon wondered what a demon-kissed would taste like, if it could get its own teeth and bite into Osian's arm or palm or—something. Did the blood tingle with aether? Or was it only blood?

Not that Moon knew what any blood tasted like. Raliel said blood was metallic, that it tasted like blood.

Moon. *Moon.*

Moon wanted Raliel to say its name again. Louder. It wanted her to snap at it, demand something with its name. Laugh its name. Find all the ways its name could sound. That's how Moon would know the shape of itself. A name was like a house.

Every time she said it, she built the demon a new foundation.

It slid into her dream again that night and made itself into Osian: small, tight, very sweet and pretty with those big dark eyes and long lashes, deep dimples, dainty wrists, but Moon gave itself black-black hair and white-white skin. Raliel liked it, even if she didn't want to admit so.

Fine.

In the dream they were in a vast plain of snow, surrounded by lovely painted mountains. One of her mother's paintings. The lines of the dream-world dripped like watercolors or very thin ink.

Raliel knelt in layers of robes that mirrored the landscape: white and gray blurring over each other. Her hands were folded patiently in her lap, and she looked at Moon with her light-brown eyes. Waiting.

Moon wanted her to say its name, so it waited too. They stared at each other, while around them the mountains dripped, ink pooling into little ponds with tiny ink flowers, then spilled away in thin streams.

Slowly, Moon smiled. It thought about bitter things, sour things, it thought about what metallic was: bloody, and it thought of the rush of ocean waves. All that went into the smile. Beautiful, dangerous.

"Moon," Raliel said finally.

"Raliel."

"What do you want?"

The question ripped through the demon; it felt its shape ripple before it clenched down in control again. She had only asked because this was her dream, and Moon had formed them conscious space here together. Why, she wanted to know, had it made this dream? What did Moon want from her right now?

But the question was so much bigger. It had told her what it wanted: to fly. To be free. To be its own.

The demon shook its head, then let go of the dream. It dissolved around them, melting ink mountains draining into the white paper valleys, until all became a smooth gray shadow.

Raliel slept, but Moon opened her eyes.

Night draped around it, dull and dark through these human eyes. Moon blinked, drew a slow and silent deep breath to enjoy the stretch and pull of ribs and skin, the drag of air through two small nostrils, down the throat, the press of diaphragm. Hair teased at her forehead, her shoulder ached gently from how she slept on it. She was chilly, but pleasantly so. Their fire was no more than quiet embers glowing with a shimmer of red-gold mesmerizing to Moon. For many long moments it stared at the rich hot color, smoothing into Raliel's body. It curled her fingers around the edge of the blanket, stretched her toes. Realized it was alone.

This crossroads shelter was no more than a sturdy lean-to, red-painted wood on two sides with a thick thatched roof, a fire pit and sigil-protected boxes of basic supplies. Raliel had gone to sleep on her blanket, head to head with Osian Redpop's blanket. But the demon-kissed warrior was not here.

Moon parted Raliel's lips to sneer softly into the night. Where was he?

Carefully, Moon sat up in her body, one hand seeking the hilt of her sword. It listened, tilting her head.

Beyond the shelter the forest shivered quietly, layers of shadows and night, colorless. No birds remained awake. Even the frogs and grasshoppers had fallen silent. There came no hint of footsteps or the light panting and shift of leather Osian produced when exercising.

Where was he?

Moon stood. For a moment it did not move further, acclimating itself to Raliel's height and balance. It had never taken control like this, moving her limbs, blinking, breathing—no, Moon realized it was not breathing for her, nor pulsing her heart, there were many things her body did on its own, without Moon's will or interference. The rhythm of her heart picked up speed as it focused attention there, on the chambers filling, squeezing, the blood rushing, pausing, arteries like filaments of heat, threading throughout her body, to every part of it, so fast! A river inside her—no, this was an ocean, with a tide of its own, in and out, in and out, a system without any moon in its sky, but changing because of other input. Her skin flushed, Moon felt the heat in her cheeks, relished it, and the crawl of it up her neck, blossoming sweat—what a surprise!

Moon laughed. Once, loud, then covered her mouth with her hands. Giggled under those soft palms.

It had a mission. It could not be distracted by the wonders of her body. Later, later it would dive down those pathways, along her spine, feel the tingle of energy snapping under her skin, deep in her bones. Moon hummed—a purr that sounded both whispering and full from inside her skull, using her tongue and lips and nose to produce it.

Then Moon crept out of the shelter to hunt Osian Redpop.

It was disappointingly easy to find him. The warrior knelt at the crossroads itself, in front of the stack of shrines built up against a hemlock tree. The drooping branches and thin needles created a narrow house for the shrines, a private space for devotion. Moon took care to walk quietly and ducked off the narrow path behind a rough-barked sugar tree.

Osian held a paper against his thigh, writing on it with quick fingers. A candle in the base shrine flickered, casting Osian in soft contrast. His frown deepened the dimple to the side of his mouth, and he tossed his head to move hair out of his face. As Moon watched, Osian folded his paper and placed it on the stone offering plate tucked into the shrine before a statue of a turtle. The turtle's eyes gleamed with glass or quartz, not the sweet blue of aether, suggesting the spirit of the crossroads slept, or . . . Moon looked up at the third of the shrines, smallest and perched at the top. Yes. The turtle spirit peered out from that one, at Raliel's height. It was a thin slip of aether arched in the shape of a shell. Two tiny eyes blinked.

Then the demon-kissed warrior took up a rock, and without warning slammed it down over his paper: a flash of aether, the sharp smell of ashes, and the paper vanished.

Oh, Moon mouthed silently to itself with Raliel's lips.

Purposefully, Moon stepped forward, toe of Raliel's boot on a bed of fallen leaves from the sugar tree. They crackled under it, and Osian leapt to his feet, turning, hand on the hilt of his small sword. Eyes wide, he unerringly found Raliel's shape in the dark and did not quite relax fast enough. Interesting, Moon thought. It barely stopped from narrowing Raliel's eyes in suspicion.

"I did not know you were so devoted," Moon said gently. Oh, its voice—Raliel's voice, felt different when it formed the sounds, when it heard with her ears and skull. It wanted to say more, but it wanted to say things *to Raliel.* It blinked, distracted again.

Osian pulled a wry smile, released his sword to put that hand to the back of his neck, rubbing almost shyly. "I couldn't sleep, Heir. I thought I would see if the spirit here was interested in a conversation."

Lying, Moon crowed silently, viciously. Osian Redpop was lying to Raliel Dark-Smile. Oh, they had to ditch him now. "I see," it said in what it hoped was a reasonable, cool tone.

"I'm sorry I woke you." Osian walked to the demon, and by now every shade of uncertainty and surprise had vanished. He smiled sweetly, big dark eyes luminous and soft in the spare starlight.

"I do not mind," Moon murmured. It wanted to shoot out Raliel's hand and grasp Osian's throat, dig her fingers into his skin, rip out the trachea. Would it be hot? Or as Moon sucked that aether out of him, would it be cool and refreshing? Demon-kissed aether must be brighter, more delicious. Mustn't it?

That would be one way to ditch him.

But Raliel would not like it. Moon had promised. It wanted too much from her to give her reason to deny it. She slept deeply, and maybe Moon's possession kept her asleep. It was unsure, new to this, and to the cold silver amulet tingling against her breastbone knotting them together.

"Do you think you can sleep now?" Moon asked Osian.

The warrior nodded, seemed to hesitate about something Moon could not read—but Raliel might've.

Moon gave in to the urge to touch Osian. It reached, but instead of grasping violently at his throat, Moon put two fingers gently against Osian's jaw. Osian's lips parted, and Moon allowed the fingers to drift along the edge of the jaw, then fall away. It turned and walked back toward the crossroads shelter. Behind it, Osian dashed to catch up but said nothing else. He seemed to breathe a little quicker. Moon ignored it, laying Raliel back down in her blanket and curling up to draw itself back into the nest of ice and amethyst under her heart until she woke up.

FIVE

THE GREAT DEMON AMBUSHED Raliel when she picked her way through a tangle of vines to the small pit dug behind the crossroads shelter. She'd woken weary, as if her sleep had been thwarted by nightmares she could not remember. It felt like she'd run miles, or suffered through triple sword practice. As she stared at the pit compost, willing herself to prepare what was necessary for relieving herself, Moon slithered up her spine like a branch of frost.

Raliel gasped and went still.

I woke last night, while you were dreaming, the demon whispered from just inside her ear.

A full-body shudder coursed through her, involuntary. Raliel blinked hard. "What does that mean?" she murmured.

later, discuss it later—now I must tell you something about Osian.

Raliel frowned.

I woke, and he was not in the shelter. I followed him to the crossroads shrine, where he used an aether-stone to send a message through the aether. He was not happy to be caught but pretended it was nothing.

"You—he . . ." Raliel took a breath and tried again. "You spoke with him."

you spoke with him, from his perspective.

"Moon."

Raliel.

She bit her bottom lip, dragging the skin harshly. Since she was on her Heir's Journey, makeup-free, without needing to perform (much), she didn't worry about bad habits like this. And it felt good. Just enough pain to ground her.

When she said nothing, Moon continued, its whisper soft and dangerous. *Osian is spying on you. He sent a secret message.*

"Maybe it was to my father," Raliel said. "That would not surprise me."

still a spy, if spying for your father.

Raliel laughed soundlessly. That was true. She let herself wear a tiny scowl and stepped to the pit to do her business.

he is not on our side. Not on your side. Leave him, Raliel. Moon did something to the nape of her neck that felt like cool needles dancing against her skin, raising the tiny hairs there. It felt delicious, on the brink of danger. *Raliel. We only need each other. Just the two of us.*

Half engaged in her bodily functions, Raliel did not answer, but she considered. It was pleasant having Osian with her on this journey, sharing the hard work of travel, making friends on her behalf, flirting. But Moon was correct: this journey had a purpose, and if Osian was keeping secrets, it was even more vital they not allow him to know of Moon's presence. Moon seemed deeply invested in being alone with her, a thought Raliel did not mind in the least.

As she finished, setting everything to rights, Raliel said, "You spoke with my voice? Moved my limbs?"

Moon grumbled against her ribs in frustration. *yes. Not the point.*

"Tell me," she said firmly. Coldly.

A long pause allowed her to hike back to the shelter and around to the small well. She pumped at it until water spilled out of the spout into the bucket. Osian nodded at her from the clearing of the path itself, where the warrior stretched, sword in hand. He smiled, but something in his gaze seemed different—hesitant—only for him to blink it away instantly. There came his smile now, bright eyes, colorful ribbons in his braided hair, a flash of dimples. Then he sank onto his haunches and shifted forward into the first of his careful sword-forms.

The moment Osian's attention refocused on his exercise, Moon clenched icy claws around her hips.

Raliel bit back a gasp and made her body rigid at the sudden pain.

Then Moon's claws softened, like fingers—no, tongues, and it licked down her thighs.

Raliel gripped the bucket tight enough her fingertips whitened. "Moon," she hissed, face down.

I like your body, the demon whispered, dragging thin fingers up the small of her back. *The way you move, the way you feel pain and pleasure.*

Bending suddenly over the bucket of water, Raliel vigorously splashed her face with the cold well water.

Inside her chest, the demon laughed, *ha ha ha,* a laugh that echoed the speeding rhythm of her heart.

Raliel forced herself into some semblance of order with long, slow breaths. "Moon," she whispered, pulling water back into her hair. "I want to be with you when you look through my eyes. Not asleep."

I did not intend that.

She nodded. "Promise."

if we are alone, it will be easy to share, to play, to run, Raliel. To run through the forest together, to find all the edges of what your body can do.

Swallowing, Raliel took a moment to tamp down the gnarl of emotions the demon's words unearthed. "Do not do it without me."

promise.

"Yes."

yes.

———

In the end, ditching Osian Redpop was so easy it was hardly worth mentioning.

They left him in the town of Silver Tree, inside the manor of the local justiciar, a woman Raliel had met several times when she came to the Palace of Seven Circles. For two days they'd relaxed as her guests, having laundry done and sleeping in magnificent beds, eating plenty of good food. Osian had even entertained the family and a few local friends of the justiciar, playing his whistle and a borrowed lap harp while he sang. It had been easy for Raliel to sit quietly and wait for the best opportunity, and easier still to leave from the rock garden in the middle of the night. She (and Moon) had climbed the wall and hopped down into the public gardens the justiciar kept for her town's enjoyment. From there, they'd gobbled up a few flower spirits, enough to fuel Moon's initial spurt of power. It spread itself into her limbs and mind, not quite taking her over, but sharing the globes of her eyes—

flicking her lashes—

the pulse of her blood—

speeding her heart—

the bellows of her lungs—

pumping great breaths—

channeling just enough aether directly through her skin to make her light-footed, fast, and full of constant electric energy.

Raliel had never felt so alive as she did running through the forest with the great demon. Her heartbeat thrilled to the sound of the wind as it tugged her hair free of the topknot, her feet skimmed the earth, pushing off with great bursts of energy so she leapt as high as she was tall. The trees waved and bent back from her crackling power, sensing the dangerous drag of aether: they would be devoured if they did not make way for her.

If only she could shift her shape like a true sorcerer, give them wings to fly!

Maybe The Scale would teach them. Not only help them understand the palace-amulet, how to change it for Moon's freedom, but teach them sorcery.

They raced day and night, never needing sleep or food. The world was their food, and Moon's strength all Raliel needed for resuscitation. On her own, the remainder of their journey to the First Mountain would have been four or five days; as it was they arrived in less than two.

At the base of the First Mountain huddled Pilgrim Reception, a small city of permanent market stalls and houses, inns and street grills. It was grand compared to the more common pilgrim settlements of wooden lean-tos and tents found throughout most of the empire at famous temples or large crossroads. But the First Mountain had been a destination for hopeful seekers of blessings and magic for centuries. The Scale—the oldest, greatest of all the empire's sorcerers—was known to be reclusive, but when they chose to make blessings or come down to offer advice, their magic was the most helpful, the most incredible. Thus, the constant influx of pilgrims sustained an entire town with no other source of income but for the visitors.

Raliel and Moon arrived midafternoon and took lodging for the night, as Raliel preferred to venture up the mountain first thing in the morning. She paid for a lovely room on the top story of an inn, with a large half-moon window that opened up toward the First Mountain, then a meal—for although Moon had sustained her well as they raced here, her body could use real food. Then they ventured out to explore the stalls.

Buying a small flask of flower wine, she wandered through the evening market, her mother's ocean-painted fan in hand, wafting air against her face. She watched as pilgrims bought tiny soapstone shrines and fried chicken and candied nuts. Toys, spirit strings, spirals of dried herbs for burning at the road temples, lanterns, candles, ribbons, hats, entire outfits even—it seemed to Raliel anything could be purchased here. They had fine instruments and books and scrolls, and, oh, Queens of Heaven, she found portraits of the imperial family at a stall that offered lovely inked portraits drawn *right there! right now!* Raliel studied the faces of her mother and father Sky, ethereal and squarely handsome respectively, and the dainty lines of ink making up the emperor's rain veil. She suddenly felt light-headed from missing them. They had to know by now what she'd done. Would they send someone after her, or hide it? She hoped hide it. If Osian had been reporting to them, they would know soon she'd abandoned her guard. Her parents would be furious.

Most of the imperial portraits did not include the Heir to the Moon, and those that did painted her younger: thirteen perhaps, and a slip of a child, though tall with long unbound black hair and large eyes. In pale robes. She did not recognize herself and said softly to the demon that she was glad.

Moon laughed at that and ran cool fingers down her spine— equally strange and titillating. Then it began to enjoy itself.

The sun set, and Pilgrim Reception lit up with colorful lights strung across the streets, and bright red and orange lanterns in every window. Raliel found herself smiling gently, feeling warmer than usual,

Moon said, *I would like this better if I could wander apart from you. In my own body.*

"I don't mind tasting for you if there's a thing you'd like," she answered very quietly. Until they found the answers they sought, Moon could only share her body, not manifest its own.

no. I want to go up the mountain.

"In the morning," she promised.

They returned to their inn, and Raliel sat on the floor before the large half-moon window to meditate, calming herself and soothing her aether-lines, which were constantly spiking and gnarled with the great demon inside. While she didn't mind being its house, it was difficult. If The Scale helped them figure out how to allow Moon to manifest itself, Raliel would be relieved.

But she'd miss its coiling presence under her heart, in that hard geode of ice and amethyst she'd made. She would miss the surprising ways it caused sensations inside her: slips of pleasure, needles of pain, twisting nausea, sudden beads of sweat down her sternum, a tingle along her scalp—as if it experimented with her body, curious and unafraid.

There was something she craved about it. Intimacy. Trust. Even when it shocked her, she liked it.

That night Raliel dreamed she was surrounded by friends. They were in the palace, in a dream-garden with flowers of vivid pink and red, gilded and frosted with silver, some with petals like mother-of-pearl but velvety soft and pliable. She had those woven into her hair as she mingled, a cup of wine in hand, slippers softly crunching the fine seashell paths. When she paused to greet a friend, they looked at her as if they knew her, as if they'd been friends for ages. Another friend refilled her wine before she asked, and someone lifted a tiny feather out of her hair that must have blown in on the warm wind. There, beside Rose Blue, was the young person who Raliel intended to make her First Consort soon. Seeing them warmed her chest. Raliel smiled because she felt like it and wondered if her Second Consort had arrived yet. Were they still being interrogated by her father the emperor? Ah, well, they could take it—that's one of the reasons she loved them.

Raliel chatted and laughed with her friends as she made her way to the First Consort, then touched her fingers to their knuckles, easy as breathing. There was her mother observing the gathering with a pleased, soft smile, and—

The hand in hers was very cold suddenly. Raliel looked down at her First Consort's light coppery fingers, rich against her white, and as she stared, the nail beds turned blue, then purple, and frost whipped up their knuckles to their wrist.

Startling back, Raliel looked at their face and saw blue lips, bruised skin, eyes as white as snow through and through.

She gasped, and her First Consort tilted their head with a sound like cracking ice. "Raliel," they said, breath so cold it puffed before them.

All around her the people were made of ice. The garden was gray and black as iron, snow fell, and the people looked at her as if she were the one changed. She the one melting in the heat of her panic. "Raliel?" they said. "Raliel?—Heir?—Raliel?"

"Stop," she whispered, and then she couldn't draw new breath. She clutched at her neck, scraping ice off under her fingernails. She shuddered with cold: the warmth inside her strangled even as she tried to stop it, as she reached for aether or laughter again. She tried to scream for help but had no breath.

Raliel thrust herself out of bed, in the dark inn room. Moonlight streamed thinly through the large windows. Her tongue hurt. There was blood in her mouth.

She'd bitten herself.

Raliel, said Moon inside her.

"Why did you do that?" she demanded hoarsely, bending at the waist. It had been horrible: a horrible dream. Raliel squeezed her eyes closed and swallowed a thin tang of blood.

I didn't know how to wake you otherwise.

"What?" she whispered.

The great demon's tingling cold hands brushed the nape of

her neck—from beneath her skin—and she shivered. *you were having a nightmare. Your pulse raced and your body continued to grow hotter and hotter. So I bit your tongue.*

Raliel shivered again and crawled back into the bed.

what are you afraid of? the demon asked.

"Nothing," she said. Moon probably didn't believe her.

"Will you . . . will you . . . be with me?" she whispered tentatively, not entirely sure what she was asking for.

I am with you.

"I . . . know." Raliel clenched her eyes shut. She dragged the blanket up over her clammy body to tuck it under her chin.

I am here. Moon whispered it in both her ears, a gentle echo in her skull.

Cold blossomed under her heart, in the geode nest. A cold, bright star of ice, prickling ever so slightly.

"More," she whispered.

The great demon sliced up from the star, raking pain along her ribs. Raliel's back arched, and she bit her bloody lip to keep from crying out. Tears sprang to her eyes.

Raliel, Moon whispered, and its chill touched her cheeks, like a strange kiss placed from underneath her skin and muscles: little cold kisses tracking the path of her tears. Comforting. Strange.

Then she felt those kisses along her neck, from the delicate hollow below her ear down to her sharp collarbone. Raliel's need to make noise transformed into a shuddering sigh as she recognized the abrupt shift in her body. This was wanting. Desire. She felt it dance up and down her skin, sparkling. "More," she whispered again.

Moon dug into her guts, and she pressed her hands over her

eyes, even as she wiggled at the weirdness of something touching the coils and knots of her insides. It was so uncomfortable, but she pressed her hips back into the bed, and Moon drifted lower.

I like your body, it said, as it had said before, and Raliel whimpered at how good it made her feel. The demon teased the hollows of her hips, caressed lower, pinched behind her knees—it tickled and she laughed. Raliel dragged one hand to her mouth, touched fingers to her lips, kissing her fingers and her fingers grew cold with Moon's frost. She wanted to do something, wanted the demon to know what she knew, but how? How, Raliel did not know. Then she parted her lips and gently bit the tip of her finger.

The great demon inside her purred. *More?*

Raliel drew a breath through wet lips, liking the sensation, the coolness of it, though her face felt hot. She wanted to be touched, but not quite like this, maybe, or exactly like this? To feel these sensations without needing the awkward interactions of another person. Alone with a demon who felt what it made her feel, or she felt what it felt—impossible to know for certain if the great demon had feelings at all. The entirety of it was difficult to untangle when she was never alone in her own body, and the great demon remained such a mystery. This old being who seemed so young sometimes, new and childish, who had been asleep and dreaming for years and woke up only recently—but still longer than she'd been alive. She liked having Moon with her. She trusted it more than she should. They were aligned in motivation and needs. For now. She could use that. She could welcome it. But. The demon was a demon. Inhuman. Dreadful. Glorious. More.

Longing burst to life in her heart, that longing for more, for ineffable more, and she needed to know what it meant. What she wanted. Who she was, herself.

Raliel shook her head. "Tonight. This is good. You're here."

Here.

It wrapped seven slithering cold arms around her waist, inside, of course, but the squeeze was just as comforting as any hug. Raliel put her arms around herself, too.

SIX

BEFORE DAWN, THEY LEFT the inn and walked up the First Mountain.

Moon warned her the forest was filled with spirits— more so than most places, and it both excited and annoyed the demon. They started up the main road leading to the temple complex, where several priests resided, tending to terraced gardens and pilgrims. But before they reached the temple, Raliel and Moon stepped off the road to climb the mountain directly, in a more demonic fashion. Raliel was fit and strong, though until this season she'd never spent any time hiking forests and mountains. It had been a month since she'd left the capital, and her forehead was tanned, her lungs adjusted, her boots molded to her feet. She was overall leaner and stronger. So choosing the rough path up was easy. With Moon inside her, it was even easier because Moon could power them both.

They climbed through ferns and thick woods, up boulder-strewn slopes. Roots worked as handles, and the trailing sura vines with their heart-shaped leaves, too. With such natural ropes and the great demon, she was barely winded at first, and able to watch for aether-webs and nests of spirit birds. Tiny silver-blue eyes peered out from tree hollows. The occasional chitter of living squirrels was accompanied by giggling spirits; birdsong was bright and vivid and *harmonized*. Raliel found herself smiling, and thought suddenly of Osian joining in on his whistle.

Despite the damp rain forest breeze, Raliel kept hot with the hard work, sweating down her spine. Moon said it could drink up so much power if she paused long enough: she did, midmorning, on a flat jut of basalt. Streaks of emerald and moongray moss softened her seat, and she crossed her legs, set down her bag, and closed her eyes to meditate while Moon gently drank up the life of the stone. The moss dried out, curling up as it died, death spreading in a creeping circle from where she sat.

The energy tingled, cooling her.

"Stop," she murmured, and Moon did with a grumpy sigh.

"We are guests."

I suppose.

Raliel didn't grace that with a response; instead, she opened her eyes to look out past the spearing redwoods and hemlock toward the spill of the lower mountain. The view was green and vivid brown, with patches of gray-black stone, and even flashes of autumn gold here and there. Smoke lifted from Pilgrim Reception. The roofs gleamed red and blue under the sun. And the sky was broadly cloudless, a pristine blue cap. She could not see the ocean from here. But she could taste humidity as she breathed, and the tingle of aether. Raliel took a drink from her water flask, then gathered everything again and continued up the mountain.

Soon they were joined by a line of goose spirits, waddling in her footsteps. Then a pair of reddish-tinged spirit cardinals flitted alongside. A fat raccoon spirit arrived, quiet but watching her with open mouth to show its tiny teeth like a grin. Raliel nodded welcome to each spirit. She bowed to an elegant spirit doe, who lowered its head back.

Dawn sprites darted out from under a fallen oak and got in her face.

what are you, they squeaked. They were tiny genderless people-shaped creatures made of sunlight aether, naked and orange, red, white-gold, and their wings sparkled and flapped eagerly.

"Heir to the Moon," Raliel said. She snapped her fingers to pop loose a few sparks of aether for them.

Moon growled jealously and dug claws into her diaphragm, stuttering her breath.

Raliel froze, except for her lips, which smiled. "Go on, little ones," she said with the last of her air. Then she waited.

For a long moment she didn't even try to breathe, instead feeling the pinch of its claws, the pressure of it against her insides. Waiting.

She won when it loosened its grip. Raliel breathed deeply and said, "It is polite to share, Moon, and you are not low on energy."

eat them, it said. And suddenly Raliel's hand reached out and grasped a dawn sprite. The demon sucked its magic up through her palm, and the sprite withered to dust and specks of faded light. Nausea—*wonder*—turned in Raliel's stomach. It—she—they had eaten it.

Moon laughed as the other dawn sprites screamed and fled.

ah no! stop, cried other spirits. *What was that.*

who.

who are you.

Raliel turned in a circle, trying to be calm despite the horrifying, thrilling beat of her heart. Her hands trembled as she held them out beseechingly. "I am here to see The Scale, to speak with the great spirit of the First Mountain. I am here, and so is Moon, the great demon of the palace."

Her voice was even, soft, but everything nearby heard.

And vanished.

Every spirit disappeared, either melting into the mountainside, diving into the foliage, or rushing off on vines of aether.

Raliel and Moon were alone with the forest and rocks, the gentle wet breeze.

With a tiny sigh—annoyed at Moon—Raliel began climbing once again.

It was not long before a single tiny bird spirit appeared, flying directly for her. Because it was alone, it took Raliel a moment to name it a starling—they were so commonly in flocks.

Raliel stopped. "Be good," she said to Moon.

The starling flew over her head, turning around in a loose circle before simply dropping to the forest floor. It was small enough to perch on a fallen brown leaf. *I bring greetings from The Scale,* it said.

Immediately, Raliel knelt, placing her hands on her thighs. "Hello, great spirit," she guessed. "I am Raliel Dark-Smile."

you have brought a great demon here.

"I have. We are allies, myself and The Scale, through my father the Emperor with the Moon in His Mouth. The demon is Moon, the great demon of the palace."

your demon is taking aether from our mountain.

Moon began to speak, but Raliel said, "That is the nature of a demon."

The little starling tilted its little head, and blue flicks of aether flashed in its beady eye. *true.*

"Moon must take, but it is mine, and with me, and so long as that is the case, it will not take more than is necessary. Not enough to harm you."

does the great demon Moon make this promise?

Raliel said nothing.

Moon grumbled again but crawled up her throat to say with her mouth, *"Yes, I will take only what is necessary."*

only what the heir deems necessary, clarified the starling spirit.

Raliel felt her face scowl with the demon's displeasure, but Moon nodded. *"Fine."*

With that they were suddenly surrounded by starling-spirits: a murmuration of them, like a cloud of silver-blue that appeared from nowhere.

Even Moon startled, and together it and Raliel stood.

The spirit swarm wrapped them up without asking, lifting Raliel off her feet and into the air.

Her stomach dropped as the mountain did, and Raliel flexed her fingers, trying to grip something—anything!

relax, the great spirit of the First Mountain said in a hundred little voices, *we have you.*

and I will not let you fall, the demon added very, very softly under her heart.

Raliel kept her eyes open as they burst out of the canopy: sunlight pierced brightly, and the sky was just as cloudless and vivid as before. Disoriented, Raliel let her fingers splay and her legs bend a little, as if she balanced on the surface of water. She breathed deeply and a little fast, and wished she flew under her own power. This was frightening more than exhilarating.

And then the world seemed to open up before her.

The mountain spread, rising in broken peaks, as wind buffeted her, and the haze of a hundred spirits cocooned her in their power, and something snapped inside her.

She was *flying*.

Raliel laughed softly, a little hysterically, and Moon purred.

The purr wrapped her spine; she felt it from her skull down to her toes. She flung out her arms like wings and opened her mouth to taste the air. Even now she was quiet, silently joyful, as the wind turned cold and brisk more than the damp of the rain forest.

They needed this! They had to learn it. To do this themselves, only Raliel and Moon.

More than halfway up the mountain, a manor stuck to the side of a cliff rather like a giant shrine. It was warm honey-brown wood and whitewash, with peaked roofs in mountain-green ceramic tiles, a tower, and curving walls.

The great spirit of the First Mountain swirled around her, flying her toward that manor. Blue and green glinted from colored-glass windows.

They landed in a half-circle tiled yard before double doors of carved honey-wood, flung open and waiting. Beyond was an entryway just as bright, lit with real candles and aether-lamps, modulating the light even and pretty.

"Thank you," she said to the great spirit as it set her on her toes and she managed to maintain balance.

Then the starlings spun and coalesced into a figure the size and shape of a person, with limbs and a head but no distinguishing features. Similar to the great demon's shadow self: when at home in the palace, it used to form into a mirror image of Raliel in size and shape, but with seven moon-silver eyes.

"May I see The Scale?" Raliel asked.

The great spirit bowed—its body lengthened until its neck was too long, its limbs, too, and it was twice her height. It walked and she followed, led through the grand entryway and a receiving hall empty of anyone. There were privacy screens and comfortable sofas low to the ground, all in bold ocean colors. The windows were blue glass, and gauzy curtains hung from pillars carved like trees that held up the arched ceiling.

She was led down a corridor and up wide stone stairs and then to a guest room.

rest, refresh, the great spirit said. *food with The Scale later.*

"Yes, thank you," she said. "Moon and I look forward to meeting them. And I hope you'll join us," she added politely.

The great spirit bowed again and dissipated.

This guest room was simple and elegant, carved into the mountain on one side, built of honey-wood on the others. A row of latticed windows and several elaborate sconces were bright with aether. There was a bed, an eating table, a shelf of tea and cups and kettles. A brazier. And through a narrow arch she found a room with a toilet closet and steaming pool rather like a fountain, constantly trickling hot water from a central statue of a dolphin. Small lacquered boxes lined the rim of the pool, and within were tiny soaps and oils, herbed salts and combs, and Raliel already felt her body melting at the thought.

She wasted no time stripping and submerging herself into the pool.

Moon woke her three times as she drifted to sleep in pleasure at the hot bath.

When finally she dragged her happy, languid body free of the water, she got towels from the hanging rack and a wonderful soft robe and wandered back to find her bags and sword leaned beside the bed, and there was a kettle on the brazier, a couple of bowls of dried tea awaiting her choice.

"Did you notice anyone come in?"

Moon said, *spirits.*

Raliel nodded, wondering if any humans served The Scale as well.

She chose a light floral tea and slowly combed her long, heavy hair. A thought flickered that she'd like for Moon to be able to comb it, or her mother. Even Osian—he'd have enjoyed it, and talked softly the whole time about nothing that mattered. It felt so good to be pampered with nothing but patience and a comb. Just as she thought it, Moon said, *I want to comb your hair.*

Surprise lifted one eyebrow ever so slightly. "Maybe soon."

She turned her back to the brazier in hopes her hair would dry faster. The diamond on the ring her father the emperor gave her glinted prettily, clean and happy. Raliel considered meditating again, or practicing with her sword—surely in a place like this, the aether-attuned weapon would spark. But instead, she didn't even put on the fresh clothes, climbing into the bed and falling immediately into a light sleep.

She woke before too long at a knock and sat up. More refreshed than groggy, she wiped hair off her face and twisted the heavy length of it into a loose braid before padding to the door. She swung it open to find a very pale youth there, dressed in the style of a dawn priest but in bold blues. He bowed slightly. "Will you join The Scale for dinner?"

"Yes, thank you. I must dress first—and may I send my clothes to be washed?"

The youth bowed again and smiled. He told her she was welcome to any of the clothing in the wardrobe and to leave her dirty things in a basket he pointed out with a spark of aether that danced off his fingers and skittered through the air to illuminate it.

A witch, then, for dawn priests dealt with ghosts and ancestors, and she'd never seen one resort to tricks. He offered to help with the clothing or anything else; when she declined, he left her to it.

Raliel first put her dirty things into the basket and then drew open the wardrobe to discover a rainbow of possibilities. For weeks she'd worn trousers and a warrior-cut set of robes, her red jacket, and boots. Tonight she had every intention of dressing up, even if it made her late.

So she chose layered skirts and an overdress-vest combination in pale pinks, the nearest to her favored moon colors the wardrobe had to offer. She added one layer of stark pure black, and an eye-peeling red belt since she had no white. It was her hair she could not manage on her own, used to sometimes two attendants or her coterie working with it. Raliel could, however, put in a few small braids and wrap it all up with the lacquered combs she discovered. Then she put on the perfumed white paint her mother gave her, across her eyelids and on her lips. Juniper filled her nose, and she smiled very sparely. She'd brought no jewels other than her ring, but she tied her mother's fan to her belt and slipped her father Sky's agate into her sleeve before sliding her feet into soft black slippers.

She waited seated on one of the low sofas, across from a tall mirror that leaned against the wall. Raliel was a faded flower with a scarlet stamen and flashes of black. As she studied herself, she realized the demon has been a little too quiet for a little too long.

"Moon?" she murmured at her reflection.

Instantly she was flooded with its tingling dark cold. Gasping, she folded her hands more tightly together.

give me eyes, it said.

Raliel avoided biting her lip in thought, then investigated the narrow chest of drawers beside the wardrobe where she'd found underclothes. One entire row was face paint and perfumes. She found a scarlet pot and a thin brush, then knelt before the floor mirror. Carefully, she painted five small red eyes in an arc against her brow. Each she dotted with a slitted black pupil.

I have seven eyes. This is only five.

"But I have two," she said, fluttering her lashes to make the point.

Moon hummed approval. *together*, it whispered.

SEVEN

THE SORCERER OF THE First Mountain waited for Raliel Dark-Smile and Moon in a stone room made with magic to seem like the ruins of an ancient temple set atop a tiny island on a night-blue sea. Once Raliel stepped in, the door vanished, as did the mountain walls, replaced with pale columns cracked and crumbling on all sides, beyond them crashing waves. Above, velvety blue sky cupped the ceiling, and tiny aether-stars sparkled in an imitation of proper constellations. Wispy clouds drifted, and the air smelled of petrichor.

In the center of the ruins was a low table beside a brazier of glowing coals, two floor pillows, and The Scale.

Raliel walked across illusory soft grass and offered the sorcerer a shallow curtsy, which they returned.

"Welcome, Heir to the Moon," The Scale said softly.

"Sorcerer of the First Mountain," she replied. She intended to behave as though this were a royal meeting. That she had not effectively run away to meet the sorcerer.

The Scale was shorter than Raliel, slender and clothed in plain white robes hemmed at the thigh like a laborer's, with gray trousers and silk boots. Their features were sharp and pretty, very distinct in the upturn of their eyes and flat, high cheekbones. Their black hair was straight and fell past their shoulders, and in the aether-starlight it gleamed with rainbows, like spilled lamp oil or mother-of-pearl. Raliel remembered the sorcerer A Dance of Stars, who had made himself so blandly handsome—the opposite of this. The Scale smiled softly as she studied them, and slowly their eyes shifted from blue to silver in little streaks: like clouds passing across the sky.

Subtle, breathtaking.

Raliel wondered if they could make it snow inside their eyes. For one stunned moment, the question nearly fell past her lips.

Then The Scale turned and gestured to the table.

In near synchronicity, they knelt at either end. The Scale leaned so that they rested on their hip, but Raliel remained in formal posture. The table was carved with an intricate landscape of terraced gardens and distant mountains, lacquered flat-over with a blue sheen. Raliel's eyes could not help tracing the delicate artwork.

Moon said, *introduce me.*

That had Raliel's gaze snapping up to The Scale, who watched her already. "Thank you," she said. "For the hospitality."

"It is your Heir's Journey, is it not? I am honored to host you. And your companion."

Raliel tilted her head in acknowledgment. "The great demon of the palace says you can call it Moon."

Moon snorted but didn't disagree.

The Scale smiled. Such sweetness and their shape made them seem no more than twenty years old. But for the shifting sky-eyes they could easily have been underestimated. Raliel would be certain not to. The sorcerer said, "You both may call me Lutha."

A breeze gently wafted away the rainy scent and replaced it with fresh brine, a crisp spring sea-smell. "This is incredible aether-work," Raliel said, glancing around at the wide-open world, knowing she was actually under several layers of mountain stone. The words didn't capture the level of power on display, and she felt slightly foolish. She bit that back behind a cool smile.

"I've had quite some time to practice," Lutha said in a gentle drawl.

Just then attendants drifted in with dishes and cups and platters of food. The attendants were hazy and translucent, like unfinished drawings—spirits without an aether glow, or magical constructs of some kind. Raliel said, "Wait," to the one that set a decanter beside her. The attendant knelt, and Raliel reached. "May I?"

It was Lutha who said yes.

Raliel skimmed her finger along the fall of the attendant's transparent hair. The moment she made contact Moon purred, and the attendant shivered as the great demon sucked at it.

"Moon," she chided, pulling her hand into her lap.

"That's very rude," Lutha said, but poured them both a cup of water-clear liquor.

"Yes, it is," Raliel agreed.

am I not a guest to be offered a meal as well? Moon demanded.

Raliel touched the lacquered table, fingers beside her cup. She glanced at the sorcerer. "Moon wonders if it is welcome here, after all."

"Are you hungry, great demon?" Lutha asked.

that is my nature, Moon said, repeating Raliel's words from earlier.

"Moon's nature—as with all demons—is to be hungry," she said.

"Everyone is hungry, but we moderate ourselves when it is polite to do so."

Moon grumbled under Raliel's heart, curling up in her little ice geode like a nesting snake. "You did promise to take no more than is necessary," she reminded it.

The demon remained silent, and Raliel lifted her cup. "Thank you, great sorcerer. And thanks to your spirit, who brought us here."

Lutha put their cup to their lips and drank; Raliel did the same. It was a taste like starlight itself: clear and mysterious. Her lashes fluttered. She sipped again. "This is marvelous."

"And excellent with the soup," Lutha said. They moved to serve Raliel, and she allowed it, being the Heir to the Moon.

They drank the soup, too, before continuing their conversation. Raliel finished her shallow cup of star liquor, then took her turn to serve Lutha a sample of the floral and fruit salad chilling beside a dish of darkly seasoned rice with thin strips of fish. There seemed no unifying theme to the meal, but Raliel enjoyed everything she tasted.

As they ate, they conversed easily and slowly about her journey, a few things she'd seen, and Lutha was careful to ask Moon's opinion once or twice. Raliel translated its answers and hoped that the sorcerer would be able to help them set Moon loose from her so it could speak for itself.

Dessert was small triangles of a soft, sweet cheese decorated with golden crystals of honey in the shape of spirit writing. Raliel picked one up daintily. "Star meadow?" she said, glancing at Lutha.

"You read? Or did Moon tell you?"

"It taught me years ago."

Lutha smiled. "Try it."

The sweet cheese melted beautifully on her tongue, begging her to close her eyes. She did, and for a moment she stood in a valley at night, surrounded by sparkling flowers that glittered and winked pale-blue-pink-white: this valley was a sea of stars. The air was clear and warm, there was no moon at all, and Raliel just knew that she was perfectly, wonderfully alone with the entire universe.

She opened her eyes with a slight gasp.

Lutha laughed gently. "I do spend some energy on magic to make the world better, but I can't resist playing sometimes."

"This did make my world better," she murmured, but nodded, for she understood what they meant.

I want to play, Moon whispered. *I want to play.*

Raliel realized she was smiling affectionately for her demon. She blinked. Wiped the smile away in favor of cool snow. "Moon would like to be able to play," she said as she sipped at the liquor. She felt tipsy from its delicate heat.

"I can imagine," Lutha said. "Is that why it came with you? Why you stole it away?"

"Yes," she answered simply. Why bother pretending? "We need your help, Lutha, to understand the palace-amulet, how it binds Moon as a great demon not to a sorcerer or house, but to a family and palace. You are old and wise, and certainly have ideas."

The Scale watched her, sliding one finger along the rim of their cup. "Because your demon wants to play?"

Moon spiked aggression up her throat, but she expected it and had prepared herself to swallow it back. She touched her chest, over her heart, and hummed too softly to be heard—only felt. She said, after the demon settled, "If that is its choice. Moon has been bound for centuries and would like a choice."

"Breaking the palace-amulet might destroy the palace. Or harm the empire."

"Lutha." Raliel was prepared for this, too. "The empire is harmed by the very existence of the palace-amulet, so long as it is a prison. Forcing the great demon to remain there, to belong to us, without choice, does harm every day. It is wrong."

The Scale watched her calmly, giving nothing away.

She continued. "Because we do not know the ramifications of changing the palace-amulet, we need information. How it works. Why my ancestors made it this way. If we understand it, I know we can find a way for everyone to get what we want. And . . . regardless, it must be done. Or at least we must try."

"And you came to me."

"As I said, you are wise and old. And the most magnanimous of all the sorcerers," Raliel said, careful to keep her voice even, away from flattery. "Will you help us?"

"You truly ought to have gone to the Fifth Mountain and asked Night Shine."

"*No!*" The great demon growled so viciously it made a harsh word with Raliel's actual voice.

She coughed lightly, covering her mouth with the back of one hand.

Lutha said, "I see," obviously quite amused.

Moon growled again, a bubbling sensation in her chest. Raliel had already argued this with Moon. It wanted what Night Shine had. Therefore, the obvious person to ask was Night Shine. Moon absolutely refused. Raliel had called it irrational. The demon had not cared.

Raliel opened her mouth to ask if The Scale knew of any *other* great demons they could ask, but The Scale said, "I have not studied the palace-amulet, so could not describe it accurately. But all the ways I know to dissolve a bond between demon and sorcerer—or between witch and demon familiar—involve mutual unbinding or destruction and death."

your parents will not free me, Moon said. *Why would they?*

"Because it is the right thing to do," Raliel assured the demon. She meant it, too.

Kirin Dark-Smile has his own priorities.

"An emperor's priorities. You cannot fault him for that."

so you agree he might not agree. Ha!

"I will convince him."

I could kill him.

Raliel gritted her teeth and refused to rise to that bait.

"What does Moon truly want?" asked The Scale, who had watched the conversation, hearing only one side.

"What?" Raliel repeated, unclear on the meaning.

"What is at the core of your great demon's desire to choose? What does it want?"

"Moon?" she asked gently, directing her focus inward.

She saw the ocean, the beach below the city bluffs where Moon had taken her this summer. She saw gusts of wind and felt the sting of salt spray. There were feathers around her, part of her: wings. And a quiet melody played on a harp, a tune Raliel knew but could not play, that invoked a yearning in her heart. Her mother's music?

Raliel nodded, and she said to Lutha, "Moon remembers part of itself that it did not used to remember. A part that flew. That was free. Had a body, a self that . . . moved and changed. Moon longs to move and change again."

The Scale eyed her seriously, with an air of infinite sadness. "We all must move and change, that is true."

"Night Shine does it. Night Shine leaves her mountain, her house. She changes shape, doesn't she?"

"Night Shine is a great demon but not exactly the same."

What changed her? I want that.

Raliel told The Scale what it had said.

"As far as I know, all great spirits and great demons need a sorcerer to bind with, in order to leave their house."

"Yes," Raliel said. "We suspected as much. And my father the emperor says we are not the equivalent of a sorcerer—we, the Imperial Triad and myself."

"True," said The Scale. "You must walk a path of sorcery to be a sorcerer."

Night Shine was her own being before she reunited with her sorceress. Night Shine was in my *house!*

Again Raliel translated Moon's words.

"Ah, well." Lutha shrugged prettily. "Night Shine was reborn more than once. And that last time the sorceress changed her.

185

Gave her part of her heart, that her great demon could live and love."

"What?" Raliel frowned. It sounded like a riddle. Or a love poem.

"I know what Shadows did, not how she did it."

"Gave her demon part of her heart?" Raliel sighed. She felt Moon under her heart, coiled and cold.

sorcery, Moon whispered.

"I don't know how to do that, Moon."

"What do *you* want, Raliel?" the Scale asked.

"Justice," she answered immediately. "This imprisonment is a canker in the heart of our empire. I want a choice for Moon, as I have a choice."

"Do you?" Lutha mused. "Have a choice?"

"Of course. I make my vows—three times. Three times I can decline."

"But if you did, who would take your place?"

"I know what you are implying, but it *is* a choice."

"You are willing to change the shape of the entire empire for this demon, for justice. What does that make you? What do *you* want to be?"

She opened her mouth, but nothing emerged.

Raliel, whispered the great demon.

Lutha watched her still, the sorrow evaporating. Replaced by something more interested, more eager.

Was she a little drunk? Flushed, at least, she realized, as her neck warmed. The sorcerer plainly stared. Moon touched her breastbone from the underside: a tentative question. What did she want to be?

More. She remembered aching for more—undefinable, impossible more. Then she stood at the window that had been hers forever. Now she knelt beneath a magical sky, in the den of an ancient sorcerer. In the house of a great spirit. She was not empty but full with her own great demon, whom she'd kidnapped! Was this more? Was this enough? What did she want to be when she went home? When she found a way for Moon to choose?

Raliel looked down at her hands in her lap, then suddenly snapped her gaze back to Lutha's. "I want to be more than enough—enough to fit into the huge space that I was born into. The—the shape of what is expected of me. Enough for my family, for my people. The entire empire. And . . . myself."

"That is heavy wanting," the sorcerer said. "And part of becoming enough is helping your friend make a choice."

"Yes," she said immediately, then hesitated. Was Moon her friend? How she wished she could look at Moon, read its eyes and shadows to know. But she couldn't. Not yet. "Yes," she said again.

Lutha smiled: sweet, carefree, and with just a hint of mischief. "I will help you."

EIGHT

R ALIEL KNELT BEFORE THE tall mirror that leaned against the floor in what was officially her room for the duration of her stay in the First Mountain.

She placed her hands on her thighs and studied herself. She took a deep breath, then another. Moon curled under her heart, restless.

Lutha had told her they'd heard of another great demon—rumors only—living in the sea, that did not have a sorcerer of its own, and perhaps it would reveal secrets to them.

Moon thrilled at the idea—loving the sea already, a sea demon seemed ideal to it. But, Lutha had warned, they could not reach the great sea demon without sorcery. Of course.

Besides, though Lutha had not examined the palace-amulet, they suspected the amulet itself was elaborate witchcraft, the sort of ritual to bind witches and familiars to power temporarily and within specific limitations. That was why specific rituals existed to bind the Imperial Triad and the heir, why the palace shrines were always invoked in specific orders and constantly tended. But the scope of the amulet and the nature of the great demon meant witchcraft would not be enough—they needed a certain amount of power to share. Sorcery was inherently malleable, liminal, ever-changing, and extremely difficult to achieve or control, but once one did so, the power was nearly limitless.

So sorcery was what Raliel and Moon must learn, whether they chose to seek out a great sea demon or to intuit their way to a solution.

"Intuit?" Raliel had repeated, aghast but trying to hide it. "Like . . . guessing?"

Lutha had laughed and nodded. "The more you learn, the more informed your guess will be."

Rather horrified to think that the great spirits and great demons inhabiting the Five Mountains were all bound by *guessing,* Raliel had excused herself for the night.

She stared at herself, at the layers of pink, the hard line of black, the splash of red that matched the eyes painted in an arc over her forehead, and then slowly put her face into an expressionless, cool mask.

Raliel, the demon muttered, but there was a tickle to its voice, like it was laughing.

"I'm not good at intuiting, Moon," she confessed in a whisper. *we will be.*

The confidence it projected comforted her a little. She wanted to ask it to make her feel things again. To touch her insides, its choice: pleasure, pain, discomfort, solace. But Raliel should not come to rely on the great demon to be with her. If they succeeded, it would leave. If they failed, it would still leave, returning to the foundations of the palace. It had to leave her, no matter what happened. This intimacy, this alliance, had always been temporary.

But maybe if she learned sorcery, she could still grasp this kind of power. Maybe Moon would want to stay with her. Be her great demon, and the great demon of the palace still. Be both theirs and free. Able to fly, housed in the palace. That was the ideal outcome. Everyone could get what they wanted. Sorcery was an easy thing for Raliel to decide to want.

Reaching out, she touched one finger to the reflection of her face: she traced the arc of five moon-eyes. "Who am I to you?"

Silence.

"Moon."

you are talking to me? or your reflection?

"The first time we met, you made a shadow-shape that was my reflection. My size, shape, my way of walking. Only you had seven big eyes blotchy like the moon."

you ate candy and I wanted to taste it.

"Like you taste what I eat now. Are you using me to taste the world?"

I want my own tongue for tasting, Moon said, and licked up her sternum. Raliel gasped.

The great demon continued licking: tiny flicks of whatever it was like tiny tongues kissing and tasting up her breastbone, along one clavicle, to her pulse in her neck. Moon licked along her artery, each beat of her heart an echo of its cold touch.

In the mirror, Raliel's dark eyes were wide and her lips parted. She panted slightly, hot inside. There appeared two tiny pink splotches high on her cheeks.

The great demon's little shadow tongues crawled up her throat, and it was too much suddenly. She couldn't breathe! Raliel gagged, flattened her palms to her face, swallowed. Tried to gain control.

Moon subsided but trailed those little tongues along in its wake as it slipped back under her heart, back into its cold geode nest.

Raliel kept her eyes closed. She breathed. Her skin tingled and the hair at her nape danced. She knew this was desire, her body hot and lit up to be touched.

Bending over her knees, she breathed in through her nose, out through her mouth.

The guest room was quiet. From the bathing room she heard the tender mutter of the hot fountain and considered slinking that way to soak again. But she was clean, and she thought for the first time in a while that even when she seemed alone, naked and relaxed in a bath, she was not.

Straightening again, she pinned her gaze on her reflection once more. "Moon. What am I to you?"

For several beats of her heart the demon didn't respond. She felt it inside her, though, a ball of shadow-tentacles, a knot of dark aether, cold spirals of inky night. Small, tightly drawn.

"Moon."

you called me your friend.

"I did."

I know you. your taste and strength, the flow of your blood and the cramp of your muscles. I know things you ignore until they are wrong or hard or shallow: pulse, breath, the slight beating of your eyelashes like miniature wings. I do not think we can call each other friends.

Raliel shivered at its low voice, the curl of it. She wondered if Moon realized how seductive it sounded. Is that something it did on purpose, or was this inherent to a demon's repertoire? "Then what?" she pressed in a whisper.

I do not know a word. human words especially are the wrong shape for this.

Nodding, she smoothed her hands down her thighs.

if you become a sorcerer, we will have a name for what we do together. "Yes."

you think you'll be bad at it.

With a tiny wince, she agreed.

focus, align your aether.

Settling into her usual posture for meditation, Raliel did.

This part was easy, as she'd done it for years. Centering, checking in with her body and energy. Waking up the points of entry: palms, soles of feet, navel, heart, ears, eyes, mouth, crown. Linking them through the network of muscles and veins and bones. Until her body was alive with sparks of aether.

give it to me.

Raliel bit her bottom lip just for a moment, an old bad habit. It grounded her. Snapped her awareness to a single point on her mouth. Then she mentally touched the geode nest where the demon curled. It was an offering and the demon took it, spreading out along every bone and muscle, along the roads she opened for it until Moon's power touched every point. For a moment her entry points drained, then Moon pushed and her aether flared stronger.

In the mirror, her eyes glowed.

what do you want to do? Moon asked.

Her breath tingled against her extra-sensitive lips, and she touched the painted moon-eyes again in the mirror.

Moon shifted the aether up through her body, a reverse rain, bringing it swirling to her forehead. Raliel breathed with the power shift, wondering if there was a sigil she should envision or draw even.

One of the eyes blinked.

Raliel gasped. She leaned forward in surprise, and Moon's amusement rippled under her skin. Staring up, almost cross-eyed, she waited.

you blink.

Just the word made her do it: when she blinked her eyes, the center red eye blinked too.

Focusing, Raliel drove more power there, and Moon grasped it, shoving it in.

A sick twist of her skin made her gorge rise, and the five red moon-eyes bulged up, little bubbles of skin; they parted with a seam of bloody red.

Raliel gaped at the five little eyes—real eyes—blinking in time. She stopped her eyelids; they stopped too. "Incredible," she whispered. Her stomach knotted loosely. She was fascinated, excited, and . . . a little bit ill. It was her, but not. That sensation, and the twitch of muscles she wasn't supposed to have, disoriented her.

it's an illusion.

Leaning even closer, she stared. The eyes moved separately from her own, despite the synchronous blinking. "We should try to do it properly, so that they're my eyes, too. Connected to my systems. My brain. So that we both can see through them."

yes that would be real sorcery, I think. to truly change you. for you to do it. this is only a trick, my brute power, not ours. but we must wait for more. I'd have to eat something, take from the mountain.

"Oh, yes. We'll practice later. Tomorrow. With The Scale."

this kind of transformation must be what would let us find the great demon in the sea. to become of the sea ourselves, breathe it and know it.

Raliel couldn't look away from her reflection. She smiled. She touched her reflected cheek, then brought a hand up to her actual face and brushed a finger against the short red lashes of one of the moon-eyes.

tickles.

"Oh," she breathed.

Then she closed her eyes and felt as Moon undid its magic, undid the transformation.

Shivering with nerves and elicit thrill, Raliel looked again at herself. Just herself, with a smear of paint like dried blood on her forehead. "Oh, Moon."

you liked that.

"I liked that." This time when she smiled, it was broad. Happy.

trace that, follow it to intuiting.

Raliel leaned toward the mirror again and met her own eyes in the reflection. They were dark, flecked with bits of glass-brown and deep winter brown, with a hazy gray circle at the boundary of her iris. She kept them open as she kissed herself on the lips.

Deep under her heart, the great demon laughed.

"Did you like that?" she whispered, and her words appeared as fog on the mirror.

yes.

NINE

THEY REMAINED WITH THE Scale for nearly half a month, and Raliel attempted to learn sorcery.

At first she was resistant to it—not on purpose, but her natural inclinations prejudiced her against the concept. Raliel was used to rules and definitive answers: here are the natural disasters that led to this famine, here the details of the trade package, this is the way to hold your sword, the fingering to achieve this chord, the sigil to draw for this and the sigil to draw for that. She'd learned so much in her eighteen years because she was good at consuming such rules and putting them into practice. Sorcery seemed entirely rule averse.

They began sitting in a dark room reminiscent of a cave, but not a cave. The floor was pale-gray granite, the walls unnaturally smooth stone that curved upward into a dome. It was only Raliel—with her demon, of course—and The Scale, facing each other as they knelt on a rug woven from several different shades of blue.

"Sorcery," Lutha said, "is liminal magic. It exists because the world is not built of dualities no matter how hard people try to define it thus. Life and death, day and night, man and woman, yes?"

"That is what we are taught," Raliel agreed.

"It's easy to think of the world that way, until you find yourself outside, or need to be outside, such a duality. When you begin searching, some liminality presents itself more obviously than others. Day and night have dawn and dusk. You must be familiar with the limitations of binary gender, thanks to your father the emperor, but what is the liminal state between life and death?"

Lutha paused long enough that Raliel realized they expected her to reply. She huffed slightly, then frowned because she didn't just know the answer. Wasn't one either alive or dead? She smoothed her mouth until there was no expression and stared at The Scale as she considered definitions of life. Heartbeats, change, consciousness. She wondered if something like a rock could be considered between life and death if it could not truly be said to ever be alive, decided no, then thought about aether, which did inhabit rocks, as well as living things like trees and people. Aether could be found in water, too, which seemed more alive, but was not . . . exactly, that she knew of, unless it was the water of a lake or river with an inhabiting spirit . . . and then it was not only water but a spirit's house.

As she considered the question, Lutha waited patiently, a pleasant but calm expression on their pale face. Today their eyes changed more slowly, the silver clouds passing in gentle billows over the dark blue. Lazy and wonderful.

Life and death, she thought. There might be moments at birth or death, or severe illness, when a person was in-between, but surely that was nearly impossible to codify. Even more difficult to test or practice. Her eyes lowered to her lap, and she played absently with the ring on her forefinger.

"Oh," she said. "Great demons."

Lutha smiled, and Moon said, *me?*

"Great demons were once spirits—alive, part of aether, but they are dead—or at least *have died*—and still retain their link to aether, themselves."

"Some ghosts are also able to affect the world, use aether," Lutha said.

"Is that why great demons are rare? Because they are . . . inherently liminal? Perfect for sorcery?"

"It is why they are coveted—more so than great spirits, though a great spirit is nearly as inherently liminal as a great demon. And even regular spirits and demons are nonbinary unless they expressly choose otherwise, which is why they are familiars to witches. Do you know the difference between aether-work with a spirit and with a demon?"

"A spirit is like a channel, a direct connection to aether, but a demon is more like . . . ready energy. They always are eating power, so it is always there for the taking—sharing. Spirits must be tapped into, but they also do not destroy what they take. Demons provide immediate but finite aether; spirits' aether is limitless but requires more effort to access. But great demons are both immediate and limitless, because they are ready energy and tapped into deep channels of aether."

"That is the exactly correct answer." Lutha smiled with one side of their mouth. "Do you know the difference between witchcraft and sorcery? Can you think of how one might use either demon or spirit to bridge into sorcery?"

"Must you be bound to them?"

"Yes, but a witch binds to a regular familiar too. It is always a relationship."

Thinking hard enough she bit her bottom lip, Raliel nodded. "Is the sorcery in the relationship?"

"Sort of."

"Do you have . . . do any sorcerers have regular familiars, or only great spirits and demons?"

"Only great, that I know of. Shadows has relationships with many kinds of spirits and demons but only works aether through the Fifth Mountain. I, too, have many spirit friends, but only Murmur shares a bond with me."

"I see," she said, though she did not quite. In the research she'd done over the past few years, looking for ways to change the palace-amulet, she'd encountered stories about all the sorcerers and their great spirits, stories that told of how they'd become sorcerers (most of them died, though somehow did not remain dead). Some stories contradicted each other: in one A Still Wind murdered A Dance of Stars and resurrected him; in another it was A Still Wind who was murdered, but not by his twin brother, by grave robbers. In most stories of the twin sorcerers of the Second and Third Mountains, they had a variety of great spirits bound with them, though all other sources agreed only one great spirit familiar at a time was possible. But witches could have as many lesser familiars as they could convince.

Lutha said, "Tell me, how did you slip Moon out of the palace?"

Revealing the silver amulet that hung from a cord around her neck, she said, "Moon possessed me through our connection that already was present. It hurt me, and so I made this. It's silver, like the moon, has both our names etched on it, along with a blessing and movement sigils, and a prayer in spirit writing. The thread is to make it unknowable to a casual witness. It puts some of the pressure of the possession into this instead of my body."

"I see."

"Is this sorcery?"

Lutha shrugged.

"Did you ask me the difference between witchcraft and sorcery on purpose, because it too is a duality?"

"Good!" They laughed and clapped their hands once. "It's slippery, defining sorcery."

"How do I *do* it?"

"You move away from binary existence. Refuse either/or. Resist all dual thinking. Then you make magic."

"Show me."

"Very well. Step out of your dualities."

Raliel frowned. They said it as if one could just do that. "But how? What is the process?"

Laughing, Lutha shook their head. "It's different for all. I found a way to be both alive and dead—to be honest, that is how many manage it, because in life and death is perhaps the most fundamental duality. If you escape it, you can escape anything. Your father . . . well, it's my understanding that once he managed some sorcery, likely thanks to being, and defining himself—to himself, perhaps—as neither man nor woman."

"You won't tell me how you managed to be both alive and dead, will you?"

"Alas, no."

"There must be a . . . path. Steps to take!"

"Rules?"

"Yes."

Lutha shook their head in a slow no.

I do magic, through you—is that inherently sorcery?

Raliel repeated Moon's question.

"No," Lutha said. "It is a great demon practicing aetherwork through a house. Like this, with the palace-amulet and this small one you made, you *are* the house. To make it sorcery, the relationship must be active. A flow, both parties participating."

"That sounds like a rule," Raliel said sharply.

Lutha laughed again.

"Tell me more," she said. "Please. More hints, more pieces of your understanding. If you give me enough information, I can make my own rules."

"That's a good way to begin, but it will take too long."

Pressing her lips together, Raliel held back a sigh and waited.

"What is the difference between awake and asleep? Can you be both?" They raised an eyebrow. "Neither? Is dreaming liminal, or is it only a part of being asleep? Can you change in your sleep? You talk, you snore, you grow . . . you're alive but you aren't aware. How does water transition from liquid to ice? When it melts again? Is snow ice or water, or its own definitive self? Sleet? Is that between ice and water or entirely different? If you leap off a cliff, before you're falling are you flying? When you begin walking and then run, can you identify exactly where you're neither?"

Raliel listened, her body leaning toward The Scale. Their words excited her, despite her lack of understanding. It felt like they built to something—they made a promise.

"What about feelings? Do you know love? Do you know

hate? How do they feel? How are they different—how *related*? How are they exactly the same? Give me your hand."

Before she thought, she did, offering it palm-up.

Lutha took it delicately in one of their own. Their skin was cool, soft, and they gently pulled her closer and lifted her hand toward their face. Holding her gaze with their sky-changing eyes, Lutha slowly lowered their mouth and pressed lips and teeth to the ball of her thumb.

Staring with slightly widened eyes, Raliel concentrated on the sensation of soft, warm lips; hard teeth biting.

"Is it a kiss or a bite?" Lutha murmured against her skin: the words skittered up her wrist, and she shivered.

Moon growled inside her and nudged her to tug her hand away, but she did not.

"Is this fear or desire?" Lutha whispered, sitting up and slowly—very slowly—releasing her hand so that it fell away with the echo of a caress.

Raliel took too deep a breath through parted lips.

Suddenly Lutha shouted! A long, high wail that shocked up Raliel's spine, and she jerked her hand against her chest.

The sorcerer grinned at her. "A scream, or a song?"

To maintain her composure, Raliel thought of her snow, the cold kiss of it, claiming her. Inside, Moon twisted itself under her heart and reached out with tiny tongues that were cold, too. She clamped down on herself in order not to squirm. She breathed deeply and evenly. She met Lutha's gaze.

They leaned back on their heels and gestured to the woven rug upon which they both knelt. It was layers and ripples of various blue shades. "Which of these colors is blue?"

"All of them," she said immediately.

"Truly?"

Taking more care, Raliel studied the patterns of silk. She might call one color cobalt, one midnight blue, one cerulean. Sky blue, rain blue, they were all blue, and all slightly different.

"They're all blue."

"And yet they are all different. Distinct."

"Blue is many things."

"What would you choose if I asked which is the most blue?"

Raliel touched a bold, bright blue.

"Why?"

"It is . . . not too dark, not light? Not defined by the sky or water or bird."

"But I have seen the sky be that very color."

"Sky blue, then?"

"If we asked others, do you think they would all say that is the truest blue?"

"Most people."

"But not all. Do people see differently? What about a bird? Or a fish? Or a great demon or unicorn? What is blue—do you think you see it exactly as I do? Or as someone born a thousand years ago might have?"

"No, maybe? I . . . don't know." Raliel balled her hands into fists, frustrated. There should have been a definitive blue. Even if the emperor must decree it. Even as she thought so, she knew it was a silly thought. Yet—she wanted, in her mind and heart, for there to be a single shared understanding of *blue*. If there was not . . . what did that mean? Raliel realized she was breathing hard.

"Good," Lutha soothed. "Now go away."

"What?" Shocked, Raliel stared at them.

"This is enough for today—"

"But we haven't done any magic."

"You'll go, and you'll think and feel about all this." Lutha smiled. "Meditate! That's good for aether-work. Good for slipping into liminality. Discuss with your great demon. Eat—and when you eat, think about smelling and tasting. How do they relate? How are they different? One piece of fruit smells one way and tastes one way—they are senses teaching us something about the same thing, and the smell and the taste might be similar, but can they ever be the same? Yet we say *this is the smell of an orange. This is the taste of an orange.* Same word, different sensations. Tongues and noses, teeth and air . . ." Lutha laughed. "Think and feel about it. Tomorrow we'll go up the mountain, and I promise we'll *do magic.*"

Raliel pushed herself to her feet. Then, watching Lutha carefully, she curtsied. Though she'd been here only an hour, she felt starving and strange.

In her room, she drank a shocking amount of water, then sat before the mirror to meditate.

"What do you think, Moon?" she asked softly.

Moon unfurled under her heart like a peony, all soft layers and full as its namesake. The sensation tickled pleasantly. *I prefer red to blue.*

Giving a little snort, Raliel said, "The color of blood?"

Blood on snow.

She gazed into her own eyes as if she could stare into the great demon's and imagined a winter landscape: soothing, cold, blanketed in drifts of white, ice coating thin evergreen trees and the glossy oval leaves of boxwoods. A frozen pond, frost against the round stepping-stones. White-cast sky promising more snow, distant white mountain peaks, curls of black forest glinting wetly. And there, before her, a splatter of scarlet blood across the winter garden, violent color that draws the gaze like a scream.

It was a good vision. Raliel liked it and felt herself settling into her body. Her eyes drifted shut as she relaxed, and she shifted into a looser posture: still precise but without the stiff-backed adherence to formality. Her hands she turned upside down in her lap, fingers curled gently. She took a deep breath, and another, and felt Moon join her. Great demons didn't breathe, of course, but Moon ruffled the petals of its peony-self in tiny waves. Soon her lungs and its flower shifted and shook in tandem.

Raliel took herself through the process of awakening her aether-threads again, the ones aligned with her arteries and bones, with her spine and throat, feet and hands. She woke it all up but only to let aether glow. Moon was a constant drain at her energy, but it balanced its drag, holding itself stiller than usual.

Soon she lost moments to breathing, to the shining silver-blue alignment of her aether, and it felt as though her body melted off her bones—or as if she were earth and aether spilled over her head, falling like rain down her body to pool in the bowl of her hips.

Raliel.

"Hmm," she hummed.

this is good. there are no barriers between us.

"Would you say we are neither human nor demon? Something in-between?"

ha ha ha, yes, or we are both, perhaps, or better yet—more.

"More." Raliel's eyes snapped open. In the mirror she was pale, calm, surrounded by dim aether-light from the lamps in her guest room, casting highlights in her hair. But her eyes—her honey-brown eyes were feverish with that thought. More.

The epiphany broke her calm, and the loose precision of meditation cracked. But like with any good meditation, she felt like she could pick off the broken shell of the experience and emerge fresh. Like a newborn bird.

More. That's what she held in the palms of her hands: not that liminal space was in between these dualities, but that it *encompassed* them. It was more. Beyond duality.

She tried this theory out on Moon. The great demon liked it. But the great demon also said the very idea of more appealed to it, being a demon who was always hungry.

Raliel laughed a little and stood to find food.

More was what she always came back to.

In the morning Lutha arrived to fetch them personally. The sorcerer said, "Outdoor shoes," so she replaced her slippers with boots from the cubby beside the door. She wondered where all of this came from. Who it belonged to, if anyone, or if Lutha had rooms like this designed and supplied for any number of types of guest. Raliel supposed if she had six hundred years and theoretically unlimited resources, she'd be prepared in such a way, too.

That made her think of another question she had, and as Lutha led her through the First Mountain's glittering stone corridors, up intensely spiraled stairs, and out onto the peak, she asked, "Lutha, my apologies for the impertinence of my question, but will you tell me how you chose this shape you wear?"

She flicked her gaze to them briefly, before focusing politely on the path ahead.

Lutha hummed thoughtfully.

"I have met A Dance of Stars," Raliel said conversationally. "He appears very different from you—obvious in many ways, and . . . strategically handsome. Stories I've heard of Shadows of the Fifth Mountain say she is gorgeous and inhuman looking. Father says he's seen her with feathers pouring from her cheeks, teeth like a shark's, and eyes that reminded him of a snake's."

Lutha guided her out into the thin sunlight this high on the mountain, leading her toward a muddy path between two boulders. They walked across a small plain of gnarled, thin grass and dead wildflowers; overhead the sky was pale blue and the wind cold. The Scale said, "If you could look like anything, how would you look?"

"Like this, I suppose," she said, choosing to be thorough in her answer as she would be on any subject she intended to master. "I am handsome and I look like my parents. I might prefer my nose less straight—my mother's tilts slightly to her left, and I think she's the most beautiful person I've ever seen. But I was born lucky, with features easily admired by everyone, and raised knowing it. When I was fourteen or so, I'd have used magic every day to clear up my skin, and for a while my feet felt overlarge, and I was clumsy. Those are all things I grew out of, or superficial. Unlike my father the emperor, I don't have any particular feelings about being a woman—or having the appearance of one. Though . . ." Raliel grimaced prettily—and she knew it was pretty—"I might use sorcery to change my insides so that menstruation is less unbearable. Not rid myself of it. I must have children as Heir to the Moon. But alleviate some of the symptoms."

"Are you certain you will still be heir when you have succeeded in your quest?"

hmm, Moon purred.

Raliel swallowed her immediate protestation, *Of course yes; that is all I know.* She tilted her head demurely. "I intend to fulfill my obligations," she said, putting the question off.

Lutha nodded once. "I look very much like I did when I was truly only twenty years old, but I have removed every physical marker of gender except the very few I like."

It was nearly an invitation to stare, to attempt to discover what gender markers the sorcerer chose for themself, but Raliel didn't.

Then the sorcerer slid her a look of pure mischief. "Sometimes, though, I look like a lion or a rosebush! Or a dragon—I have enjoyed being a dragon."

Raliel laughed delicately, and the great demon inside her grumbled about wanting to be a dragon. The grumbling warmed her; Raliel imagined hot red-gold scales running down her forearms, armoring her cheeks and spine. A dragon named Raliel, or Raliel's Moon, or Moon Caught in Raliel.

Suddenly Murmur, the great spirit of the First Mountain, appeared. It was a scatter of blue-silver starlings, spinning around them like confetti. Raliel felt her pulse speed and stutter.

"Try to catch as much of it as possible," Lutha said, and Murmur fled in every direction, an explosion of aether.

"What?" Raliel turned her version of a gape at them—eyes only a little wide, lips slightly parted.

"Run! Chase them—catch the great spirit of the First Mountain, and we will show you the secrets of the universe!" Lutha urged, laughing. "You said you wanted to play!"

go! said Moon. *We can do this!*

They ran. Raliel lifted her skirt and took off. She chased, grasping at tiny aether-birds, and sometimes they melted into her hands, filing her with a burst of energy; other times they slipped free. The sorcerer dashed behind her and sometimes tugged her hair. She spun, ready to pull back, but Lutha danced away. It became an elaborate game of tag, across the mountain meadow. Raliel ran, and laughed, and furrowed her brow in concentration. Moon pushed her faster, feeding her energy, but never enough—there was always more of Murmur.

Raliel tried to give up. She begged off when her lungs ached, laughed and bent at the waist to catch her breath. But Lutha said no, always pushing. Moon dragged magic from the meadow in great black bursts that left furrows of dead grass behind, and they gave chase again. Still, it was not enough. Raliel understood this game could not be won; she could not catch the great spirit, not in essence or entirety.

But she kept trying.

Until hours passed, and she and Moon had made aether-nets, had set traps, had asked sweetly, had caught Lutha instead—surprising the sorcerer into changing their own shape. They became a slippery snake and slithered out of Raliel's grasp. Moon tried to pull on their aether, but the snake shot up into a little dragon and flew over them in a long arc of feathers and scales.

Finally Raliel fell to the ground, flat on her back. She panted, closed her eyes, and let herself sink against the cool earth.

"How do you feel?" Lutha murmured, leaning on an elbow beside her.

Without looking, Raliel stretched. She said, "Melting. Tired. Hungry."

"Part of the world?"

A thoughtful frown was merely a line between her eyebrows as she considered. "Yes . . . ," she admitted, not having realized it was a good way to describe this feeling.

not separate from it, Moon whispered wonderingly. *You could become it. I see, we could turn to stone and dirt, your hair flowers. As you have imagined before. At dawn in the forest.*

"Yes," Raliel said again, more of a contented whisper. She let herself imagine it again: her bones roots and muscles earth, becoming a part of the great weave of aether, like a mushroom sprouting up through earth but connected through intricate mycelia to others like it, to decay and rebirth.

"Learn to hold this feeling. This experience," Lutha said lazily. "Be it."

The Scale didn't allow her to go to sleep, or to eat. All day they fasted together, drinking only a light tea, shifting between meditation and hiking. Lutha took her to the side of the mountain where she saw the distant ocean and asked her if it was green or blue or gray. Raliel wanted to know why the sorcerer was obsessed with shades of blue, and Lutha said the sea was a mystery and mystery was a good place to find liminality.

When the sun set, they sat on pillows the sorcerer produced from nowhere, and they watched the sky. Lutha told her when they thought night had fallen, when the liminal dusk gave way to perfect night, and pointed out all the stars. They liked constellations because they were points without defined shape, and certainly they shifted as the stars curved across the night. "What I see as the great ox is not exactly what you see, and stars are . . . well. Fire and light and color—when you free your great demon maybe you can discover the nature of stars together."

"I would like that," she said softly, touching her hand just under her breasts.

me too.

"If we manage it, Moon," she whispered deep in the night, "will you choose to go back with me?"

I don't know. Would you, if you were me?

"Yes. If I was with you."

The great demon purred.

"Keep her awake, Moon," Lutha said. "Can you do that? Keep her body from falling into sleep?"

yes, the demon said, and just then pinched her bladder.

"Ah!" she cried. And stood to go relieve herself, grumpy and sleepy in the dark. "Be nicer," she said.

All night the demon teased her and made her remain awake. She asked why, and Lutha said, "To put you on the edge of what you know and feel. Alcohol would work, and some teas and fungi, but this is more controllable, and matters more if you can understand how your physical form will do this to itself. That is another duality to break down: body and spirit."

That made sense to her, in her slightly addled state. And she drifted, discovered a well of giggles in her belly a few hours before dawn. Everything made her laugh. She sang a little, harmonizing with Moon, and then with Lutha, until they were a quartet because Murmur the great spirit whistled along with their ridiculous melodies.

Lutha lifted her into their lap, wrapping their arms around her. "Look," they whispered in her ear. She leaned back as if they were a nice reclining chair, until her head knocked against their shoulder. "There is light in the east."

It brought tears to her exhausted, giddy eyes.

"You tell me when you think it stops being night and becomes morning."

"Already," she said right away. "It is morning."

"Is it?" Lutha laughed.

"Dawn, gloaming, liminal light—it's all morning. Morning might begin when the stars descend once more, hours ago. It's maybe been morning for hours. Maybe when we're in morning, morning is inherently changed from when we were looking at it from nighttime or back at it from the afternoon. Maybe it's arbitrary, and everyone would define morning differently—but you asked me! And I say it's *all morning*." Oh, Raliel felt silly and free.

The Scale kissed her temple. "Good."

Pleased as ever by a tutor's approval, Raliel hugged herself and leaned into their very strong chest. Behind her was the sorcerer, within her was her demon, and all around her the First Mountain and the entire sky. She felt very content, very powerful, and very safe. That alone threaded a needle of concern, but for now she did not sew it down.

TEN

AVING DITCHED OSIAN REDPOP, who may or may not have been in secret communication with her parents, Raliel had, on her first full day with The Scale, asked if a letter could be delivered to Osian. She wrote, *Osian, apologies for the abrupt departure. I have rushed ahead to visit with The Scale at the First Mountain. If you would be so good as to follow in this direction and await my return in Pilgrim Reception, I would be glad. I enjoyed my night at the Silver Broom in town, and recommend it. I left some belongings in storage with the owners. Also, the local grape wine is good. I should not be more than a week or two. If longer, I will send another letter.*

Moon complained she was too kind to Osian, too forgiving. Raliel reminded it that to their knowledge Osian had done nothing wrong. He ought to be allowed some privacy, though she admitted his behavior was suspicious. They would remain on guard but treat him with friendliness and respect in order not to make anything worse.

Murmur the great spirit had delivered the letter itself, which Raliel expected would impress and delight Osian. When

Murmur brought a response, Raliel read it warily but found herself laughing.

Heir, it began plainly, *I am sure I was not concerned about your safety; nor did I pace all night long in worry and set out immediately, thinking my head would grace the end of a pike the moment your father Sky became aware of my situation. Certainly, royal bodyguards lose track of their wards all the time and it's of no concern whatsoever. I am glad to hear you only abandoned me out of excitement, and I shall await you at the Silver Broom. Give The Scale my regards. Yours, Osian.*

Meanwhile, Raliel tried to discover her way into liminal space in order to practice sorcery. Alone in their guest room, she and Moon sat before the mirror and attempted smaller shape-shifting, as they had the first night, and they could do it to a certain extent, but it left them both drained of aether and exhausted. It was like the palace-amulet: limited witchcraft with incredible power behind it. Not sorcery. The Scale continued overseeing her attempts, giving her playful exercises and aether-games, and made suggestions for Moon to help. None of it worked. Raliel could not manage to shed her dualities.

"This is the only foundation I can give you," Lutha said. "Unless you prefer to remain here indefinitely. I think two things are holding you back: first, it is one thing to understand what you must do to break dualities but very, very difficult to convince your body of it. Your body is the part of you that must understand what aether is, to make it into food. Second, the palace-amulet."

Moon said, *yes I think that as well. The amulet limits me—us. It's fixed.*

"Moon agrees," Raliel said, balling her fists in frustration. "So

Moon must be free or we cannot do sorcery—yet we cannot free it without learning sorcery!"

The Scale pressed their lips into a line. "If my friend Murmur were bound as Moon is, based on my limited understanding of the amulet, we could not be bound as familiars, as we are. But at the same time, I do not believe a great spirit could be bound to the palace like that. Demons are fundamentally different from spirits, in how their aether exists and interacts. The palace-amulet is more than a house. More fluid in some ways but still powerfully imprisoning. And if you will not speak with Night Shine, I am at a loss without more time and experimentation. Moon and Night Shine are the only great demons I know."

we can still do it without Night Shine.

Raliel pressed her lips together. After a moment she said, "Why do you refuse to seek her help?"

she . . . she tricked me. Moon said it so hushed and quiet, Raliel thought it was embarrassed.

"Is avoiding her worth the risk of never understanding this?"

Moon grumbled, *we can seek the sea demon.*

Lutha leaned toward her. "May I see the amulet you made to allow the Moon outside of the palace?"

Raliel pulled aside the collar of her robe and vest, hooked the thong with a finger, and freed the amulet. When it wasn't against her skin, she shivered at the odd sensation of loss. Moon curled under her heart, heavy and cold, so nothing *was* lost.

Taking the amulet in both hands, the sorcerer studied it, leaning their head close. Raliel was used to their porcelain-smooth skin, inhumanly perfect, the curve of their lashes, and the slope of their nose, and even the rainbows glinting in their sleek black hair. But she'd never be used to the cloudy blue sky of their eyes. This close, she saw the shape of the clouds, puffy and summerfull, slowly blotting out the flecks of blue. She took a soft breath through parted lips and swallowed it.

Lutha hummed and peppered the amulet with tiny sparks of aether: they appeared like glitter, and she felt it in her breastbone. Moon murmured, *tickles*.

The sorcerer ran their thumb along the black silk threads, closed their eyes, and took a few deep breaths. "I like this," they said quietly. "Simple and elegant. I can make it better though."

"Better how?"

A sneaky grin spread across Lutha's face. "Moon will be able to possess something else without losing connection to you."

ah! Moon cried happily.

They were in Lutha's small workroom, built of living red wood in a perfect sphere—like working in the heart of a massive king tree. When Lutha chose, they could open little shelves and alcoves where various books and scrolls and tools were stored—and yesterday they pulled a bowl of spiced nuts out for a snack. Right now a net of tightly woven aether-cords spread across the base of the sphere, creating a flat floor upon which they sat. The aether lit the room well. Lutha left them and slid their fingers against the warm, bright wood. Their fingers sank in, as if the wood swallowed their hand, and when they pulled it free with a little popping sound, they held a thin black stylus.

Returning, Lutha knelt and lifted their eyebrows in a question. Raliel nodded, and the sorcerer used the stylus to rearrange the weave of black silk she'd knotted across the face of the moon amulet.

It was quick work, whatever Lutha did: Raliel couldn't quite tell, but she suspected it was spirit writing, etched directly into the silver with aether.

"There."

Moon filled her body with a sudden burst of lightning. She gasped and stood. *nothing to possess here!*

"Moon eagerly requests a chance to practice," Raliel said, laughing because she could not quite suppress the demon's elation.

Lutha smiled brightly and took them out onto the mountain— low through the front gates, so there were trees and rocks and birds and beasts.

The demon thrummed. It heated Raliel's skin like a flush of pleasure. She walked carefully out into the trees. "Will you begin with a solid old thing?" she asked, putting her hand to the rough bark of a pine. Its needles tented around her, dulling the sunlight and easing the wind. Raliel shivered in the cool shade, despite her flushed cheeks.

yes.

With no further warning, Moon slid toward the amulet. Raliel cupped her other hand over it, so that she held both the amulet and the tree. She closed her eyes and focused on the sensations as Moon gathered itself in the silver and spooled out like thread. With a spark, like an arc of lighting, it leapt from the amulet to the tree and—

It was gone.

Raliel gasped hugely and nearly fell to her knees.

Weeks into this, she'd forgotten the weight of the Moon. Now, without it, she could float away.

Lutha touched her shoulder. Lightly, just a reminder.

"Moon?"

A low groan of wood emerged from the tree.

Raliel leaned against it, pushing her forehead to the rough reddish bark. "Be careful."

The amulet on her chest was ice-cold. When she pressed down through her robes, it burned coldly enough to brand her flesh.

Then Moon swarmed back into her: an entire hive of bees forced through a funnel the size of the amulet. She whimpered, and Lutha caught her elbow.

I did it! Moon trumpeted.

"Yes," she whispered, still recovering. "Next time be gentler when you return, please."

ah, yes, I will—if I can.

They practiced for a few hours, moving through the damp forest. Moon possessed several trees—only one of which it killed—and a doe it found in the shadows of a blackberry bramble. It attempted to take a thin waterfall, but the energy was not enough, and the same they found with a bright-red cardinal. Perhaps it would do better with a handful of crows, or a mountain cat. Moon was eager to seek out a wolf. But they'd need to experiment with the finer details. Moon was ecstatic, and that left a weary smile on Raliel's lips by the end of the afternoon.

As Lutha led them back into the mountain, the sun glared low in the west, violent gold and pale pink. The sorcerer opened their mouth to speak, but just then, behind her navel, Raliel felt a strange pressure. She frowned and put her hand over the belt of her gown. She tilted her head and concentrated.

"Raliel?" said Lutha.

The pressure sharpened. Raliel gasped and Moon grunted. The demon clasped on to her rib cage like fingers through prison bars. Raliel clenched her teeth against the pain. "Something is . . . ," she gritted out through her teeth.

Lutha cupped her elbow but did nothing further.

hold . . . on, Moon hissed.

The pressure hit her, an inside punch, and Raliel doubled over, falling to her knees. "Moon," she whispered.

But Moon reached for the First Mountain. A babble of voices skittered and pleaded inside Raliel's skull, someone yelled in distress—her mother?—and there was a sharp tear inside her. Raliel cried out and caught *whatever* it was, desperate to hold on.

She couldn't. It slipped away, ripping at her flesh and bones, like pulling her spirit out of her body!

Then a burst of aether flooded Raliel from outside, and it was over.

She slumped forward, abruptly drained and exhausted. Lutha caught her, arm around her shoulders, cradling her to their chest.

"Raliel?"

"Moon," she murmured.

the emperor, Moon said darkly. *they tried to tear me away from you.*

Raliel shuddered. She leaned her head against Lutha's shoulder for a moment, delicately nauseated. "My father the emperor wants Moon back."

TRUST

THE UNICORN

THREE HUNDRED YEARS AGO, give or take a decade, Esrithalan the unicorn was minding its own business at the edges of a massive hurricane. Esrithalan enjoyed the gusts and unpredictable drag of such storms, allowing itself to dissipate into a shape rather like a long flag of silk, to be buffeted and snapped by the wind and rain. (This only worked when there was no dragon behind the storm, and no great owl spirit of the sky, and certainly none of the Queens of Heaven present to look unkindly upon a unicorn using a hurricane like a pressure massage.)

Suddenly it heard—well, hearing was the closest possible metaphor for the sense Esrithalan had that mortal creatures did not—the distinctive pop of a spirit dying and becoming a demon.

The sound was unmistakable and, in this case, alarming, because to be heard above the raging storm, it had to be a great spirit giving way to a great demon.

Swallowing a groan, Esrithalan formed itself into a solid shape that would more readily invoke gravity and plummeted down through the hurricane like a solid gold chamber pot.

It landed lightly on four dainty hooves along a thin stretch of beach awash with a muck of seaweed and sand and churning ocean water.

The newborn great demon rolled just offshore in the furious tide, battered by the wind and stinging rain.

Esrithalan backed away to watch, finding a small shelter against the cliffs.

The demon flung seven arms around and seven tails, too, and screamed and growled from seven round mouths that spun and sucked at all the aether kicked up by the hurricane. It was a lot. A perfect feast for a newborn demon, and Esrithalan leaned against the wet sandstone cliff and watched.

Very likely, the great demon would keep the hurricane raging for days, upsetting the balances of aether and nature. Either it would spin itself out and die, or grow so large a Queen of Heaven would appear to intervene. Being so near now—and certainly if a Queen arrived—was dangerous, even for a unicorn. But it wasn't every day a great demon was born, and Esrithalan decided to remain and watch and perhaps be the first to hear the demon's new name.

Esrithalan, shaped like itself—scraggly and goatlike, with cloven hooves, fine silver hair, and a curving single horn between its eyes that sliced up against the dark afternoon storm like a rainbow—knelt in the lee of the cliff and watched.

The great demon pulsed and grew, tendrils of sickly green-black shooting out to plant in the sand and try to root. But the tide pushed and pulled and the demon screamed in frustration. It flopped into the ocean again, but of course could never house itself in the sea. No, it would need to move, and soon, to find something firm and foundational, with enough power to be its house.

But the afternoon passed, and the night, too, and the great demon refused to climb up the cliff seeking a mountain or lake to decay.

Esrithalan witnessed several spirits approach as if to explain, as if to help the demon, only to be eaten in a snap and crack. This new great demon was throwing quite the tantrum!

Late in the night the moon rose, and only then did Esrithalan realize the hurricane had passed: the great demon was so determined to flail on the shore, to demand the attention of surf and sand, it had released the storm.

And now, under the bright, bulbous old moon, it stopped. The great demon stilled, and all its eyes and mouths and arms and tails focused on the moon. It reached into the sky, then leapt high only to crash down again. Water cascaded up the beach, tearing at the sand. The demon drank on the strings of aether, dragging especially from the strong threads that led up and up the cliff to whatever sat atop them, and once it had the power, it managed to hover over the earth, just slightly, and its arms moved like wings. But the great demon could not fly: it had to be rooted to the aether of the world.

It leapt again and again, and Esrithalan felt pity in its pearl heart. The great demon reached for the moon, and then it dove toward the reflection on the black sea. But the sea spat it back onshore.

The great demon dragged on the aether-threads again, swallowing and hungry, and Esrithalan began to hear voices crying out from down the beach. Humans.

With a cranky sigh that flapped through its blocky goat teeth, Esrithalan prepared to change again. The unicorn, when pressed by absolute necessity to subject itself to human form, preferred that of an ugly little girl. So that is what it became just as three humans ran into view. They tripped and struggled on the rough, soaked beach, wincing and holding up hands to block the sudden red sun blossoming on the horizon.

Two of the humans appeared to be of the man sort, one a woman, and the woman and one of the men had the shaved heads and scalp sigils of witches. The third carried a sword on his back. They all yelled at the demon, tossing sigil sticks, and the two witches raised a banner between them with glowing talismans that might temporarily bind the great demon.

They were saying they wanted to help it.

Interesting.

Esrithalan walked out on its awkward little-girl legs, and when the great demon spun to face the three humans with all seven mouths open, the unicorn yelled in its wavering little-girl voice, "Stop at once!"

The humans did, shocked, and the great demon did as well, unable to ignore the unicorn's thrum of pure power. It slid toward Esrithalan in the shape of a great black serpent with seven multifaceted amethyst eyes focused on it. With its tail, the great demon encircled the three humans.

what are you? it hissed, seven forked tongues flicking.

"A unicorn, obviously," Esrithalan said.

The three humans shared a startled look through sweat and fear as they attempted to avoid touching the coiled demon-snake penning them in on the sand.

I had the moon! The demon yelled, voice sharp as lightning.

"Hmm." Esrithalan suspected the demon had been a tidal spirit, a great spirit that earned its aether by the constant give-and-take of the tide. Or a dragon. Or both—that was possible.

"We need you to stop eating all our aether," said the woman, and then the sword-wielding man added, "We had an idea for your house!"

The great demon swung its head toward them. *my house is here!*

"No, I don't think it can be," the same man said. "But my—my witches think—can you just listen?"

It had been putting its fangs nearer and nearer to the man, even while the two witches cut their arms and bled onto sigils to throw up a spiky aether-shield.

"Unicorn!" cried the man witch. "Can you help us?"

"With what?" Esrithalan crossed its little-girl arms. "You're doing fine."

The great demon laughed, *ha ha ha.*

Esrithalan couldn't help it and laughed too. But brighter. Maybe a little like a donkey.

Sunlight caught the newborn great demon's scales, and they began to smoke in tiny greenish wisps. The waves splashed and the demon's tail rolled a little, dipping into the ocean. *I will not leave the sea.*

"But there are caves," said the man with the sword. He pointed at the limestone cliffs. "And they go all throughout there, and there is a tunnel leading from one up into a warehouse—my family's. It isn't a mountain, but they're cliffs and caves, and we'll build a palace there."

why.

Esrithalan had to admit that it wanted to know too. Humans never bargained with demons—or even with each other—unless they wanted something.

"To stop you from destroying our entire city! You're taking all the aether anyway. This would help us make it a house instead of just a meal."

how.

Esrithalan pressed its lips together and tilted its head. None of these humans had a channel of aether strong enough to indicate they were a sorcerer. Each was well connected to the threads of aether the unicorn could see, and . . . to each other. "Oh," it said.

But the woman witch spoke first, "You make the cliff, and the foundation stone of the palace your house, and we'll feed you as we grow it all. It could work!"

"You aren't sorcerers," Esrithalan said.

I will make you husks of skin and tough leather muscle, the great demon said silkily. *your bones will be brittle, and when I throw your carcasses into the sea, you will drift and drift.*

Esrithalan laughed again—it liked this melodramatic great demon. Too bad it had never met the thing when it was a great spirit and probably easier to talk to.

The three humans looked at Esrithalan as if it were the scary thing, not the great demon. Oops. Sometimes Esrithalan forgot unicorns were supposed to be neutral and sweet.

how can you stop me from consuming you? the great demon insisted.

"We think . . . ," the sword human began, and the woman witch added, "We think together . . ."

Then the third of them, the quieter man, whose thin beard was slick to his face with sweat and salt spray, held out both his hands. "We aren't a sorcerer on our own, but together we are . . . closer. We are not man *or* woman, but both and more than both. With the three of us, our magic is unbalanced and in-between—we can hold a balance and also stand inside that balance. I can write it in the language of spirits, where it makes perfect sense. That's what makes a sorcerer, isn't it? How a sorcerer becomes part of aether and can bind to a great spirit. Or a great demon."

I don't know, the great demon snapped. *I only know the moon and the tide and . . . and*

and

Its voice faded, and all seven eyes winked closed. As if it struggled to remember.

"We are more together, and also bound," the sword man said. "Together. We bound our hearts together, with our bodies and our magic. It should work."

"It will work," Esrithalan said suddenly. It clapped its little-girl hands in delight. "But not for long. Because you are all human, and the last test for a sorcerer is stepping beyond life and death—you must find a way to be immortal."

The giant snake suddenly vanished. In its place stood a little child the same age or so as Esrithalan's shape. Only the demon didn't seem to be boy or girl, but a shadow child, small and slender, with seven small pearl eyes. (No, eyes like seven full moons.) And seven fingers on each hand. *I need a name,* it whispered.

"So will they," Esrithalan said. "That's what is at the core of a sorcerer's binding. New names, shared names."

The woman witch reached out and touched each man on the shoulder. "I know how to make us immortal," she said in a tone hushed by awe.

"I will witness," Esrithalan declared, and it snapped into its unicorn body. "And then I will bring your new names to the Queens of Heaven to be written on the rolls of the gods."

The great demon blinked its seven full-moon eyes and said, *yes.*

ONE

R ALIEL WALKED BACK INTO the Silver Broom sixteen days after she'd ditched Osian at the justiciar's
manor.

It was evening, just in time for dinner and bed. Then they'd
get up early and start the trek to the ocean. From Pilgrim
Reception it was only half a day's journey to the shore, but the
great demon Lutha knew of lived farther west. It would take
three days of constant walking at Osian's pace. Moon grumbled
vaguely about why they had to meet back up with Osian at all,
but Raliel wouldn't leave Osian behind again—for her parents'
sakes mostly. She had a letter in her pocket, ready to send on its
way in the morning:

> Mother, Fathers—I am well. My friend is well. I am of
> sound mind, having taken this risk willingly and for a
> very good cause. Please do not interfere. If you continue
> your attempts to draw us back, it is possible the effect will
> be catastrophic. We will return in the spring, as planned.
> Osian Redpop remains with me for company and safety.

*He understands what is at stake. I intend to spend part
of the winter at the Mountain of One Thousand Falls if
you would like to send word to me there. I love you all.
Please do not worry. Raliel.*

Most of her assurances weren't true—yet. But she was certain
she could win Osian to her side. Moon was less sure, but willing
to let Raliel try.

She intended to tell Osian about the great demon traveling
with them. That way, she argued, she could speak with Moon
anytime she liked, and Moon could catch beasts to possess—
maybe even the wolf it wanted. Besides, building trust with the
people was part of the point of her journey, and she could start
with one person. It made sense when she laid it out for Moon,
though the demon could tell she was anxious about confessing.
If Osian reacted badly, Moon promised to possess him until they
could dispose of him. "Respectfully and safely," Raliel had said.
Moon had meanly pinched her bladder but agreed.

The Silver Broom was alight with green and red lanterns,
music spilling through the open door. It was not a rowdy song,
but a pleasant harvest lament, a suitable background for the
conversations at the full tables. Raliel stepped in, and almost
immediately the proprietor scurried toward her, a wince of
denial in place. Then the old woman recognized her and grinned.
"Ah! Young Liel, welcome back. Your friend has kept your room
for you—he's back there, entertaining Salang and Forest. Will
you join him, or head up?"

Raliel looked through the crowded dining room to the
round table near the back, spying Osian easily. His charisma lit

the corner, and his curling hair was in a messy topknot, giving him enough added height to measure up to the pair of brewers he was sandwiched between. He noticed her and lifted a hand.

"I'll join him." She squeezed the proprietor's arm and asked for wine and whatever was best from the kitchen. She wove through the tables, paused to nod respect at the woman playing a round guitar to accompany her singing.

When she was several steps away, Osian called out, "Welcome back, beautiful!" His voice directed the eyes of everyone present to Raliel. Her sword was sheathed over her right shoulder, and otherwise she was dressed in much richer attire than when she left. The Scale had insisted on outfitting her with new magical wool and silk robes and snow-proof boots. She'd agreed as long as everything remained shades of gray and white and fit under her dark red jacket.

"Osian," she said coolly but with a slight smile. She flicked her eyes to his companions, and he introduced Salang and Forest Heaven's Own Brew. Forest poured Raliel wine from a squat carafe as she sat.

She lifted it in a salute and sipped, pleased by the flavor and the immediate flush it brought to her cheeks. "Exquisite," she said.

"Just like you, lovely spirits both," Osian flirted. His messy topknot glistened as if he'd just bathed, and he was missing his outer jacket, wearing only a loose tunic over his trousers. Very relaxed.

The innkeeper approached with a tray of soup and bowls of roasted vegetables and steamed redpop. She set down the food and smiled softly, giving Raliel a little bow.

Osian borrowed readily from Raliel's bowl, chattering with

the brewers and the soldiers at the table next to them, as well as with a trader who passed by and the child who belonged to a handful of pilgrims eating simple boiled vegetables on long benches behind them. Raliel listened absently, her attention more on the musician, and said nothing. Osian slid her cup nearer to himself and refilled it, offering it back with a soft smile.

There was something behind the smile, and Raliel assumed it was a promise that when they were alone he'd pepper her with questions.

The great demon growled. Raliel petted the small triangle of skin accessible where her collars crossed under her throat.

I could possess someone right now.

She dug a nail into her skin with just enough pain to deny Moon.

A great laugh erupted around her, and she blinked, having missed the end of the story that sent Osian rocking back, clutching his stomach with laughter.

She stared at the line of his neck, the shine of his teeth. He was so bright.

I don't like it.

Raliel glanced down at the table. It was awkward being suddenly unable to speak back to Moon. She'd grown used to the ease of it in the First Mountain. Frustrated, she finished her cup and held it out for more.

Forest obliged and asked what she'd been doing while she left her Osian to wait.

"*My* Osian?" she murmured, lifting a brow.

"Oh well," Osian said with a candy smile. His dimples flashed, and he fluttered his lashes. "Only if you don't mind."

she minds.

"As long as you behave," she teased, then wondered if anyone could tell she was teasing.

Forest snorted. Her husband, Salang, punched Osian lightly. *don't flirt with him,* Moon snarled.

Surprise had Raliel frowning, and Osian asked what was wrong.

"I am tired from my journey . . . back to you," she added to play along, despite Moon. It was only a little stilted.

Osian smiled like the sun. He hopped up, pressing past Salang to lean his forearm on Raliel's shoulder. His copper-brown eyes glittered in the lamplight like new coins. "To bed it is!"

Raliel thinned her lips—that was a little too far. What if these people realized who she was? The heir must remain untouched. As she thought it, Raliel realized the wine haze in her mind was heavier than she expected.

high alcohol, Moon muttered. It stuck out tongues of shadows from its nest under her heart, tickling up behind her breastbone in that dangerous way.

Swallowing the gentle flicker of desire, she stood, knocking Osian off-balance when he swiftly removed his elbow from her shoulder. But he laughed. They bade good night to their table companions and headed for the rear stairs.

There was only one room, the same one Raliel had slept in before climbing the First Mountain. Lantern light from the street pushed through the half-moon window, clashing red and green across the floor. Osian's things were set out neatly, on the foot of the bed and on a short table beside the privacy screen. The inn had a shared bathing room, but this room included a shallow basin and a full pitcher with towels for quicker ablutions.

"I'll take the floor," Osian said, and proved his preparedness by producing extra bedding from under the bed frame.

Raliel opened her mouth, but the demon-kissed warrior said with a half smile: "Don't think that now we're together again I'll let you out of my sight!"

After a considering pause, Raliel nodded. She'd permit it, at least until they were on their way in the morning and she explained about the demon. So she set down her sword, propped against the wall by the bed, removed her jacket and leather vest before sinking onto the low bed to remove her boots. Immediately, Osian perched on the edge of the straw mattress beside her.

"Are you going to tell me a story, or must I drag it out of you?" he said softly.

In answer, she took the second pillow and shoved it into his chest. "Sleep first. Stories in the morning."

"I see, I see." Amusement coated his voice.

They prepared for bed, taking turns behind the privacy screen. Moon remained silent, coiled tightly in her chest. Together, Raliel and Osian put out the lantern beside their door and in the darkness touched the small dream blessing carved into the single brick built into the wooden wall.

Once she settled under the blanket, she turned her face to the night sky she could see through the window and sighed a very, very soft, "Good night," for the great demon.

There was rustling as Osian settled too, and a quick lullaby whistled with only lips and teeth, and then silence spread in their room but for the muffled bustle from the rooms beneath them.

Raliel's eyes had been closed for no more than a few breaths when Osian said, "Heir?"

"Yes."

"May I ask you one thing?"

"So long as the answer does not require a story."

He paused, and in the darkness Raliel felt the hesitance. She didn't give him anything to end it, but waited.

"Why did you come back to me?"

"It wasn't fair to leave you in the first place," she answered, glad she knew the answer. She didn't apologize further but could admit this much again. "I needed to move faster and could without you—why is a story that can wait until tomorrow. But I didn't leave you because of anything you did, or are."

"Thank you, Heir," he murmured.

"Osian."

"Yes?"

"Call me my name."

"Raliel. Raliel," he said again, slower, as if practicing.

She imagined his curving mouth as he said it, then imagined a whiter version of that mouth doing the same, with a softer voice, and maybe even how it might sound whispered right against her ear.

Raliel woke suddenly, eyes snapping open at the pain of cold wire tightening against her throat.

It did not squeeze. She stared up at Osian Redpop, bent over her in the darkness, hands to either side of her neck.

Raliel opened her mouth to gasp—to scream—and saw Osian's eyes shining with tears.

Then Moon surged and Raliel's back arched: she choked

as the demon leapt into Osian in an arc of blue-white aether.

Osian stumbled back, loosening his grip on the wire, and Raliel sat up. She flung it away.

"What the—" Osian growled—lower, darker. It was Moon in his body.

Raliel touched her throat. No blood, not much pain. He hadn't pressed down, hadn't yet tried to . . . murder her. The bed tilted beneath her as her skull pounded. Shock beat cold punches against her bones, falling, draining. Raliel closed her eyes and took a deep breath. Another. In through the nose, out through the mouth.

When she looked again, blinking in the dim moonlight, Moon in Osian's body crouched near the bed, wrists balanced on his knees. Staring at nothing, blinking slowly.

"Moon?" she whispered.

It looked up. "Raliel."

"He . . . tried to kill me."

Their gazes locked together. Raliel shook her head. Too stunned to process, much less think anything through.

Osian—no, Moon—rolled his neck and stood too fast. It stumbled backward a couple of steps. Raliel could only stare as Moon stretched legs and arms, twisted its torso, and touched its face. It scrunched up its expression, then ran Osian's hands into the braided hair, catching in knots. It stepped again and fell to Osian's knees with a soft grunt.

"Moon," she hissed.

Slowly Moon lifted Osian's face and grinned up at her—ferocious, wild. It stood, shoulders just hunched, head tilted oddly. Osian, but off-key. Osian, but a loose, feral puppet. It sent a shiver down Raliel's spine.

She liked it.

"Moon," she said again, more of a gentle threat.

"Raliel," the great demon answered, then turned on Osian's heel and ran. It slammed into the door and fumbled with the lock. It flung open the door and dashed out.

Shocked, Raliel took a moment to give chase.

She had to drag on her trousers and tunic, then her boots without socks, and grabbed her sword and jacket as she ran after that damned great demon.

Stumbling down the narrow staircase, Raliel hoped they hadn't woken anybody else with their banging around. When she reached the dark dining room, she paused: nothing stirred, but the front door swung open, allowing in very spare light.

Raliel only knocked her hip into two tables as she hurried across the floor and out into the depths of night.

Pilgrim Reception slept under the starlight, windows dark, lanes silent, carts battened down. A flash of movement turned Raliel west down the market street, jogging with her sword in hand. She caught up with Moon around another corner; it waved cheekily and darted away again, leading her deeper into town. "Moon!" she whisper-yelled.

Its laughter rang back at her.

She huffed, fighting a flush of irritation. And a smile. Moon had said it wanted to play.

Running, she tried to catch up, until Moon vanished down an alley. Raliel stopped, turned, and ran the other way, attempting to cut it off down the next street.

When she burst into the crescent courtyard, Moon waited, leaning insouciantly with a shoulder against the central well shrine. A tiny wisp of a spirit peeked through the vines, climbing up the mossy bricks. Moon batted lazily at it.

"Moon," she said, and stopped halfway to it. A single lantern swayed from the lintel of the building behind her, glowing softly yellow.

The expression on Osian's face was both mysterious and more raw than she'd ever seen. The demon looked at her through those pretty eyes with dark intensity, and she remembered it in her dreams: Osian's shape but with stark black and white coloring; none of this sweet softening of the demon-kissed blue and violet. The knives strapped to his legs, the fit of the leather jacket, the dimples that appeared when Moon smiled its own devastating version of a smile. Raliel's pulse raced. She stared, stunned.

"Moon," she said, a bit shaky—which was intolerable. Taking a deep breath, she closed her eyes. She was ice. There was snow in her veins, in her mind, sprinkling her heart with calm. When she opened her eyes, Moon stood directly in front of her.

She gasped, and the moment her lips parted, Moon kissed her.

It cupped her head with surprising delicacy. Osian's lips were dry and warm, tasting of the mintgrass he chewed and hints of hearty gravy from their dinner. Raliel didn't move, her hands stuck at her sides, pinned in place by her disbelief. She was frozen indeed, but her eyes drifted shut as Moon kissed her with Osian Redpop's pretty mouth.

Their kiss was tentative, exploring, a brush of lips, a mingling breath, just the hint of Osian's tongue and Raliel's teeth.

Moon slid Osian's hands down her neck until his thumbs brushed the corners of her jaw with just enough pressure she shivered and leaned involuntarily closer. She'd never been kissed at all, much less with curiosity equal to her own. It was different from the demon kissing her from inside. Less invasive but somehow stranger, because another body was involved.

Realization crashed through her, and Raliel shoved the demon away. She wiped her mouth with the back of her hand, glaring at it as it stumbled back.

"Raliel!" Moon said, gasping, eyes wide, and then it laughed. "This feels *good*. The body—it's hot and strong. And . . ." The demon frowned, exaggerated and almost silly on Osian's face.

"We must return to the Silver Broom and interrogate him." Raliel held out her hand, forcing it not to tremble, refusing to be concerned with touching Osian's skin. Without his permission. With—no, it was too much to untangle when she'd just been nearly *assassinated*.

But Moon wasn't listening anyway, its gaze turned inward. It blinked several times. Raliel licked her lips; they were hot. She took another deep breath. Snow, she reminded herself. She was snow, not—not this melting.

Moon shook Osian's head. "Oh my, my." It laughed once, a low bark that sent honey-shivers down Raliel's spine. Then it glanced up at her with Osian's chin angled down, so that it was looking with those big lashes as frame.

"Raliel. Osian Redpop has been lying to you about something else. Lying to everyone."

TWO

A S THEY RETURNED TO the guest room through the quiet streets, Moon explained what it had discovered. "This body is not demon-kissed. It is entirely human, just like yours, but with"—it tilted Osian's head thoughtfully—"an overlay of sorcery, like someone carved a sigil diagram into his flesh and transformed it."

"Sorcery?" Raliel frowned. Osian was not demon-kissed. Osian had saved her mother's life. Osian had been hand-chosen by her father Sky. Osian flirted and laughed and made friends. He made her like him.

Osian had tried to kill her.

She clenched her jaw, seethed a little through her nose.

Moon touched the back of Osian's knuckles to Raliel's hand. "The transformation is too . . . fluid . . . for witchcraft alone."

She swallowed and nodded. "We should interrogate him."

They arrived back at the Silver Broom and upstairs undisturbed.

The moment they were alone in the guest room, Raliel said, "Tie him up."

Moon headed for Osian's pack. The gait was different, stiffer than Osian's compact grace.

While Moon dug into Osian's bag, she lit the oil lamp beside the door. Double-checked the lock.

The great demon said, "Only these cords for tying the canvas. They're strong but not long."

"We can use the blanket. And his wire. Lie down. I'll tie him to the bed."

After stripping Osian of all his knives, Moon did so, and Raliel first tied both ankles to the foot of the bed with the blanket. It was awkward and poorly done, but if Osian struggled too hard, Moon could possess him again. Then she used the canvas cord to tie his wrists together. Moon tried to pull them free and couldn't easily. It nodded and raised them over Osian's head.

Raliel's pulse thrummed. She resisted the hundred questions flipping through her mind and climbed onto the bed. She straddled Osian's waist, scooting up to get her thighs around his ribs. Moon pulled Osian's mouth into a grin, and Raliel took a second to regret her position. "Behave, Moon," she murmured, stretching the same wire over Osian's throat with which he'd held her down. Leather-wrapped loops at either end allowed her to grip tightly. There was no doubt this wire was intended as a weapon.

The great demon lifted Osian's hips slightly, nudging at her bottom. It licked Osian's lips. "This is fantastic. I want to keep it."

"I want to talk to him."

"I wish I could get these hands on—"

"Moon!"

Moon slithered back into her, skimming up her thighs to her navel, curling where it belonged. It pressed little shadow-fingers against her ribs, like climbing a ladder.

Before she could speak, Osian himself groaned and winced. He moved his arms, only to jerk at the bindings on his wrists. His eyes flew open.

Raliel gently pressed down on the wire. "Osian Redpop, do not move."

Underneath her, Osian's entire body tensed. He stared up at her, lips parting. His chest moved in a big breath, but he clearly strained to hold still.

"You attempted to assassinate the Heir to the Moon," she said coldly. "*Me*. Explain yourself."

"I—I didn't."

Raliel scoffed just as Moon tightened its grip on her ribs. Her scoff stuttered, but she only lifted an imperious brow. "Oh? You had this"—she shifted the wire on his neck, cutting into the flexed tendon to the right side; she did not look away from those big eyes—"against my neck. Right here, in this bed. What other reason is there than murder?"

"Raliel—"

"That permission is revoked."

Osian licked his bottom lip, nodded small and frantic. "Heir. I was supposed to hurt you but did not. Had not. I could have, but I hesitated."

that is his excuse! Moon hissed, sounding on the verge of impressed.

Raliel did not allow herself the luxury of reacting. She kept her voice cold. "Then you are guilty of conspiring to assassinate me, if not for having gone through with it. Hardly a difference in consequences."

Osian shut his eyes, and actual tears plopped out of the corners, rolling down either temple. "Yes."

Loosening her grip on the wire ever so slightly, Raliel waited. Moon simmered just as coldly, like cracking ice.

The warrior—the traitor—looked up at her again. "I deserve your wrath, Heir. Do what you must." His eyes glinted with so much feeling, Raliel could barely stand it. He continued. "Believe me, I wish I had not—I hesitated because I did not want to hurt you."

"You have lied about so much, I do not know what I could possibly believe."

Something like surprise flitted across Osian's face.

tell him, Moon snarled.

"You are not demon-kissed."

Osian sucked in a sharp breath.

Raliel waited again. She'd long learned to allow others to fill in her silences. They would give themselves away.

Over his head, Osian's hands clutched together. His knuckles blanched. Raliel looked back at his face.

He said, "How do you know?"

Glad he had not bothered to deny it, she leaned back. It settled her weight on his stomach. His torso fluttered as he shifted and tried to breathe. She put the wire across her lap, back straight as if she sat for tea with her mother. "I have a demon familiar. It stopped you from harming me by possessing you. Making you its house. And while it lived in you, it felt the lines of sorcery."

"A demon . . . possessed me?" His brow wrinkled. "That was not a . . . dream."

To Raliel's consternation, Osian licked his bottom lip just as Moon had, and she wondered if Osian remembered the kiss. She pushed the concern away. "No, it was not."

"How . . . long?"

"An hour."

"I mean, how long has . . . ? Did you have a demon with you the entire time?"

"Yes."

"What is its—"

"Stop." Raliel glared. "Tell me who wants me dead. Tell me who you are. Is my family in further danger?"

Osian stared at her, and slowly his body relaxed. His lashes flicked softly as he glanced down and away, and when he grimaced, it was almost a smile. One of his dimples flashed. "My mother wants you dead—no, she wanted your father the emperor to hurt. My name *is* Osian. My mother is Syra Bear Mistress, and my—my father was Skybreaker, the sorcerer of the Fourth Mountain."

Inside her, Moon exploded into tiny tendrils of cold. Raliel gasped, dropping one end of the wire to press her hand to her chest.

"Raliel." Osian started to sit, but Raliel slammed her forearm against his throat. Pressed until he could not breathe. His bound hands lowered fast, nearly smacking her head. She turned over, and Moon flung itself back to Osian's body.

Raliel rocked off the bed, catching herself on hands and knees against the floor. She breathed. Eyes closed.

"We can go," Moon said, in his raspy Osian voice. "I can walk him wherever you want. I can kill him."

"No." She flattened herself to the wooden floor, exhausted. "We'll take him to the nearest justiciar and turn him over. That's in . . . Shards of Summer, unless we want to go back to the one we ditched him at . . . which I don't. But they're both in the opposite direction of the sea."

She heard shuffling on the bed above her, and Moon touched her hair with Osian's hand. "Turn him in?"

"Yes."

"Ugh."

A weary laugh spilled from her.

Moon smiled, leaned down. "Then we should take him with us to the sea first. If we meet the great demon and it eats us, it won't matter what happens to him."

"Cheerful thought."

"I like this body. I don't mind taking it with us for longer. Then I have more time to convince you to let me eat him instead of turning him in."

Raliel studied the dim light flickering on Osian's face, as it wore Moon's vindictive delight. She said, "Let's try this again."

Once they'd repositioned themselves into the original arrangement, Raliel straddling Osian with the wire to his neck, she nodded and Moon darted back into her.

Osian choked on a gasp.

Raliel waited until his bleary gaze flew to hers and said, "You can't hurt me. My demon will take you and suck all the aether from your body until you die."

247

The warrior nodded. He swallowed carefully, the wire a black line against his blotchy skin. "I . . . won't."

"Why does your mother want to hurt my family?"

Osian swallowed tightly. "Revenge."

"Shadows of the Fifth Mountain killed Skybreaker."

"But . . . the former empress, and your father Kirin, sent an army, and in the end did nothing to Shadows. My mother believes your father is responsible for the lack of justice. He is the emperor and should have done something."

Raliel narrowed her eyes. "Your mother is incapable of taking revenge on a sorceress and her great demon. So she turned to what seemed an easier target."

". . . Maybe," Osian murmured.

"She sent you, falsely demon-kissed, to what? Infiltrate the palace and hurt me? Why did you save my mother? Why did you wait so long? We were alone for weeks. Why?" Her voice rose, and she struggled not to push the wire through his neck to his spine.

Oh, Raliel realized. She was *angry*. Hurt. Furious with herself, too, for liking him. For admiring his way with people, his charisma and pretty smile. The ease with which he held himself, the flash of dimples like a gift. Those big eyes framed with such lovely lashes.

She should have known immediately—there was no flash of blue light deep in his pupils. The flecks of demon-kissed violet in his irises had been all she'd seen. But her own father Sky was demon-kissed. She should have known.

"Osian," she said again, a quiet command. "Explain."

"She sent me, like this, to infiltrate, yes, and hurt the emperor."

"You waited because you were plotting."

"Yes . . . though not only."

"Did you save my mother to get closer to us?"

"It was instinct," Osian said quickly. "I saw the sigils and just acted. I . . . I am a good guard."

Moon snorted, and Raliel echoed it.

"I am." Osian held her gaze. "I liked working there. After so many years in the capital, I was . . . I . . . disagree with my mother. But she's my mother."

what does that mean, Moon said.

"It means he cares for her and wants not to upset her."

Osian startled. "The demon asked that?"

"Yes. Is your mother a sorcerer? Who is her great spirit?"

it's good, powerful shape-shifting, Moon said. *subtle.*

"No. Mother is not. The spirit—my father's great spirit survived his death. Crown, it is called."

"This is sorcery," Raliel said, nodding at his face.

Osian winced, sliding his gaze away. Again, Raliel waited him out, and eventually he said, "There were two others. The twin sorcerers, with their great spirits. They helped Mother."

Inside her, Moon snarled.

Raliel stared down at Osian. The implications were enormous: two of the living sorcerers plotting against the empire. She remembered A Dance of Stars exuding his understated power, smiling at her in the palace. He wanted a great demon, the emperor had said. Wanted the Fourth Mountain. Maybe they already had the mountain, if the great spirit there welcomed him and his brother.

Ice slicked down her spine as she thought of the danger the

empire was in if the twin sorcerers realized Moon was no longer in the palace.

Raliel, Moon whispered.

"It's speaking to you?" Osian said.

Raliel ignored him.

Osian took a deep breath. "It may use me if need be. Or . . . want be. I deserve it."

"No," Raliel said at the same time Moon said, *yes!*

"If I can be of service," Osian reiterated. "Let me serve you."

"How could I possibly trust you?" She put as much snow and ice into her voice as possible.

Osian nodded, eyes sliding away with an air of sorrow.

Raliel stared down at him. At the false streaks of demon-blue and violet. She thought of chasing Moon through the streets of Pilgrim Reception, the laughter it made, so loud and wild. Its delight. She kept thinking about kissing Moon, even in this terrible position, betrayed and angry. She wished she'd had another moment to breathe and think before taking Moon back. Now she couldn't ask it why it kissed her. Was it only because it knew she found Osian beautiful? Did it think a kiss was a way to learn possession better, or an individual? Did it just think of it and act on impulse? Or had it wanted to, after weeks in her body, of getting to know her inside—did it want to know her from the outside, too?

She did not touch her lips again. She did, though, want to.

What she did not want to do was go home. Not yet. Not without learning how to give Moon its choices. They would always be vulnerable if Moon was a prisoner.

As she thought it, she glared coldly down at Osian. He bravely held her gaze, barely wavering.

Raliel, Moon crooned inside her. *you should sleep. we'll leave at dawn.*

"You can hold him that long?" she asked. Osian startled, but she ignored him.

if not I'll wake you.

"Promise?"

promise.

As the great demon slid into Osian once again, Raliel relaxed. She did not know if she'd sleep well, but she untied the cords around Osian's hands, and when Moon opened those arms for her, she sank down against the hard, narrow chest and drifted immediately off.

THREE

T HEY LEFT FIRST THING, to the proprietor's dismay.
She patted Osian's cheek, and Moon managed a vague
smile shape for her, and she curtsied to Raliel. Her
eyes nearly disappeared under smiling wrinkles when Raliel
slipped her extra money. They ate breakfast purchased at the
pilgrim stalls: hot pies with vegetables and potatoes, and for later
they got a bag of salted fish and four meat buns. Moon made
ridiculous faces at the food, almost slathering in excitement at
the flavors until Raliel hissed it needed to at least pretend to be
human while they were surrounded.

It took Raliel a bit to grow used to her backpack again, hooked
over her shoulders and pressing her sheath to her spine. But she
was stronger than before. She paused at the shrines stacked up at
the edge of Pilgrim Reception to light incense and leave the last
of her pie crust at the feet of a raccoon statue. The spirit of the
little shrine winked at her, its aether-blue eyes sparkling.

The journey to the sea was awkward and messy. Moon spent
hours of every day possessing Osian, and the rest they kept the
traitor tied up. Though Raliel had considered acquiring horses,

controlling him mounted would be more difficult, and Moon had no experience whatsoever riding. Raliel barely did herself.

So they walked.

Moon possessed Osian for the entire first morning, but by the afternoon it needed to recharge its aether, which it could not do through Osian. Not without burning up his aether-channels. It worked through Raliel only because of the palace-amulet linking them, making her a piece of its house. The demon helped Raliel tie Osian's hands behind his back with fine rope they'd bought in Pilgrim Reception. Then it slipped into Raliel. The cool slithering comforted her, and as they walked she held out her hand to weave her fingers through the air—she'd been practicing catching aether in such simple ways since living on the First Mountain.

"Wow," Osian said as he came back to himself. He managed to hold his silence for half a mile before asking where they were headed. Raliel told him what The Scale had told her: "We're aiming for just beyond a village named Jellyfish Rest, which has a cove with a white sand beach and dark waters, too, because the sand drops away fast into very deep waters. A trench, it's said. We'll know the right place because far out in the water are three islands small in circumference but tall, like pillars rising out of the waves. They're home to nothing but pelicans and seals. At night, just an hour past sunset, in between the pillar islands the water glows."

Osian's eyes grew wide. "What is it?"

Raliel clenched her jaw, remembering herself. She did not answer, but said, "Afterward we're taking you to the nearest justiciar to be turned in."

"You'll continue on your own?" he said, as if he had any right to be concerned.

She turned a cold glance on him. "I have never been on my own since I met my demon."

I like it when you say that. yours.

Osian grimaced. He was quiet for another bit, as they trudged through a patch of muddy road, churned up from recent rain. Though the mountain range loomed in the east, the land to either side of the road was flat, pressed into small furrows by plentiful streams that gave the breeze a pleasant musicality. When they entered woods again, spruce and evergreens turned the light green; their trunks were painted with moss and rainbow lichen. Ferns crowded the narrow path, and meadows of weedy wood sorrel hid little rabbits and root mice.

Moon said, *I want to catch a rabbit and race alongside you.*

They stepped off the road while a small cart pulled by a cow with blessing ribbons tied around its short horns passed them by. The driver did not even glance at Osian's bound hands. As Raliel nudged Osian back onto the road, he said, "Is it the Moon?"

Raliel pursed her lips.

clever, whispered the demon.

"There were rumors, in the palace," Osian continued softly. "You had a close connection to the great demon—closer than most heirs."

"It is."

"I thought . . . Everyone thought the great demon's house is the palace itself. It should not be able to leave."

Moon answered before Raliel could, driving forcefully into

254

Osian's body. It shuddered, then turned for Raliel to untie Osian's hands. That was the end of the conversation.

They avoided crossroads shelters in the evenings, unable to share space, instead camping alone out under the trees. Moon used Osian to gather firewood and help place the canvas shelter and roll out their beds, but then they tied Osian to a tree, sitting up.

"This is so strange," Osian murmured, taking in the change in his situation from hours before. The small camp, the dark forest. He tilted his head at the trill of a frog. Then he stared at the fire for a moment, at the small pot of water Raliel had set to boil, and he raised his eyebrows at her, wiggling his shoulders to emphasize his bound state. "Is the heir going to feed me by her own hand?"

"Moon enjoys eating," she said lightly.

Moon purred under her heart.

Once Raliel had made tea for herself—and she did tip a water flask to Osian's mouth—she settled down to wait for the buns set on a rock near the fire to heat. Her sword she'd slammed into the earth, where the sigils burned into the steel tugged at aether to store up for the great demon. The forest here was lush; it could spare plenty.

Osian whistled.

Raliel startled at first, but the whistle became a gentle melody, a song she recognized as a lullaby. She allowed it.

That night she slept while Moon listened with her ears for any movement from Osian—but it seemed he slept, too, reclined in discomfort against the tree. In the morning Moon possessed him to relieve the body and splash it clean in the nearby crescent pool of a stream. Then Moon ran ahead, stretching Osian's legs. It tripped, laughter floating back to Raliel.

The joy she inadvertently experienced at the sound felt awkward.

When Moon dashed back to her in Osian's body, bright with merriment and arms flung out to embrace the whole world, Raliel realized she'd made a strategic error.

"What?" Moon asked, stepping right into her space. Osian's demon-kissed eyes glinted with purple-blue shadows, gorgeous, but Moon leaned in, frowning. She could feel its breath on her lips.

She said, "If we leave him with the justiciar, he can tell everyone you're with me. He can tell them a lot."

"I said we could just kill him."

Raliel pushed the demon out of her path and strode on, angry at herself. At Moon. But especially at Osian.

When they stopped to refill their water at a well shrine, Raliel tied Osian to a tree at the edge of the grove and welcomed Moon back into her. The spark of power startled a little fish spirit that swam over the surface of the well water in an invisible pool of aether. It fell into the real water with a tiny splash.

Moon laughed inside her. Raliel filled her water and crouched before Osian. She held his gaze, reminding herself of cold and snow, and tipped the water for him. He drank, watching her steadily. A drop of water glistened at the corner of his mouth, and Raliel thought about Moon kissing her with those lips. She jerked the water flask away. Osian blinked.

Raliel stood so that she looked dramatically down at him.

"You will not tell anyone about Moon. You will keep my secrets, Osian Redpop. Or Moon will eat you."

The young man's mouth dropped open, and he blinked again rapidly. Then swallowed. "I will keep your secrets if you keep me with you."

what.

"You have no leverage," Raliel said.

"I have your secrets."

"Moon would be happy to eat you right now."

"Why doesn't it, then?" Osian's mouth flattened into a grim line. He raised his chin.

Raliel clenched her jaw. "I have not allowed it. Yet."

"You don't want to."

She held herself still as ice. Stared with her best cold, imperious expression.

Osian shook his head once. "Raliel." His voice cracked, no longer challenging, but softer and more intimate. "You don't want to kill me."

"But I will," she whispered.

"What can I do to prove I mean you no harm?"

A single loud laugh barked out of her: raw and impressed.

Osian did not glance away, but something shivered through him—effort maybe, or fear or determination.

"You cannot," Raliel said.

"I went to the capital knowing my mother would ask me to hurt someone. You, one of your parents, probably. She did not say so with so many words, but I understood what she would want, because of what she had lost. But I was barely fourteen when she sent me to the Warriors of the Last Means. I had no

257

reason not to believe her. To me your father the emperor was a villain. Skybreaker went to the Fifth Mountain to rescue him and was murdered for it, and nobody cared. Nobody in the capital, in the palace. I went, believing in my mother, but also . . ." Osian closed his eyes. "I knew she was struggling. I knew . . . her violence wasn't the only way. I had other mothers, other aunts, and they were good. They are good. It was difficult, Raliel."

Raliel flinched at her name. But she hardened her expression. Hardened her whole self.

"I went to the palace expecting to hate it. To be hurt by indifference or judgment. But do you know what I found?" Osian shook his head. "Acceptance. Your father . . ." He drew a ragged breath. "Your father may have done terrible things—maybe not! But he . . . Every day he puts on different rings, different clothing, different hair, and people notice. People see. He is the emperor, but he is also . . ." Osian bit his lip. Looked away for the first time. "I didn't have to pretend anymore, in Kirin Dark-Smile's court."

Moon grumbled.

Raliel frowned. "You did. You lied about your family. Being demon-kissed."

Osian's frown was confused more than anything. "I mean, my—who I am. I . . ." He struggled against the ropes binding him to the tree, grimacing. "This would be easier free," he muttered, but then his lips quirked up. "But easier isn't something you're interested in for me."

"Explain yourself."

"Moon didn't tell you?" the young man murmured.

Moon hissed. *tell what.*

258

Raliel sank down to her haunches. "Tell me what?"

"I . . . Why?" Osian looked down her neck, to her chest, as if he thought the demon lived in her heart. As if he could meet its seven moon-eyes. Raliel reached out and nudged his chin up. He said, "When I was younger, before I came to the capital, my mother, my family, everyone assumed I was a girl."

For a moment Raliel didn't understand. Then she remembered what Moon had actually said: *this body is just like yours. not demon-kissed.*

Just like yours.

"Oh," she said.

Osian said firmly, "But I am not. A girl."

"Father made you feel . . . welcome."

"I stopped pretending, Heir. I stopped pretending to be anything other than what I am. And in the palace, after a few weeks, nobody cared. They just accepted it. Called me . . . It was . . ." Osian closed his eyes again, and this time a tear slipped out of one eye, falling straight and perfect down his cheek. "He could have murdered my father personally, could have been a tyrant, cruel, awful, anything, and to me it wouldn't have mattered as much as whatever he did to make people *care*. About who I am, not who I . . . seem."

Raliel felt herself aching and turned away.

Moon said, *this is because he doesn't have a penis?*

Raliel laughed. Tears prickled her own eyes, and she squished her face up, trembling with slightly hysterical mirth.

Something behind her shifted, and she realized it must seem to Osian that she laughed at him. She clenched tight, stopping the laughter. Then she said, "Moon thinks humans are ridiculous."

Osian laughed a little, too. Darker than anything she'd heard from him. "We are."

I am not a man just because I possess someone with a penis, the demon said.

"And I'm a dragon," Raliel whispered. She turned back to Osian. "So? You still tried to kill me two nights ago."

"I had to. I have . . ." He paused, drew a very deep breath. "Will you unbind me for this? I swear I will not run, nor attack or attempt to do anything you do not command."

Raliel studied him. "Moon?"

Osian blinked but otherwise did not react.

Moon said, *I suppose it is safe enough.*

She strode behind the tree and took a moment to untie the knot.

Osian wisely did not move until she returned to face him. He shifted, leaning forward, but did not stand. Instead, he knelt before her. Tilted his face up. "Heir to the Moon, I have been in communication with my mother, occasionally, and she knew of this journey. When you left me, I told her where I was going, and she sent a message to me through a shrine in Pilgrim Reception. It said, 'What are you waiting for?' Nothing more or less." He lowered his head but clasped his hands before him. "I was waiting for nothing. I was afraid and uncertain. But it had been trained into me. This was my purpose. How could I deny my mother?"

"Now you do," Raliel said. "Now you wish to go with me, to remain with me. That denies your mother."

"I failed her."

"We stopped you."

"No—I hesitated." Osian looked up at her. "It could have been fast enough your demon could not have stopped it. But I hesitated because I did not want to hurt you, even with her voice in my head. I couldn't try again."

it is mutual blackmail, Moon said. *he has a secret of ours, but if we choose we can have him imprisoned or executed, or I can drink up his delicious life.*

Raliel nodded. She felt sick. Knotted and clammy. "You cannot hurt me, even if you want to, or try. Moon is with me, and it will annihilate you."

"I understand," Osian said.

"I do not trust you, but we will try to continue on. After the sea, we head north."

I want to meet his mother.

"I want to meet your mother," Raliel repeated, because she agreed.

Osian's face jerked up. "What? No—she wants you dead."

Raliel smiled and felt the great demon beneath her skin, making her smile worse. They said nothing.

She picked up her things and walked away. Osian scrambled to follow.

He trailed her, remaining just behind, but eventually he started to sing a gentle work song, good for steady walking and harmonies. Raliel did not sing back, but Moon did, from the ice nest below her heart.

FOUR

MOON DIDN'T KNOW MUCH about love, but it did understand possession, and it felt possessive about two things: Raliel Dark-Smile and the entire ocean. *mine mine mine,* it felt, and struggled not to say.

When Raliel walked out onto the beach, Moon vibrated inside her, and she laughed a little, breathless with its energy. The white sand glared under the sun and brought the tang of tears to her eyes. Moon relished the glint and expanded to every part of her body as she lifted her gaze to the sea itself. Water fluttered like a thousand ruffled skirts as the wind blew steadily toward shore, toward them.

go in go in, Moon said.

Raliel stared out at the bright, flickering waves, to the three pillar islands in the distance. They rose like giant fingers, a massive old beast reaching its hand out of the ocean. The sun sank just to their west.

"This is the place?" asked Osian from behind. Raliel didn't turn, keeping her eyes on the sea, which Moon appreciated. The demon had liked being in that strong little body, liked running and laughing, liked looking *at* Raliel instead of through her.

Liked shocking her with the kiss, liked tasting her too, and liked exposing Osian for being a liar. It had told Raliel late last night that honestly it liked Osian more now. Before, Osian had been funny but annoying. Charming, useful, but stifling. Now Moon was impressed. Now it knew Osian was bold. Ambitious. The lie of being demon-kissed had been precisely chosen to gain him the advantage he sought, without doing great harm. Moon told Raliel this was an excellent quality in a friend.

After her surprise subsided, she'd nodded in agreement.

The fact that he'd been a sleeper assassin and spy was several major points removed from his favorability column, but it did give them something very concrete to attack, a mission for the rest of the Heir's Journey, a goal they could actually express: to put an end to Syra Bear Mistress's quest for vengeance.

But not today.

Today belonged to the sea.

Oh, it smelled bright, like salt and seaweed, rot and reclamation. Moon thrummed! Raliel rolled her shoulders and flattened her palm down her forearm as if she could press away the little goose bumps running along her skin and lifting her hair.

go in, Moon demanded. *I want to taste it! breathe it. we will fly through the deep water together, Raliel Dark-Smile.*

It felt her gasp, and she shivered. She wanted it. To fly with Moon. She . . . desired such a thing. The great demon could feel the desire welling in her hips, in her throat. Moon liked knowing how it could make her feel and touched tiny fingers of itself to the hot places in her that slowly knotted up.

Moon teased like the tug of the tide, aching as it drew out out out to sea.

"I'm worried," she whispered.

about what!

"Sorcery. I . . . we've barely managed transformations. The eyes, the hair color. But breathing? And . . . It isn't sorcery. Just power."

Raliel's heart sped, rushing blood to her face. Moon retaliated with a surge of cool aether, flooding her chest with it like a medicinal compress. *Raliel,* it soothed. *Raliel, we can do this. I am the great demon of the palace, and you are Raliel Dark-Smile. we have come this far. I have the whole ocean of aether to draw upon.*

"I'm worried," she said again.

scared.

Her jaw clenched. She nodded.

The great demon did not know scared any better than it knew love. It said, *use it.*

"Use it?"

fear. energy. make it yours, mine. ours.

"Ours," Raliel murmured. "Ours." She drew a deep breath that seemed to ground the vibrations of her bones and breath. "We need it," she said. "Or you'll never be free. It's worth it."

yes

"It has to be." She took another deep breath and slowly let it out. She stepped forward.

"Wait," Osian said, and Moon growled.

But Raliel turned. "You stay here. We're going under, to try to talk with a great demon."

"Under!" Osian caught her hand.

Raliel allowed it, though Moon felt a sizzle of surprise up her spine. She turned her hand so that their palms grazed together. "Yes. To visit with a different great demon."

His entire expression seemed to widen in horror. "Raliel, that's . . . too dangerous. You can't go under the ocean, and great demons . . ." Osian's grip tightened.

Moon hissed, raising through Raliel's throat to push the hiss aloud through her teeth. But Raliel held her lips in a firm line and swallowed it back. She did, though, jerk her hand free of Osian. "Stop. This is what is happening," she said.

"But—"

"No. You do not have a say in this, Osian Redpop." Raliel lifted her chin. Moon felt her gather her inner snowscape and put it in her eyes. Oh, Moon liked that. "Wait here, and if it all goes wrong, you will be free of us. You can tell your mother anything you wish. Tell everyone."

"Queens of Heaven," he muttered, and glanced up beseechingly.

"Osian." Raliel put her other hand to his face, almost tenderly. Her thumb brushed his cheek, and Moon wondered if she was thinking about touching him when Moon has possessed him. Kissing had been weird but good—slick, warm, sloppy. Tongues were for eating and talking, and this was somehow both! Moon wanted to do it again, the way it wanted to eat another river spirit or taste demon-kissed blood. It should ask Raliel if she'd liked it.

Moon was so enveloped in its thoughts that when Raliel spoke again it was quite surprised.

"You couldn't stop me if you tried," she said, and smiled a little cold smile. She stepped away, letting go of his face and hand, even as Osian's mouth fell open. Through the corner of Raliel's eye, Moon could see the promise of his tongue. But Raliel wasn't looking.

She faced the sea again and bent to remove her boots.

Behind them, Osian sighed hard. "How long will it take?"

"Moon?"

I have no idea.

"If I'm not back in . . . three days? Go."

"Three days!"

"Probably less." Raliel put her socks into her boots, then dropped her bag, unbuckled her sheath and sword, and began removing her outer layers of jacket, vest, and robes. "Should I . . . leave anything?"

as little as possible. Moon suspected the shape-shifting would be difficult enough.

In the end Raliel left on her trousers and the thin under-shirt. She shivered in the cold wind, and her toes where the sea grasped again and again with the tide turned vibrant pink.

Osian asked her to take at least a knife. His were all in her bag, tucked away where Osian couldn't use them against her. It wasn't a terrible idea. Osian avoided looking at her nearly naked body, gaze averted, but when he finished speaking, he looked right into her eyes. "Please."

Raliel and Moon agreed, and she strapped it on with one of Osian's thigh sheaths, though the salt water would ruin both.

When they were ready, Moon coiled itself around her spine, slithering up into her skull. *this will be wonderful*, it said.

"Yes," Raliel replied in an eager whisper. She stared over the water again, the setting sun hot orange near the horizon. The pillar islands were directly south of where they stood on the beach. A half mile out, Moon guessed.

"Be careful," Osian murmured.

Raliel stepped into the water. Cold swallowed her calves. She stepped again, and again, until the incoming waves rushed around her thighs, sticking her thin trousers to her skin. She shuddered, hugged herself.

I'm here, Moon said.

"I know."

The ocean was on fire with the setting sun; it shoved and pulled at them, waves hitting harder and dragging more desperately as Raliel stood hip deep in the water. Shoved. Pulled. Shoved.

She closed her eyes and centered herself. Moon went with her, focusing its shadows and fingers of aether. It felt as her threads opened, the aether-points in her feet and hands, belly, heart, mouth, crown tied together with a flare of her power—Moon's power. Theirs.

It concentrated, knowing what it wanted, knowing how it should work, to pull her out of her shape and into a shape that could thrive in the ocean—see, hear, talk, swim, breathe.

"Do you feel the aether of the sea?" she whispered. Waves crashed around her. Pushing. Dragging. The sand slipped out from beneath her feet: even the earth wanted the sea.

Moon looked through her skin and eyes. Unlike the land where aether followed threads and nets, where aether streamed and lifted and tangled in roots and rivers, the aether of the sea spread everywhere, filling space, and shifting, sliding, lilting, billowing in currents and tides. Moon moaned softly, unable to help it, and Raliel opened her lips to let out the delicate cry.

oh the sea, the sea! Moon reached for it, lost to longing, and it remembered the sky, too, where the aether was wind and clouds, spun by heat and rain.

Raliel dove into the next great wave.

It was dark, loud, cold, but exhilarating. Moon laughed, and Raliel stroked deeper with her arms, kicked with her legs, just as Moon had told her to do, just as they'd practiced in her dream last night.

But Raliel held her breath, squeezed her eyes closed.

This was the only way to prove she could walk a path of sorcery. *most of us find sorcery between life and death,* The Scale had said.

open your mouth, the great demon commanded, and she did. Ocean flooded in, tangy, bitter, the salt of the whole world coating her tongue, making her pallet into a cave, rushing down her throat.

Moon pulled aether through her skin, through her mouth—there was so much!

It took and took and took while Raliel choked and flailed. She had to, had to, get to air!

Moon took control, stopped her muscles: for a long moment they hung there, suspended in the sea, aching from the heart out, rigid fingers, burning eyes.

Dying.

Then Moon exploded the aether it had gathered outward.

Raliel's back arched, and she clenched her jaw. Black and golden spots burst in her vision, her skin tore, her heart stopped.

Moon wove, shoved, screamed wordless magic, and then her name, her name, her name.

Raliel!

Raliel, catch it, help me.

do this.

be this!

She did. She curled her fingers in the water and shut her mouth. She opened her eyes again to burning-cold water, greenish-black misty in the evening. They were so deep, falling, floating.

First air: the great demon twisted the lungs and forced them to be what a shark's were, redrew connections, tore and reknotted, made infinitesimal filters and fringed gills.

Second eyes: thin inner lids, a wider pupil for more light light light.

Third skin, fourth hands, fifth bones and muscles until she was a person-shaped fish, sleek and sharp and strong.

Moon let her go, and Raliel gasped. She breathed the water, jerking, and stared out at the murky green ocean she'd kicked up to churning. Light from above, glinting, shimmering, and out to sea: gorgeous shades of blue-black-green, shadows and there—

Light.

A brilliant star glowing silver-gold.

It looked how Moon felt, how Raliel felt as she dragged fingers through water, catching on the membranes between her fingers. She pulled herself forward, then spun, laughing with a mouthful of ocean. She curled up and stretched and swam a little. Her black hair turned in a spiral around her face, and she spread her hands down her body, up again to touch the edges of her gills, the sleek change of her skin. Again she made a bubbling sound that had to be a laugh.

Moon liked it too.

They'd done it: they were a sea monster.

And the ocean pushed at them, drawing them toward that underwater star. Raliel grinned, and Moon thought, distracted, it should have made her teeth sharp. Oh well, next time!

the star, it said, and Raliel nodded.

They swam, reveling in the sensations, through the sea. Light tinged gold from the setting sun barely filtered toward them, but the star was a perfect beacon.

A flight of silver-striped fish darted past them, and they sank to go beneath a few bobbing jellies. Raliel reached out toward one of the pale orbs, but Moon tugged her hand away, nudged her stomach to make her go forward again. She laughed and obeyed.

The pillar islands thrust up from the edge of a dark ravine in the ocean floor, a gash, a crack, stretching like a smile. Coral and seagrass clung to the black rock, waving in the currents. Bright pink and yellow grasses and anemones lived up the pillars too, striping them and giving them splotches like the lichen on standing stones. In the center of the pillars a thin plinth rose, seemingly grown of corals, and upon its top glowed the star.

No, Moon realized. A tree. An aether-silver tree, reaching branches like veins streaming up up up toward the surface. Its roots crawled down down down along the pink coral plinth.

There was no other obvious place to look for a demon or sorcerer here.

They swam deeper, strong strokes and easy kicks, as if Raliel had been born to this—like Moon knew, *knew*, itself had.

As they neared, they saw the nearest of the great pillars was covered in spirit sigils. Writing!

Raliel neared it without needing Moon to suggest it. She caught herself against the rough black stone and brushed away a tangle of grass. Moon read:

Build a god with breath of salt

Raliel followed the lines of sigils, around and around, lower and lower against the pillar, and they read the entire poem:

> Build a god with breath of salt
> Bones of coral, volcanic steam
> Sand and teeth and dolphin dreams
> Build its heart with scales
> With fins and gills
> The songs of whales
> Build its temper with shipwrecks
> The tongue of oysters chewing pearls
> The smile of a shark
> But always its blood is our blood

As Raliel paused her hand against the final sigil, Moon asked, is this about a demon, or a god?

Before Raliel could find a way to answer, something dragged sharply at her hair.

She cried out, voice strange and thick and low, and together they kicked, turning. Raliel put her back to the pillar, ignoring the sharp pain as hair was pulled from her scalp. Grabbing Osian's knife, she held it blade-down, and faced their attacker.

A creature floated before them. Person-shaped, with two legs, two arms, a single head, but there the resemblance ended: its round eyes were far apart, covered in a sheen of membrane, its nose mere slits and its mouth lipless with very sharp lines of teeth showing as it sucked water. Beautiful green-blue scales covered its body, overlapping and dangerous, with spines on its elbows and knees, at its hips, and five flares of them in rows along its skull. It was small, like a child, but Moon thought it was fully grown.

It moved its mouth and one hand with an intention that spoke of a language.

Raliel shook her head, attempted to speak back.

The creature gestured at the pillar. "Oh!" Raliel said, though it was mostly a burst of water. She moved to the pillar and drifted up its length to a strip of basalt that had no spirit sigils. She looked back, and the creature had followed. Staring at them from the distance of an arm's reach.

With a finger, Raliel drew the sigils that appeared just below this space: *bones of coral*.

She did it again, and a third time, looking evenly into the sea creature's strange eyes. The creature reached and spread its fingers; it pressed two against the basalt and wrote a sigil. *bone*, then added the plural signifier.

Delight, like laughter, bubbled in Raliel's throat, and Moon purred, proud of her.

Raliel wrote, *meet sea demon*.

With a flick of its long-boned feet, the creature flattened its hand over the sigil for demon.

Raliel turned to gesture at the silver-aether tree, then wrote *meet sea demon* again.

The creature did not respond. Except bubbles, a stream of water, burst out from behind its ear, as if expelled in frustration.

use the poem, Moon said.

Raliel moved around the pillar to tap the sigil *god*.

The creature drew the god sigil.

Raliel wrote, *meet god*

After a moment staring at Raliel, the creature wrote, *what are you*

of air

The creature expelled water from behind its ears again.

Moon said, *I'm going to shift you again, welcome it*

Then Moon flexed the aether woven throughout this shape of theirs, breaking the smooth sharkskin, letting it peel away to reveal hardened dark green-gray scales. It lengthened Raliel's bones, made it mirror the creature more, while the creature clutched the pillar, staring.

Raliel curled over herself at the sensations, jaw clenched as Moon pushed these changes, but she did welcome it. She reveled in the alluring sensations; as did Moon. It gave her thicker chest armor and slicked shadowy fingers against her scalp until spines burst out through her long black hair. Suddenly Raliel flung out her arms and legs, spread like a starfish, and arched her back.

The sea creature's elbow spines jutted out, and it shoved away in shock. But it did not flee.

Raliel reached to the pillar and against the basalt wrote, *meet god*

Only hesitating a moment, the creature made its way to the end of the long spiraling poem. It caressed *blood is our blood*

Then, below the blood sigil, it added, *feed.*

oh! Moon understood. *give the tree your blood. summon the demon!*

273

Just then, more of these sea creatures appeared out of the distant ocean waters. Various shades of green and blue, a few with streaks of white and eye-popping orange spines. More of them reached out their scaled hands.

Raliel bowed her head, then suddenly turned and swam hard for the silver tree.

It gave off a cool power, familiar to both Moon and Raliel. Pure aether. As it glowed, aether stripped away from it in wisps like smoke, fading into the wilder aether of the ocean. Moon wondered if the tree *was* the demon.

Raliel stopped moving, holding herself carefully in place against the push of the currents, and reached for a slender white branch.

Blood, Moon whispered.

She paused, then took Osian's knife and cut her hand open. Salt water stung badly but blood blossomed bright red, a sweet puff drifting on the little currents that warred among the three pillars.

A tingle of power slithered down her spine.

Immediately she grasped a branch of the tree, teeth bared, and smeared its blood to the glimmering wood.

The sea exploded.

They were knocked back by a wave hard and heavy as stone, flung away. All Moon could do was wrap Raliel's arms around her head as they careened through the water.

They slammed into rock—one of the pillars—and water pressed so that she couldn't move or breathe. The sea itself bound them in place. But Raliel struggled to look.

The sea demon was *there*.

Massive!

Moon laughed in glee—in *terror.* In glee.

The sea demon filled the space, swarming around the tree, a thousand jagged teeth and whip-thin tentacles, scales and spines and black ink.

Raliel yelled through the water *great sea demon I am Raliel Dark-Smile, I*

The sea demon opened a single mouth, and its roar was stronger than the tide, blowing them back.

DEMON! it screamed. *I DEVOUR YOU! I DESTROY YOU! MINE THIS IS MINE GET OUT GET AWAY*

Fear pinched Raliel's heart. Her bones were pure ice. Moon hissed, *we need it*

Raliel clutched at her heart, the bleeding palm trailing threads of blood in the water like magic. Her shape shuddered, her bones unraveling.

Raliel, Moon said desperately. She did not respond. She held on to herself, and Moon felt her panic, her determination to quell it. She dug her nails into her bleeding palm and drew in a huge breath of water.

But she was shaking apart.

Moon needed to talk to the sea demon! Moon needed—it *needed*—it needed to keep Raliel alive.

The great sea demon billowed even larger: Moon reached for all the wild ocean-aether it could and ripped.

A burst of power lit them up like a starburst, as if the ocean salt itself popped with aether.

That power thrust them free of the pressing ocean, and Raliel angled her trembling arms forward like an arrow. They shot away.

The sea demon gave chase.

FIVE

OSIAN REDPOP WAS FAMILIAR with waiting. Soldiers, especially those trained for the palace, learned early how to wait without growing complacent. And to look good doing it. Osian wasn't too concerned about how he looked at the moment, internally bedraggled from being repeatedly possessed, raked over the coals for multiple offenses, and caught out in the demon-kissed lie he'd lived and breathed for ten years.

What he wanted to do was collapse on the beach and stare out over the water in a daze, anxious and eager and honored and afraid and maybe the slightest bit in love. This tangle of emotions knotted up his stomach to the point where he thought stretching physically on the ground might be the only cure.

But he didn't. He couldn't. He needed to remain vigilant. So Osian settled himself as he always did: taking his slow time moving through basic breathing exercises, then footwork dance, and finally, as the sun disappeared under the ocean horizon, he picked up his sword to run forms.

He'd missed his sword the last three days. The weight in his hand, the poise it brought him, the soft leather of the grip made him remember himself. But tonight it wasn't enough. Panting hard, he lowered it until the tip skimmed the sand. The ocean rushed in and out, the tide pushing closer to him. It reached with foam hands.

Far out at the pillar islands, black now against the streaks of gold and pale violet in the southwest sky, Osian noticed the surface of the ocean glinting with light. As if a bright moon had appeared in the sky and reflected off the choppy waves.

Osian stared at the light for a while, then turned and stomped up the beach to the pile of their things. He flopped down, boneless in the lack of witnesses. He found water and a bun. Ate them. The wind was cool but not cold, brushing hair back from his face; overhead the stars slowly peeked out of the midnight blue. A few clouds drifted inland. He could hear nothing but the crashing of waves. The rhythm wasn't perfect, but he matched his breath to it, sinking into a shallow meditation.

Suddenly he snapped out of it, gasping for breath, clutching his chest with both hands.

He had no idea what had jarred him, but the physical panic reminded him of stumbling back every time the great demon let him go.

Osian closed his eyes, recalling the heat in his cheeks that first night, when he'd been poised to cut Raliel's throat, determined, pushing himself, but incapable. Afraid. Weary. So incredibly sad. Then her eyes had snapped open and he'd—

Woken up tied to the bed. With a wavering ache in his legs and lungs like he'd been racing. His mouth had felt just slightly bitten. Being possessed had been all-consuming; he only remembered it like a dream: swaying lanterns, empty shadowed market, running, a laugh, a kiss.

That's the part he was really angry about. He'd wanted to kiss Raliel Dark-Smile himself since the moment he saw her, and obviously, of course, had not. Would not. But he didn't *get* to be angry about that. Because of the lies. Instead, he'd begged forgiveness. Put all his truths into his eyes, his voice, his dimples. He'd watched her tuck her anger away behind that cold facade.

To get back the softer trust, the warmth she'd just begun to offer him, Osian had told her everything. The important parts, if not the details. Picked her side. Even though his mother would hate him. Never forgive him.

Osian Redpop was unfamiliar with questioning his own integrity. Strange, perhaps, for a spy, for a secret weapon sent to infiltrate the imperial palace. But Osian had always known what was right: Obeying his mother. Obeying his commanders. The two had never been in conflict. He learned, he worked, he surpassed expectations. He learned to be himself. To like it. He reported sometimes to his mother.

In ten years he'd seen Syra only twice. Each time she'd seemed frail—not older, but ill, feverish. The light in her eye focused entirely on him. Osian knew if he betrayed his mother, she'd lose the only tether she had to life. To reality. Something in her had been torn away when his father was killed, something nobody could give her back. She could do it herself, maybe, but she wouldn't. She'd mourned Skybreaker for twenty-four years. Half her life. All of Osian's.

Sometimes he wondered what his childhood would have been if his mother had loved his father just a little bit less.

It made him shy away from love, himself. Choose flirting and smiles instead, friendships too precarious and brief to risk deeper connection.

Then he'd been possessed by a demon. Experienced the disorienting sensation of being known. It was terrible. But also— a relief. Something knew him. A demon, but still. Moon knew him. Every shred of him. Maybe it was mostly intoxicating.

Osian snapped to his feet. He left the bags, picked up his sword and Raliel's, and jogged up the beach in the darkness, toward the little crossroads shrine set at the edge of the rain forest, where sand and stubbly grass became ferns and mud.

When he reached the shrine, he dropped to his knees and placed the swords to either side of his legs. The shrine was built of small stones glued together with crumbling plaster, in the shape of a pointed hood. A tiny dragon statue snaked against the back, curling up and down around an offering plate scattered with ashes.

From his pocket he pulled his paper, with the last of his thin charcoal sticks tucked into a ribbon. He wrote quickly against his thigh: *Mother. I am stopping this. I love you.*

He lit incense and prayed softly to the crossroads of land and sea. Then he rolled his letter placed a small river stone over it. He cut his tongue one final time and spat the blood onto the stone. Osian took a shaky breath, then slammed the butt of his sword against it until it shattered.

Message delivered, Osian returned to the stretch of beach for his vigil. His hands trembled slightly, and he held his own and Raliel's swords tightly. It was done.

He felt . . . good.

Osian would not be welcome at the palace again after this, but if he could remain honest, that should be enough. He could do almost anything else, with his memory and skills. And maybe—maybe—Raliel would allow him to go with her for the rest of her journey, and he could be her friend.

Unburdened, Osian had just begun to settle down on the sand for the long night vigil, when the surface of the ocean exploded upward.

A massive wave of black water rose, spraying in a great sparkling arc halfway between the shore and the pillar islands. It was so large it blocked the pillars, blocked most of the sky. Osian gaped, backing up. He stumbled over the bags, then cussed at himself. He was, if not demon-kissed, an elite imperial warrior. Better than this.

He drew both swords and stood at the edge of the tide, blades bared to the sea.

The wave crashed down, shoving wave after smaller wave toward him. A bulbous shape rose—broad-backed and wet, black and red, rough as raw pumice. Then it vanished again, with another great wave. Osian's pulse pounded. He shifted his weight.

When the creature appeared again it was a lot closer.

It burst up: this time in the starlight Osian saw teeth and tentacles; he heard a shriek and a long wail like a flute's off-key scream.

He'd never seen anything alive so huge.

The tide ruffled furiously, lapping at his ankles. He clenched his jaw. If he didn't see Raliel soon, he'd back off. This wasn't a monster to fight for fun.

It roiled tentacles, reaching, and dove again. A wind that smelled of old fish and briny rot gusted at him, and before he could gag, he saw a tiny splash among the angry waves near to shore. A head? A head! Arms!

"Raliel!" he yelled, leaping into the ocean. His boots soaked immediately, water dragged at his legs, and he kept going. "Raliel!"

Sea spray scoured his cheeks rough as sand, and he yelled her name again as she struggled to shore. She was gray as death, skin ragged—scaled?—hair tangled—her eyes were huge black orbs.

Osian froze for a second, breathless. But it was her. He knew it. "Raliel, I'm here. Come here!"

He held both swords high, wishing he could activate the aether-sigils on hers to make it shine like a beacon—even if that drew the monster, she'd get here first.

Then a tentacle slapped beside her and she dove sideways, flailing.

Osian was waist-deep and it was so hard to move, to shove himself against the driving waves. "Raliel!"

He thrust a sword at the tentacle. Scales deflected the sword, and he jabbed with the other, up against the scales: that worked better, but was not nearly enough.

Behind him Raliel struggled still, disrupting the sand and water. Osian struggled to hold his stance as he slashed at the tentacle. She did something and a burst of aether shoved around him, blasting the monster back. Her cry garbled, like a wet cough, and Osian turned to grab her, to help her, but the monster shrieked again. A pressure of air shoved him aside, and the tentacles chased after Raliel. Osian gritted his teeth and threw himself at the nearest one. It knocked him under, but he drove his swords up. His sword caught in scales and was torn away. He let it go.

His lungs burned as he attacked with both hands on the heir's sword: one on the grip, the other on the counterweight for leverage and force. He rose out of the water, salt stinging, blood in his mouth, and the monster loomed over him, blocking the whole sky as seawater rained down on him. Osian did not look for Raliel. He felt magic driving at the monster; he felt magic on his skin, and with a yell he stabbed at the monster. He was between tentacles, small and too close to be easily grasped: he hit hard, sliding the sword between ridged scales.

The monster screamed and reared: Osian was dragged underwater. He choked. He felt fire on his thigh and side. Water was a thousand furious hands pulling and pushing at him. All he could do was hold tight to the sword and try not to breathe. He felt a tentacle around his leg and with one hand grabbed a knife from his thigh sheath and stabbed down.

His head burst out of the water and he breathed: he choked again, coughing, and couldn't see, but a silver-blue light drew him in one direction. Osian did not swim well, but his toes skimmed something and he tried. Oh, he tried.

"Osian!" he heard as a huge claw swung at him. He twisted, but it caught his side, throwing him up, up, up and he fell again, slamming into the waves. Osian was nothing but pain, caught unable to breathe: sharp pain, empty black overwhelming pain! He felt air, sea spray, reached with one hand and cracked open his eyes just as light whipped over him, a web of lightning, and then a roar blew out his ears and Osian fainted.

SIX

B Y THE TIME RALIEL and Moon dragged Osian up to the edge of the beach, she thought she would shake completely apart. Freezing, aching, somehow also on absolute fire, she panted, struggled to breathe with her barely reworked lungs, and finally collapsed. Osian still held her sword, clutched to his chest. His mouth was slack, thin blood pinked across his teeth, his clothes and body were waterlogged.

Raliel leaned back, holding him against her chest, in her lap, and wrapped her arms around him. He breathed raggedly. So did she.

Night pressed down against them. The ocean shoved loudly at the beach, churning waves leaving streaks of bloody foam against the sand.

Moon crouched next to her, looking like a second Osian— dream Moon, Osian copy, pitch-black hair and frost-white skin, huge eyes, dimples gouged to either side of its frown.

Was this a dream? Raliel blinked hard. She held the real Osian, both of them covered in blood.

Moon had blood on its face, too. Looking at her.

"Raliel," it said. Stunned.

It wasn't inside her. Raliel couldn't feel it under her heart. She was *looking at it*. With a shaky hand, she reached out and touched its jaw. Its skin was smooth and cold under her fingers. Then it vanished.

Raliel's back arched at the shock of bright, sharp aether. It tore through her, in through her open mouth and eyes, her palms. Raliel gasped loud and hugged her arms tighter around Osian. She pressed her cheek down against his head. The wind was so cold, but her heart was hot with Moon's power. It sucked and pulled from the land: she felt the hiss of it, like a dim echo of Moon's roar when it had grabbed hold of the ocean-aether and with raw power driven them away from the sea demon.

Then on the beach: Moon next to her. Manifested. They'd transformed, but not completely. She couldn't catch her breath. Her insides were—off. "Moon," she whispered, shocked and in pain. Her body hurt. Bled. This was not all Osian's blood.

hold on, Moon said inside her.

Shivering hard, Raliel clenched her teeth. She felt hot, not cold, but maybe it was shock, fever, she wasn't sure. She pressed her eyes tightly closed as Moon filled her with magic. Finished reworking her lungs and bones and flesh.

Raliel thought, *If this were sorcery, I could do it myself.*

Osian groaned quietly. His breath was shallow, too. Raliel needed to get him to a healer. There was a town two miles west of here. Jellyfish Rest. "Moon," she said, more a whisper than words, "stabilize him, too, if you can. Get inside him, if you must."

The power flexed inside her. Sparked. Raliel sneezed. It

popped her ears, and she felt dizzy. Wrapping herself around Osian, she tried to think what to do. Fire. Warmth. Dry clothes.

you're not injured anymore, Moon said. *just exhausted. when I go to him, it will be worse.*

"Do it."

just to keep him alive.

Raliel nodded, then whimpered as Moon jumped from her hands and lips to Osian's head and chest. Osian, in her arms, stiffened. Then Raliel noticed nothing but the vast, spinning emptiness of fatigue. She grasped at consciousness, and failed.

When she woke, she was warmer, still embracing Osian. Night remained thick. It couldn't have been long. Moon was a cold weight under her heart.

get up, Raliel. you can. we'll pull aether. leave everything, we can get new things.

"My—my mother's fan. Father's agate."

Moon did something against her sternum that felt like a sneer. Raliel ignored it, carefully putting Osian down and struggling to the dark lumps of their bags. She was in no pain, just trembling. She fumbled with the ties but managed to pull out almost everything. Then she stripped fast of her soaked shirt and trousers. She dressed in most of her remaining layers, pulled on her boots, and from the tiny side pocket she pulled her diamond ring and replaced it on her forefinger. She tucked her other gifts, fire papers, money, and a knife into her belt, then grabbed Osian's bag.

The warrior shivered where she'd left him, still unconscious. Raliel undressed him quickly, jaw clenched. It was difficult because he was loose and couldn't help—but Moon did. They got him in dry clothes but had to put his wet boots back on. By the time that was finished, she sweated down her spine and her fingers were stiff as sticks. "Can you help me carry him?"

She wanted to ask if it could manifest again. How it had done it. How.

Moon said, *no, I don't know. but I can make him walk.*

That's what they did: Moon possessed Osian, and Raliel helped drag him to his feet. They stumbled, in sand-covered disarray, to the town.

Raliel recalled very little of it, barely aware of more than putting one foot before the other, her arm around Osian's shoulders. Moon said her name sometimes, in Osian's gravelly, ocean-wrecked voice, and she said his in return. They trudged. They found the road. They reached the town gate at dawn and slumped against it. It was the best she could do. As they slouched down to lean against the wood in the darkness, Moon said Osian's leg was inflamed, three left ribs broken, and he had scratches and massive bruises, plus damage to his throat and lungs, but only from nearly drowning, not from broken bones or ruptured anything. "He'll survive, probably," Moon wheezed from Osian's mouth.

"Good," Raliel sighed. Her head lolled back against the gate. She heaved herself to her feet and pounded on the slats of wood.

Immediately her heavy pleas were answered. A gatekeeper hurried to get more help, and Raliel and Osian were taken to a nearby inn. Osian was carried to the second level (Moon jumped back to Raliel before she let go of Osian's hand), and the warrior was put into a room while Raliel explained they'd had an accident on the beach with a demon. She didn't bother hiding her identity, but begged them not to send word anywhere—this was her Heir's Journey, and with the generosity of the town, she and her companion would thrive. A healer pushed past her to fall at Osian's bedside, and as she began, she ordered Raliel to explain what she knew. Raliel did her best without giving away anything magical about how she knew Osian's injuries. The healer ordered everyone but her assistant out, though Raliel remained. She kept out of the way, kneeling by the foot of the bed, and put her hand on Osian's ankle.

Three nights ago he tried to kill her. Tonight he had saved her life.

For an hour the healer worked, murmuring to her assistant. They used small sigils to knock moisture out of his lungs, then a chest compress to draw more out slowly. His thigh wound was a deep gash from the sea demon's claw, and the healer cleaned it twice with different tools, wrapped it with another compress and two blood-drawn sigils. She told Raliel once the infection was defeated she'd sew it up. Moon whispered to Raliel, *I can slip back into him when she leaves and help.*

Raliel tapped her finger against her chest because she couldn't speak.

Osian's ribs would have to heal on their own, and the healer said he'd be off his feet for a couple of weeks at least. Again Moon silently disagreed. When Osian was packed into bed and sleeping instead of unconscious, the healer flat-out commanded Raliel to get into the other bed and submit to examination. Raliel allowed it, uncertain how strange it would be that she had so little injury in comparison. But the healer said nothing except that Raliel was going to collapse from exhaustion. She was given a small restorative potion to drink and ordered to sleep. Raliel promised. She gave the healer money, asking it be spread to all who'd helped tonight.

"Today," the doctor grumbled, glancing at the bright sunlight.

Raliel closed her eyes, intending to begin interrogating Moon the moment the doctor was gone, but fell asleep instantly.

———

Moon had overestimated its ability to heal both Raliel and Osian, thanks to a lack of access to aether. If Raliel could have ventured outside of town to find a spirit or two, or drawn sigils for summoning aether, they might have banked enough to help, but as it was, the first day they relied on what Moon had done initially and the healer's skill. Raliel slept for nearly a full day and night, waking early at the following dawn. She felt sore all over, and her head pounded from thirst and hunger. After checking on Osian, she stumbled to a washroom to relieve herself and drink several gulps from the pitcher before it occurred to her to moderate what she threw into her stomach.

"Moon," she said, voice rough.

here. you are healthy, just out of sorts. we expended every drop of your power. our power.

"Can you do more for Osian?"

you eat first. I won't leave you unless you're in the room, right there.

"Yes," she agreed vehemently.

The innkeeper's husband, called Rugo, set up a bath in the other guest room, currently unoccupied, and had food, water, and tea brought to her. Raliel ate a bit and fell asleep in the tub. Moon woke her before too long, and Raliel wished it could help her with her hair. It hung wet and unwashed past her waist. Perhaps she should have chopped it all off before this journey.

"Do you know how you manifested?" she whispered.

unsure.

Raliel nodded reluctantly. It may merely have been a combination of transformation, the wild ocean-aether, and her panic that had led to the right circumstances.

Osian did not wake until later that afternoon, once the doctor returned to change his bandages and sew up his thankfully uninfected thigh wound. Raliel insisted on remaining to help and learn exactly what needed doing, so that she might do it herself. It was during the stitching that Osian's eyes fluttered. Raliel held his hand, murmuring his name to remind him of her presence, and smoothed his brow, tracing the lines of demonkissed blue.

The doctor said Osian was doing well, all things considered.

Thus passed three days, while Raliel recovered almost entirely, and Osian slowly drew near enough to health that he could remain awake for most of the day. Raliel and Moon left twice to meet the innkeeper's family, to eat with the mayor and other townsfolk. She did her best to warm her smile and speak of her travels, asking many questions of the people to set them at ease, but she demurred often, promising them a better time when her companion Osian woke. It seemed to charm them, her concern for him, as well as her interest in their lives. Raliel and Osian's abandoned belongings had been returned from the beach, and those who'd been sent to investigate her demonic accident reported a great swath of dead forest at the edge of the beach: curled, blackened with rot, drained of aether.

Raliel said she had drawn on aether to protect herself and Osian, and the rot must have been the result of the sea demon. The townsfolk had stories about the sea demon, though they called it a monster, and knew it appeared when the glow rose from the heart of the three pillar islands. It had never ventured to shore before, never bothered them so long as they did not stray beyond the pillars after the sun set.

That night, lying in bed, she whispered to Moon about what had happened to them in the ocean.

"It *was* a great demon, wasn't it?" Raliel remembered the sheer power it had wielded, that billowed off it like warring currents. Its form, so strange and monstrous. A regular demon would take the form of the spirit it had been: a dolphin spirit or spirit of a reef. Not a bizarre combination of tentacles and claws and fins. "The spirit languages on the pillar island called it a god. The little sea person worshipped it."

no god. Moon made a sound like a snort. *I would know a god.*

"A demon, then."

yes. it was not possessing a great whale or abyssal squid. but manifested like Night Shine. it must be a great demon. and it must have a sorcerer in order to manifest beyond its house. spirits and demons cannot leave their houses. we know this. only great spirits or great demons can do that, and only with a sorcerer.

"No, that's not quite true," she said, and Moon poked her rib at the disagreement. But she continued. "At the palace, you can manifest. Inside the Palace of Seven Circles, when you are with all of us, inside the palace-amulet, you can give yourself physical form. Without a sorcerer—because you have the amulet. And my parents. It has only been since we left—since I stole you away from your house—that you could not. Night Shine does it away from her house, because she has a sorcerer. But . . ." Raliel thought about the song etched into the basalt pillar. What she'd managed to read of it: *build a god with breath of salt, bones of coral, volcanic steam, sand and teeth and dolphin dreams. Build its heart with scales . . . the songs of whales. . . . The tongue of oysters chewing pearls, the smile of a shark. But always its blood is our blood.* "Moon . . . the song on the pillar, it makes it seem like the sea people create the sea demon. Their god. They build it like pilgrims, with flesh of the sea and their own blood. . . . Do you think they—all the sea people—are its house? A different sort of amulet? Like my parents all are bound to you? 'Build a god with breath of salt,' it read. I wish that the great demon would have talked to us instead of just attacking!"

Moon purred in thought. Raliel touched the silver disk amulet that rested against her heart. This had allowed her to remove Moon from its house, but the price had been its ability to manifest, to be itself. Then The Scale had tweaked it in order to allow Moon to possess other temporary houses.

Finally, Moon said, *maybe you are correct about the sea people, but there must be more to it. I cannot do what it did. it hit you physically. it touched Osian. it displaced water with its body, not with only aether. everything I do is aether-based, even in the palace. that's why I cannot taste: I am not manifest. not like that. not like Night Shine.*

"You did, though. On the beach. You were there. I touched you."

I remember, but I was . . . confused, desperate.

"Was it sorcery?"

seemed so. we used so much power, and you almost died, you were breathing air and water both. maybe that was enough in-between. we were many things at once, and so it worked? but I thought it would need to be more than sorcery—I would have to be your familiar, too. we would need to make a bond of our own.

"We have managed sorcery, grasped at it, but cannot hold it. Maybe the palace-amulet binds us too much into one thing for us to be liminal, or . . . move beyond it?"

if so we are still as stuck as always. want to break the amulet, but need sorcery to do so. cannot do sorcery without changing the amulet.

Biting her lip, Raliel wondered what they were missing.

In her dreams, Raliel raced through the water, swimming, clawing herself through dark salt water. Moon chased her, Moon screamed and laughed behind her, and when it caught her by the ankle, talons hooked through her flesh, catching her bones. Pain burned up her leg. She choked on the water, choked like she was only human, and Raliel gasped awake in the dark inn room.

Raliel, Moon soothed.

She shuddered, holding the blankets close to her chest.

The room was small, with space enough for the two low beds, an eating table, and a desk but little else. The walls were pale wood with only a single long painted banner across from the window and a privacy screen folded unused at the foot of Osian's bed.

"Raliel?"

Osian. His voice wavered between a whisper and gravel.

Hopping up immediately, Raliel crossed the slight space in the dark and perched on the side of his bed. "I'm here," she murmured, touching his temple. "Are you thirsty?"

He curled his fingers around her wrist. "You had a nightmare."

"Hmm. I am fine. Let me get you water."

But by the time she returned, he was asleep again.

he belongs to you, Moon whispered.

"What?" Raliel's surprise pushed the word aloud. Osian shifted on the pillow.

you heard me. because of this, he is yours. take him back. forgive him. he will do anything for you now.

"We'll see."

SEVEN

R ALIEL AND HER COMPANIONS remained in the town of Jellyfish Rest for six days. The healer was more than shocked at Osian's swift recovery but couldn't deny that he *was* recovered.

Raliel and Moon had begun to venture out by the third day to stretch her legs and speak freely about the sea demon and everything they'd learned transforming together and from The Scale. While hiking, they drew extra aether to bring back to the inn so that Moon could possess Osian awhile and repair his broken bones and deepest gashes more quickly. It was uncomfortable for Osian but a necessary price. Osian expressed his thanks every time. When he climbed out of bed on his own and took his first solo bath, feeding himself and doing everything necessary without breaking into a sweat on day four, he bowed deeply to Raliel and stayed there until she lifted him out of it. She didn't release him, letting her hands slide down his arms to clasp his hands instead.

They read to each other most evenings, until Osian was well enough to join the small crowd down in the dining room. Osian did well reading the adventures, adding voices and the occasional commentary. Moon commented, too, and Raliel laughed a little, able to share his thoughts with Osian as she couldn't on the road so many weeks ago. That reminded Moon of his critiques of Osian's stories and led to a vibrant but strange debate between them, with Raliel as a reluctant, eye-rolling moderator.

Laughing so often relaxed Raliel, though she breathed cold into herself every morning and maintained distance despite sitting perched on the same low bed as they read at night. Raliel preferred the poetry, though it was not all very good—she liked poetry of the seasons, of landscapes and intricate invocations of light and earth and sky. These poems were overwrought love poems, entertaining in their own way, and occasionally surprised her with an absolutely heart-wrenching perfect line to steal her breath. Moon liked when it felt the poetry change her body.

In the mornings they did stretches and gentle paired sword-forms—with a new sword for Osian purchased from the local blacksmith. Osian talked about his childhood most easily when exercising, and Raliel discovered so did she.

It was a revelation—she'd never spent time like this with anyone but her parents and her coterie, but they already knew what her life had been like, her schedule and preferences. They weren't resigned to complete honesty. They didn't ask why she loved the standing harp over the lap harp or the round guitar, or all stringed instruments over the flute and whistle. For Osian such questions were just conversation, and at the same time he listened as if her answers hid the secrets of not only her heart but perhaps the entire galaxy. She showed him the sigils on her sword, what they meant and how they worked. When he asked if his new sword could be awoken to aether, she promised to try.

On the fifth day, Moon and Raliel discovered the key to manifestation in lines of that very overwrought poetry.

until the morning bruise
dark sunrise on your shoulder
kisses manifest in flesh

Raliel worked the lines silently against her tongue as she walked along the beach with Moon curled under her heart. She made it a tuneless song, a rhythm, as she picked up pretty spiral shells. They reached the two-mile mark, and she headed for the forest to return along a deer path easy to cull for an aether-meal.

"Moon," she said. "I've been thinking about manifestation."

The great demon purred as it reached with her hand to grasp a branch and drink up a cold tingle of power.

"Night Shine has a *body*. One that she shape-shifts rather like a sorceress herself. Because she was reborn in the palace. She is different from Lutha's great spirit Murmur, different from your palace form, that cannot eat or feel. Night Shine was reborn through a piece of the sorceress's heart, Lutha said. Flesh and blood. And the sea demon . . . it was manifest. Not possessing a monster—there are no monsters like that except built by magic. And the sea people feed it blood."

yes.

"My blood was everywhere that night. When you manifested. We did sorcery, and my blood . . ." Raliel stopped walking. "There was a blood ritual I read about, where dawn priests used blood to force a demon to *end* a possession."

Moon shivered inside her. *should we make the attempt?*

"I am willing," she whispered back. "How?"

I do not know. I can touch your blood. As the demon spoke, it gripped her heart, and Raliel gasped at the pain—it darted through her chest to her back as though she'd been stabbed.

"Ouch," she hissed. The demon released her, and she bent, catching herself on her knees, head hanging. Heat surged up her neck to her cheeks and ears; her pulse pounded in her skull. Moon went still as she breathed herself cool again. Then she took Osian's knife from her belt and held the blade to her forefinger. She cut, not too deep.

After the heart-squeeze, it barely registered. Blood welled quickly into a single, glorious fat drop.

Moon pushed through her arm to her hand, a web of frost, and the blood vanished.

But a dark shape appeared before her, wavering. The great demon trying to manifest.

"More," she said, and cut again, making sure it would bleed harder, and only vaguely aware she should have chosen a different location on her body.

Blood dripped and a shadow-hand caught it. The hand solidified and blood vanished again, in lines like deeper black veins through the shadow. Suddenly seven eyes appeared, perfectly round and moon-gray white. Raliel felt the cold pressure of the silver amulet on her breastbone. She dropped the knife and dug for it, revealing it to air. The entire time she stared at the seven eyes.

A shadow, her height and size, a mirror of shadows wearing too many eyes, formed right before her. Raliel panted shallowly, in anticipation and wonder.

Moon touched her.

Moon *touched her*. A cold brush of something like fur against her finger, then palm. She laughed in shock—then the great demon burst apart, and Raliel staggered backward under the force of Moon driving hard through the amulet again.

Power surged inside her rib cage. She closed her eyes, catching herself.

Raliel, Moon whispered, and made a sound like a whimper and a gasp.

"Moon."

it worked. just enough.

Raliel was covered in sweat. She wiped her brow and shuddered all over. Picking up the knife, she balanced it on her palm. The light seemed too bright, and the wind through the forest rushed harshly in her ears. "Again?"

I have an idea.

She pressed the wound on her finger again. It hurt more this time but bled eagerly.

brace.

Raliel did, shifting into a strong foot base, as if going on the defense with her sword.

Moon dragged aether into her body, in a huge, sharp tug: grass browned and curled dead in a circle three paces wide, with Raliel at the center. She gasped, mouth sticking open. Her body ached suddenly, but it wasn't pain—it was a soreness born of well-worked muscles.

There was no transition this time except an afterimage of aether-threads in front of her, replaced immediately by Osian.

Dream Osian. The white-skinned, black-haired, aether-eyed

Osian Moon had made again and again in her dreams. And that night on the beach.

It wavered, its skin shivering unpleasantly. Its eyes blinked—became gray-silver mottled like the moon. Unnaturally plain shirt and trousers covered it and boots that looked drawn on, not real. Painted in thin watercolor ink.

But Moon stood manifest, there in the world.

Raliel stared. The amulet was brittle-cold in her hand.

Moon wriggled its shoulders, rolled them, widened those eyes. It was so cute—dangerously, shockingly adorable in this menacing Osian form. Then it grinned, and its teeth were ever so slightly sharper. Not so much the teeth would give its game away, but enough to unsettle. Raliel found herself nodding slowly. Dizziness swept over her.

"Raliel," it said, voice softer and slightly deeper than Osian's. Like a careful caress rather than a joyful poke.

"Moon."

"I think . . ." The demon tilted its head, and its hair didn't quite behave like hair, floating with too much intention as it slid loose across Moon's back to sweep its shoulder. Because Moon considered how hair should follow the gesture, rather than letting its hair do what air and gravity dictated.

Raliel felt a new, foreign sensation pool in her belly. An awareness of . . . she did not know.

"It will not last very long, like this," Moon finally finished its thought.

"I am dizzy, a little. I can manage, but we should . . . practice."

"Only your blood will work. Or your parents'."

Reaching with her bloody hand, Raliel grasped Moon's

wrist. It was solid. With just a bit of giving skin over the knob of bone. She gripped tighter. "Moon," she said, and looked up at its lovely eyes. They stood so close. Moon's gaze was level with her mouth.

For a moment the ground tilted under her. Moon leaned nearer and caught her arm. It snorted, a little half smile on its face. Raliel's lashes fluttered in her disorientation. "Did you take . . . more than blood?"

"I had to channel it through you. The aether. It's all through you. That is what sorcery would make easier, I think . . . if you had your own links to aether. If you were a sorcerer, I could do this forever."

"Moon, you have a voice!" she whispered, delighted, cheeks pink and mind swimming as though tipsy. "I like it."

"Ah, my heir, here, here," the great demon murmured, and then the grip on her hand vanished.

She stumbled, surprised to be alone, but Moon slithered its cold-snake fingers throughout her body and caught her from the inside. *Raliel,* it said inside her, sounding as before, a purr, a whisper, a beloved voice only in her mind.

Together they breathed there, standing with the same feet and heart and flesh. Breathing in time, slow, inviting her aether-channels back to their controlled dimensions.

"We did it," she said softly, when she felt strong again. She tucked the knife away and took them back to Jellyfish Rest.

EIGHT

THE FIRST THING MOON said to Osian, from a body all its own, was, "Osian was your father's name too."

It happened on their first full day on the road north. They'd started off early, with a horse and plenty of supplies, and a packet of letters to be delivered to the crossroads station. Raliel had sent her own letter nearly a week ago now, to the Emperor with the Moon in His Mouth, relating a few details about Osian's confession so that her father could bolster any necessary defenses to the palace on the off chance Syra Bear Mistress or the twin sorcerers took further action. It should arrive within another week, depending on the weather. She had not mentioned the ordeal with the great sea demon, nor her work with Moon.

They had considered returning home. So much had happened, and now that Moon knew how to manifest physically, the palace would not be the same kind of prison. They could work on the palace-amulet in the capital, safe. She could continue studying the path of sorcery.

But this was her only Heir's Journey. If they did not manage to change the palace-amulet, this was their last chance to be a little free. Moon had said, *we have been gone nearly two months. there should be snow already in the northern mountains.* By the gentle longing in its voice, Raliel understood it wished to keep going too.

Besides, a reckless part of Raliel wanted to confront Syra Bear Mistress herself. Challenge her. Take care of this problem on her own. Prove she was strong enough—good enough—to be emperor someday, by vanquishing such an enemy. If the twin sorcerers were there, Raliel and Moon should face them together. Maybe—and this was the truly reckless part—becoming a sorcerer required such a risk, such desperation. Between life and death, between night and day, between girl and dragon.

Perhaps it was a bad decision, but they were in accord. They would go north, to the Mountain of One Thousand Falls, to spend the winter in snow and sorcery practice and visit Whitelar Town, where Osian had grown up. Confront and arrest Syra Bear Mistress for plotting against the emperor. They did not mention that part to Osian—yet.

The horse they had now was a gift from the people of Jellyfish Rest, despite Raliel's protests, for the honor of aiding the heir on her journey. It did make travel easier, if not faster, as all their belongings could be piled on the horse without overwhelming it in the slightest.

They stopped for lunch at a small meadow where the road bent around a very old oak—the sort with crags hollowed out and claimed by animals both living and spirit. A low bowl was carved with spirals of blessing sigils and a small dish set into the wood so long ago that the bark had curled around it like gently gripping fingers. Before departing, Raliel poured a bit of wine and offered sparks of aether, then turned to Osian. "Once the horse is ready, hold a moment."

"Moon," she murmured, and the great demon shivered under her heart. Raliel took the knife she'd never returned to Osian and cut open her hand. It was easier to cup the blood, and when Moon returned to her it could heal this slick wound in moments. They'd practiced. Moon thought eventually she could use her own aether to heal herself.

"Raliel!" Osian jumped toward her, dropping the lead so it slapped the ground gently at the horse's hoof.

"It's fine," she answered, focused on the blood pooling warm and viscous in her palm. Moon rushed through her veins to the cut and made a dramatic flourish of splatter as it dragged the blood up and away in an arc, then formed itself between one blink and the next.

Moon appeared in his dream-Osian form, and Osian flung himself between Raliel and Moon, sword out, crossed defensively.

Osian stared at his mirrored face.

Dizzy and bemused, Raliel took a few breaths to ground herself again, and with a smear of remaining blood drew a sigil to pull aether into her hand. The influx of magic settled her. She made a fist and pressed it over her chest where the amulet sat between her clothes and skin.

Moon winked at Osian, and Osian's lips parted. They continued to stare until Moon stepped in, forcing Osian back in a strange dance. Moon moved again, raised a hand, slunk nearer, then to the side, teasing. Osian did not try to match the movements, but only backed away if Moon got too close. He finally sucked in a breath and said, "Moon?"

And Moon smiled slowly, dangerously. It said, "Osian was your father's name too."

Osian gasped yet again.

"Let's keep walking." Raliel took off as she spoke, grabbing the horse's lead. At first she heard nothing to indicate they followed; then suddenly, Osian jogging. And the light, measured pace of the great demon. Raliel let herself glance over her shoulder at the pair: one real and one shade, built the same, in every detail of appearance but for stark colors, and yet they moved differently. One strong and compact with a soldier's training; one sinuous grace that sat ever so slightly off the frame it wore.

"It's true," Osian said. "Skybreaker was called Osian before he was a sorcerer. That's . . . everything I know about his previous life."

"He was the brother of the First Consort."

"How long ago?"

"First Consort Sting-in-Honey. But . . ." Moon paused. "I remember little because I was sleepy. It was several generations ago."

"Five," Raliel said. "First Consort Sting-in-Honey was the mother of Fire Smile, the sixth Emperor with the Moon in His Mouth. My grandmother's grandfather."

Osian drew a rallying breath. "So perhaps he was two hundred years old when he died. Or thereabouts?"

Moon said, "He came to the palace! I remember. He came to the palace suddenly, dropped out of the sky. A sorcerer. He'd just made himself one. I don't know how. I didn't care. Then."

"I wonder if The Scale knows," Raliel said.

They fell quiet for a time, until Osian asked how they'd managed Moon's new skill.

Every day they practiced, sometimes more than once, depending on how long the manifestation lasted. They tried using Raliel's aether but Osian's blood, or Osian's aether as Moon possessed him and Raliel's blood. The latter came closer to working, but the former was useless. They meandered along the north road, though the days shortened and the farther they traveled the colder it became. Fewer people joined them on the roads, and the smaller crossroads villages and shrines shuttered for the season.

For three days they were rained into a crossroads shelter, reliant upon damp wood and the food stores in the waterproof boxes beneath the low beds. Raliel had to hide how much she enjoyed those days, with no goal, no direct future or pressures of travel making decisions. She could stretch and do abbreviated sword-forms with Osian, experiment with Moon, and they realized when she did not exert herself with even something as simple as walking, her aether and blood lasted much longer. Moon manifested itself for the entire last rain day, and Raliel fell asleep leaning against its cool shoulder while the fire danced across both their faces.

Late in the night, once Moon's body flickered out and she curled alone in her blankets, Osian whispered, "Raliel, are you awake?"

"Yes."

Nothing immediately followed. "Osian?"

"What will you do with me, when this is over?" Osian kept

his voice soft, as if there were anyone else to wake. The shelter was damp and chilly, for the fire had dimmed to glowing coals. Outside wind splattered rain against the thatching, making a dull, peppering sound and a quiet, persistent rustle.

"Do with you?" she repeated.

"Because I lied. Because I . . . betrayed you."

Raliel tilted her head against the thin pillow, searching for the glint of his eyes in the dark. "What do you want to happen?"

She imagined she could hear him swallow. She definitely heard him sigh. "I want to go back with you. To the palace. I want to serve. I want everything I was working for. For myself, I mean. Not what my mother wants. I love her, but . . . I think whatever happened to my father, it isn't your fault, and probably isn't your father's. Besides, our fathers are . . . our fathers. They aren't us."

"Do you—do you want to go back to serve the palace, or to serve me?" Raliel tried to make her voice even, plain. She thought of invoking her icy facade but didn't want to sever this quiet intimacy. The tentative connection.

"Whatever I am allowed. And . . ." A gentle huff like a wry laugh sounded from his bed. "Some people would say those are the same choices. The palace, the heir."

Raliel laughed a little too. "They are. And they are not."

Raliel, complained Moon. The great demon was sleepy, because her body was sleepy, and it had spent vast quantities of energy remaining physical so long.

"If I had to choose, you." Osian sat up. She saw the shape of him in the dim red glow of embers.

Pushing herself to sit, too, she said, "Good. Then start now."

"Start . . . ?"

"Serving me like it's for the rest of your life."

In the intimate hour, with rain cocooning them in this pocket of no-where, no-time, Osian got out of his bed and knelt beside hers. The fire behind him gave him a hot aura, but she could see the glint of his eyes and the movement of his mouth as he said, "I will, Raliel Dark-Smile."

Because they were alone, just the three of them, and Osian had promised, Raliel reached for him. She put her fingers gently against his jaw. Then she let her hand fall.

NINE

I T BEGAN EXACTLY AS the full moon crawled up over the canopy of hemlock and redwoods. They'd made camp in a meadow covered with low ferns and smooth brown rocks easily built into a firepit. The horse slept standing where it was hobbled beside a redwood with long, luxurious branches and needles that brushed and danced in the cold breeze like hair.

Raliel had not yet pulled off her boots to sleep, instead watching Moon, fully manifest, move around the meadow setting little signal sigils. Every time it planted one successfully, it grinned at her over its shoulder. Its hair had gotten more lifelike, its grin no less vicious. Osian tuned his flute, ready to play them a lullaby he was teaching Raliel while Moon invented lyrics. Raliel allowed herself to slouch as she sat cross-legged before the fire. Relaxed, nearly. It was too cold to truly relax, and Moon had begun flirting terribly with Osian most evenings, as if to bring them all into a pile for warmth and sleeping. Raliel tolerated it, and in fact enjoyed the antics, but she wasn't certain still where she landed with regard to this complicated reality of her great demon manifest enough to touch her, to lean against her, while the pretty, loyal, betraying Osian laughed and winked.

It began as a cold hook in her gut.

Raliel did not recognize the sensation initially: she rolled her shoulders, wondering if she'd eaten something slightly off earlier, and it was giving her gas.

Then the hook snagged up into her heart and the amulet on her chest burned colder than anything—*anything*—Raliel had ever known. Suddenly she knew it. She recognized it, slapping both hands over it as she cried, "Moon!"

Osian and Moon both grabbed her, to either side as she bent over, groaning against the pain.

Moon said, "What—I feel it, what is . . . ?"

"The emperor," she managed to hiss, twisting her hands to grab Moon's wrist and arm. She dragged him closer, as if she could press his forehead to hers and jerk him back inside her, melt them together.

"Raliel," Osian said. "What can I do?"

"We need power," she said through gritted teeth.

Aether exploded around her. The burst of light blinded her: Raliel cried out at the pain, the shock. She flung up her hands. Energy sucked through her, pulling, aching, screaming. A great, vast strength reached over miles and miles to fist around her heart and demand.

The cold amulet burned her, falling into her skin, burning flesh black with cold.

Raliel shoved away from Osian and Moon. She had to get away before she hurt Moon with her father's power. She scrambled back, a crab-crawl, awkward but as fast as she could manage. The pull came again, and she screamed. She *screamed* with everything she was. Her spine arched. Her tongue was cold fire. She became nothing but a screaming star.

"Moon!" Osian yelled. "Here, take my hand!"

Something popped inside her, and Raliel stopped screaming only to gulp breath and begin again.

"Take my hand!"

Everything was light. And pain.

Light.

"Take my hand, Moon!"

morning bruise

brilliant sunrise on your shoulder

heart

kisses manifest in flesh

pain

light

Nothing.

KNOWING

THE SORCERERS

THE CROWN OF THE Fourth Mountain was not ideal neutral ground, but it would have to do. There were few options when it came to a space for parley among the empire's immortal sorcerers.

The sorceress of the Fifth Mountain was first to arrive: called Shadows these days. She arrived under her own power, a creature of black-green scales, sinuous as a snake and winged like a bat. When she set a delicate foot to the scruffy grass of the mountainside, she instantly became a woman with long hair streaked black, brown, volcanic-red; dark-tan skin; and large slit-pupiled eyes—one life-green, one death-white—and an expression set into casual disdain. Her dress did not flutter in the cold wind, as if the layers of pink and black silk were carved from marble. Alone, she turned to gaze out beyond the cutting peaks of the Fourth Mountain toward the waning moon as it set. Snow would come before dawn. The clouds throwing themselves against the stars in the north promised it.

Shadows had been a sorceress for a century, or thereabouts. Since she'd thrown off her home and family and gone tearing into the world full of desire and anger, since she'd clawed her way up the Fifth Mountain and, half-dead, half-despairing, half-wild with longing, had begged with broken hands for the demon to let her in. "I am a sorceress," she'd yelled, willing it so. "I will bargain with you, power for power."

The demon had appeared, like a woman scaled green, wearing nothing but luxurious silver hair that spilled from its head and a mouth of shark teeth. It had laughed at her but brought her inside to heal her and listen to her jokes. That's what it called every word she said. Jokes. And it said it liked funny things. Like bumblebees and hail. And humans. When it had laughed enough, it ate her up and spat her back out a sorceress.

Since then Shadows had lost her great demon Patience with a chunk of her own heart and gained Night Shine, a wife as ridiculous as the world could invent. It was for that demon wife that Shadows had come to this mountaintop.

The second to arrive was the sorcerer of the First Mountain, flying exactly like themself: a slender youth with oil-black rainbows of hair, humble robes, bare feet. The Scale dashed through the cold night air as if running across a field of flowers, bright eyed and having fun.

They hopped out of the sky and onto the scrub grass and smiled prettily at the taller Shadows.

The Scale had been a sorcerer for more than six hundred years. They'd come from the other side of the First Mountain, from a land of poets and thirteen genders. After being struck by lightning and seeing the whole of the world light up with aether, they'd left on a quest to find its source. On the First Mountain with the help of a great spirit called A Murmuration of Stars, they discovered no source but themselves, and that was enough.

The sorceress inclined her head at The Scale. They nodded back, approaching casually, and stood beside her with their fists on their hips. "So, you are concerned."

She blinked slowly, giving nothing away.

The Scale nodded again, in agreement, as if Shadows had delivered a speech. She knew this was an act on the part of the oldest sorcerer—not that they truly saw through her. She hoped.

Third and last to arrive for the parley were the Second and Third sorcerers, twins who appeared out of a shadow and stepped in tandem onto the rocks opposite Shadows and The Scale.

These mirrored each other in physique and coloring: white on white on white, the white of The Scale's lightning, the white of Shadows's left eye. Broad and masculine, large hands loose at their sides, long tunics and tight trousers woven of moonlight.

Shadows swallowed a scoff. Did they think they'd come to intimidate humans? Shadows's wife was a great demon—these two had none but spirits and lesser demons at their call.

A Dance of Stars and A Still Wind had been sorcerers longer than Shadows. Born together, they'd studied magic together—one through witchcraft learned to make familiars, the other through the priesthood learned to talk with the dead—and they had lived together as guardians of an ancient cemetery filled with ghosts, tucked up against the Third Mountain. Together they shared food and friends and seven familiars, bound to both. They died together, too: first one, murdered by grave robbers and dragged back into his body by his priest brother; then the other, stabbed by his witch brother in order to be dragged back the same. They both were alive and both were dead, their hands filled with aether and their hearts with ambition.

Silence stretched between the four sorcerers, where once had been five. Shadows had killed Skybreaker more than twenty years ago, never regretting it for a moment. She put that into her unbalanced gaze as she waited to see what the twins would say.

They would speak first, though perhaps pretend for a while otherwise. One of them—A Dance of Stars—was impatient. Or The Scale would weary of this game and speak simply to end it. They had no interest in petty reputations.

Shadows liked silence. Liked the anticipation of Night Shine's bright laughter cutting it to pieces.

Tension rippled between the twins, and Shadows nearly allowed herself to smirk. One tilted his head; the other pursed his lips.

The Scale laughed softly. "This is ridiculous," they said, sliding a look at Shadows. She shrugged.

The oldest sorcerer, appearing the youngest, spread their hands, palms up. "Why are we here, Sorceress?"

"The sorcerers of the Second and Third Mountains continue to stray out of their bounds," she said coolly.

"Bounds!" said A Still Wind with a sneer. "What boundaries affect sorcery?"

"The great demon of the palace is not yours to take," she said.

A Dance of Stars shrugged one hard white shoulder. "The great demon is not in the palace."

"And you continue to threaten there."

"Threaten!"

A Still Wind took over: "Are we not welcome in the house of the empire?"

A Dance of Stars added, "There is another demon's house empty now."

Shadows grinned, all her teeth sharp and jagged as a shark's. "The Fifth Mountain is never empty now, no matter where Night Shine walks. And I recall how at my weakest, without a demon at all, I tore Skybreaker to pieces. You would do well to remember too."

At the old Fourth Sorcerer's name, a roar broke the side of the mountain: the rock trembled, and a great bear spirit appeared, mouth wide, teeth hooked. Its eyes shimmered with rage as it glared at Shadows.

But the sorceress of the Fifth Mountain met its angry gaze and did not move. If it liked, she would fight it, and destroy it, too.

A Dance of Stars soothed the bear spirit with a calming hand.

Shadows bit back her surprise as the old Skybreaker's familiar allowed the touch, and more, allowed a soft gift of aether from sorcerer to beast.

"Interesting." The Scale spoke up finally. "You have taken on the Fourth Mountain's bear."

"Together," A Still Wind said. "We share it, and our own." He looked piercingly at Shadows, to tell her especially she did not know how strong he and his brother were—together.

She remained unafraid. But it was cause for suspicion. The twins actively gathered power, and a simple parley would not be enough to warn them off the capital and the great demon and the heir. Shadows looked to The Scale, wondering if they would choose her side, or remain neutral. The Scale loved humans broadly, but not so deeply as to often concern themself with anything other than balance.

Shadows did not love humans, or the empire, but she loved her wife, and her wife loved the imperial family.

Fortunately, The Scale stepped toward the twins. "You may not cause harm to the heir or the triad in order to take the great demon of the palace. I will stop you should you choose such a path."

"This is hardly a parley," sneered A Still Wind.

His brother leaned into him. They pressed together and glowed a fractured silver-blue. The great bear spirit dissolved into them, and the glow disseminated wider: a storm of power.

The Scale did nothing to display their strength. No shimmer of aether, and the little twinkling clump of their great spirit merely hovered as it had for all the long minutes of this gathering. The Scale said, "I have no need to parley. This was Shadows's idea."

She gnashed her teeth. Wind shoved around her, gathering her hair into snakes, and she, because she was not The Scale, let her hunger to rid the world of them show in her grin. They should never have tormented her wife twenty years ago, taken Night Shine apart to understand her, to make her theirs. Night Shine had been too much for them, but Shadows would prefer to make them pay. "You will not take the great demon of the palace."

A Dance of Stars laughed, quickly echoed by his brother. Their mouths gaped black and violent red, marring the white-white-whiteness of these shapes. "And what if," A Still Wind said, voice merry, "Raliel Dark-Smile offers her demon to us, freely and willfully?"

Shadows closed her mouth. A trick waited in the sorcerer's words, but it was the kind of trick obeyed by spirit and demon and sorcerer alike.

Indeed, The Scale said, "If the heir gives her Moon to you, then with you is where the Moon belongs."

As one the twins thrust out a hand and each sketched a sigil for "end." It meant completion. It meant the turn of seasons. It meant a deal had been struck.

The Scale did the same, their sigil softly gilded as if by dawn light.

With little choice, Shadows made her own, twining it with darkness.

The four sorcerers pressed their sigils together in unification. It was done.

The twins waved at her, one almost respectful, the other cruelly, and they stepped back into their shadow and vanished.

"What have we done?" Shadows demanded of The Scale, who tilted their head and studied the space where the twins had stood. "Lutha," she added pointedly when they remained quiet.

The Scale turned that changing-sky gaze on her, and she saw the clouds floating in the hazy blue of their eyes. They said, "This is what Raliel and that great demon asked me for, Shadows of the Fifth Mountain."

"What is?" Shadows whispered.

The sorcerer of the First Mountain smiled, but it was a grim, ancient thing. "Choice."

ONE

M OON DID NOT LIKE this feeling. Not at all.

It knelt in a huge circle of death. Blackened and bent grass, charred brambles, and ferns curled in on themselves, wavering in the air like smoke. The breeze touched them, and they burst into ashes. Streaks of gray and white spread like rays of a poison sun from exactly where Moon knelt. Trees bent away, as if afraid of the nothing energy, the emptiness. There was no aether here, none but what coiled inside Moon, and the tiny, shallow puffs that gasped from Raliel's lips.

She sprawled beside the demon, lips gray, brow furrowed, unconscious, and covered in a film of sweat.

Pressed against Moon's knees was what remained of Osian Redpop.

In death the young man looked sunken and wrong. Moon stared at the details of his face, upset and disliking it. The demon-kissed colors and textures were gone. Stripped out of skin and hair. Just dark-brown curls remained now, tangled, and cream-peach skin, blotchy from the sun. What else had Moon stripped away?

Life. Power. Osian was empty. While Moon was absolutely full of aether. Burning with it, like a volcano rumbling to release itself, or a churning, constant waterfall. So much power crackled within, Moon ought to be gloriously happy.

But, instead, the great demon stared at Osian's body and frowned. Osian should be in motion. Osian was always in motion. Little flickers of thought, his eyes darting to take in everything. Lips twitching to hide a smile. Emotions flying through the delicate skin around his eyes. Lashes, tongue, fingers fingers fingers, tapping out a silent song.

Moon had seen death. Moon knew death. Caused it.

Osian Redpop's aether—his life—filled Moon to the brim and past. Overflowing. Moon could fly to the stars, shine like the Moon it was, light up a thousand nights with this power.

Moon, here! Take my hand!

The great demon had heard, taken that hand, gripped it and pulled. Power to shove back through Raliel, along the palace-amulet threads stretching far far far all the way from here to the palace and blast it back into Kirin Dark-Smile and his husband and his wife. *Leave us alone! Stop hurting Raliel!*

Moon had taken what Osian offered without hesitation, without considering limits.

Osian was dead, all his life burning in Moon.

Moon did not like this feeling.

It knelt, hands flat against its knees. Staring at the dead man. It leaned down and blew a gentle breath against Osian's lips. Nothing. It put its eyes right against Osian's cheek, flicked its lashes. Nothing. It did not move its hands. Could not touch. Not again.

Then Moon slammed aether back into Osian's body.

Months ago, Raliel had died like this. When Moon crashed through her the first time, it possessed her. It had brought her back, sparked her heart and brain again. Osian had only barely stopped breathing too.

Moon felt the spark of Osian's heart. Felt the beat. Felt it stop.

Aether pooled.

Filled the arteries.

Moon shoved again, flared aether into the heart.

Osian's body twitched. His mouth fell open. But he did not wake.

Beside the great demon, Raliel shifted on the ashy ground.

Moon turned and put its body between Osian and Raliel. It touched her forehead: clammy but all right. Just in aftershock. It could sense her aether turning, stretching. It should get into her body again and take her away from here. Before she saw. Tell her Osian left. Moon sent him back to the palace to warn off the emperor. Find a slower, kinder way to tell her the truth.

But Moon didn't do that. It was too full of magic, and too *upset*.

Instead, it took Raliel's hand. Squeezed it. Set it down again on her stomach, then returned to its position, kneeling against Osian's body, hands flat on its thighs. Waiting.

Breathing.

Air pulled through its mouth, down its throat, into lungs that expanded, held, disseminated, expelled, then collected once more, pushing air up and out again. Moon breathed. It had observed Raliel breathe like this, to calm down, to make herself cool night sky, frozen winter. Moon swayed like the ocean.

Moon wished Osian's body had turned to ashes too.

Raliel moaned softly, a little sigh like a kitten. Moon didn't move. Something twisted inside itself. Was it cold too? Clammy like Raliel. Was this sweat?

The great demon panted a little, listing sideways as if an invisible force tugged at it, tender and inexorable: the ground is better. Lie down, the force said. Under its knees, the dead earth tilted, too.

With a gasp, Raliel sat up. She flailed, reaching, and knocked her hand into Moon's arm. It turned and clasped her forearm. "Raliel," it said in its almost-Osian voice.

"Moon. Oh, ow." She pressed her free hand against her eyes, then dragged it up over her brow to dig into her hair. "What happened?"

"The emperor."

"Oh, yes, I remember. It hurt. I cannot believe my father hurt me." She groaned and leaned toward Moon, who leaned back so that she could press against its shoulder.

Moon brushed its cheek against her sweat-damp hair. "Raliel, I fought back. Osian . . ."

"Is he all right?" Raliel lifted off Moon and twisted, looking. It took a second for her to glance in the right direction: down. Then her body went absolutely rigid. Moon held tight to her forearm. "Osian!" she said in a terrible voice, jerking away from Moon to throw herself over Osian, gripping his shoulders. "Osian!"

Moon let her. It did not know what else to do. But watching was worse than waiting. Worse than wondering. Watching Raliel shake him, then push open his mouth, then finally dig her fingers under his jaw. Moan his name.

"He has a pulse," she said. She laughed.

"He does?" Moon stuck two fingers into Osian's mouth, just the first knuckles, and focused.

Air. Motion.

Raliel laughed again, high and soft, and tears fell out of her eyes. She leaned against Moon. "He's alive."

It had worked. Moon had brought him back. It liked this feeling better, except for the canyon of panic still open inside it, under its skin. It did not tell Raliel it brought Osian back—it had killed him in the first place, so hardly deserved praise.

Raliel wiped her face. Blotches of pink marred her lovely cheeks, her lashes clumped together. Her lips were too pale. Moon hated it. This was also a bad feeling.

"Don't cry," it whispered. "Please." It kissed the corner of her eye, tongue soft against the curl of her lashes.

Raliel suddenly stopped resisting, melting against the great demon. She did not stop crying as she folded over, her face pressed to Moon's. It wrapped arms around her, lifted her onto its lap, and held her tight while she wept. Her hands found its waist, and she hugged it back.

Suddenly Osian sucked in a huge, wild breath and leapt to his feet—only to crash back down to his knees, then fall against them. Raliel and Moon caught him, and easily, naturally, drew him into their embrace.

TWO

N IGHT SHINE EXPLODED INTO a million tiny shards when the great demon of the palace returned fire.

Elegant Waters had braced the moment the ritual began. She had the most training in witchcraft between herself, the emperor, and The Day the Sky Opened, though she had rarely used it in more than twenty years. But it had convinced them to allow her to hold the most precise point of the sigil matrix. Thus, Elegant Waters was ready.

The full moon shone down on them like one of the great demon's eyes, accusing, she believed. It had been only the three of them and Night Shine, the fickle, disorienting great demon of the Fifth Mountain, in the Consorts' Garden, standing in three points with Night Shine floating in the center, just above the matrix drawn in milk infused with their imperial blood. Now Night Shine had vanished, shattered in the aftershock of the magic.

Elegant Water's ears popped, then muffled again. She worked her jaw and swallowed. It did not help. She blinked, slowly sinking to her knees on the lawn. Moonlight cast the garden in cool blue-gray, pure and cold. They'd lit no aether-lights or candles, relying on that big moon.

The lines of the sigil matrix bent and frayed on the ground, distorted as if something from the east had cast a spear and pierced the matrix. Elegant Waters touched the damp milk. Aether reverberated up her finger.

"Raliel," she whispered.

Across from her, the emperor collapsed on his haunches. "Night Shine," he called sharply. A command. Then he looked at Elegant Waters, and she read a flash of pain on his beautiful face. It cleared out, making way for hard anger. "Night Shine," the emperor demanded.

Sky said, "Are you both all right?"

"I am," Elegant Waters said. "Emperor?"

He shook his head. Like all of them, he wore a simple red robe over trousers and bare feet. His hair was in a loose knot, his face unpainted. Elegant Waters was unused to her husband the emperor seeming so young. Even when he spent the night in her room, or they reclined all three of them in his, the emperor carried his smile like a mask across his mouth.

Elegant Waters wondered what she looked like. Afraid? She felt afraid. A constant hum of fear had plagued her since her daughter left weeks ago. No, not since then—at first it had been gentle worry but bearable. Then they realized the great demon was gone. They realized what Raliel had done. Then the fear had snapped its fangs into the base of her skull and refused to release.

Suddenly Night Shine appeared, with a slick popping sound. She fell from a few paces in the air and hit the ground hard. The seashell gravel crunched. Sky went to her side, helped her up by a gangly elbow.

The demon shook herself like a dog. Her hair was brown and spiky as winter blackberries, her eyes black expanses of night filled with pink-blue-yellow sparkling stars. Otherwise the great demon looked like a sixteen-year-old girl in a ragged dress with her toenails lacquered black. She grimaced. "That hurt. Are you all hurt?"

"Not physically," the emperor snarled. He stood as well and skidded a foot through the milk and blood matrix.

"Is it your aether?" Night Shine said, turning so she faced the emperor with her side pressed flush to Sky's chest.

"My heart."

The demon scoffed, but the melodrama warmed Elegant Waters. She knew her husband, and when he was truly furious or absolutely devastated, he was as cold and calm as a frozen lake. Standing gracefully, Elegant Waters smoothed the lines of her robe and gazed at the emperor. He said, "I am furious at Raliel and the great demon of the palace, and I do not know if I will forgive either of them."

His honey-brown eyes glinted dully in the moonlight, and he didn't look away from Elegant Waters. She held his gaze. She was cold and tired. So very tired all the time. They'd had to do this. Had to drive the great demon home, because of what was happening to the three of them.

It had begun as lazy resistance to waking with her schedule in the morning and had progressed the longer Raliel was gone into frequent naps and a constant dullness to her senses. She'd hidden it from both of her husbands for the first month. Until the

329

emperor had tripped in the corridor and his self-recriminations had led to Sky confessing his own lack of strength. They'd turned to Elegant Waters, and she had nodded slowly.

Missing the great demon took a toll on them. They were the only cornerstones of this great foundational amulet, and the demon pulled constantly. Elegant Waters was not a vivid dreamer, but the emperor said that his were thin and pale compared to the wonders and nightmares he'd lived with since being enthroned.

They'd made the first attempt to drag Moon home because Kirin and Sky and Night Shine were afraid that if the great demon of the palace tried hard enough, it could snap the amulet and the ricochet might kill them. Or if it used too much power, even accidentally, it could drain one or all of them.

Elegant Waters had been afraid, but not of that.

"Why did she do this?" the emperor had whispered the first night after they discovered Raliel's trick.

Elegant Waters hadn't thought he needed an answer, but Sky said, "It's something you'd have done."

They'd been in the emperor's bedroom, a large but astonishingly simple chamber with windows in the ceiling, dominated by a bed and a long low table decorated with several tea sets, ink and paper, and books. A mural wrapped the walls, of a springtime mountainscape, with five peaks and rolling rain forest canopy, rainbow birds, dragons of the air and water, misty clouds, and tiny people going about the daily business of the empire. The emperor and his consorts had huddled in the center of the large low bed, a turquoise lacquered tray balanced between them. Steam coiled up from the teapot, and only Elegant Waters held her little blue clay cup.

"This isn't my style," the emperor had said, despite Sky's side-eye. "It is not. I never risked the palace, the empire. For what?"

Sky shook his head.

"My motivations were selfish when I was her age, but I knew my duty," the emperor continued.

Elegant Waters had set her cup back upon the tray with a click. It was not overly loud, but both husbands looked immediately at her. "Not selfish," she had said in her hallmark cool tone.

The emperor narrowed his eyes to slits. "Do you know something we do not, wife?"

"I know my daughter."

He'd sucked in a shocked gasp, and Sky frowned. "Elegant Waters," the First Consort had said, chiding.

"The Day the Sky Opened," she answered.

They both stared at her. Sky's jaw clenched. The emperor did not blink, radiating hostility at her.

Elegant Waters had held firm, though it had been a very long time since she felt so apart from them. Since before the enthronement, even, before this powerful amulet had connected them to each other and their triad to the great demon in the first place. "My daughter is not selfish. She is entirely too *selfless*. Without even thought enough for herself to try to be happy. She did this for a good reason. Justice, would be my guess."

"Justice," Sky repeated, shocked.

The emperor's hostility faded as he studied Elegant Waters in speculation. She said no more. She rarely said as much as she already had, when the conversation mattered.

"Justice for whom?" Sky asked.

"Moon," the emperor said, deflating. He fell back against the pillows and cushions of his bed. "The great demon itself. She asked me once if the demon is our prisoner."

Sky settled a large hand on the emperor's flat stomach. "She asked me the same."

Elegant Waters nodded, but Raliel had asked her a slightly different question. She'd asked if they were *all* prisoners.

The demon Night Shine had appeared in their garden the very next day, ripe with eager gossip.

Their first attempt to bring Moon (and Raliel) home had not worked, obviously, and Night Shine had left to consult with her sorcerer Shadows and returned after a week with a complex sigil matrix and a hundred questions. They'd agreed, however, to wait, because the tiredness was something they could deal with for a little while longer.

Elegant Waters had nursed the tiny seed of fearful hope that Raliel was happy on her journey. And hopeful fear that the daughter who returned would be unrecognizable to her mother.

Then, three weeks ago, the palace-amulet had exploded with aether, dragging all three of them unconscious. The only silver lining had been that it was late, after dark, and none of the Imperial Triad had been among the public.

Night Shine had panicked, built them each a seed of aether, something she called a heart-shrine, to wear. Containers for aether to drain should they need them again in an emergency.

Shadows of the Fifth Mountain had sent word that Raliel and the great demon had performed sorcery, huge and powerful and brief. It was the kind of magic that might change both parties, and all the sorcerers in the empire would have felt it.

That proved true seven days ago when A Still Wind, sorcerer

of the Third Mountain, arrived at the palace with his great spirit and asked to be admitted.

Night Shine pretended to be the great demon of the palace and denied them with a roar and seven glaring eyes. A Still Wind pushed back, but gently, a feeling sort of magic, and the emperor worried the sorcerer knew it was a ruse. Knew the great demon was gone. They were vulnerable for the first time in centuries, and the twin sorcerers had been waiting for such an opportunity.

Thus this second, more powerful full-moon ritual to force the great demon back into the palace.

Elegant Waters's ears rang with the aftershock of power. She ached in her jaw where she'd clenched her teeth.

Night Shine pushed slightly away from Sky in order to throw out her arms and declare, "Let's try again right away! Whatever the great demon did that slammed me back like that, it almost certainly can't do again! We can get it."

The emperor pursed his lips, and Sky nodded slowly.

Elegant Waters said, "No."

All three of them rounded on her.

The Second Consort lifted her chin. A cold sea breeze brushed hair back off her face, and she wished to give in to the chill and shiver, hug herself. Run inside and curl around a steaming cup of tea, then tremble and weep.

"No?" the emperor said dangerously.

"Why?" Sky asked.

"It's too much of a risk."

Night Shine shook her head, and little flecks of silver and pink like sparks scattered out of her hair. "No risk. This isn't hurting Raliel."

"You don't know that, Shine," Sky said.

"I said no," Elegant Waters repeated.

The emperor stalked across the night garden, smearing the milky sigil with his bare toes. He put himself in her space but did not touch her. "Don't you want her *back*?" His voice cut into her.

Elegant Waters looked into her emperor's eyes, at the honey-gold and warm brown, and said nothing in response to such a senseless question. But she did lift her hands and place them gently on his jaw, brushing her cold thumbs against the soft skin of his cheeks. She gazed at him, willing him to match his breathing to hers, to cool himself down. He'd said it before: his heart hurt. The emperor did not make wise choices on such occasions. That was all right, Elegant Waters was here.

His face fell first, out of the stiff anger, past hurt, and into an uncertainty that fluttered his lovely lashes. "Why didn't she talk to me about this?" he whispered. "Did I do this to her? Secrets and demons and . . . Was there something I could have done differently?"

"Always," Elegant Waters said. She swallowed her own fear. "Once, Kirin Dark-Smile asked me why I should be his consort. Do you remember? I said because together we would make children more beautiful than both of us."

The emperor snorted softly, and behind him, Night Shine laughed. It was a pretty, breezy thing that trilled like a flute.

Elegant Waters held her husband's face. "You agreed with me, and isn't she? Isn't she more beautiful than both of us?"

"Yes."

"And so that is the reason you invited me to stay, but do you know why I did?"

"You couldn't resist me," he answered with that characteristic hooked smile.

She let herself return it, because he was not entirely wrong. "I stayed because I belong here. I knew it. I felt it the moment I saw the city. I knew I was not Elegant Waters of the Mountain of One Thousand Falls. I was Second Consort Elegant Waters. That was my real name. My true name. This was my place. I knew it like I knew how to breathe."

"El," he murmured. His hands came up to curl around her wrists. She did shiver then, because his hands were just as cold as hers. They needed to go inside now that the ritual was done, and they were drained, weary, freezing.

"I was younger than Raliel is now," Elegant Waters said firmly. She glanced over at Sky, walking up behind the emperor. "But I trusted myself, though I was terrified. Of you—both of you. But I did it. I stayed, and I fought for it, in my own way. I don't regret it, and have not for twenty-one years."

Night Shine appeared next to them in a blink. Small, pale, and luminous, even in the robes of a palace servant. "Trust Raliel," she said to Elegant Waters. "That's what you mean."

"Yes. We're going to trust her with the entire empire some-day. Why not begin with this, now?" Though the demon had spoken, Elegant Waters answered with her attention entirely on the emperor, her hands anchored to his face, his hands on her wrists.

Sky took a breath deep enough his wide shoulders lifted and settled under its strength. "It's so dangerous."

"I can ask Selegan to check on her, and Shadows is already aware of everything we know, especially regarding the other sorcerers," Night Shine said. "I'll remain here, still. This isn't my house, but I can keep it from falling to a great *spirit*," she added with acid disdain.

The Emperor with the Moon in His Mouth did not smile but pulled his mouth into something more like a distant ocean horizon. "Trust our daughter," he said, and it became more than acquiescing; it was a command.

THREE

RALIEL DARK-SMILE AND THE great demon of the palace arrived in Whitelar Town at the base of the Fourth Mountain three weeks after Osian nearly died.

Moon and Raliel rode hastily acquired horses, as the one from Jellyfish Rest was dead, having been caught in the aether backlash. Osian slumped against Raliel's back, his shoulders pinned with dozens of sigils for strength and balance. Moon had grumbled that even if he did die, his body would last a hundred years.

Osian lived, but barely, and both Raliel and Moon were determined he'd remain that way: whatever quasi-sorcery his mother, Syra, and the bear spirit Crown had performed on his body had unraveled when Moon stripped power out and through him in such a violent burst, leaving Osian trembling between consciousness and dreams. They'd done their best to investigate what was wrong, but neither had the experience to solve it quickly. There were no healers specialized in sorcery anywhere at all, and no great library without returning to the palace or to The Scale. Even if they chose such an option, it might take weeks more to figure out how to help him. But Osian's mother knew exactly what had been done to him, so they'd brought him north as fast as possible. Despite the risks. Surely she would help her own son. Raliel had a lot to bargain with, after all.

The sky rippled in layers of gray, low and dark. Even without wind, the air bit at Raliel's cheeks, pinking them. She purchased a hood to tie over her hair and protect her ears, and her red jacket that had come with her all the way from the palace did the rest. For Osian she'd purchased a thick wool and silk cloak and tied it awkwardly around him. In one moment of lucidity, he'd said he felt like a ladybug wrapped in a spider's web. Moon did not feel cold, and rode at their side in a solid black version of Osian's uniform. Not a hint of color ruined the demon's look, not in its eyes or lips, even. Moon was harsh black and white contrast, inhuman. The flawless pearl-white skin, the gray-silver full-moon eyes, the sleek, inky hair that spilled and drifted in ghostly slow waves all worked to make Moon stand out clearly as what it was. When they went into a town, people veered away from it, though Raliel expected they assumed Moon was a spirit or a powerful witch, not that it was a demon.

Sometimes Raliel glanced at it and felt as though a gorge deeper than any ocean separated them. Like this, it was so familiar it tipped over into completely alien. They couldn't know each other; they couldn't be *friends*. It was unnatural, impossible. The demon's mind worked too differently. Its needs and capabilities were unfathomable. Other times she caught it frowning to itself, or blinking in its perfectly even, perfectly measured way, and Raliel thought she'd never understood anything in the world as well as she understood Moon. It showed its guilt in odd moments of laughter, sudden and harsh, followed by soft inquiries in Osian's direction, wondering what story Osian would tell in response to that bent old juniper or to share a song that had popped into its head despite Osian's lack of consciousness. It occasionally poked at Osian, tried to make him perform some proof of life, and Osian just as occasionally managed a wan smile or tapped his finger on his leg in accompaniment.

Twice on their jouney they were stopped by Warriors of the Last Means with letters from the emperor. Raliel took them coldly and burned them as soon as she could. She refused to acknowledge any communication with her parents, not after they'd nearly killed Osian. After the second letter, they avoided towns and crossroads entirely.

Traveling off-road was more difficult, especially with the horses. But by now Raliel was strong. Despite no more resting at warm inns, despite bathing in cold ponds and waterfalls that froze her blood, she thrived. She slept hard when they stopped and flourished on the simple food they foraged. Osian could barely keep anything down, but Raliel pushed aether into his body while they rode, her fingers twined with his against her stomach.

To Raliel's surprise, they were visited at night by spirits. No demons crept near enough to Moon to be noticed, but spirits of the forest with curiosity to match their power risked it. Perhaps the spirits were less wary because Moon had drawn on such an explosion of aether that it could now hold its blood-manifestation solid and did not constantly draw aether from everything it touched. A great blackberry spirit climbed up the tree under which they camped once, all thorny vines and purple berry eyes on little wavering stalks. It did not speak. A trio of fox spirits trotted up laughingly on a different night and challenged them to riddles. Moon invested so hard in the game it leaned on its haunches, balanced forward on fingertips, and its face grew slightly leaner and she saw the ghost of a bushy tail. It didn't seem to have realized what it was doing to itself. Until it won, and laughed so hard in such pure delight even the fox spirits rolled with amusement. Raliel nearly smiled. Osian, curled with his head against Raliel's thigh, did.

They met a mushroom spirit whose house was so large it told them what was happening three miles away, at the edge of its mycelial fingers. A rat spirit tiny in appearance drank half a flask of wine, revealing itself to be a great spirit with an entire underground burrow of connected spirits who all enjoyed the shared liquor. A wildflower spirit crackled as it walked toward them, dry and sleepy thanks to the oncoming winter. The most beautiful was a waterfall dragon, slithery and bright, that floated over the stream at the base of its fall, seemingly made of clear crystals and mist.

Raliel asked the waterfall dragon if it thought its luck and magic might help Osian, and when it offered to try for an equivalent gift, Raliel kissed the lovely agate her father Sky had given her and dropped it into the waterfall. Moon remained far back while she helped Osian to the edge of the pond. The dragon coiled long tails of water around Osian's ankles, crawled up his body, and kissed him. A surprised Osian opened his mouth and the dragon spilled itself inside.

Almost instantly Osian shook all over, and his lips paled drastically.

"Stop!" Raliel cried, gripping his shoulders from behind.

Moon appeared behind her, holding her in turn, and tore through her at Osian and the dragon.

The dragon burst back out of Osian, hissing and snapping its tails. *Demon!* It snarled and dove into its pond, which boiled briefly with its anger.

Osian jerked in Raliel's hold. Blood trailed out of his nose.

They did not stop again until they reached the base of the Fourth Mountain, where Osian had grown up.

Four Ridges Manor was tucked up against a granite cliff alongside a thin, powerful waterfall that arced out from the overhang and crashed into a deep pool before sliding out in two different streams: one rushed under the wall of the manor; the other spilled toward Whitelar Town in a cheerful babble over smoothed red and gray stones. The manor wall was built of massive timbers and rough granite blocks as tall as Raliel. At each of four corners a tower rose, capped with a sharply peaked roof of dark slate. Smoke rose in six columns from beyond the wall, slow and pale.

Raliel dismounted, and Moon held both horses, standing beside hers to put a hand on Osian's leg to prop him up while Raliel climbed the shallow steps to the wooden gates. They were plain and polished rich brown, with a bell on a rope that ended with a raccoon coin. She pulled it and heard the dull gong echo inside.

The door opened in a few moments, just enough for a person to step out. She was older than Raliel's mother, with copper skin and short black and silver hair, wearing a cloak of heavily braided wool and thick boots. Outwardly, her features and stature presented very masculine, but Osian had said only women called this place home, and Raliel had been raised by a father with a constantly shifting gender. After looking Raliel up and down, the older woman flicked her gaze to Moon. Her eyes widened slightly. Then she looked at Osian, slumped on the horse. "Osian?"

"Windsong," Osian whispered. His eyes drifted closed, but he managed a slight smile.

"He is very ill," Raliel said. "He needs his mother's magic. Have you a way to contact her?"

"Yes." The woman shoved the door fully open, and Raliel stepped aside to allow Moon to lead the horses in. She followed, and the woman closed the door behind them.

"I'm Windsong. I raised him, with most of the rest of us here. Who are you? Why is he not in the capital?"

"I am Raliel Dark-Smile. This is my friend Moon, and Osian is my companion for my Heir's Journey."

Windsong paused in obvious but very brief shock before she bowed at the waist. "Heir. Welcome to Four Ridges. We can put you in the teahouse while we send for Syra."

Lovely, simple buildings of bright wood and plaster spread within the boundaries of the manor walls, few higher than one level. Lanterns danced in the cold breeze, strung across lanes and allies. Chickens wandered, feathers fluffed; Raliel heard the clang of a smithery, and somewhere someone played a flute. A handful of women approached them, looking between Moon, the horse's obvious burden, and Windsong.

"Osian?" called another of the women. "Sunrise?" said another, and Raliel smiled. It was a good nickname for him.

Osian's head bobbed awkwardly, and he lifted a hand, but his smile was painful. "Auntie," he said.

Raliel stepped forward. "I am Raliel Dark-Smile, and Osian was injured in my service. Anything you can do for him will put me in your debt. He needs his mother."

A woman with mounds of long black hair bound in three buns rushed forward, putting her hands on Osian's knee—nearly shoving Moon out of the way. Another woman followed, arm going around the first woman's shoulders, and she glared at Moon. Moon sneered back, then wiped its face of expression, ducking around to hide beside Raliel. Many of the women shot it suspicious and fearful looks.

More and more women appeared. They were all older than Raliel, a few wrinkled enough to be grandmothers. Most were pale ivory or light copper, but there was a woman with skin darker brown than Raliel had seen outside the palace. A few had the shaved heads of witches, and they all dressed in heavy wool layers, trimmed in fur and bright ribbons.

"Let us care for . . . him. In his childhood home." Windsong eyed Osian affectionately.

Raliel looked to Osian for an answer. "Please," he said, voice hoarse. "Aunties, I need to remain with Raliel. She is . . . I am . . . I should be near Moon if something . . ." He trailed off.

It was his illness exhausting him, but it sounded like a dramatic pause.

"But, Osian," said a woman with more wrinkles than Raliel's grandmother Love-Eyes.

Osian took a breath and coughed, listing to the side, and the women on either side caught him. He stood on his own, carefully stepping away. "Aunties. Raliel is good. Moon is good. I will be well with them until Mother comes."

A new woman stepped closer. She wore bright blue and her eyes were a startling pale-brown, like sunlight. "I am Tali. I nursed him because his mother was ill," she said, with a dazzling smile despite the fat tears that plopped off her lower lashes as she patted Osian's cheek. "Come with me. I will settle you three in our finest room."

Windsong remained with Moon to care for the horses while Tali and Raliel each took one of Osian's elbows. Tali took them to a house with long silver bells clinging to the eaves and round windows with their shutters flung open. "We have two other guests at the moment. They shouldn't bother you."

The room was large enough to have two screened bedchambers, a common dining area, and a bathroom. Once Tali had promised food and left, Raliel nudged Osian toward one of the beds. "Sleep as long as you need," she ordered. Then, as he stumbled around the screen, she followed and crouched to help him off with his boots.

"Ah, Raliel, you shouldn't," he protested, bending too.

She batted his hands away. "You nearly died protecting us. Again. So stand there and take it."

Osian pressed his mouth in a line under her sharp glare. He looked so different without the demon-kissed coloring. Younger and more vulnerable. Which, of course, he was not. It had always been an illusion. Raliel drew a deep breath and softened her expression.

"What are we going to do?" Osian asked.

"We are going to rest. Until your mother comes."

"She'll hate you."

"But help you?"

Osian looked away. He was too pale, too wavering, the bruise of his bones under his paper-thin skin filled her with fear. Raliel did not force him to speak. She'd leave her forcing for Syra Bear Mistress.

Once his shoes were off, it was quick work to remove his outer layers and tuck him into the low bed. He passed out before she'd finished gathering his things for the laundry.

When Raliel emerged, it was to Moon standing in the middle of the floor, their shared bag slumped against his ankle.

She blinked. It should be disorienting to see the stark lines of her dream-Osian-Moon in the rich blond of the wooden room, against green and teal hangings and in bright sunlight streaming through the latticed windows. But, instead, she felt a surge of relief. Of gladness.

"Bath?" it said.

Raliel nodded.

The tiled floor of the small bathroom was quite cold, but a fire burned in the stove, directing heat through several pipes for a warming rack and easily heated water. Raliel used a bit of Moon's stored aether to heat it faster, then stripped and got into the tub. Moon picked up her dirty clothes, rolling them for laundering, as she scrubbed at her skin with a soft bar of apple-smelling soap.

The great demon dragged over a short stool and set it beside the tub. "Hair?" it offered, and Raliel glanced at it. Nothing showed on its stark face—its pretty, dimpled, sweet face borrowed from Osian. Then Moon blinked and lifted brows so that it seemed to gently plead with her. Raliel sighed softly and sank deeper into the water, burying herself in it so that her hair floated and sank too. She wiped her cheeks as she held her breath, heat prickling her eyelids, her lips, filling her nostrils until she gently blew them clear and sat up, careful not to spill over the rim.

Moon gathered her hair and slowly worked in soap. It kneaded, combed its fingers through, lathering well and saying nothing. Raliel brought her knees up to her breasts and held them, letting her eyes drift shut. "Sing something," she murmured, and the great demon hummed one of her mother's slow, sweet compositions.

Raliel relaxed slowly, nearly to sleep, except for the tender tugging of her hair and the splash of water keeping her alert. Moon let its fingers brush the nape of her neck, the shells of her ears, and when it finished rinsing her hair of soap, twisted the weight of it into a knot and slid two hair sticks to secure it. Then Moon rubbed gently down her neck and squeezed her shoulders. "We should contact your parents."

Raliel groaned. She did not want to. The demon slipped its hands back to her neck and curled its fingers gently around her throat. Shivering despite the steamy water, Raliel pushed back to lean against the tub, and Moon shifted until its arm came around her neck instead, embracing her. Its sleeve touched the water, its elbow pressed to the silver amulet she hadn't removed. Moon pressed its cheek to hers.

Its voice whispered past the corner of her lips, and Raliel leaned into it. "Raliel. My Raliel."

Being here in its embrace, hot in the water, she felt safe. And

Osian was as safe as could be until his mother arrived. So finally Raliel said what she'd feared for weeks, "I think . . . something must be wrong in the palace, Moon. They wouldn't have risked hurting us if they didn't need us—you—back. They are sending messages with the Warriors of the Last Means for a reason. But if I talk to them, I'll know, and I won't be able to stay away. I'll take you back."

"They couldn't hide my absence forever. They need me home. To protect the empire. Their reputations." Moon's lashes brushed her temple as it blinked quickly.

For a few breaths they remained so, until Raliel whispered, "Is it home to you?"

"Yes," Moon answered immediately. "But that doesn't make me want to return. I like being out with you, like this. A self of my own."

"I like it," she whispered. "I like you with a self of your own. I wish we had more chances to . . . enjoy it."

"We'll keep enjoying it," Moon said ferociously. "We can now. I don't know if—I don't know if you're a sorcerer. I don't know if what we're doing—what we've done—*counts*. I don't know what will happen if we can change the amulet, if we can make it a real sorcerer binding. But I won't stop trying. I won't go back unless you promise not to stop too."

Raliel thought back to the promises they'd made to each other. On the beach at midsummer. To help. To do no harm. "I promise," she whispered.

FOUR

R ALIEL DRESSED, AND AFTER Moon combed her hair she offered it more of her blood to gobble up. Together they headed down to the lobby to brew a pot of tea.

Seated at one of the low tables, already with a steaming teapot and two cups, were a beautiful woman the Second Consort's age and an androgynous youth with watery blond hair cut sleekly at their jawline. The two turned immediately to Raliel and Moon.

Raliel nodded and made her way to the wall of tea sets. She knew neither.

Before she could begin selecting, she heard a sharp gasp behind her, just as the great demon hissed, *"Selegan!"* and flew at the youth with inhuman speed.

The great demon grabbed the blond youth by the neck and flung them away in an explosion of aether. The youth twisted into a dragon—a very small dragon, hardly larger than it had been as a youth—with three tails, a long feathered mane, horns, rippling silver-rainbow scales, and bright blue eyes. It hung in the air, wingless, exuding waves of bright aether that forced Raliel to shield her eyes with a raised hand.

The dragon's companion had not moved from her seat at the low table. The woman's perfect posture held, and she gracefully lifted a teacup to sip, watching.

Raliel stared at the dragon. Moon had called it the Selegan River. But here at the Fourth Mountain they were days and days away from its house. Raliel hadn't even known a river spirit could do such a thing. Was it also a familiar to this woman sipping her tea?

As Moon had not attacked again, but glared at the dragon, fists clenched at its sides, Raliel chose to continue selecting her tea, forcing a semblance of calm. Turning her back to the room was difficult, but she managed, picked a tray with a deep red pot and cups painted black and red.

"The third drawer from the left has a very crisp winterberry," said the beautiful older woman, her voice as lovely as her face.

"Do they have juniper or evergreen?" Raliel asked, thinking of her father's favorite.

"Two drawers below that."

"Thank you," Raliel said, and found a satchel that smelled sharp and cold. As she carried the tray to the hearth for hot water, she glanced at the great demon. "Moon," she said firmly.

"What are you doing here, Selegan?" Moon demanded.

The dragon landed on two feet, back in their youthful shape. Sixteen, perhaps, neither particularly masculine or feminine, wearing traveling tunic and boots in all the blues of a mountain stream. "We came to see the heir, on behalf of her family," they said, and bowed.

Raliel lifted her eyebrows. She nodded to the dragon, then looked at the woman. "I am the heir," she said, giving the woman a chance to introduce herself in return.

From her seat the woman smiled without showing teeth. Her eyes changed: from homely brown, one melted into a deathly yellow-white like old bones and the other brightened into a brazen green. "Shadows of the Fifth Mountain," she said simply.

The sorceress of the Fifth Mountain. Raliel held herself very still. Was the great demon Night Shine here too?

Moon's entire body wavered before it caught itself and solidified. Its shoulders heaved with the effort, then resettled, and its hair drifted up as if suddenly untethered by gravity.

"Sorceress," Raliel said, and nothing more before bringing her tea to the same table. She sat across from the sorceress. Moon stomped over and joined her, a scowl marring its pretty white face. And then came the dragon-youth, slipping silently over the tiles to perch across from Moon.

The four of them remained silent as Raliel's tea steeped, and she poured it for herself and Moon, even knowing the demon wouldn't partake. Then she offered some to the sorceress and politely poured. The tiny honey pot she'd found with the tea sets had a little dipper of pale wood, and the honey curled off it in perfect little streams Raliel found soothing. The Selegan River asked for some, too, once Raliel had added hers. Raliel handed it the little pot, and the youth grinned, using their finger to scoop out a large golden dollop.

Moon scoffed, as if above such things.

Raliel drank her tea and studied the sorceress, who studied her back. She said, "Why did they send you?"

Moon said, "The sorceress of the Fifth Mountain is not *sent* anywhere."

Ignoring him, Shadows said, "They wish to know you are well, to offer aid you require, and remind you of your duties to the palace, to the empire." Shadows's voice soothed Raliel just like the honey, very silky and confident. Even wearing plain black and brown robes and a long braided wool jacket like a pilgrim, something about the sorceress exuded refinement and skill. Raliel wondered if it was an aura she actively cultivated with magic.

Moon leaned forward. "Where is Night Shine?" it asked quietly, dangerously.

"In your palace, of course," Shadows replied. She met the demon's gaze without fear. Which made sense, as she was the only other confidant of a great demon in the known world.

"Doing *what?*" Moon seemed to be a little larger than usual. Its hair and eyes crackled with shadowy aether.

"Guarding it against danger. From Syra Bear Mistress, apparently. And the twin sorcerers of the Third and Second Mountains, who have been inquiring lately."

Raliel remembered the appraising look A Dance of Stars had given her in the palace corridor, and her father's bitter warning that the sorcerers wanted a great demon.

"We all felt it," Shadows said. "When you and your great demon stepped into the paths of sorcery last month. All masters of the mountains know—that is why they attacked the palace."

"A Dance of Stars?" Raliel demanded as Moon hissed through blunt human teeth.

"A Still Wind, but"—Shadows shrugged with all her elegance—"those two do nothing separately. They want your demon."

Beside Raliel, Moon rippled. It clamped down on its power, but she could feel it seething.

"Is everyone all right?" Raliel asked.

"Yes. Night Shine held the sorcerer off, and they will not be allowed to attack again. A compromise has been reached between the mountains."

Moon bared its teeth again. "What is the price of this compromise?"

The sorceress turned her death-white and vivid green eyes onto Moon. She studied it for a moment, and her expression seemed to soften into something like fondness. In response, Moon snarled.

Shadows laughed lightly. "No price for you."

The Selegan River suddenly said, "Raliel Dark-Smile, I've wished to meet you for all your life—but especially since I heard your name."

Smiling as much as she could manage under the circumstances, Raliel said, "I am glad to meet you, Selegan. I haven't had a chance to swim in your waters, but I have admired the glint of light along your length and the way you cradle the western city."

The youth looked down as if to hide a flush they could not experience. "You would be welcome in my waters," they murmured.

Raliel finished her tea and set the cup down. She turned fully to Shadows. "Sorceress, how did you give your great demon a piece of your heart?"

Shadows laughed once again, her expression warming further. "Enough with the pleasantries, I see."

Raliel waited. Beside her, Moon leaned on its elbows, eyes vivid black and fixed on the sorceress.

"Magic, of course," she said. Then she grinned, and her teeth were layered and jagged as a shark's. "It was no trick. I simply took out a piece of my heart, because I am a great sorcerer, and I gave it to my demon to fuel its transformation. Just as you have done something"—she slid a look at Moon—"traded something of her body to achieve this manifestation. Not a piece of your heart. Blood? Sex? And away from a house, indeed. Unless you are its house, Raliel Dark-Smile?"

"Partially," Raliel admitted. She breathed deeply and poured more tea. She did not look at Moon. And she did not think about sex.

"Why didn't it work?" Moon demanded. "Why did your demon appear in *my* house?"

"That I do not know, though I have theories. Tell me what you really want to know, and I will tell you the theory that fits it best."

Moon bared its teeth in a sneer, those dimples it stole from Osian flashing, and Raliel touched its wrist. She said to the sorceress, "You lost your familiar, then, yes? You gave Night Shine your heart, and she was reborn a living demon far away. But you were bound until then, weren't you? A true shared binding?"

"Yes." Amusement fled Shadows's face.

"How did the binding change then? Your sorcerer-demon bond."

"That part was only a question of names."

"Names?"

"Names, yes. Names are all that matter for the binding, whether witch or sorcerer, familiar or great demon." Her tone said, *You should know this.* "We changed my great demon's name when I gave her my heart, and it changed our relationship, her entire self, her power, her heart, her life."

"That's all it takes, even for a great demon's bind?" Moon slouched. "My binding is different from most."

"But does anything else power the great amulet of the palace? You exchange names and vows, and the power of the amulet takes over, yes?"

Moon nodded.

The sorceress lifted her eyebrows as if to say, *That's all it takes.* That and an incredible amount of pure aether.

"So all Moon must do is change its name," Raliel said softly. "No heart, no sorcery. Just, change your name." Growing incredulity heated her, and she struggled for her snowy calm. That was too simple, too easy. The Scale would have known that!

Moon pushed away from the table. "That's too easy to be true!"

Shadows said, "It is not *easy* to change the name of a great demon. You cannot simply say, here is my new name. It must be fundamental. An earned name. A name you know in every fiber of your being. And even with a new name, old ones can do harm. If enough people with power remembered Shine's old name, they could use it, believe in it, and harm her strength—her heart, too. Names can reveal us, or hurt us. They make, remake us, but they can completely undo us too. Destroy us. What we are called matters. I expected you to know such things, considering the name you chose for yourself, Raliel."

Raliel winced slightly. She'd picked the name of a deliciously infamous dragon, whose name had lived beyond its death, in violent song. But when Raliel had been a child, she'd only thought it was thrilling and beautiful. She'd been seven!

"But the humans," Moon said, turning back, "the humans change. Their names. The palace-amulet must require something else."

But Shadows said, "No. The Emperor is always the Emperor with the Moon in His Mouth, and his consorts always the First and Second Consorts. They fit themselves, their names, to the amulet names. They change to the always-names."

Raliel said, "I put your name on this," and touched her fingers to her shirt, over the little silver amulet. This was such a vital conversation to be having in that simple tearoom. Raliel thought the world outside might have vanished. And she thought if Osian were present, he'd be laughing. A little awed, too.

"This entire time we have been struggling to make me into what I want to be, and I only needed a new name," Moon said.

The Selegan spoke up. "Do you really want to be someone entirely different? You change if your name changes. Live or die or become something new. You could end up a thousand miles away, or unrecognizable to yourself and everyone."

"But I would be free." The quiet longing in Moon's voice silenced the conversation for a long moment.

Shadows studied the great demon as if suddenly understanding something. But she merely said, "None of us is free."

FIVE

SHADOWS OF THE FIFTH Mountain departed as soon as she finished her tea. "I've seen you're alive, and I'm not a babysitter," she said, before dragging the reluctant Selegan River with her. Raliel and Moon returned to their room. Osian remained sleeping, and Raliel sat on the edge of his bed, staring down at his slack, wan face. His breath seemed thinner than before. Slower. Soon, if they didn't find help, he wouldn't wake up at all.

"We made the palace vulnerable," she whispered. "You and I, Moon."

"We knew when we left that the palace would be vulnerable," it whispered back.

"But now they've attacked. The sorcerers. And when Syra comes here, she'll know too that the great demon of the palace is not in the palace. It's a good time for revenge."

Moon frowned. "Obviously we're going to kill her before we go."

Raliel's mouth fell open. She'd known she'd have to argue hard for arrest over death, but Moon didn't even give her an opening.

"Not until after she heals Osian," Moon reassured her. As if that were the concerning part.

"We can't even trust her to do that."

Moon wrinkled its face. "Oh, we can make her do that."

"Prove she was right about the imperial family?" Raliel asked softly. The great demon only rolled its eyes.

For two days they waited. Osian woke in the afternoon of the first day and insisted on being bundled up in the tearoom to receive a stream of visitors. Raliel and Moon remained at his side, feeding him aether and propping him up. Raliel played her role perfectly: glad to meet all his aunts, complimenting them, and, of course, providing stories of Osian's bravery and cleverness upon request. None of them mentioned what his mother had expected of him. Perhaps they did not know. Some of them apologetically stumbled over his name and his pronouns, but none of them were surprised to see him without demon-kissed markings.

One of the aunties with priestly training, Blush Hunter, finally broke and asked Moon why it wore Osian's face.

"He is very handsome," the great demon said.

Blush Hunter lifted her eyebrows, but Windsong laughed. "We have always thought so, Moon," the latter woman agreed.

"Raliel likes it," Moon added without prompting, to which Raliel flattened her lips and Osian glanced at her, smiling shyly—but broad enough his dimples made an appearance.

In the evening, only Windsong and Tali remained with them. They shared a simple meal, and Osian put up less fuss with Tali helping him than he did when Raliel tried it. Moon urged them to tell stories about Osian growing up and frowned when Tali referred to the five-year-old Osian as a she before wincing and apologizing. Osian said, "I never told you otherwise. You could not have known."

"Did you think you would not be welcome here?" Windsong asked gently. "You must have known I, myself—"

"This is a place for women," Osian interrupted. His lashes fluttered nervously. "You're a woman. I am—not."

Silence surrounded them for a moment: Osian and his aunts held each other's hands, and Raliel remained quiet, too, glad they could have this. Moon stared blatantly.

Windsong said, "I am glad you were able to live openly in the capital." She slid her dark brown eyes to Raliel. "Thank you for facilitating that."

"My father," Raliel began to protest.

Both aunts nodded. Windsong laughed a little. It was oddly light, breathy. "Heir—"

"Raliel," Raliel murmured. "Please."

Then the older woman smiled easily as a child. "Raliel. Your father is the reason I am here. I came to Four Ridges because of the stories I heard about Kirin Dark-Smile. Good and bad—there were both—but part of them after his Heir's Journey always included who he *is*. Who he made himself, or"—she waved a hand—"who he allowed himself to be, and then fought to be. Knowing that helped me be strong enough to try myself."

"Oh." Raliel did not know what else to say. When Osian had said similar things, she'd been so emotionally compromised for other reasons, and Osian was only a single person. But for others to think this same thing about her father, about his life, was a revelation. The emperor had always just been himself to her. Choosing rings, choosing himself, changing himself. Even when he was arguing or sneering, flirting, laughing, he was just her father. People admired his poise and beauty and his sharpness. People complained about him, about his decrees and suggestions, about how ferocious he tended to be, how stubborn and inconsolable. He changed laws, ordered taxes, moved pieces of the army however he liked—those were the things Raliel had thought mattered. Changed the empire and the people. That's what he taught her, what everyone taught her.

Glancing down at her hand, Raliel rubbed her thumb over the small diamond ring on her left forefinger.

The emperor had affected Windsong's and Osian's lives fundamentally just by refusing to hide himself. That daily choice rippled out and changed people, just as much as any decree or command. Just as much as his mistakes led to thirsting for revenge.

Raliel reached for Moon, overwhelmed by the sudden edges of ineffability.

Moon wove its fingers with hers.

A long time ago she'd thought she couldn't be like her parents, putting their masks down with each other, falling in love, serving the world through themselves and their relationship to it. She couldn't because she didn't know how to make a mask when she wasn't certain who she was beneath it. More and more, Raliel suspected she'd always known who she was—since she gave herself this ridiculous name.

And it was this: a solitary diamond, cold and strong, on a finger twined with a great demon's.

Syra Bear Mistress arrived suddenly and without warning.

Raliel and Osian sat on his bed, trading lines of poetry back and forth—mostly Raliel, because Osian's exhaustion made it difficult to recite for long. Their knees touched lightly. Moon sprawled on the floor on his back, eyes closed but frequently taking one of their stanzas and unknotting it with quick word-play into something new.

Once or twice the great demon slipped and added puns in a different language, and Osian pouted until Raliel did her best to translate. She took his hand and drew a sigil for sharing aether on his palm.

"It tickles," he said, but did not pull away, only curled his fingers up around the invisible sigil protectively. Blue-white light flashed briefly, though Osian couldn't see it, and sank into him through the lines of the sigil.

"Thank you," he murmured.

Raliel thought about kissing his wrist. She glanced at Moon, whose wrists tucked under its head as it stretched languidly. Before she could wander too far down the path of tracing the line of its neck to chest to stomach, from downstairs they heard a door slam and a voice yell, "Where is my son?"

"Mother." Osian tried to leap up but stumbled. Moon slithered in a way no human body could and caught him. The demon raised them both to their feet: they mirrored each other perfectly.

Nerves bubbled in Raliel's chest, but the angle of Osian's lean against Moon's chest solidified her resolve. She would demand Syra's aid with Osian and allow no harm to come to any of them. Moon had previously vetoed her argument that it wait up here, to seem less a threat, to be her secret weapon. And so Raliel buckled her sword belt over her shoulder. The weight of the blade pressed comfortingly.

Together they went downstairs.

Syra already prepared tea at one of the tables. Raliel had only a moment to study the woman: overly thin with light-brown hair falling loose but for a few small braids. Ragged silk flowers wove through them, limp like old mushrooms clinging to a tree.

Osian, between Moon and Raliel, stepped forward. "Mother."

She froze, back to them. As she turned, her worn gray robes rustled against the floor. "Osian," she said, almost regretfully.

It was an odd reaction. Osian did not appear to think so.

Raliel found Syra beautiful in the way of antique furniture or heirloom teacups: lovely, sleek, finely made, and if out of style, still retaining the echo of details that once had been glorious. She seemed drawn, as if she'd been ill for a long time too, but Syra's eyes were the same merry brown as Osian's, and in her grimace sat the ghosts of his dimples.

"You brought the Heir to the Moon here?" Syra said quietly. "Alive."

"I did."

Syra approached. She did not go to her son, but Raliel. "So. You are Raliel Dark-Smile."

Raliel nodded once. It was not a bow. This was not respect.

The resignation in Syra's gaze did not falter as she slapped Raliel across the face.

Shocked, Raliel stepped back, but she grabbed Moon's wrist before the demon retaliated.

"Mother!" Osian cried, and took hold of Syra's arm.

Raliel's cheek burned, and the sharp sound rang in her skull. She blinked away stinging tears and faced Syra again.

"Thank you for the excuse to have you executed," Moon hissed, jerking its wrist from Raliel.

Syra hummed. "The palace needs no excuse." Then she actually seemed to notice Moon, and her lips parted. "What are you, wearing my child's face?"

Moon grinned, showing sharp teeth, and five more eyes bulged out of its forehead. They blinked in time, and the demon said, "I am the Moon, and I can eat you before you can scream."

Raliel shifted between them. "Lady Syra," she said. She ought to keep the upper hand if possible. "Whatever else may be between us, your son is ill and we need to know what you and the great spirit of the Fourth Mountain did to change him."

"My son . . . ," the woman murmured, glancing to Osian. "Windsong's message said you were ill, but unless it is magical, I cannot save you." She took his face between her hands.

"It is magical," Raliel said.

Moon said, "I stripped his disguise away, and it hurt him beyond what I expected." The demon's voice managed to make the fact more of a threat.

Syra, who thus far did not behave with the madness Osian had warned them to expect, but with a rather weary, defeated air, said, "We traced new lines of aether into your body. Placed them over others, twisted through some. If it was stripped away violently, those lines and channels might've knotted, or torn. If the energy cannot move as it should, you will be exhausted, unable to regulate your temperature or digestion. It seems already worsened enough your body cannot process sleep, nor take sustenance from food."

"Can you help him?" Raliel asked. If it was only torn or knotted aether-channels, surely the priests and witches in the palace could reorder them, or smooth them. But they were far away. Maybe the women here could help.

Syra said, "I could."

"Will you?" Osian asked. His jaw muscle shifted as he clenched it. Raliel could barely imagine what he was going through, standing before his mother like this after everything. And her not leaping to his aid or comfort. Raliel wanted to put her hand on his back but refused to undercut him. That might turn Syra entirely against them.

"Perhaps," Syra said, too casual.

Moon snarled.

Raliel allowed herself a moment to breathe and recall the snow inside her. This was a palace battle, not one her sword could help with. But ice could, and politeness. "We will find someone else if you will not," she said lightly. Easily. Arrogantly. She was the daughter of Kirin Dark-Smile, and partner, if not sorcerer, too a great demon. Raliel tilted her chin up and gave Syra Bear Mistress her best princess glare.

The woman smiled. "Drink with me. We will discuss my price." She gestured to the nearest table, set with a pale-pink teapot and cups cut to look like balsam trumpets. Lovely, easy to spill.

Osian needed to rest, and so Raliel did not hesitate. Though she would make sure Syra drank first.

Raliel helped Osian sit, then folded herself down with every ounce of grace she could manage. Moon knelt at her other side, and Syra lowered herself across, haltingly, as if her body hurt her.

Syra poured tea for the four of them, and before anything else, Moon reached out and plucked up Syra's cup and Raliel's and switched them. It did not bother looking away from Syra as it did so.

The older woman smiled, cradled her new teacup, and lifted it in salute.

Raliel did the same, as did the rest.

"This smells of aether," Moon said.

Surprised, Raliel realized she could smell it, indeed: a hazy ozone like the sea after a storm.

"It is a tea I make myself on the mountain. Invigorating." Syra narrowed her eyes at Moon, daring. "The power I have used is harsh on my human body, too."

Moon did not back down, though it had already switched the drinks. Raliel nearly reached to touch its wrist, but with a pretty sigh, Syra drank her entire cup in one scorching draft. She reached for Raliel's and took that, too, drinking it in full. Then she returned her bright brown gaze to Moon. The great demon flattened its lips. "Fine," it said.

Syra went through the process of pouring again, sliding a new cup to Raliel.

Osian held his cup against his lap but did not drink. His expression screamed of tiredness, confusion, hurt. Raliel wanted this over with.

She sipped. The tea sparked on her tongue—it was pleasant. She breathed deeply through her nose, thought of her own mother, her fathers, sharing tea with all of them in the Moon's

Recline Garden early in the morning, when it was the emperor's preferred evergreen tea, sharp, astringent, kissed with honey.

Syra's hand trembled as she set down her empty cup. One finger skimmed the edge of the petal carved into it, nearly tipping it over. The skin below her eyes was shaded with bruises. Raliel remembered Osian had said she was sickly when he was a child, and now remained so, it seemed. Sacrificing health for magic she was unsuited to.

The tea in Raliel's belly continued to sparkle.

"Ah, Raliel Dark-Smile," Syra said. "Thank you for this opportunity." She blinked, blinked again as if having trouble focusing.

Raliel leaned nearer. "Are you well?"

"Ah, ah, well enough. Is the tea to your liking?" Syra smiled, and the dimples she'd passed to Osian deepened, drawn firmly in place by lines around her mouth.

"Yes." Raliel took another sip. It warmed her throat as she swallowed, and she flicked a glance at Moon, who lifted one eyebrow to say it did not know anything. There was not very much room in the delicate cup, and Raliel finished her tea with her fourth sip.

"I would like water," Osian said, shifting as if in pain. Moon stood to fetch it, but just then Syra suddenly grimaced wildly.

"Lady—" Raliel snapped, and Moon jerked forward to grip Syra's arm. But the woman pulled away hard enough she fell back, landing hard on the tiled floor.

"Thank you for bringing them to me, Osian!" Syra declared, laughing. "It is better to do it myself!" Her cheeks flushed quite suddenly, and she widened her eyes to glare at Raliel.

As their eyes met, Raliel felt a slow, strange dip in her stomach. As if it pulled down, swung up, and flipped over. A great tidal wave crackling with tiny sparks of aether. She opened her mouth, tongue peeling off the roof dryly. It was difficult to draw a deep breath, and as she tried, the air stuttered.

"Raliel," Moon said, throaty. It gripped her face, its palm cold on her cheek—so cold! Raliel was used to its skin being cool, hers being so too, but this was shocking. She had to be aflame to experience its touch like ice.

Raliel tried to stand up, but the room tilted.

Osian called her name, and Moon, too. Their matching faces, with matching concern, floated before her.

Syra Bear Mistress laughed again, high-pitched. She leaned back to the floor, hands splayed like white spiders against the tile. Raliel looked suddenly at her empty cup, then flung her hand to spill Moon's and Osian's—she missed! The distance it looked and how her hand reached were incorrect. Her perception . . . her . . .

The great demon threw itself up and outside, yelling for help louder than a human possibly could.

"Oh," Raliel said, closing her eyes tightly. They'd been so foolish. Long fingers of lightning whipped out from her stomach, up and down and out, piercing her aether-threads. Her body ached suddenly, all over, fighting another tidal roll. Raliel murmured, "Moon. My sword . . ."

The laughter spilling from Syra's mouth was more like choking, like hard sobs. Maybe she was saying "justice," maybe slurring nothing at all. Raliel stared.

Osian fell to his knees beside his mother, pushing her to her side, telling her something Raliel did not understand.

Raliel had never been so hot, never. She felt as though her blood had become strings of lightning, searing fire! She was ice, but she was *melting*. She fumbled to unbuckle her sword belt; it slipped off her shoulder and crashed to the floor.

Syra Bear Mistress's back arched, and blood spilled from her nose. Then she froze, slumped. Died.

SIX

M OON COULD NOT BELIEVE how long it had taken it to learn that with humans involved things could always get worse.

Its roar for help shook the lintel of the door, and the lanterns strung up and down the lane bobbed as if in a strong wind, and silver bells hanging from the peaked roofs tinkled bright and wild. A woman appeared, wide-eyed, then another. Moon yelled again, for a doctor, then rushed into the guest house lobby so fast it disappeared and reappeared between one step and the next.

Crouching over Syra, it grasped at her neck to shake her, demand a cure, but her body jerked loosely. She was dead already. So fast!

Moon spun.

Raliel sat on the short stool, legs crossed and back straight, all proper posture, but completely rigid as she struggled to remove her outer jacket. Her eyes were closed, her jaw tight. And a faint tremor ran up and down her body. Osian knelt behind her, leaning fully against her, an arm around her waist. His skin shone with sweat, and he met Moon's eyes. "Help her."

"Raliel," Moon said, creeping nearer. Her knuckles had blotched pinkish she gripped her fists so hard against her thighs. Bright red streaked her cheeks like a rash, ran down her neck, and blossomed at her collarbone. If it opened her robes, it knew it would find vivid red spreading down her chest.

She did not respond to Moon. It felt heat radiating off her, sharp and brilliant like lightning, not fire. Aether rippled around her—Moon felt it inside itself, too: the connection, the threads knotting it to Raliel with her blood, with her amulet, with her name and vows, all of it trembled. Moon pressed firmly on itself, testing. It was solid. Aether thrummed powerfully.

"Raliel," it said again, a warning now, and put both hands on her cheeks. Aether rushed out of her and into it, ragged and powerful as a waterfall. Moon grunted at the effort of refusing the aether, the struggle to *not* latch on and drink drink drink. That would clean her out in seconds.

Instead, Moon focused and pushed back, forcing aether to halt and turn, shoving it with raw strength back up the waterfall.

Raliel cried out, shying away. She raised her hands against Moon, and it caught her wrists as she flailed. It stopped working aether, and she shuddered, eyes flying open but unseeing.

"What's wrong?" Osian asked. "Do you know what the poison is? Mother was—I don't—"

"It's her aether."

"Does she need more? Take mine—whatever you need, please."

Moon snarled, "You don't have any to spare."

"I don't care."

"Nor do I." Moon glared at Osian. "But she does."

Raliel suddenly slumped forward. Osian held on, slowing her fall, and Moon caught them both. Lowered them to the ground before putting Raliel's head against its thigh. Her magic flickered and spat, a huge mess of churning power. Her threads, her aether-points, rejected their natural paths. She was unspooling, her channels peeling apart. Moon hugged her tight and started to panic. It was a demon. It took. It took and took and could not heal.

"What happened!" someone cried. There were more voices. Someone dropped to their knees beside Syra's corpse, and Tali appeared beside Moon. The woman put the back of her hand to Raliel's forehead.

"Poison," Osian gasped. "Mother poisoned Raliel—and herself! She—"

Moon interrupted, "Syra is dead, but Raliel's aether is under attack. The poison attacked her aether?" it guessed. This feeling was terrible: Moon was unravelling too, cold cold cold.

Another woman nudged Tali out of the way. Her hair was recently shaved, and the shadows of sigil tattoos wavered through the hair. A witch.

"Don't push aether into her," Moon said, almost shoving Raliel into the witch's arms. "She cried out."

The witch nodded as together they laid Raliel down on the floor. Raliel moaned. Sweat curled her baby hairs, sticking them to her forehead and temples. Moon smelled the sharpness of it, the aether-sweat, like salt water and lightning.

"—the tea," Osian said. He gestured weakly at the balsam trumpet cups.

Ignoring him, the witch used a polished white birch stick

to touch Raliel's crown, her throat, and then her palms, while holding her hand over Raliel's heart. The witch's eyes flickered with blue aether.

"What can we do? Blankets? Ice? Fire?" Tali said. She knelt with them, and Moon only then realized the woman had a hand on its shoulder. It was . . . comfortable. Moon's insides clenched. It held to Raliel's ankles, anxious.

The witch didn't answer right away, then slowly shook her head. "Her aether is . . . disintegrating. The poison, whatever it is . . . tainted it all somehow."

"Can I . . . ? Can we do anything? There must be something." Moon did its best to speak firmly, without desperation. Under its hands, Raliel's ankles spasmed, popping with aether-sparks. It swallowed a yell.

"I do not know how to counteract it. I . . ." The witch closed her eyes. She drew a sigil on Raliel's skin with the birch wand, then yelped as the sigil sizzled. Raliel gasped: her neck arched and she didn't close her mouth, panting now instead, shallow and fast.

Moon shoved forward, pushing the witch and Tali away. "Raliel."

The witch said, "I can't clean it. All her aether needs to be . . . replaced, flushed somehow. At once."

"Can I—" Moon tried to pull on her aether, gently, not voraciously.

She shuddered again.

Moon's hands were ice-cold. It felt off, sputtering.

"Keep going," the witch urged. "Carefully."

"I am careful," Moon snapped. It breathed through its teeth, concentrating. It was so very difficult to moderate its drag. Better if Raliel woke to push—she could feed it better than it could take from her. The channels were too connected. There was too much chance of it stopping her heart like it had all those months ago, when they first experimented. Her heart had stopped. Like Osian's had stopped. Moon was only death for these people, for everyone. Taking, hungry, wild. It couldn't do this. It was made to devour.

Moon was sweating now too, little jagged flecks of frost hardening on its temple, at its cheeks, across its lips and knuckles: an ice blush, blue-silver hives.

Suddenly Raliel fainted. Her limbs went limp, her mouth slack.

"Raliel," Osian moaned.

"Oh no," the witch said, grabbing her wrists again. "Her . . . There's nothing to replace it! Stop."

The demon stopped. It stopped so hard it didn't breathe and its heart didn't beat. It was completely still.

"When you take her aether, nothing follows. The poison . . . I don't know. I can't tell. I'm not a doctor, and our best healer knows nothing of aether-work except for how it affects blood and breath."

"What do we do? Can I take her home? Somewhere? Is there—" Moon hissed to stop itself from asking if she had *time*.

The witch sat back on her heels and stared at Moon. "You're a demon. By nature you drain, take, even as her familiar."

"I'm not—not exactly." Moon squeezed its eyes shut, frustrated. When it opened them, its lashes shattered as it broke apart the ice.

"But if you were a spirit, a great spirit with your own aether, all the aether of a mountain . . ." The witch looked past Moon at the dead Syra. Then snapped her gaze back to Moon.

"The great spirit of the Fourth Mountain," Moon said. It surged to its feet. "The bear can help."

"Crown," said Osian urgently. "It's called Crown."

Moon picked Raliel up. She was nothing, fire and air in its arms.

SEVEN

R ALIEL RECALLED VERY LITTLE of the race up the mountain. She burned, carried by a demon of ice, its arms hard as it ran, pulling on so much aether the great spirit of the Fourth Mountain could not possibly miss their arrival. She heard Moon whispering to her, her name, exhortations to live, to hold on to her aether even if it hurt.

It did hurt.

Raliel tried, but it was like snakes of fire, hissing and spitting inside her, burning where she touched. She was not made for this heat! Scorching from the inside, she felt her bones crack, her fat pop, her skin flake, and her muscles melt. Her blood evaporated into wisps of red smoke. Her eyes were pools of lava in her skull. Only where she pressed against the cold, cold Moon did she feel relief at all. And the edges of its power, the aether it dragged out of the mountain, soothed her only enough to cling to it, to waking. Her jaw ached from clenching it.

"Raliel, Raliel, hold on," Moon whispered, its breath a frozen relief against her ear. "If you don't, I'll let go. I'll push back inside you and nestle under your heart, just me and you, even if it unravels me, too. I don't want that. You don't want that, but I'll do it. I'll try to give it all to you if you don't stay awake, alive."

With all her reserves, Raliel hugged the great demon's neck and tried to laugh. Tears squeezed past her lashes and turned into smoke.

Suddenly they stopped.

what is this, called a booming voice.

Raliel winced away.

"This is Raliel Dark-Smile, Heir to the Moon. And I am Moon, the great demon of the palace." Moon spoke too loudly as well. She buried her face in its neck. "She has been poisoned. Her aether is diminishing. But you can save her. Will you?"

save her.

"You're a great spirit—you can. Give her a transfusion of aether. Yours is endless. You can heal her. Will you?"

bring her here.

They moved again. Raliel tried to crack open her eyes, but the light slashed into her brain. She shied away, trying to shield herself.

Her pulse beat so hard in her chest. A hammer. Thunder. Crashing waves. The entire world beating. It hurt.

She thought, Syra Bear Mistress knew this great spirit. It had been bound to Skybreaker. Why help her? Why did Moon think—

I will help if you put this on, the bear spirit said.

Moon tensed around her. Lowered. Knelt. Set her on hard—cold!—stone. It felt good. She twisted her fingers in its jacket. Forced her lips to part, and with breath hot as smoke, tried to say, *Wait, wait, don't trust it—*

375

But her great demon did not wait. "Do you swear you will help her?"

I do. On the strength of the Fourth Mountain, my great house.

"Very well." Moon shifted somehow, then hissed a long breath. Her bones hurt. Her skin itched with sensitivity, too much, everything was too much.

Then all was power: vivid silver-blue aether suffocating her, lifting her, tearing her away from Moon. Raliel gasped; she sucked searing magic down her throat and—

Blinked.

Raliel opened her eyes.

She felt fine.

A little tired, as if she'd slept too long. She lay on something soft, a thick rug? Light filtered through a gauzy curtain around her.

The rattle of a chain drew her attention, and she turned her head. Beside the low bed Moon crouched, head lowered, elbows on its knees, and hands dangling. A collar around its neck. And a chain looped over its shoulders like a stole. Its black hair curled and sighed to its own breezy gravity, as usual, bringing Raliel a modicum of comfort. "Moon?" she said, more of a gentle cough than a word.

It jerked its head up, eyes wide and oh so black. Completely black, without pupil, iris, sclera. Not even the gray-white of a full moon. Solid, impossible black.

"You're awake," spoke someone beyond Moon, a cheerful voice.

Standing in the room—solid stone walls marked with crawling, glowing aether-sigils—were two men and three beasts. The

376

twin sorcerers, Raliel recognized. They looked exactly the same: blandly handsome, gilded, draped in crimson and maroon, long bloodred hair pinned up with elegant golden crowns. Their eyes were the silver of aether-light.

And the beasts: a massive bear, a tiger, an eagle who fluffed its wings as Raliel stared.

"We have met, Heir," said one of the sorcerers. It had to be A Dance of Stars, who'd spoken to her at the palace on Midsummer Night.

Raliel pushed herself to sit. Her arms trembled with exhaustion, a mark that she was unwell, despite feeling strangely healthy. She bit her lip, glanced at Moon, who had not taken its eyes from her. She felt for her aether: it trembled too, just like her arms. It was . . . slow. Stuck. No longer burning, but nor did it flow. It was like cold honey, hardening inside her, in a knot under her heart, in long sticky strings in her legs and arms, gummy in her head. "What's wrong with me?"

stopped the poison, said the bear spirit. Its fur bristled, dark brown and tipped in streaks of silver.

"I am not better. It is still corrupting my aether."

"They did not heal you," Moon said, its voice like tumbling rocks. The chain shifted over its shoulders, clanging. "They want to make a bargain."

"Why are you wearing that?" Raliel murmured, struggling not to list sideways. She lifted her gaze to the twin sorcerers. "Moon is no threat to you. Release it. Confining it is an insult to the emperor."

A Dance of Stars laughed. "I do not mind insulting the emperor."

377

The tiger spirit slunk nearer to Raliel, huge blue-silver head tilted to watch her with one beautiful eye. *you nearly have made it your familiar. but we want it for our family.*

"Your family?" Raliel frowned. Her mouth was so tacky. She needed water.

Before she could ask, Moon was up, sitting on the edge of the bed, offering her a cup. She took it, and A Dance of Stars summoned a chair from up through the floor and lounged into it, relaxed and intent upon her. A Still Wind remained standing, but held out his hand to the eagle spirit: it rubbed the side of its enormous sharp hooked beak against his palm. Lovingly.

"They're all bound," Moon said quietly. "Crown is their familiar, too. It is not just one sorcerer to one great spirit, but all three of the great spirits bound to both of them, them to each other."

Shock punched through her, and she looked at the twins. But said nothing. She hadn't known that was possible. To share familiars with others. It seemed not dissimilar from the palace-amulet.

Finally A Still Wind spoke, mirroring her thoughts. "You see, the imperial family's bond is not the only unconventional sorcery in the world." His voice was softer than his brother's.

Raliel handed the water cup back to Moon, then put her hand on its knee, where it had hooked up on the bed. "You want Moon. You want me to give it to you."

A Still Wind did not change his expression, remaining cool, distant. Despite his easy looks, he seemed the most inhuman thing in the room. It was A Dance of Stars who grinned. "We want Moon to choose us. Join us."

"It is bound to me. To the palace. It cannot."

The eagle spirit ruffled its feathers again. *hunt now.*

A Still Wind nodded, and the eagle vanished into a wisp of aether, drifted away.

"Aerin tends to be easily bored," A Dance of Stars said with false apology. "But Crown and Beauty are more than enough to hold you and your demon."

"You can't get away with this. Shadows said there was a compromise." Raliel said it, even suspecting the twins either did not care or had a loophole.

"This falls into the allowable actions of what we agreed to."

"Unless you die," said A Still Wind.

"But then," laughed A Dance of Stars, "you will still be dead. So."

"What is your proposal?" Raliel demanded calmly. She straightened her posture, lifted an eyebrow, thought of her mother. Though she was covered in weird sweat, hair falling around her, vulnerable in a bed, she would behave like the Heir to the Moon.

"Your great demon will give us its name so that we may bind it with us, and then we cure your poison. Very simple," A Dance of Stars said slowly, like to a young child.

"And when it refuses?"

"We unbind the poison and let you die. When it—and your family—is vulnerable in the aftermath, use force to take it anyway."

Rage exploded in her chest. Raliel clenched her jaw against it, pressed her mouth closed. But she glared. Her fingers dug into Moon's knee. The surge of emotion dragged at the poison, and it sparked, too. Raliel gasped, tears filling her eyes with crunchy, salty irritation. "How dare you," she said.

"Be careful, Heir," A Still Wind said in his gentle way. "If you aggravate the poison, it will kill you faster."

"I'm going to die from it anyway," she said breathlessly, hating the sound of her weakness.

"Hmm, I don't think so," the sorcerer said, glancing at Moon. Raliel couldn't help but follow his strange gaze.

Moon stared at her with huge black eyes, too big in its face—Osian's pretty face, made inhuman with moon-white skin and that solid black hair, those solid black eyes. It was utterly still. "Raliel," it whispered.

"No," she said.

yes, said the tiger. And the bear said, *you will.*

"Live for each other, or die for each other," A Dance of Stars said. He leapt to his feet. Bowed with a smile. "You have until dawn to decide. Until then, our hospitality!"

They left, followed by Beauty and Crown, who seemed to suck all the warmth out of the room in their wake.

Moon slumped toward Raliel. "I am sorry," it said, low and whining. "I should have—I should have looked elsewhere. A different spirit, anything else."

Raliel lay back down, unable to keep her spine straight a moment longer. "Did they all plan this together? Syra and Crown and the twins? How?"

"I don't know."

"Osian?"

"With his aunts. He did not drink the tea." Moon stretched out beside her, its head on her shoulder. "I wish I could possess you. Slip back inside."

"The chains?"

"Yes. If I could, maybe from inside you I could do something about this poison. I tried pushing aether into you, but it didn't work. The witch said it must be a full, powerful transfusion of aether. A great spirit could save you."

"I see." Raliel tried not to worry. Tried to tamp down the anxious pattering of her heart.

"I'm sorry," it said hoarsely.

"I know," she whispered. "Let me—help me up. Let's find food. Drink. I need to be a little stronger."

Moon stared at her for a long moment. Its eyes were less horrible now, threads of moon-silver gathering among the black. "I won't let you die," it said.

She waved its words away. She was not prepared. Needed fortification to win this fight. "Food. Then argue."

The great demon's lips twisted as if to hide a bark of laughter, refusing to give her its amusement. "Fine."

EIGHT

I T WAS EASY, IN the Third Mountain, to find a pretty young
servant to direct them to a dining room and bring them
an extravagant meal: water, hot wine that steamed sweetly,
honey cakes and tiny smoked fish to eat in a single bite; chicken
in plum sauce and rosemary cheese, roasted purple carrots
sprinkled with dark sugar. Raliel ate until her stomach rebelled
and drank until her cheeks pinked. She felt full, light-headed,
and well. Moon watched her, smiling with amusement and a
certain horrible fondness she glanced away from.

It told her what it knew about the poison, everything the
Four Ridges witch had said and what the twin sorcerers added
while she'd been asleep. The great spirit of the Fourth Mountain
had made an aether-net to hold her in stasis, to keep her aether
from flowing at all. If she broke it, the poison would start eating
her again. She shivered at the spark of pain that thrilled up and
down her body. Raliel breathed narrowly through pursed lips
and avoided Moon's accusing gaze.

"A great spirit could blast through me, purging and replacing
the aether in my points and threads," she said, to be sure she

understood. "But you cannot, because you couldn't replace the aether you dispelled with anything."

"And if I did try, I might destroy your aether-channels, destroy your ability to touch aether. My nature is destructive. Consuming. Not like a spirit," Moon said bitterly—she'd never heard it regret itself.

Raliel's heart ached. Softly, she said, "I could live like that. Without magic. If I have to, if we both lived."

"It isn't a real choice, Raliel. I can't promise anything—I killed you once already. And Osian. This would be raw, desperate. Much, much more dangerous. It would probably kill you no matter what. I can't practice! There would be no second chance. I won't."

Raliel swallowed, skimming her finger along the rim of her wine cup. A fluttering anxiety groped at her stomach. Her throat felt thick. Choking her.

"No," Moon said, halting her finger with its cold hand. "Stop thinking it. Besides, I can't even try with this chain, this collar. They have to remove it, or I have to destroy it. Which would take a lot of power, and they would notice immediately. Stop me."

"I know what we need," Raliel whispered, shaking free of its touch and finishing the final sip of clear wine. It burned gently down her throat, forcing back her queasy stomach.

Moon lifted both eyebrows.

She took a deep breath, relishing the tingle of sharp alcohol brightening the back of her tongue, the sting.

But the great demon's gaze flicked past her, toward the windows. "Raliel, wait."

It stood and held a hand out to her. She took it, and Moon

pulled her up. She swayed against it. With an arm around her, hand fitted to her waist, the great demon turned her and led her toward the tall arched windows. "Look."

The night beyond wavered strangely: streaks of clouds shrouded the moon, but the world was not dark; it glowed. The entire night glowed softly. In flux, motion, like the inside of a silent waterfall.

Raliel's lips parted, and she started forward before she even realized it, rushing. Her hands touched the panes of glass, and they moved, swinging out to allow her to step onto a balcony.

This was snow.

It was snowing.

She could hardly breathe. Tiny stars, millions of them, floating down, drifting prettily in the grip of the mountain wind. Raliel gasped: it shook like a little sob.

Cold air embraced her, little snowflakes caught her hair and lashes. She blinked, tilted her face up, and snow kissed her cheeks, her lips! She sobbed again: no, it was laughter. Bright, sweet, painful laughter stuttering her breath, squeezing her throat and heart.

Raliel's slippers crunched on a fine layer of it as she walked across the balcony to the stone rail. She pressed bare hands to freezing crystals gathered there and leaned out. The mountain fell before her, jagged and harsh, but limned in white, gleaming silver traces against the spearing evergreens and fanged cliffs. She looked up to see nothing but a soft veil of white-gray descending, hanging like her mother's ink paintings. The entire world swirled white and black. Brilliance and shadow and shadows that gleamed themselves.

It was more beautiful than she'd imagined. Slippery and sharp, she wanted to touch it—she wanted to taste it.

Laughing, she held out her hands with open palms. They trembled. Snow landed on her fingers and the delicate lines of her palms and melted, became water just slow enough to witness. She shuddered—it was so cold! Her shudder was a laugh, too, both. Her teeth chattered in the wake of a strong shiver; Raliel opened her mouth wide and made it into a cry: "Ha!" she yelled, and her breath was visible. A puff of warmth.

"Moon!" she called, and her demon was beside her, short and perfect, looking at her with two eyes like moons, a little smile promising dimples and all that vast black sea of hair catching snow. The snow did not melt against Moon but stuck like tiny diamonds. Speckled its hair like stars. Blended into the deep, pallid white of its skin.

"Sorcery," she said to the great demon.

It frowned.

"I need to transform my *own* aether. If I were a sorcerer, I could. You could feed me power. I could use it." She was laughing again, with tears in her eyes. "A real bond, you and I. We've done sorcery, transformed together, shared power. It's been the palace-amulet holding us back, fixing us into a structure, into a pattern. You know this. You said as much. I wanted to find a way to free you without breaking the amulet, without shattering what my family has built. But that's not an option. Maybe it never has been. We have to break the palace-amulet. It will happen anyway if they take you away from me, with your true name. So we do it on purpose. Break it and bind ourselves together, sorcerer and great demon familiar. Truly, forever, step into the realm of sorcery. Then I am safe, and you are safe."

"Raliel, you don't—"

"I have to!" She shrugged and turned, made it a dance, face to the sky. Her feet slid, slippers soaked with snow, toes numbing. Her parents would understand. Not because it would let her live but because she had to do this: it was the right thing for Moon, for the empire. They could not be built upon a prison. No true good could come of something rooted in injustice.

"Raliel." Her name burned urgently across the snowy balcony, and Raliel stopped. She turned to it as it said, "You should let them have me."

"Never."

"They are dangerous—they'll keep trying."

"I won't give you to them, not like this. I have spent months trying to help you be free, Moon, to choose! I will not help you be bound against your will."

"It would be my choice. Beauty told me it is good, being a group. I could—do more."

"Blackmail is not choice, Moon."

"Raliel!"

She made her face expressionless. Cold as this snow. "We are going to do this. Break the amulet. Bind ourselves in partnership. This is what you wanted!"

"It's not that easy," it argued. "We've been through this. Breaking the palace-amulet, you achieving permanent sorcery, saving you, rebinding ourselves—hard enough with a universe of time, but with the sorcerers and their great spirits waiting, knowing? They have to take off this collar. They won't give us a chance to thwart them. It's so much. What makes you think you can do it now? Where do we even begin?" Moon sounded desperate.

"It's only a name," she whispered.

The great demon fell still, unblinking. Not even pretending to breathe.

"Moon," Raliel said with all the blurring, winter world in her heart. "Can you change your name for me?"

Moon stared at her. The edge of fear tightening its eyes melted slower than the snow dripping down her cheek. It looked at her, looked and looked, until it was not afraid. It was soft and serious. "Yes."

The breath gusted out of her. She threw herself forward and hugged it. Its cold nose pressed her neck, and she shivered. Raliel held on, tighter and tighter, as her muscles spasmed. Oh, this was not just cold, not just relief; it was fear.

Her knees gave out, and they sank to the hard, snowy balcony. She pulled Moon, though it grunted and tried to stand her back up. She pulled it to the rail and leaned there, drawing Moon with her until they tucked together and snow fell around them. There was no heat to share, for Moon did not generate such a thing. It was a cold great demon, made of shadows and ice crystals. That was fine with Raliel because she'd made herself the same through long practice.

Snow fell, and as her breath quieted, fear muffled by strange wonder at the perfectly natural, perfectly alien snow, Raliel began to hear it. Gentle brushing, softly hollow moans of wind through naked branches, against the peaks of the Third Mountain. Her mother used to sometimes whisper, *Hush hush, shhhh,* when she plucked a particular lullaby on her lap harp. It sounded like this.

Maybe she'd never hear it again. Her mother's harp, her father Sky's grumble. The emperor's laugh. Maybe Moon was correct and this was too much. She couldn't do it. Sorcery was so large. So much. An ocean. Fear was too. How could she hold it all? Contain the entire world?

"Can something very big feel very small?" she whispered. "In order to fit inside something else that is small?"

"You aren't small," Moon said immediately.

She snorted softly, leaned her cheek to its head. A shiver slid down her spine, melting ice.

"I am very big," the great demon added. "And I more than fit inside you. You were my house, the best house I ever had. That little space under your heart."

A tear squeezed out of her eye, and before it could freeze to her skin, it slipped into the demon's hair. She pressed nearer, but the chain jangled.

Moon grumbled and shifted it, snaking an arm around her waist. It pulled her close.

She held it and took its other hand, linking their cold fingers together. Her knuckles felt like rocks, her fingers stiff. Her toes, hidden under her legs, were numb and tingly when she wiggled them. This cold was like nothing she'd felt. Nothing she'd imagined. How nice would a fire and fur be, to snuggle together with just enough heat to share and live. "What will your new name be, Moon?"

"I can't tell you. If I say it, I'll change. When I name myself, that's the beginning."

Raliel leaned back to look at it. "Can I tell you something ridiculous?"

"Yes." It met her eyes, and she saw herself reflected—blurry, snowy—in the deep blackness.

"I don't want you to change."

Moon grinned. The tilt of it was so very *Moon* that suddenly Raliel remembered this face was molded after Osian. She hadn't thought that in hours. The awareness had slipped a bit. This had become Moon's face. Moon's face, too. "I don't think Osian would mind," she murmured, and the great demon kissed her.

Just cold lips to cold lips.

Their linked fingers slid apart, and Raliel cupped the demon's jaw; it tangled its fingers in her hair. The chain dragged against the rail. With her lips on the demon's, pressed, gentle, Raliel dug her freezing hand into her robes and found the silver amulet. She pulled it out, and with a strong tug snapped the cord. It hurt, a line cut along the back of her neck, momentarily hot with the pain.

Moon looked, parting the kiss to touch their foreheads instead. Raliel cupped the amulet in her palm; the great demon cupped her hand. The silver gleamed through the layers of black silk threads tied around and around. "Moon Caught in the Tide, Great Demon of the Palace," she said for the last time.

"Raliel Dark-Smile, Heir to the Moon," the great demon said.

Together, knowing what the other expected—wanted—they twisted to put the amulet through the gap in the stone rail. They held it out over the edge of the mountain, into the swirling snow. At the same moment, with the same held breath, they let go.

NINE

THROUGH THE SNOW, DAWN was impossible to see coming. It simply arrived. One moment the world was bright night, churning falling snow-stars; the next the world gleamed too sharp for comfort. The clouds glowed evenly, filtering sun, and the snow fell like quartz droplets tumbling through gray light. The mountain appeared, harsh granite and scraggly grass barely ripping up through the layer of snow.

Raliel remembered telling Lutha that it was all morning. Everything after the stars came out. Morning always. And more than morning—more had always suited her. Wanting more, imagining more. Believing herself to be more. She could *do* this. She had to.

She stood on shaking, numb legs, one hand in Moon's, and looked out again, at the snow, the world. The running ink of evergreens slashed up through ice. Her heart clenched in pain. She put her free hand against her chest. Strange not to feel the circle press of the amulet.

"I can do this," she whispered: the words took form, misty and amorphous, but visible. Liminal, she thought.

Moon turned her to face the mountain. Through the glass doors the dining room glowed warm with fire and aether-light. The table where they'd eaten was set with more food and steaming tea. Raliel strode to it, ignoring the needles pricking her legs, her fingers, her nose, and chapped cheeks. She poured tea into two cups and held one against her heart. The steam warmed her chin, her lips. Smelled of roses. Roses, here in the cold winter. She considered roses lush flowers of summer, culti-vated in the palace gardens to bloom again and again in yellow and sunset orange, tiny heads clustered in brambles, daring her to touch. Raliel had never seen one wild.

She drank the tea, and it burned. Wincing, she took the second cup she'd poured and downed it, despite the discomfort.

Taste, smell, different and same. She thought of the color blue—every color that was blue. A cascade of blues, rippling one after another in her mental eye: blurring. Every blue and all blues. She bit her lip: she couldn't imagine it perfectly. But she told herself she believed in it.

She would fling herself off this cliff of cold white and into every blue.

"Call them," she said.

Moon gazed into her eyes for a moment, then pulled hard on the aether of the mountain. It grimaced, and the chain shook, flashed blue-white.

Almost immediately a great spirit appeared, falling from the ceiling—no, leaping: Beauty, the tiger spirit of this Third Mountain. It landed gracefully, like a house cat, but huge, taller at the shoulder than Moon. Its eyes gleamed, and its slit pupils wid-ened and narrowed again, sparking with silver. Then the eagle spirit,

Aerin, glided through the stone wall and curved its wings, tilting into a circle. The dining room was just large enough for it to soar.

Crown, the bear of the Fourth Mountain, walked through the door with the twin sorcerers. They moved in tandem, dressed in matching gold and red robes, face and shoulders, eyes and plain smiles the same.

One said, "You have chosen?"

Raliel lifted her chin. "Take the chains off, and the great demon of the palace will tell you its name."

The other twin said, "If it does not, we will break the binding on your poison and you will die."

"I know."

Moon said, "I know."

The tiger stalked forward. Raliel held her breath, ridiculously, and Moon stared at it, even as the tiger leaned into its space, little beard at its chin sparkling, and took the chain daintily in its teeth. It huffed, said, *I told you, remember, it will be good with us,* then snapped through the chain.

Moon instantly spun to face Raliel. It put its hands on her face, leaned in, and said directly to her, but loud enough for everyone to hear, "My name is The Moon Died for Raliel."

Power exploded around her.

It surged, it crackled cold and deadly in the air. A scream, a snap of lightning. So much in angry motion, the entire mountain tilting.

But for Raliel everything stopped.

Her lips peeled apart in horror—in *wonder*—and as Moon fell to pieces, she did too. She witnessed it, heard it, *knew* it. And in knowing Moon, she knew herself. She knew what she was.

And more.

TEN

ELEGANT WATERS WAS PLAYING her harp when the palace shivered. Dawn had broken. The sky through her windows glowed a soft pink-gold around fluffed clouds that hid the actuality of the sun. The Second Consort knelt alone on a floor pillow, in her sleep pants and silk shirt, with a thick winter robe tied around it all. Her hair was down, freed of its night braid to breathe while she plucked notes of a new composition and waited for her husband the emperor to emerge.

She heard him, his soft footsteps beyond the open doorway leading into the emperor's bedchamber. Last night Sky had stayed with him, and Elegant Waters had not, leaving when she felt sleepy, though her two husbands had been far from finishing their round of four generals—a strategy game that bored her. She'd slept uneasily, as had become her habit in the weeks since their last attempt to draw the great demon home. Worry, she was certain, though sometimes Elegant Waters believed she could sense the lack of the demon in the walls, in the floors.

When she composed, she expected Moon to be listening.

Since it left with Raliel at the end of the summer, she'd done this alone.

The emperor emerged, box of ruby rings in hand, his hair braided in the messy way that meant he'd done it himself.

Elegant Waters nodded to him and plucked the most recent measures of her new song. He plopped on the edge of her bed, box cradled in his lap, and listened. Unguarded this early, he seemed more beautiful than when under his layers of expressions and ink, loops of braids, embroidery, dark smile.

"Do you," the emperor began, and the palace trembled.

She gasped, gaze flying up to his, just as the emperor grimaced and arched his back. He fell onto the bed, and his ring box slid off his thigh: it hit the floor with a crack. The lid opened like a mouth and spit out twelve rings, rubies bright as blood spatter.

Then Elegant Waters felt it, ripping through her. A cord of lightning, slicing her in two, easily as if she were butter.

Aether swallowed her up.

She saw snow.

Her mountain, the drifting black lines of trees, the jagged spill of cliffs. Snow. Ice falling, sliding through gray skies.

Waterfalls. Crystal-blue arcs slicing through the gray-black-white. So many. A thousand waterfalls, reaching, slowing, freezing. Everything stopped, and at that moment the snow gleamed in its purest form: filaments of ice, patterned into impossible stars.

Elegant Waters fell back into herself, sobbing and bent in half. She was so cold. She smelled blood.

It was her fingers: cut against the strings of her harp where she'd gripped too tight. Elegant Waters released it, wincing at the fresh sting of pain.

She stood, shaky, and looked to the bed where the emperor slumped, dreadfully pale. "Kirin," she said, climbing onto the mattress to shake his shoulders. "Kirin."

"Kirin!" called Sky from the emperor's bedroom. The First Consort stumbled as he careened into her room, clutching his chest with one large blue-tinged hand.

The emperor snapped open his eyes. "The demon," he said, voice harsh as if he'd been screaming.

"Raliel," Elegant Waters answered.

The palace trembled again, as if with an earthquake. She felt it, saw the sway of the ink drawing that hung beside her bed, saw the shiver of the privacy screen beside her wardrobe.

Sky clambered onto the bed with them. "Are you—" He touched Elegant Water's cheek, and she nodded once. They both looked at Kirin.

"It's gone," he said. "It's *gone.*"

Yelling outside their room drew their attention, and then a distant but impossibly loud rumble shook through the walls.

"Was it holding the foundations in place?" Kirin said, incredulous, and threw himself up, pushing past both his husband and wife. He stopped suddenly, staring down at the spill of ruby rings.

Then Night Shine appeared: drew herself out of the air with a pop. The temperature of the room heated instantly, like she was a bonfire pretending to be a girl.

Elegant Waters stood and stepped between her husband the emperor and the great demon of the Fifth Mountain. "Night Shine. Take me to the Third Mountain."

"El," Kirin began, "you can't—"

"She can leave," Sky said, almost choking on it. "The demon is—we can all—"

But Elegant Waters ignored them, staring at the churning black-red flecks of lava in the demon Night Shine's huge wide eyes. "My daughter is there." She'd seen it: her Mountain of One Thousand Falls, at the base of the Third Mountain. Ice, and Raliel.

The demon swung around, grabbing Elegant Waters up into her arms, and threw the both of them together out the window.

Glass rained, slicing at Elegant Waters, who clutched at Night Shine, holding on to flesh that changed under her fingers: skin, muscle, feathers, scales, and more arms wrapped her, held her just as tight, and Elegant Waters felt the new throb of wings pushing, lifting them: a heartbeat. She clutched what she could, found tears in her eyes, and heard only the roar of the wind. To herself, she whispered her daughter's name over and over again, a refrain, a prayer, never stopping, never, until they were far away, surrounded by cutting snow, and she began to scream it aloud.

ELEVEN

T HE MOON DIED FOR Raliel roared.

(A scream, or a song?)

It reached with every particle of itself out and out, changing, transforming, and Raliel said, "I am Raliel Dark-Smile," reaching too. The great demon bent, flared—it grasped the furious great spirit of the Third Mountain and destroyed it in a starving, aching drag. The power of it flooded, exploded, and it moved for another even as it shoved that power at Raliel.

She caught it easily: it crashed through her like a waterfall, unrelenting, stripping her of all that she was except for exactly what she was.

(More.)

(Not between life and death, between day and night. But both. Beyond.)

Then came another wave of it, pounding, ripping, pure horrible gorgeous aether.

Raliel caught that too and turned herself inside out. She maybe screamed; she definitely hurt. But she kept catching, kept dragging, pouring, making herself a waterfall, a high, arcing, inevitable waterfall of silver-blue aether.

The Moon Died for Raliel took again and again—bear, eagle: two great spirits so surprised, so unguarded, the demon devoured them as it unraveled under the onslaught of its own consummation.

Then—the sorcerers. Too tied to their familiars, bound by names, bound by blood and love: they went together.

More and more and more, the magic careened from the great demon into Raliel until she was scoured thrice over and filled up again: floating off the stone floor, mouth agape, eyes wide, seeing *everything*.

And she took it. Put the aether into the corners of herself: veins, elbows, teeth, belly, everywhere inside her bones, the little channels of marrow turned white-cold. Raliel made of ice. Raliel translucent. Raliel interconnected snowflakes.

Raliel embodied again.

She fell hard to the ground, joints jarring, bruised on knees, hip, hands scraped raw. Her spine bowed, and she heaved for breath.

Every piece of her ached. Trembled.

It had been fast. It had been a hundred years.

Carefully, Raliel cracked her eyes open. She stared at her hand splayed against the gray granite beneath her. It flickered with shadows, rippled into scales the color of snow, tinged blue like mother-of-pearl. Then it was her plain human hand again.

Her stomach rolled. She spat a string of bile on the floor.

"Moon," she whispered.

She remembered that infinite moment when they were

bound. Sorcerer and great demon. Familiar. Oh, familiar—known.

It meant to know. Be known. To recognize.

The Moon—her familiar.

Raliel recognized that her familiar was gone. She was herself. Poison-free. Alive. Huge with sorcery. Her heart pounded.

Tears flooded her throat. She swallowed them.

Sitting back, she glanced around the room. There was nothing with her. Nobody. Then the stone trembled. The mountain groaned.

It was empty, too. Spirits gone. Sorcerers gone.

Raliel was alone in a dying mountain.

She breathed. She dragged herself back out onto the balcony—into the snow.

Shivering, curled on her side, she held on to the piece of herself she knew: that cold, beautiful amethyst geode under her heart of blood and flesh. The Moon's nest. Empty and shadowed. She held it as her body rippled and changed, slid between states, between boundaries, scale and skin, air and flesh, and Raliel put herself into the nest, safe among shards of crystal and reflecting ice.

Holding on.

Breaking apart.

Holding on.

Until she heard her name like a harmony countering the song of the wind. Her name, her name, and hands on her shoulders pinning them back into shoulders, lips on her cheek—her cheek, hers—and arms lifting her up up up into the sky on the wings of a great demon.

TWELVE

I T WOULD TAKE RALIEL a long time to relearn how to be
alone.

When the great demon of the palace died, part of the
wall of the sixth circle collapsed, killing two people. In the
spring, Raliel would go herself to take blessings to their families, discover the names of their cousins and grandparents, and
remain a week to help repair a neighbor's fence.

They would tell stories about her, in the years that followed,
they and others she encountered in her travels: Raliel Dark-
Smile walked confidently throughout the land, but slowly for
all the stops she made to listen to the complaints of mushroom
spirits and coax smiles from the emerging wildflowers. Upon
arrival in any village or town, she would ask if there was help
she could give, like rethatching a roof or attracting a fresh, merry
rabbit spirit to the town's fertility shrine. They said she especially
enjoyed sharing a bonfire with the townsfolk and could be per-
suaded into telling stories of her Heir's Journey—the Last Heir's
Journey, some would call it. She might mention The Scale, or
a demon-kissed warrior with dangerous secrets, or waterfall

dragons and a deep-sea demon. Raliel might look up at the gibbous moon as it floated among stars and wisps of clouds. She might say that when the moon grew so, it was the opposite of the bright sickle-smile of the crescent. This was when the darkness smiled.

The moon had a dark smile, too, she would joke.

Like the tide, she would come and go from the palace. Seeking every corner of the empire on her own two feet—and very occasionally with wings or fins, but she did not tell stories about that. She would swim the entire length of the Selegan River without taking a breath, darting between fish and under flat-bottomed boats, and laughing with the dragon. Transformation was *hard* without a familiar, but she wouldn't go about finding one.

She would visit the Fifth Mountain and the First, as well as the emptier ones where people needed to be resettled or given magical aid. She'd organize the women of Four Ridges to assist her, and reach out to monasteries and a few local covens for help shoring up the dangerous parts of the empty mountains. And she would wander. She'd meet stinky pond scum demons and glorious lightning demons. Once she'd spend a week chatting with the colorful demon of a nurse log, tending to its lichens and fungi and iridescent beetles and handfuls of earthworms. She'd meet spirits, too, and liked raccoons and foxes and braided the tail of an impressive spirit stallion once, but of course she preferred the attitudes of demons. She would meet a storm dragon outside Shards of Summer and get so close it would nearly tear her to pieces. Recovering with her father Sky's extended family would be a revelation of noise, and she would tell them, who had such strong demon-kissed blood, that the sorcerer of the

First Mountain had taught her *blue* was the key to sorcery. But she thought it was relationships.

That's why she would try to forge them everywhere she went. And it would work. The heir would become known for steady strength and listening skills. For an ease with spirits but a fondness for demons that allowed her to negotiate most issues better than a witch or itinerant priest.

And always, always, she would return to the sea.

Because she was like the tide.

She'd return again and again to the palace, to her family, to her future.

But before all that would happen, the first winter she was home, when her mother Elegant Waters and the great demon Night Shine brought her back to the arms of her fathers, Raliel had to rebuild her most fundamental relationships: with her parents, and her friends, and the silent, empty walls of the palace.

It was easiest with Rose Blue, Salri, and Averilis, for none of them were upset. They welcomed her back and listened as she haltingly told them what she'd done and why and then asked for their honest opinions. She listened in return. She squeezed their hands, and she thanked them for being her friends when she did not know how to reciprocate. She said if they wanted to go home, or serve someone else, they should. If they ever wished to leave or change, those were their rights.

With her parents, it was different. Elegant Waters refused apologies, ferociously insisting that Raliel had done no wrong. Her mother was so stubborn, Raliel hardly knew how to talk to her, and so the death of the Moon hung between them. With her father Sky she knelt and asked forgiveness, not for taking the demon, but for lying. And for giving his agate away to a dragon. Sky said he was proud of her and put a large hand on her cheek, brushing with his thumb as if she were the one with tears in her eyes. Raliel and her father the emperor circled each other coldly for several weeks until one dawn Kirin appeared at her bed and dragged her half-sleeping self up to the Moon's Recline Garden for evergreen tea and silence. A waiting silence. A silence for quietly placing down burdens.

So she reached out a hand and let her skin pebble into small mother-of-pearl scales, dry and glistening like a snake's. "I can be anything," she whispered.

Her father's amber eyes lifted to hers, and he said, "Good."

"I'm not sure I should be in the line of succession," she added. She didn't know if she'd age or die or anything.

But the emperor immediately and dramatically rolled his eyes. Then he slid one of his ruby rings onto her thumb. "If you can be anything, you can be mine, too."

That was that.

Shadows of the Fifth Mountain and the great demon Night Shine brought Osian Redpop to them two weeks after Raliel herself had been returned, when things were still chaotic and the imperial family sorted rumors and stories and decided what to tell the people. Osian was unconscious and remained that way for nearly three months.

Balmy spring winds were blowing off the ocean when he woke. Raliel attended his bedside in relief. "How do you feel?"

Osian's lashes fluttered, bright brown against still-wan cheeks that slowly flushed under Raliel's regard. "Better," he said. "Stronger."

"The sorceress Shadows unknotted your aether, and you were asleep and healing for the entire winter season. You're in the palace and safe. And free."

"Can I stay?"

Raliel took his hand, laced their fingers together. "Please."

He smiled, tiredly but real. Dimples flashed, and Raliel caught her breath.

"What happened to Moon?" Osian asked.

"Scoot over," she said, and when he did, Raliel lay down with her head on his pillow and told him face-to-face, their hands clenched together between them, exactly what Moon had done.

The first time Osian joined her at an official function as her personal guard, whole and glowing with readiness, Raliel nearly managed a smile backed by nothing but joy.

Alone in her room, Raliel stood at the window and put fingers of aether into her belly, pressed and explored the slick, dark spaces inside her. Changed her lungs, her breasts, her jaw-line, and put it all back. Tapped the sparks of desire waiting in the cold. Nothing dragged claws up the insides of her ribs in response. Nobody sneered under her heart. There never was laughter echoing in her skull or hissing commentary.

She put her cheek to the wall and listened: only the sighs of the wind and distant conversations, the faint presence of the city all around.

It took a month for mice to appear in the cellars and remain.

They kept up the shrines cut into the stairwells and red-washed walls, but nothing withered the flowers. Nothing dried out the bowls of tea. Maybe, Raliel thought, someday there would be smaller spirits flitting through the corridors, or some of the flower demons in the gardens would finally dig their roots deep enough to claim offerings.

At the end of the winter, Raliel heard a soft harp song from a waiting room in the seventh circle. It was her mother's song.

Raliel paused at the entrance to the music room. Elegant Waters played a lullaby with repeating cascades of notes, a tumbling melody like layered waterfalls. It was from her home on the Mountain of One Thousand Falls, and she used to play it for the great demon.

Pushing in, Raliel listened quietly. She folded her hands and closed her eyes until the notes faded. When she looked, her mother had one hand flat to the parquet floor. Her lovely pallid face held tightly with grief.

"You can visit home now," Raliel murmured, going to kneel beside Elegant Waters.

"This is my home, little emperor," Elegant Waters said. She took her hand from the floor and pressed it instead to Raliel's knee.

"You could take me, then."

"Yes. Someday I would like that."

They sat together, listening for anything to break the silence.

There came only the creak of footsteps overhead, the slide of wood as other doors opend and closed.

Raliel tried very hard not to break in half.

Her breathing quickened. This was why she kept busy, kept moving, listening, plotting, planning, kept to practice and education, to as much and as many responsibilities as she'd ever had. Silence and sorrow were only for those moments alone at her window. But oh, she missed her Moon.

Raliel erected a little shrine on the beach, near the tunnel through the bluff.

Built with seven chunks of salt crystal quarried from near the Second Mountain, the shrine arced over a crescent-shaped tide pool. Each crystal she carved with runes for the moon and seven blessings, and blue ribbons tied in place. The pool was shallow but alive with dark-orange starfish and pink anemones, the occasional crab or even an indigo octopus. Wind caught the whistle mounted at the crest of the shrine and sang a low, sad song.

When the moon was full, Raliel went to the shrine to drop candied petals into it and reinforce the blessing aether. Someday the sea would take back all the inland salt, and the shrine would be gone again. It was that sort of shrine: changing.

One night Raliel knelt at the edge of the sea, where the tide met the shore. Waves dragged sand from beneath her, saltwater foam curled against her toes, her skirts were damp, trailing, and she thought about her Moon. Of course she did.

She reached forward and buried her hands in the sand, where it was pressed flat by the constant rush of the tide. Ocean rushed toward her, lapped at her fingers, knuckles, wrists, then pulled away away away.

She whispered its name to the retreating sea.

When the water returned, she sparked her aether until her bones glowed, visible through her skin. She let it melt out of her, into the saltwater. Pushed her aether into the sea, and again, as it receded, whispered its name.

Maybe if she fed the tide herself, if she listened, if she offered it the possibility of a name, a spirit would manifest. A spirit of change and bitter salt, sands both smooth and raw, cool, cold, and itchy on the skin. A spirit like the wavering reflection of the full moon risen just a little into the stars in the east. The moon was reborn every month. Rebirth was what it *is*.

"It won't work."

Raliel startled at the voice: beside her was a . . . well, a very ugly little girl. Her eyes were too small and far apart, her cheeks narrow, her nose long, and her lips a thin line over a jutting chin. She looked like a goat.

The little girl smiled at her, revealing gaps in her blocky teeth.

"Why not?" Raliel managed. They shouldn't have been able to hear each other over the crashing waves, considering how softly they both spoke.

The little girl shrugged bony shoulders.

"What are you?"

"Ah! What do I look like?"

"A goat."

The girl laughed, and then she *was* a goat. No, its fur was too long, too silky, and its ears pricked forward like a delicate pony's. It tilted its head to stare at her with one eye like a pink-tinged pearl, and a horn grew out of its forehead, in a cute arc that shimmered just like its eye.

Raliel bit her lip, sat on her heels even though it would make her robes totally soaked. "Esrithalan."

"Hi, yes. I just thought you could use some company. Then I realized what you were doing."

"And it won't work."

The unicorn shrugged—odd in that form.

Raliel felt her belief settle like a rock in her stomach. She looked out to sea and twisted her fingers through the ends of her braid as she'd done when she was a child. The ocean reached for her, and she said, "Would you like to go swimming with me?"

"I'd love to!" the unicorn said, and dashed into the surf, kicking up whitecaps and sand with its tiny hooves. Then it was a fish, vanishing through the underside of a wave.

Raliel chased after, pulling aether into scales and gills, giving webs to her fingers, elongating her toes, and when she dove, it was almost—*almost*—like Moon was with her again, changing her from the inside until she could breathe the thick wilderness of its tide.

It was not long after that she secured permission from her parents to take their blessings and her own to the families of the two who had died when Moon's death broke the palace foundation.

"Can I walk with you?" Osian asked.

"Not this time," she answered. "But maybe the next time, and the next after that, too."

Osian bowed—he understood, she thought, better than most.

She put on the rings from her father the emperor, hugged her father Sky, took the harp her mother handed her, and kissed Osian's cheek. She waved to Rose Blue and Averilis and Salri, and left.

Raliel Dark-Smile walked out of the palace and out of the capital unburdened and eager. She walked, and she breathed, and she allowed her eyes to turn mottled white-gray like two wide full moons. She was alone, but she smiled.

THE LAKE

NORTH, NEAR THE THIRD Mountain, a lake spread four fingers out from a rocky beach, through steep mudbanks and red-barked pines. Hazy mountain peaks kept sleepy watch in the northeast, and the sky reflected on the glassy surface, bright blue. It used to be called Tylish, but for several years the locals had said it was Moon's Lake, because from dusk through dawn a glow emanated from the depths: a sphere of light, a silver ball, like the full moon's reflection—even on nights when there was no moon at all.

After long enough—a handful of years, an entire decade—the name changed. They made it official with the nearest justiciar.

Probably what happened is that the lake had a dragon. Young, playful, sinuous, with sharp teeth and scales like mother-of-pearl. It slept curled up, tails and limbs tucked tight to itself, and when it dreamed, its aether sparkled and shone, strong enough to light up the lake and attract the pleased attention of others. So the moon of Moon's Lake was simply a dreaming dragon.

During hot afternoons it flung itself around, splashing arcs of water to make rainbows, chasing fish to tease, pressing its claws to the murky mud and raking them gently to loosen water grasses like combing beloved hair. It leapt into the sky and floated like a cloud, drifting here and there—but not far; it was too young to venture away from the wet-rock-mud-magic smell of its house. It breathed water and spat streams of it at cranky geese. It sang songs in hollow notes, haunting and tender, and it laughed at strange things: flirting dragonflies and iridescent tadpoles, ladder mushrooms, spider spirits weaving webs against the ground, even rain. It liked rain.

When it snowed, ice traced sharp fingers against the edges of the lake but did not take firm hold. The lake dragon hovered just beneath the surface of the water, eyes and neck ridges visible, occasionally the swish of one of its tails, and stared up into the gray-white snowing world feeling like it was inside a crystal globe built of ice and love. It loved snow.

People came with carved toys and strings of agate, gifting them to the dragon in return for a blessing or promise of softer storms in the area.

The dragon snapped its teeth at people, laughing, and tried to lick the bravest children. It took a baby once—but gave it right back! It shed scales sometimes and nudged at the rippling waves to let them wash onto the pebbly shore. Anyone who picked one up could carve a name and make a charm. The dragon liked that; said with a wiggle of its tongue that those charms protected the wearers no matter how far they wandered, so long as they could see the moon in the sky.

The spirit of Moon's Lake was young but strong, and stretched its water-mist-ice wings in wide arcs in the sun, liking the glint of itself, the kiss of warmth melting against its scales. It liked to be beautiful.

A few dawn sprites built a nest among the exposed roots of a hemlock tree, and the dragon brought them hearty water grass to weave better floors and sometimes let the sprites sun themselves on its belly, out in the middle of the lake.

When the spring brought morning glories and yellow sun-eyes to visit, the dragon made its eyes change colors too and crawled into the grass at the banks to reflect pink-purple-gold back at the meadow. At the end of every summer some of the trees tucked among the evergreens transformed scarlet and orange, like bonfires here and there against the dark green. The dragon rolled in the mud, streaking itself brown-orange, and laughed at the autumn world.

And it snowed.

And the dragon was happy.

One day, in the summer, when the lake dragon floated along with the rippling water, three dawn sprites stretched against its moon-white belly scales, a sorcerer appeared at the crescent beach and sat down where she could skim her fingers into the lake water.

The dragon knew this was a sorcerer because from every direction aether slipped and slithered toward her, for kisses and smiles, to touch and spark and dance away again. The sorcerer cupped her hands against her knees and let aether pool in her palms. She smiled softly out at the lake, one side tilted higher than the other. Her eyes were as moon-gray and mottled white as the dragon's belly.

It sat up, spilling dawn sprites into the lake with tinny little shrieks.

Sinking into the water, it stared at the sorcerer. At her back was a sword bright blue with power, around her throat a silver circlet pressed with sky agates. She wore plain clothes, like all the people the dragon had seen: trousers and robe and jacket, each in white and dark gray. Her hair was black and bound up in a knot, decorated only with a silver comb shaped like frost. The sorcerer smiled at the lake dragon, though its eyes barely showed above the surface of the lake. And she smiled at the dawn sprites flicking wet wings at it before diving off to their nest.

The dragon swam nearer. The sorcerer waited.

Nearer and nearer it slithered until it sank its claws into the drowned pebbles just at the edge of the beach. It said through all its sharp teeth, "Did you bring me a gift?"

The sorcerer laughed. She tossed aether from the pool of her palm up into the sky—much like the dragon splashed arcs of water for rainbows—and when her hand lowered, she removed the silver circlet from around her neck.

"Will this do?"

It was gorgeous, glinting like an arc of sky with little dots of blue. "I like it. What do you want in return?"

"Tell me your name."

The dragon opened its mouth to say its entire name but caught itself in time. Narrowed its rippling-water-blue eyes.

The sorcerer laughed again, soft and pretty. She leaned forward and touched the circlet to the water. "Here. Nothing in return. This is an offering to the dragon of the lake."

"Moon," the dragon said, and snatched the circlet.

Her smile fell away.

"It's the name of my lake," the dragon said.

"I know."

As the dragon drifted farther from the beach, it put the circlet around its arm, then took it off and put it on its head like a crown. Then it stuck it into its mouth and tasted the color of the sky agates, the lightning flavor of the metal. Bit down, enjoyed the scratch of its teeth. Then put it around its neck like the sorcerer had worn it. That necessitated shrinking itself just a little.

It flicked its tails and returned to shore. "I like it. What is your name?"

"Raliel," she said softly.

"Hmm," said the lake dragon. "I know that name. Do I know you?"

"A long time ago, this lake had a different dragon. Did you know that?"

Moon bared its teeth and hissed.

The sorcerer laughed again. "The dragon died, and for a long time the lake was only a lake, no demon or spirit or dragon. But I heard, recently, that a dragon lived here again, for nearly ten years. And the name of the lake changed. We track such things in the capital, as much as we are able."

"The capital is far away, at the sea," the dragon said. "Is that where you are from?"

"My house is there," she answered. "But I am from every road that crosses between the Five Mountains."

The dragon liked that kind of answer: riddling, mysterious. "Will you put my name in the capital, where you keep the name of the lake?"

"Not yet." The sorcerer pulled her legs up to her chest and hugged her knees. She looked small and young as she stared at the dragon.

"Why not yet?"

"I want to find out what you will become first."

"You're a sorcerer. Do you want me for your familiar?"

"You think you're strong enough for me?" She smirked.

The lake dragon burst out of the water, showering her with a cold splash. She laughed, wiped her face. It hovered over her, wings spread and dripping tiny droplets like mist. They shimmered, made rainbows with the sunlight, and the sorcerer's eyes widened as she took it in. Admiration played across her cheeks, and something infinitely sad—longing the dragon did not understand.

"If you want to be my familiar, I wouldn't mind," she said, gaze roving along the misty rainbows, beyond, and then her eyes fell shut. "But I have managed for a decade without any, and I can manage more."

The dragon dropped to the beach and turned into a young man, sitting cross-legged like the sorcerer, wearing clothes like hers but black and white, hair in a knot like hers and black as the night sky, and made its eyes moon-gray and mottled white—just like hers. It knew itself to be a great mimic.

Her lips fell open, and she gasped.

"You don't like it?" The dragon frowned, spread its arms, and looked down at its chest, at its shoulders and hands. They seemed very nicely formed.

"I do," she said quickly. "Especially the dimples."

"Dimples!" The dragon winced, and the sorcerer reached out and with one finger poked the side of the dragon's face. It batted her hand away.

She reached into her jacket and offered the dragon a single

pink sugared flower petal. It stuffed it into its mouth. The petal was sweet and melted on its tongue. "More?"

The sorcerer emptied her pocket, holding the little candies in both hands.

One by one the dragon plucked a candy and put it into its mouth. One by one they melted, sweet, honeyed, feather-light petals, and the sorcerer watched. After a while the dragon paused and asked, "Do you want one?"

"I know what they taste like," she said.

So the dragon shrugged and ate the rest, and the sorcerer remained on the beach until the sun set and twilight blushed across the sky, and until the first stars appeared. And then she stayed a little while longer.

ACKNOWLEDGMENTS

Thank you to all the usual suspects: my agent Laura Rennert, my editors Karen Wojtyla and Nicole Fiorica, and everyone at McElderry Books for once again shepherding my work through the publishing process. Having you invested in Raliel's story was worth the moon.

Thank you to Natalie C. Parker, Justina Ireland, and Adib Khorram, who bore the brunt of my existential angst during the writing of this book.

Thank you, Robin McKinley: your books brought me to myself when I was a child and being able to know you as an adult has been meaningful in ways I, a writer, have trouble expressing. Some of how I feel is woven into the lines of this book.

Thank you, Karen Lord, for giving me the poem "The Question" by Theo Dorgan. The poem and our conversations about our mutual work helped me develop the book's sense of transformative change in relationship with identity and the liminal world. You'll understand better than most that ineffable *more*.

And thank you to my readers who embraced Night Shine, the Sorceress Who Eats Girls, Sky, and especially Kirin Dark-Smile. I hope this next generation captures you as deeply.